Menopause in Manhattan

Menopause in Manhattan

*A tantalizing tale
of trials and tribulations,
triumphs and tuna melts*

Anne Kleinberg

Bestsellers Ink

[B]

ALL RIGHTS RESERVED

Menopause in Manhattan is a work of fiction.
Names, characters, places and incidents are the product
of the author's imagination or used fictitiously.

The scanning, uploading, and distribution of this book, via
Internet or any other means, without the written permission
of the author, is illegal.

Copyright © 2011 by Anne Kleinberg

Author Website: www.annekleinberg.com
Book Website: www.menopauseinmanhattan.com

Published by Bestsellers Ink
MMXI
Caesarea • New York
www.bestsellersink.com

ISBN: 978-965-91575-0-1

Cover Photograph by Moshe Cohen

Cover Art by Charles Fazzino
© Charles Fazzino
Exclusively Published by Museum Editions, Ltd.
www.fazzino.com

Dedicated to

Women everywhere who think they can't –

Oh yes you can!

One

It looked as if a holiday piñata had burst open in the middle of The Cutting Room floor. Garlands of holly draped the styling stations, mistletoe twigs dangled from the ceiling, a large silver menorah graced the reception desk, and pots of bright red Amaryllis plants lined the window ledge of the Greenwich Village salon. Even some of the workers got into the spirit by donning elf hats. Oddly, Elie Sands was oblivious to it all.

She sat in the waiting area nervously tapping her foot. If they don't take me in the next five minutes, she thought, I'll leave and manage on my own.

Today was not the best of days to be taking time off; things were especially hectic at the magazine. A recent blizzard had cut power for two days, employees were preoccupied with Christmas shopping and vacation plans, and there was the usual end of the year craziness. And like always, there were pushy designers angling to get their work published, advertisers demanding better page positioning, and staff members promoting an edgier orientation for the magazine – more architectural projects, fewer decorative ones. As executive editor, she had to shoulder a great deal of the responsibility, and she was feeling the burden.

"Good afternoon, Elie. Happy Christmas! I mean, Happy Hanukkah!" Lisa, the stylist, walked over and kissed her. She was a wisp of a woman, with a blonde pixie haircut, aquamarine eyes and a strong British accent.

"Shall we do something different today, darling? Maybe burnished pomegranate?" She mussed her hands through Elie's hair. "It would be brilliant on you."

"What am I, a fruit platter?" Elie said, pointing to her head. "No burnishing and no pomegranates. Just the usual cut and color."

"A few highlights maybe? Spikes? What about coloring your hair platinum? Come on, let's make a statement."

"Let's? Since when are we partners? As for a statement, here it is. Dye the gray and stop being such a *nudnik*. When I decide to go platinum, it will be my own natural color. Until I have the courage for that, please make me as beautiful as you can, with what you've got here." She squeezed Lisa's arm affectionately and returned to her thoughts.

This evening was the celebration of her fiftieth birthday. She had hoped for a quiet dinner with Philip and the girls, but her husband pushed for a blowout party with personal and business acquaintances. They compromised – immediate family and close friends, at a restaurant in Little Italy.

Elie could hardly believe it. How did she get here, married for almost thirty years and the mother of two grown daughters? She stared at herself in the gilt-framed mirror, looking for signs of age.

Her dark brown hair fell from a side part, framing her face in waves of relaxed curls. She kept it chin length and dyed, to disguise the creeping gray. Her skin was smooth, thanks to good genes on her mother's side. A few lines played on the corners of her eyes and mouth, but people said her smile lit up a room, so she didn't obsess.

She considered her body, which fluctuated between a size ten and twelve. She would have preferred to be thinner, but she hated exercising and loved to eat. Overall, Elie was satisfied with the way she looked.

She tried to relax while Lisa worked, but her mind was racing. She worried that sparks might fly tonight. Her two best friends had not spoken to each other for over twenty years. They had a mutual dislike due to an ancient argument, and her husband disliked them both. Her mother-in-law, a matriarch who ruled with a manicured fist, might try to run things while her own mother would no doubt stay in the background. She let out an audible *oy* and Lisa laughed.

When she finished blow-drying, Lisa held up a mirror to show off the back. Elie looked straight ahead, turned both ways, smiled and nodded her approval. She would have to be careful showering and applying makeup, but with the new outfit she had purchased for the occasion, she was fairly confident she would look great.

She left the salon and headed back to the office, hoping for a few calm hours before she had to go home and get ready.

When she arrived, her assistant ran into her office, dumped a pile of papers on the desk and exclaimed breathlessly, "Elie! Where have you been? It's Armageddon around here."

"Slow down, Keira. What are you talking about?" Elie was used to the dramatics. The young woman was intense, which contradicted her quirky looks – tall and gangly, with henna colored cropped hair and green glasses.

"Anthony Montecristo was here. He stormed in and started threatening. He was badgering Heather, demanding to see Walter or you. She's such a twat, she started shaking and stuttering. Walter was who knows where, you were gone; I heard the racket so I stepped in."

She took a breath and continued. "I invited him into your office, told him to calm down, and asked what his problem was. He was ranting that if his job in Luxembourg gets pulled, he's going to take the magazine to court. What a tyrant! I calmly explained that you and Mr. Lavigne were out of the office, but that I would do my best to help him. I said I would look into his story and get back to him. Can you believe this?"

Elie sat back, stunned. Anthony Montecristo was a celebrated interior designer with an international following. His most recent project was the renovation of a three-hundred-year-old castle in Luxembourg, and he had given *Interior Design & Style* the exclusive on it. It was a major coup for the magazine and as of yesterday afternoon, all was fine.

As she grasped the situation, Elie started to seethe. Not only did Keira have no authority to manage this sort of problem, but her approach could have caused serious damage. Client relations were beyond her scope of work and, apparently, a field she was not equipped to handle.

"Keira, I understand that there was a temporary crisis here, but why did you think it was your responsibility to deal with it?"

"What would you expect me to do?" She stood with her hands

on her non-existent hips, waiting for a response.

"Heather is the receptionist and she is supposed to take messages. I do get that you were trying to help, but you really overstepped your bounds. It was inappropriate to speak to Mr. Montecristo in the manner you described; you may have insulted him. *And,* it is certainly not your position to tell him to calm down or that you will get back to him."

"But Elie ... you were out with your visiting daughter or whoever, Walter was not in the office, *again*, and the others here can only deal with room settings. What choice did I have?"

"If you insisted on interfering, you might have simply said, 'Mr. Montecristo, I'm Elie Sands' assistant and I promise to convey your message to her as soon as she returns.'"

"Well, I think I handled it pretty well."

"That's apparent. Okay, I'll take it from here, thank you."

As Keira strutted to the door, Elie glanced at the pile of papers she had dumped on her desk. "What are all these?"

"Oh, I forgot. They're more of the usual. You know, the stuff I have to deal with on a daily basis when I'm not putting out fires." She turned back to grab the pile and a few of the papers flew onto the floor. She stooped down to pick them up and left the office in a huff.

Elie decided to ignore the incident for the time being and get back to the most pressing work on her desk. Soon, the buzzing of the intercom interrupted her thoughts.

"Elie?" It was the receptionist. "I have Mr. Hendricks of Hendricks Thompson Furniture on the phone."

She wondered why she was being bothered with this. "He needs advertising, Heather; he probably wants to change his ad."

"No, Elie. He asked for Mr. L. and when I said he wasn't in and I'd be happy to take a message, he insisted on speaking with you."

"Okay, put him through."

She picked up the receiver. "Hi James, it's Elie. What can I do for you?"

"Hey, Elie. I have an unpleasant request. I'm going to have to pull the big ad campaign we had scheduled."

Elie felt punched.

"Why, James? What happened?"

"I just got a call from Anthony Montecristo. He was ranting like a lunatic, insisting that I stop doing business with you people. Carrying on about some project of his in Europe that was canned. He said he came to your office to settle the matter, but some upstart patronized him and ... you know what? It doesn't matter. He has me over the coals."

"James, apparently there was a misunderstanding." Elie tried to think fast, hoping to salvage the situation.

"Look, it doesn't matter. I feel like crap about this and I would never cave in to such intimidation. But, I'll be brutally honest with you. We've had a dismal last quarter, the spring doesn't look promising and the summer will be dead. No one buys furniture then. They're all visiting chateaus in the Loire Valley or screwing their nannies in the Hamptons."

Elie started to bite her lower lip.

"Montecristo has orders in with us for nearly half a million dollars. That's a shitload of shekels, if you'll pardon the expression, and I cannot afford to snub my nose at it. The guy swore he would cancel his orders with us and hand all his business over to my competitors if I don't cooperate."

"James, it will all be worked out. Montecristo can be a bit impetuous, I'm sure that story will run." She said it without having the slightest idea if she was right.

"Elie, it doesn't make a rat's ass of difference to me if the story runs or not. Believe me, I know you people are reputable, I've been doing business with Walt since he started the magazine. But Montecristo has me by the balls. He's blackmailing me. I made light of it at first and didn't take him seriously. I'll tell ya, that guy is one vindictive son of a bitch. If Montecristo goes, Elie, so goes a major chunk of my business." He stopped for a moment, and then continued.

"I'll make this up to you. Don't you worry, Walter knows I'll make good on the ad campaign. Hopefully I'll be able to run it soon, just not in the issue as planned."

"I see. I am so sorry about all this James. May I ask Walter to phone you?"

"Sure, you do that. And again, I'm really sorry Elie."

She sat in the chair, feeling all her energy draining away. She wondered why she hadn't followed her initial instinct that morning: coffee, Sudoku and a lingering day in bed.

She buzzed Walter's secretary, Denise, and left a message for him. What a pity, she thought, that he could not have some peace with all that was going on with his wife.

After some time, she heard a beeping sound coming from her purse. How ridiculous, Elie thought, she hated talking on the cell phone, now she had to receive messages from it? It brought to mind what one of the office interns told her – that she set the alarm on her phone as a daily reminder to take her birth control pill. A world I'm just not prepared for, Elie reflected.

The message was from Philip, wishing her a happy birthday and saying he would probably be home on time. She was grateful, at least, for that small piece of good news.

When Elie entered the apartment, she found her husband standing in the foyer, flipping through the mail.

"Hi! You're here! I'm so glad."

"I just arrived a few minutes ago. Luckily, my plane landed on time. Happy birthday, babe. Ready for your big night?" He kissed her.

"I think so. Although, with the day I've just had, I'd be happy to stay home and put my feet up. I guess there's no chance of that, though." She waited for a response but Philip was reading something.

"Do you like my hair? I had it done this afternoon." She took the mail that he handed her and followed him into the kitchen.

"It looks like it always does. I don't know why you don't try going blonde for a change." He took a bottle of Vouvray out of the wine refrigerator and poured two glasses. "Where's my girl? I thought Lexi would be staying with us."

"She decided to stay at Chloe's apartment for a few days. They're getting in some quality sister time."

"Oh, nice. So, here's to your fiftieth, a celebratory drink to start off our evening." He raised his glass to hers. "And, a present to go with it." He took a small Cartier box out of his pocket and handed it to her.

"Wow! Thank you Philip. Should I open it later, at the restaurant?" She was disappointed at receiving the gift in such an unromantic way.

"No, now. I want you to wear them tonight. I also bought you a great Murano piece, limited edition. It's in the living room, but open this first."

She did as she was told. It was a pair of diamond earrings. "Oh my, they're gorgeous! But so extravagant! They must have cost a fortune."

"El, why do you always have to refer to the price of things? I can well afford it. Put them on."

She took off her pearl studs and replaced them with the diamonds. They were exquisite – large, square-cut stones set in platinum. She kissed and thanked her husband, choosing not to mention the fact that he bought her a very similar pair for their twenty-fifth wedding anniversary, two years before.

Elie suggested they move to the den to catch up on each other's news. After their older daughter moved out, they remodeled her bedroom and it became Elie's favorite spot in the apartment.

The sofa was from the Pinstripe Collection of Sands Home Furnishings, Philip's company. She had it upholstered in charcoal gray linen with hot pink piping. The coffee table was an antique steamer trunk discovered at a flea market in Connecticut, and the rug was a pastel Dhurrie. Above the sofa, she had hung black and white photographs of the family. For the first time since living in the apartment, Elie had decorated every inch of the room according to her taste, not Philip's, and she loved the result. He did not.

As they drank the wine, Philip spoke about the company and described the new furniture designs that he and his Italian partners had been working on during his trip. Then he went on to list all the business parties he had attended in Milan.

"You know, El, it's getting old. I am so over these furniture festivals by now. Lots of press, all the who's who of the design and architecture world. Wait until our party out at the Hamptons.

We'll show them! What's happening here? Anything I need to know about?"

Elie thought for a moment. "Well, let's see. It's been great spending time with Lexi. I took off a day and we went shopping, got some great stuff for her and her stepchildren. We drove out to Queens and spent time with my mother. And, as I told you on the phone, we had dinner with your folks. Nice evening."

Elie took a sip of wine, and then began to talk about her work. As she mentioned the mystery of the Montecristo affair, Philip interrupted her.

"Babe, I think we should get ready. I don't want anyone to have to wait for us. I'll shower in the girls' bathroom." Although both daughters were living elsewhere, the bathroom was still referred to as theirs.

Elie showered carefully and applied more makeup than usual, going for a dramatic effect. She used a kohl pencil under her lower lashes, outlined her lips and applied two coats of mascara. The outfit she had purchased for the occasion was a Guy Laroche winter white pantsuit. The jacket had a low-cut neckline that boosted her cleavage, and a cinched-in waist that flared out and covered her backside, which she always thought was too big. The slacks were straight-legged, ending in a cuff. With sexy high heels and the new diamond earrings, she felt quite glamorous.

Philip sported a navy jacket, gray slacks, a light gray shirt and a Missoni striped tie. Elie looked at him and thought that for a man in his mid-fifties, he was still quite striking. Tall, well built, his thick dark hair peppered with gray, the crow's feet surrounding his dark brown eyes only adding to his charm. She was turned on by how attractive he looked.

"What's with the pantsuit? I thought you'd wear something black and sexy." He glanced at her as he took his keys from the foyer table.

"I just bought this and I love it. Anyway, I'm getting too old for black. It doesn't look as good on me as it used to. I think I look okay, don't I?"

"I guess. El, what's the deal with the fancy soap in the bathroom? I smell like a bordello."

It took her a second to relate to what he was saying. "Umm, Gloria must have put it in there. I suppose we ran out of the regular."

"I hate that flowery French crap, it's so pretentious. Why do we even have that kind of soap in the apartment? Get the regular kind and instruct Gloria not to put that stuff in there again. Come on, let's go."

Elie was annoyed by his comments, but she decided not to make an issue out of it. She took a black Pashmina shawl from the hall closet and wrapped it around her shoulders, hoping it would be enough to keep her warm. They left the apartment and headed down to the garage.

They arrived at Casa di Venezia and were delighted to find the restaurant's private room looking ridiculously festive. Besides the usual salamis in red fishnet bags, baskets of plastic ivy hanging from the ceiling, and the panoramic wall mural of Venice, there were hurricane lamps flickering on the red and white checkered tablecloth and balloons and streamers strung everywhere.

With the loudspeakers cranked up and a tenor belting out Italian opera classics in the background, the owner, Alfredo, popped open a bottle of champagne and regaled Elie.

As friends and family began to arrive, the atmosphere became joyful. The Sands' daughters showed up first. Lexi, looking older than her twenty-six years, was modestly dressed in a turtleneck sweater and skirt. Chloe, younger than her sister by two years but decades ahead in style, wore a chocolate brown, scooped neck body suit tucked into stretch pants with a wide leather belt hugging her small waist. She was stunning and Elie had to restrain herself from commenting on the revealing outfit.

Syd Sorenstein, Elie's best friend and upstairs neighbor, made a grand entrance enveloped in a sheared black mink coat. Her shimmering silver hair was swept off her face, flaunting her oversized hoop earrings. As always, she had glamour written all over her.

"Hey there, my gorgeous fifty year old friend!" She hugged Elie.

"I see you're wearing mink. Not very PC. I would have taken you for an animal rights activist." Philip smirked as he kissed her hello.

"And I would have taken you for someone who knows that his opinion doesn't rate a bleep on my radar screen. Now, where are my precious girls?" She turned her back on him and walked off in the direction of Chloe and Lexi.

Sophia Stein, Elie's mother, walked in next. Even at seventy plus, the traces of her beauty were evident on her face. She was the personification of elegance and grace.

Soon after, Philip's sister and brother-in-law entered the restaurant. Sandy, a slightly plump and perpetually smiling woman, was the wit of the family who could always be counted on for entertainment. Her husband, Richard, was a reserved man who appeared content just to be in his wife's company. Elie's mood lightened whenever they were around.

Elie's boss, Walter Lavigne, followed them. He kissed Elie, shook hands with Philip and introduced himself to the other guests.

Philip's parents were the last to arrive. Max Sands was a tall, distinguished looking man with a full head of gray hair. He was an old-fashioned sort of gentleman, exuding charm and warmth, and he was adored by all.

Tillie Sands, on the other hand, had an intimidating air about her. She was small in stature but enormous in presence. She wore designer clothes, anointed herself with expensive jewelry, doused herself with Shalimar perfume and proffered opinions on every possible topic. She was an acquired taste, and Elie was still working on the acquisition.

There was no sign of Elie's friend Michael Delmonico, but Philip insisted on starting the evening. He asked the guests to take their places around the large table and instructed Alfredo to bring out the food.

A parade of servers began streaming out of the kitchen. They set down platters of Chicken Cacciatore, Steak Florentine and Shrimp Scampi, followed by lasagna, Spaghetti Bolognese, sautéed escarole and a variety of fresh salads. For Chloe, who was vegetarian, and Lexi, who had recently become kosher, there were fish and pasta dishes. The waiters poured the wines, keeping a watchful eye out for empty glasses.

The setting was intimate and the mood was bubbling. People ate and drank, passed plates of food and spoke animatedly. When a platter was empty, it was refilled. After an hour, the guests begged for an end to the feast, no one could consume another bite. Philip asked Alfredo to have the table cleared. Then he nodded at Chloe, who stood up and gently tapped her glass with a knife.

"Attention, could I have your attention please?"

It took two more attempts before the room quieted down.

"My older sister, Lexi here, says she's suffering from jet lag, but I say she's playing the shy card. In any case, I shall be your Mistress of Ceremonies this evening." She turned to her mother. "Mom, I've asked a representative of each family to prepare a few words in your honor. And for once, you have to remain silent and just listen. We are in charge tonight. So, without further ado, I would like to ..."

"Why do I get the feeling that I'm about to be roasted?" Elie looked up at her daughter and winked.

"No comment." Chloe turned towards her grandmother. "Nonna, as you produced my mother, would you kindly be the first to acknowledge her birthday?"

Sophia stood up at her place and clasped her hands together. "My darling, Eleanora, how do I express in words how much you mean to me?"

Normally reserved, Sophia opened up for the occasion and reminisced about Elie's childhood. She complimented her daughter on the way she built her life – with a wonderful husband, two beautiful daughters, a lovely home and an important career. The smile on her face faded only when she mentioned her late husband.

"I suppose the only thing I can be sad about today is that my sweet Aaron is no longer with us. When our daughter was born, he said that she was the best Hanukkah present a man could wish for. And although we were never able to have more children, we were always so grateful for the gift of Eleanora."

Sophia ended with an Italian blessing for good health and long life. Even after sixty years in America, Italian was still her preferred language.

Sandy was called on next, and she began with a description of the first time Philip's family met Elie.

"Gee, we're going back so many years now. I recall that Richard and I were sitting around planning our annual July Fourth family barbecue. Philip, the brother too busy to ever call me, phones and says he wants to bring his girl up to Scarsdale for it. I thought, *yahoo*, we're finally going to meet the mystery lady! And maybe, just maybe, my big shot brother is going to settle down and stop being such a playboy. He didn't admit it, but I knew why he wanted to bring Elie. So that she could meet the boss. Because without our mother's approval, there was never going to be a *chasaneh*. No marriage. *Nada!*"

Philip objected, as did his mother.

"Hush up little brother, it's my turn. As for you, Mama, you know this is the *emes*. I speak only the truth." Sandy often threw out Yiddish-sounding words just to tease her mother, because Tillie made believe she didn't understand the language of the old country.

"Can you just imagine how nervous I was? I hear that this Elie person is in the interior design business. Did I need this? Some gorgeous young chickadee with an eye for detail checking out my home? My humongous house that looks like a cement factory on the outside and a *tchotchke* palace on the inside!

The big day arrives. They pull up in Philip's pretentious little convertible. Remember that ridiculous red MG of yours Philly?" She shot her brother a mischievous look. "I had *purses* bigger than that car!

But before the cute couple can even step into the house, my kids pounce on them. 'Uncle Philly is here, Uncle Philly is here', they're yelling. The poor girlfriend looked like she was about to faint. So, what did I do? I rescued her! I grabbed sweet, shy Elie, whisked her off to the kitchen, and asked my mother to take the children outside." She looked at Elie. "Wasn't that kind of me, Elie?"

"It sure was, Sandy." Elie was laughing and shaking her head.

"We got through the afternoon relatively well and I was thinking that it's all going to be just fine. *Then* it happened. My mother, bless her heart, starts the interrogation. I tell you folks, the steaks on the barbecue were *nothing* compared to the grilling that poor girl got. I felt so bad for her."

Tillie glanced at her husband, expecting him to defend her, but Max just put his fingers to his lips.

"Mom begins by asking Elie about her background, whether she is an Ashkenazi Jew, like us, or Sephardic. She knew that Sophia Stein was born in Libya, that her family fled to Italy to escape persecution, and that later on she followed her older brother to America. Continuing in her roots research, Mom discerns that Elie's dad had been a refugee from Poland. That much information she had yanked out of my brother. But Mom needs to know *exactly* how Elie was raised." Sandy turned towards her mother. "Remember, Mama, how you wanted all the details of Elie's upbringing?"

"No *Sandra*, I do not remember that." Tillie was noticeably annoyed.

The only person in the room who did not seem intimidated by Tillie's response was Sandy, who kept on talking. "Elie, after that inquisition my mother put you through, I couldn't believe you were relaxed enough to take off your cute shoes, with the bows and kitten heels, and play Twister on the grass with the kids. And then, remember you helped me in the kitchen and we talked about how we both loved Julia Child and were addicted to her show on PBS? And you complimented me on our home. You told me it was so lovely and welcoming. Boy, was I was flattered! Like, how could I not love you?

To sum up, I think it's a damn miracle that you put up with my brother all these years. But honey, I am so glad you did. Richard and I, and of course our Amy and Eric, wish you at least another fifty marvelous years on this planet. We love you to pieces, sweet Elie." Sandy threw a sweeping kiss to her sister-in-law and sat down, to the sound of applause.

"Do I need this aggravation from my own family?" Philip exclaimed. "Who's next?" He crossed his legs and looked impatient.

"Hang on, Dad," Chloe piped up. "Why don't you have another drink?"

"I shouldn't. I have to maintain my perfect body."

Everyone laughed and began to tease Philip about his vanity.

It was Tillie's turn, but before she could speak, Walter walked over to Elie, whispered in her ear, touched her shoulder and walked out of the room. Tillie waited for the door to close, then cleared her throat and began.

"I shall now set things straight." She turned to face her daughter-in-law. "Elie, my dear, it is not true that I interrogated you when Philip brought you to meet us. I just wanted to know a little about your family. After all, a mother should be familiar with the girl her only son intends to marry. Don't you agree, dear?"

Philip glanced at his sister, she caught his look and they both chuckled. "Oh come on, Mom. You gave Elie and me such a hard time. So, how about this? Almost thirty years we've been married!" He was a bit drunk; otherwise, he never would have taken on his mother.

"Philip, I will thank you not to interrupt me." She glared at him for a second, and then continued. "Once we knew that Elie was a good girl, from a good family, we had no objection."

"Yeah, because after all, we're descendants of Russian nobility, right Ma?" Sandy rolled her eyes, while everyone else snickered.

"Oh, here we go again. Pass me the Moscato. I can see this night is never going to end." Philip reached for the bottle, which was handed to him by an amused Richard.

Tillie went on to talk about the Rosh Hashanah lunch at Sophia's house when the two families met for the first time. "You made such nice Sephardic food; it was really a lovely afternoon, dear."

Sophia smiled in acknowledgment and overlooked the fact that Tillie, after all these years, still had to throw in a reference to her background, and always with an air of superiority.

In a span of just a few minutes, Tillie wove into her remarks that Elie and Philip's wedding was not as she would have liked it, that she and Max bought the "kids" their home, that they took the girls on extraordinary trips as Bat Mitzvah presents, and that they handed Philip a ready-made business. She ended on a note about Elie being worthy of their love and wishing her many more happy and healthy years. "Because, as I've always said, if you're healthy, you're wealthy!"

As Tillie sat down, Max stood up. "May I just add that our family has been enriched by having Elie Sands in it. And if I may borrow a blessing from our forefathers, you should live til a hundred and twenty. And I hope I'm around for a good many of them!"

"Hear! Hear! Amen!" The guests were raising their glasses and toasting.

Suddenly the door to the room swung open.

"*Helloooo!* We're here! Did you start without us? Ah yes, I see you did. Well, we will just have to catch up."

It was Michael Delmonico and his partner Daniel. As Michael made his way around the table, kissing everyone on both cheeks, removing his leather jacket and adjusting the scarf around his neck, he continued to talk, to no one in particular. Daniel discreetly mouthed to Elie that he was sorry they were late.

"You would not believe what happened. I was at the Metropolitan Museum overseeing the last details of the black tie soiree they're throwing for some fashionista. I know, I know, what's a famous interior designer like me doing working on a fashion party? Well, I promised a friend I would supervise the design.

It was a d-i-s-a-s-t-e-r! The flowers were gladiolas and I had specifically ordered calla lilies. The napkins were polyester. Can you imagine? *Polyester!* What a bunch of Philistines. Well, I just threw a hissy fit, and it worked. It took a major effort, but in the end, I got everything straightened out." He stopped to take a breath. "*Sooooo*, what did we miss?"

Philip shook his head and passed him the bottle of wine. Alfredo was summoned from the kitchen and asked to bring back the food. Michael feigned objection, saying that he was so nervous he couldn't eat a thing, but he gave explicit orders to the waiters as to what he wanted. He was oblivious to the furtive glances and grins around the table.

Michael's sudden arrival caused Elie to laugh, and to indulge in a bit of nostalgia. His lateness may have been unintentional, but it was typical. Michael always had to make a grand entrance, the more conspicuous, the better.

They met during their first year of college, at the Fashion Institute of Technology. Elie enrolled hoping to be a big interior design star, Michael enrolled knowing he would be. Almost from the start, they became the best of friends.

When not in class, the two would sit in the Fashion Diner on Seventh Avenue, sharing gossip and tuna melts. Michael always had something to say, about the professors, the other students, their work, their fashion sense or the lack thereof. He never ran out of topics or criticisms. Elie usually listened and laughed.

The roles the friends played in each other's lives were established early on. Michael insisted on creating a fuss over everything, and he needed constant attention. He was narcissistic, fastidious and opinionated. He was also entertaining, boyishly handsome and extraordinarily talented. It was clear to Elie, the professors, and all the students, that Michael Delmonico was a rising star.

Elie was the calm and rational half of the duo, always the voice of reason. She adored Michael's sense of humor and felt honored that he chose to hang around with her. Ever since her best friend, Devi, moved away in high school, she had longed for that intimate bond with someone. She found it in Michael. He glided effortlessly into the roles of confidante, tutor and wardrobe advisor.

Michael finished his tirade and Chloe resumed her position.

"Next, I would like to introduce someone who has provided a constant and nurturing presence in our lives, because … she lives upstairs! I have known her my entire life and I love her very much. Financial consultant to the rich and famous and mom's very dear friend, I present to you, Ms. Sydell Cohen Sorenstein."

Even at sixty, Syd Sorenstein was stunning. Her perfect skin, deeply set gray-green eyes, sculpted cheekbones and striking silver hair produced a head-turning beauty. She wore a black silk caftan with iridescent threads woven through it, something she "picked up" in Marrakesh, and her arms were covered with silver bangle bracelets. She wore a large emerald ring on her left hand, next to a diamond wedding band.

She winked at Chloe, which Elie did not miss, and faced the others. "My, my, we are so formal this evening. Doesn't it seem like this is turning into an Elie fest? Shouldn't we add some of the naughty stuff?"

"You wouldn't dare!" Elie called out.

"Try me." Syd responded. "Okay, I'll keep this PG rated. I met our dear girl eons ago in the lobby of our building. She was struggling with a baby carriage and packages, but was too shy to ask the doorman for help. I, not usually the friendly or helpful type ..."

"You can say that again." Michael said it a little too loudly.

Syd glared at Michael, and then continued. "Where was I? Oh yes, so I saw this woman in distress and I gallantly stepped in to offer assistance." She bowed and gracefully waved her arm.

"You actually kidnapped me!" Elie loved that Syd was talking about their first meeting.

"Indeed, I did. I convinced you to come up to my apartment. And I am certain that when you walked in, you wanted to *plotz*." She looked from Elie to the others again. "You see, we were living in the penthouse of a Central Park West building, the same one as now, only it looked more like a student dorm. Anyway, the apartment decoration is another story." Syd shot a piercing glance at Michael.

"From that day on, Elie and I became best friends and we have remained so all the ensuing years. Naturally, I had to take Philip as part of the package, so be it." She smiled at Philip, knowing that her comment would elicit a response.

"Who invited this woman?" He was now too inebriated to try to hide his feelings.

"Quiet, Dad." Chloe interrupted. "Aunt Syd is like family."

Syd regaled the guests with stories of shared cooking lessons (Elie benefited, Syd did not), bridge lessons (they both gave up), shopping jaunts, baby and dog sitting, and the sad times when her husband was ill.

"To be completely honest, Elie has been a treasure in my life. She calmed me when I was nervous, nursed me when I was sick, and gave me pep talks when I needed them. No, allow me to clarify that. The pep talks were when *she* figured I needed them, not necessarily when *I* needed them." She raised her eyebrows and looked directly at Elie. "Could have done without some of those, darling."

Without waiting for a response, she went on. "My darling Julian was very fond of our Elie and she was such a source of comfort to me when he was dying. Oh hell, let me not get into that."

While Syd spoke, Elie thought back. Initially, she had been intimidated by Syd's strong personality, but she learned to regard her as an honest and forthright person whose friendship she cherished.

"So, in conclusion, I would like to say that I adore having you as my dear friend and neighbor. I am delighted that you chose our little hi-rise on the park in which to build your nest and I hope that the powers that be will grant you many more lovely years on this earth." Syd reached across the table to take Elie's hands in hers.

Elie smiled and bowed her head in acknowledgment. She was starting to feel uncomfortable with the tributes and was about to say something when her daughter interrupted her thoughts.

"Now, ladies and gentlemen, it gives me great pleasure to call upon Michael Delmonico, interior designer *par excellence* and Mom's friend for more years than I've existed. Michael, would you please say a few words about my mother?"

Michael delicately wiped his mouth with his napkin, adjusted his scarf and stood up. He ceremoniously cleared his throat.

"Good evening, ladies and gentlemen. I met my darling Eleanora in design school, at the illustrious FIT right here in *le grand apple*. I was there to learn about our glorious profession, while she was there to … actually I haven't the faintest idea what she was doing there." He turned to face Elie. "You never did catch on, did you sweetie? Isn't that why you chose to get into design via the back door as a magazine editor, rather than interior designer?"

"Don't you start with me, Michael." Elie bunched up her napkin and aimed it at him. "I know you're going to make it sound like I was totally hopeless."

"Well, dearie, if the Manolo fits … Anyway folks, allow me to share one particular antidote."

"That would be anecdote," Philip gloated, rolling his eyes.

"Whatever. So, we were sitting in our History of Ancient Furniture class. I, naturally, was paying close attention. Eleanora, naturally, was not. All of a sudden in walks this guy – rather, in *swaggers* this guy. He looks older than us, and straight, so I don't bother checking him out. However, our girl here? She gets all *gaga*. The teacher is droning on and on about ancient Greece and

Klysmos chairs, and Eleanora turns to me and says, 'Never mind the Greek furniture, how about the Greek god who just walked in. Isn't he the dreamiest?'

So I'm like, yeah, he's okay, but not really my type. You want him? You can have him. But *nooooo*, our Eleanora here first has to find out if he's Jewish. Because Adonis or no Adonis, if the guy isn't Jewish, well then it just ain't kosher. Right, Mrs. Stein?" Michael waved at Elie's mother. "And lo and behold, what happened next? That guy turned out to be Philip here and she deserted me for him! Can you imagine?"

Everyone laughed, except Philip.

Michael pushed back his dirty blond hair. "We used to have such fun. Gossiping about the other students, their *horricious* taste in clothes ..."

"I think you mean horrific." Chloe corrected him.

"Yeah, yeah. Anyway, we were ever so perfect and the other students were so very ordinary. That's how we spent four glorious years together. Oops, sorry about that, three years together. Miss E. went off to Israel for one year. I cannot vouch for what she did there. I can surmise, but I better not say."

"That's enough, Michael. Your time is up." Elie pointed to her watch.

Both Chloe and Lexi perked up and called out to Michael to provide details.

"Nope, sorry girls. Can't fill you in on those days. I wasn't there to witness them. But I can tell you about some adventures your mom and I had in Chicago, when we attended the Neocon convention."

"Michael, that's really enough now!" Elie raised her voice, the crowd laughed and Philip signaled the waiters to keep pouring the drinks.

"Ah, Neocon! Do you all know about Neocon? Not the political movement, but the convention of office furniture companies that takes place in the Merchandise Mart in Chicago every year. Everyone who is anyone attends, and then they forget that they are supposed to go to the showrooms to see the new furniture lines because they're too hung over from partying the night before. I won a trip there because I was the best student, of course, and I took Elie as my roomie. Oh my word, did we have a ball! I nearly got married in the back office of one of the showrooms and Elie got ..."

"*Michael!*"

"Okay. Okay. Let me think, what really happened? Oh yeah, she got a job, that's it! She met the legendary Walter Lavigne and he offered her a job because he liked some article she wrote about his magazine when she was working for the student paper. So, my best friend gave up a career in interior design to become a rising star in the world of publishing. You know what they say – if you can't do it, write about it."

"Excuse me, but did you think we would continue with our friendship after this little speech of yours tonight?" Elie interrupted.

"Oh hush up, girl. You'll never give me up. You're addicted to me. Now seriously, what I want to say is that I love you, Miss Eleanora. You are an extraordinary woman, from every point of view. You are funny, pretty, well-dressed – that is when you obey my fashion advice – and you are a wonderful friend.

You married Philip even though I thought you could have done much better, but you did produce two divine daughters with him. You have brought much joy into my life and I'm sure my darling Daniel here will agree. We love you to pieces. *Mazel tov* on your fiftieth birthday, my sweet. And that's a most genuine *mazel tov* coming from this Catholic boy and his devoted partner."

To the applause and laughter of the guests, Michael bowed and sat down.

Chloe then took a piece of paper out of an envelope and spoke. "This is a letter sent to Mom from the wife of the American Ambassador to Israel, Mrs. Devorah Strauss Young, known to us as Devi. She is Mom's oldest childhood friend."

Elie instinctively put her hand to her heart, touched that Devi had remembered this occasion.

Chloe read Devi's letter. It mentioned childhood experiences shared by the two girls: playing dress-up, going to synagogue services and escaping before the rabbi's sermon, obsessing over cute boys, passing notes in class. There was a reference to Enoch, the black boy Elie had a crush on, and the girls' subsequent interest in civil rights. Devi wrote about her brother, Josh, who helped them with their math homework and put up with their incessant giggling. He even took on their dares to eat everything they piled on his plate at the Passover and Hanukkah dinners that Elie shared with the Strauss family. Then the letter touched on a part of Elie's life that no one else knew about: the year at Tel Aviv University. The girls had spent their junior year of college there, and it was life changing for both.

As Chloe read Devi's final words aloud – wishing her friend happiness and the successful pursuit of dreams yet unfulfilled – Elie felt a lump in her throat. She quickly wiped away tears that were welling up in her eyes, hoping that no one noticed.

Chloe put the letter back in the envelope and handed it to her mother.

As the crowd was commenting on Devi's words, Alfredo walked in and whispered into Philip's ear. Philip nodded and within seconds, a procession of waiters marched in carrying trays of desserts.

Tiramisus, éclairs, cannolis, amaretto cookies and mini ricotta cheesecakes were distributed throughout the length of the table. Alfredo brought out more Vino Santo and Moscato and it looked like the party would never end.

Lexi, who had been sitting quietly all evening, got up. "Actually, if it's okay, I *would* like to say a few words." She looked at her sister and took a deep breath.

"As you all know, I moved to Israel a year ago. I married a wonderful man who was widowed, and became a mother to his two little children. I really love my life there, but I will never stop missing what I have here. In honor of my mother's birthday, I would like to say a few words directly to her. No doubt my loquacious sister can say this better, but I'll do my best."

Lexi looked at Elie. "Mom, you're the best. You were always there for us. You *schlepped* us to after school activities, led our Girl Scout troops, baked us our favorite cookies, chaperoned our class trips. You let us pick out a new Barbie doll every year, for no other reason than we wanted to add to our collections.

You arranged the most amazing parties and sleepovers for us. The kids in my class couldn't wait for my birthday, because they knew I'd show up with some dazzling cake, covered in candies. You even managed through our teen years, although admittedly, I was a joy, while Chloe was quite a handful."

Chloe reached over and playfully slapped her sister on the arm and Lexi slapped her back.

"Mom, I think you're a really fine person, as a mother and a human being. I love you so much and I hope that when I reach the age of fifty, I can emulate you."

Elie sat smiling with one hand folded under her chin. She touched Philip's arm with her other hand.

"To tell you the truth, I agonized over what kind of gift to bring you. I wanted something special that would express my love. But I couldn't come up with anything even faintly appropriate. And then I realized, I already had the perfect gift for you!" Lexi swallowed, as if to stall for time and courage. "I won't be able to provide it for another six months, but I think when it comes, you'll love it. Mom, Dad, I will be presenting you with your very own grandchild. And I really hope I can be as good a parent, to him or her, as you have been to me."

There was a second of silence and then a roar rose up from the table. Elie jumped out of her seat and rushed over to hug her daughter. Philip followed, and all those in the room shared the family's joy. The party was turning into an evening way beyond Elie's expectations. Lexi couldn't continue. She sat down and reached for a glass of water.

It took several minutes before Chloe could speak. "Wow! Who can follow that? I was planning to say something, but after my sister's beautiful words and her amazing announcement, I'm speechless. Dad, would you like to take over?"

Philip went back to his place. "That's one hell of a tough act to follow. Imagine – we're going to be grandparents! Lexi, it's wonderful news, cookie." He took a deep breath and looked at Elie.

"My darling wife, it is hard for me to believe that you have reached the grand old age of fifty. And now I realize that pretty soon I'll be sleeping with a grandmother! Umm, I'll have to consider that."

"As will I, Philip. Don't forget – I'll be sleeping with a grandpa."

Elie smirked.

"Okay, point made. You know, El, you don't look much older than when I first met you. You were such a sweet, naive girl in those days. You had that long dark curly hair, which you were forever trying to blow dry straight. And you had that annoying habit of tapping your foot when you got nervous. Now look at you! All I can say is that it has been a pleasure spending this last quarter of a century with you, and as far as I'm concerned, you've still got it! Not bad for fifty years on this planet. May you stay as beautiful as you are right now." Philip motioned for the guests to join him in a toast and he kissed his wife on the lips.

He sat down and told Elie it was her turn.

She stood up, took a deep breath, then another. "I feel embarrassed, but so grateful to you all." She hesitated, playing with a tissue in her hand. "This evening has gone way beyond my dreams. I feel so blessed for what I have in life. I'm thankful for my generous husband, my darling girls, a great job, a family I can count on and friends who support and encourage me. We are all healthy, knock on wood, and just when I thought things could not get any better, Lexi gives us her wonderful news."

Elie went on to acknowledge everyone in the room individually, giving credit to each for the unique contribution made to her life.

"It's getting late. I would just like to add, that for a woman of fifty, I could not possibly ask for anything more than what I have right at this moment. I hope you will all celebrate future birthdays with me and as a final message, allow me to say ... *fifty rocks!*"

The guests laughed and applauded and Elie made her way around the table kissing and thanking all in attendance.

When the evening wore down, there was a final round of hugging, kissing and promises to get together. Michael whispered into Elie's ear that he had news to tell her and she had better call him. Lexi went home with Chloe, and while Elie gathered up the presents, Philip settled the bill. They left the restaurant loaded with gifts, including a box of cannolis from Alfredo.

As Philip drove uptown, Elie was on a high, spilling out all her good feelings. She raved about the lovely tributes and the wonderful friends and family she had. When she finally stopped talking, she looked at Philip, waiting for him to agree that it was a perfect evening.

"It was nice, but I could have done without your fan club."

"What do you mean? Are you talking about Syd and Michael?"

"Of course, who else? Who does that *schmuck* think he is, coming so late? And Syd, with that mouth of hers? I've never understood what you see in her. I think if we were keeping the party small, it should have just been family. But whatever. Everyone enjoyed it and Alfredo did a great job."

Elie was silent. She didn't want to get into it with him and wasn't willing to spoil the magical feeling she had. She had just enough alcohol left in her to ignore his comments and stay floating.

Two

Elie had planned to take Friday off, but there were too many loose ends left at the office. She decided to go in for a few hours and then meet her daughters for a shopping spree.

She greeted Heather at the reception desk and asked for her mail.

"Already spoken for. Keira took in the first batch when she arrived. I also gave her a note for you from Mr. L."

At the entrance to her office Elie was surprised to find the door open, knowing that she had closed it the day before. After putting away her jacket and purse, she headed over to Walter's office. She had worried about him after he left the party, and she needed to discuss the Montecristo problem with him.

She looked through the glass wall and saw that he was not in. She left a message with Denise and on the way back to her office, ran into Keira.

"Hey, Keira. How's it going?" She decided to ignore yesterday's outburst.

"Don't ask. Too busy. I took some stuff from your office earlier and was trying to plow through it. I made some notes for you. Want a cup of coffee? I'm on my way to get one."

"Sure, that would be great. Thanks."

Elie walked back to her office thinking about Keira. She had hired her right out of journalism school and it was a good decision. The young woman had proven to be worth her weight in gold, generally predicting Elie's needs and coping well with the masses of work. However, lately, there was something strange about her behavior – she was becoming unpredictable and testy. Elie wondered what was at the bottom of it, and how it would affect the projects that needed to get done.

Because of her promotions at the magazine, Elie's workload had intensified, as had her responsibilities. When she was first hired, she was the gofer girl, going on photography shoots in order to ensure that the rooms were set up correctly. Now she was considered number two in the hierarchy and, although she wasn't expected to, she kept abreast of developments in every department of the magazine.

She demanded that all articles and photos pass her desk before publication and on occasion, when Walter wanted a special angle, he requested that Elie write the article herself.

Keira walked into the office, her arm hugging bunches of papers to her chest and a coffee cup in each hand. "Here you go, your morning Java and another zillion requests for fame and fortune."

"Ah, I see you are excellent at juggling. Here, put it down on my desk."

"I went through these letters already. Most are from unknowns and aren't worth much, but I indicated with a Post-It the ones I thought might have potential."

"Great. What's happening with that Arizona story I told you about last week? The luxury retirement community on the golf course in Scottsdale. Have you dug in yet?"

"Ah yes, *the* place for blue-blood octogenarians. No, I haven't had a chance. I'll try to get to it today."

"Keira, it's very important. I want it to run in the May issue. Please make that your priority."

"Okay, okay."

Elie ignored Keira's impatient tone. "I'll go through some of this, but I'm going to leave early today so let's talk next Tuesday. I'll be out on Monday; it's my last day with my daughter before she flies back to Israel."

"No problem. Oh, there's a note for you from Mr. L. on the top of the pile. I'll be plugging away if you need me. *Ciao.*" She left the office and closed the door behind her.

Walter's note was simple: *No to Montecristo project – must find sub. Talk to me.*

There was the partial answer to her question, but she was anxious to know the rest. She was trying to keep herself from panicking. Pulling that story off the editorial calendar was bad. Another project would have to be found as a replacement. And fast!

Elie glanced at the letters on her desk, all from designers, architects and owners requesting consideration of their projects. Understandable, since publication in *Interior Design & Style* conferred superstar status on designers and prestige for their clients.

She always felt mixed emotions when tackling this part of the job. She did not relish the position of sitting on high, judging who's in and who's out. Although she kept in mind that it was interior design and not brain surgery, the projects' initiators felt differently. She was always amazed at people who had such utter confidence in their work.

Their letters often began with something like *I am sure you will be astounded by my design on this Boca Raton chateau* or *This villa is the quintessential post-modern, deconstructionist expression*. A favorite was *This office should be on the pages of your magazine because it is a sublime rendering of minimalism in the work place.*

As a student, Elie had never possessed that kind of confidence. Perhaps that was why she became an editor and not a designer – not being certain enough about her own creative talent.

There was a knock on the door. Walter popped his head in, startling her. "Hey, someone in here looks very serious and I have a feeling it's not because of that project in Scottsdale. I heard you were looking for me."

"Hi! Good morning, Walter." She sat up straight. "Not to worry, Keira is taking care of the Scottsdale story."

"She better get her ass moving. I want a good piece. I'm glad you're giving her some of your load. You're too protective of her. What am I paying her salary for if you supervise her all the time and don't let her get her feet wet?" He sat down in one of the two chairs facing her desk.

"I've already reminded her that it's urgent. Walter, I wanted to talk to you." Elie went over to the door, closed it and sat down next to him.

"I was concerned when you left the party early last night. We missed each other at the office yesterday and there was so much going on. Is everything okay?"

"There are a few things happening."

"Care to share?"

"No, not right now. Your party was lovely Elie, but Katherine is not doing so well and I wanted to get home to her."

"Oh?" She waited to see if he would continue.

"It's been confirmed that she has Alzheimer's disease." He crossed his legs and brushed some lint off his pants.

"Oh, Walter. I am so sorry. I was hoping that there would be another reason for her behavior, something less serious."

"I'm afraid not."

Elie didn't know what to say, and felt that whatever she offered would sound lame. "Katherine is such a lovely woman, it's so damn unfair."

"Katherine is a remarkable woman." Walter leaned back in the chair and looked directly at Elie. "Did you know that she gave up a very promising modeling career when she married me? She was quite a looker. On top of that, the connection to her family was all but severed. Imagine, their Texas debutante marrying this tough New York Jew. And a Jew in publishing yet, with hardly a pot to piss in."

"It must have been very difficult for you both." Elie was touched that Walter was opening up to her.

"Yes, it was. I could not believe that this goddess of a creature was willing to disregard everything she held dear in order to build a life with me. And you know what? Not once in all these years, and I am talking fifty years now, not once did she complain, or throw it back at me. I've been one hell of a lucky bastard."

"What will you do?"

"I'm considering options. I've been thinking of moving her to our house upstate. I'll have to find a suitable companion, but she really loves it up there, much more than our apartment here in the city. You should see the joy on her face when she's in the country. There are horse stables nearby, and as you know, a small lake on our property. Maybe being close to nature will bring back her old self."

"Will you join her there?" Elie wondered if Walter was about to make a major change.

"I intend to go up every weekend, and I will try to stay one or two weeknights. I think I need to slow down a bit anyway. I am past seventy now. Maybe it's time this old goat took a break."

"Excuse me? I don't think so. I cannot imagine this magazine without you. You are *Interior Design & Style*."

"Don't be silly. I am not this magazine, I just founded it. No one is irreplaceable, and it would be wise of you to remember that. The magazine can move ahead without me. But, let's not get carried away. I'm still here, no need for eulogies yet. I just thought you should know about Katherine's situation. No one else knows. Well, Denise does, but that's it. I'd like to keep this between us."

"Yes, of course. And I know it sounds trite, but I mean this with all my heart, if I can be of any help at all, please think of me. You know, don't you, that I would do just about anything for you. I owe you the world."

"Eleanora Sands, you owe me nothing, nothing at all. Don't talk like that. I would not have asked you to work here if I did not believe you had great potential, and you have proven me right, ever since that day I hired you right out of design school. Now, enough of this mushy stuff. Why did I come in here? You summoned me, did you not?"

"I did want to check on your situation, I was worried. I also found a note here from you about the Montecristo project. There was a bit of a flare-up yesterday between him and Keira. *And,* I got a call from James Hendricks canceling their ad campaign. One batch of bad news on top of another, I'm afraid."

"Yeah, I know about it all. That damn fool. I've lost all patience with these designers. What a piece of work that Montecristo is."

"What happened?"

"I was here late on Wednesday in order to finish up some things. The phone rang and since I was the only one around, I answered it. It was the owner of the estate."

"The client with the castle in Luxembourg?"

"The one and only. He must have been really fuming because it was the middle of the night over there. He started shouting at me, saying that he does not want his estate to be used in our magazine. That he's going to sue Montecristo for embezzlement and breach of contract and if we use the story about his home, he'll sue us too. Seems that our Count de Monte Crisco did not fulfill his obligations, and this guy is very displeased. Big time."

Elie laughed at Walter's intentional mispronunciation. "What did you say?"

"What do you think? I told him to stop being a namby-pamby, that I'm not the address for his temper tantrum, and that he should shove it."

Elie laughed. "You did not. Seriously, how did you react?"

"I told him I was very sorry to hear that there had been problems, that of course I will respect his wishes, but that I hoped he would settle his differences with Montecristo and not prevent us from using his home in the magazine. I told him that according to the photographs I saw, it was spectacular and he did a marvelous job respecting the integrity of the property, that his ancestors would surely be proud and that I hoped he would change his mind. And that we were considering making his estate the cover story. Some crap like that."

"Walter, I'm sure he signed a release form. We do have the rights if you want to run it."

"No thanks. I'm not taking that route. Legally we're covered, but why risk it? Because we spent thousands to send a crew over there? I'd rather shoot Crisco in the balls; it would give me greater pleasure and be worth every penny of the money lost."

He played with a paperweight on the desk. "Obviously that story can't run in the September issue as we planned. I am not a happy man right now – I wanted to make a big splash with it after the summer vacation. Elie, this would be a very good time to have one of your brainstorms. I also have a call in to the Crisco kid to get back to me ASAP. Problem is, he left last night for Santa Fe – supposedly to a spa to rest his nerves. But I know that he's using it as an excuse to get his face done."

"No! How did you find that out?" Elie snickered, admiring Walter's uncanny ability to know what was going on everywhere.

"What, you don't know me by now? I can find out anything. So do not think you can keep secrets from me, kid. I have my methods!" He winked, got up from the chair and walked out of her office.

Two minutes later, the telephone buzzed on the direct line. She picked it up and heard: "And Eleanora, don't protect that assistant of yours. Get her to finish that Scottsdale story or I'm going to give it to someone else and it won't be pretty for her! And no *dreck* about handicapped accessible bathrooms and extra wide corridors. You know what I mean." He hung up.

Elie shook her head, smiling, and thought about Walter. He was a larger than life character. At first, she was intimidated by him, but over time her admiration and respect for him increased. He was a natural in the business world, knowing what would sell, which designers were headed for greatness, and what the public wanted. In addition, he was honest and straightforward.

She recalled one particular instance, many years ago, when she had gathered up her courage to approach him with a question. She wanted to know, within the scope of her work as a photo shoot assistant, about room authenticity – whether she had to remain faithful to the space if she thought there was something out of context. It was her job to spruce up interiors with fresh flowers and timely journals. But what about accessories? What if the client had placed some awful vase or sculpture in the room? Leave it, or remove it in order to conform to a design style?

She was surprised at the severity of his response. He took the cigar out of his mouth, sat on the front edge of his desk and peered across at her.

"Eleanora, we have a responsibility to the public. We do not choose rooms because we like the interior designer and want to promote his or her work. We select projects because of their contribution to good design. It is our job to share wonderful settings with the public. To show people what good taste is, to offer them a glimpse into the world of elegance and fine interior decoration."

He continued. "Now hear this! If a goddamn red plastic Buddha is sitting in the middle of a Georgian dining room table, do you think we should show it? Do you want every person in America to think that's okay? If a homeowner displays his Erté sculpture on a fireplace mantel in a Moroccan sitting room, do we show it on the pages of our magazine? No! We do not! We show authenticity, accuracy, whatever you want to call it, when it works. When it does not, we make it right! Now get your rear out of my office and let me go back to thinking about my stock portfolio."

Elie knew he was kidding about the stock portfolio. He was then, and now, the most devoted man she had ever met when it came to business. He reminded her of her father-in-law. They were both impressive men – smart, quick-witted and in spite of their advanced age, still commanding. Now that she was Walter's most trusted right hand, and by all accounts the prime candidate for his replacement, she wondered if she could ever measure up to the challenge.

Elie spent the next two hours dealing with high-priority matters, then she left to enjoy the remainder of the afternoon with her daughters. If last night had taught her anything, it was that time passes too quickly and one should grab life's opportunities.

After a successful shopping expedition through Bloomingdales, Elie came home with the girls and the family shared a Friday night dinner. Although they had never been religious, Elie had always tried to maintain the Jewish tradition of lighting *Shabbat* candles, reciting the prayers over the wine and *challah*, and sitting down to a home cooked dinner.

There was talk about the birthday party, the people who were there, the presents Elie received, and the letter from Devi. The girls wanted to know about that year in Israel, but Elie brushed them off. The subject was changed to Lexi and the impending birth of her child. Although pushed to reveal the sex, Lexi said she didn't want to know until the birth.

By Sunday afternoon, Elie was alone. Philip had left on another business trip and Lexi was back at Chloe's place. After spending most of the day absorbed in the newspaper, she began to feel restless. The excitement of the party and Lexi's news had kept her on a high, but now the reality of being fifty was sinking in. She also felt sad that her daughter would be returning to Israel in two days and she wouldn't be able to share the pregnancy with her. She decided to improve her melancholy mood by taking a walk through Central Park.

She bundled up against the December cold and headed into the park, where the landscapes, winding pathways, the lake and the city views always cheered her. After an hour in the frosty air, she'd had enough. Craving the warmth of home, she walked back towards her apartment.

She noticed the answering machine blinking with two messages. The first was from Philip. He said that all was fine, his battery was low and to call the hotel or showroom if she wanted to reach him. The second message came on.

"Miss Eleanora, your birthday party was a smash, darling. We loved it. Now will you please call me already, I have to spill my *gargantuan* news."

She laughed upon hearing Michael's message and looked forward to a gossipy chat with him.

In spite of their different backgrounds, Elie and Michael shared a solid bond – a genuine concern for one another and a mutual passion for the world of design and decoration. Each believed that an aesthetic, well-designed environment fosters harmony.

As a young child, Elie loved playing with all the elements: forms, colors, textiles and layouts. She could spend hours drawing and decorating imaginary rooms. Then, at the age of eleven, she met Charlotte – her mother's decorator friend – and that was it. She knew that this was her destiny.

Charlotte was the most glamorous woman Elie had ever seen. There was a Sophia Loren look about her – she had cascading auburn hair and an ample cleavage, which was always exposed. She dressed in jewel-toned fashions and wore large, dramatic pieces of jewelry. She lavished attention on the little girl, thoroughly captivating her.

On a few occasions, Charlotte took Elie to the D&D building on Third Avenue, the bastion of furniture and decoration showrooms. She introduced her to all the major houses, like Scalamandre Silks, Brunschwig Fabrics and Stark Carpets. She taught her the differences between damask and tapestry, voile and chenille. She showed Elie paint samples and patiently elucidated all the subtle variations that could exist in "plain" white – as in cream, vanilla and egg shell. Wherever she went, Charlotte was treated like royalty, and Elie felt like a princess when she was with her.

Michael, on the other hand, had chosen the profession for different reasons.

At the age of twelve, when left alone after school one day, he felt the urge to redecorate. Tackling the living room, he pushed the sofa to the other side of the room, then the armchairs, coffee table and rolling TV cart. Although he was a slight child, he found the strength to move everything. When he was done, he surveyed his work and felt very pleased with himself, thinking it all looked much better this way.

When his father came home that night, drunk and stumbling, he walked into the dark living room, fell over the chair, cut his lip on the edge of the coffee table and landed on the floor. That is where he stayed until morning, when found by his wife, who had just come home from working the night shift. He woke up hung over and furious, and he knew just who to blame.

He stormed into the bedroom that Michael shared with his younger brother, pulled him out of bed by the neck of his pajamas, dragged him into the living room and threw him down on the sofa. Then he exploded.

"You think this house is yours, you little shit? You think you can do what you want around here? Well, you're going to find out once and for all who's boss."

He ripped the belt off his pants and beat Michael with it. While the boy pleaded with him to stop and whimpered that he didn't mean it and that he would put everything back in place, his father ignored him and kept shouting and beating. Then, he dragged him down to the basement and ordered him to stay there.

"You want to fuck with my things? Live down here for a while and you'll think again about whose house this is."

Michael's mother stayed in the kitchen during the outburst, nervously smoking a cigarette while fearing for herself and her younger son, who was cowering behind her. When he was finished, Michael's father locked the door to the basement, threw the key on the kitchen table, warned his wife not to let the boy out and went to the bedroom to get ready for work. She waited for several minutes after he left before going downstairs to release her son from his prison.

"I decided right then, that one day I would make the world beautiful, and people would pay me for doing it." Michael told Elie. "I would become rich as Croesus and give my mother enough money so that she could leave that monster and buy herself a beautiful home. I was determined to make it big and that bastard of a father would know that I achieved it all from moving furniture around. Funny thing is, I needn't have worried. My father deserted us not long after that incident, he just disappeared from our lives and was never heard from again. And no one ever missed him."

Elie poured herself a glass of sparkling water, sat down at the kitchen island and reached for the telephone. Michael picked up on the first ring.

"Hi there, friend. How are you?"

"Hey, doll face! How is fabulous and fifty Eleanora?"

"Not bad. Funny that you called earlier. I was thinking about you today."

"What's funny about that? You should be thinking about me every day. I am the first person you should think of when you wake in the morning and the last face you should see before you drift off to beddy-bye. So tell me, what was the occasion that brought me to the front of your *cerebellium* today?"

"It's cerebellum. I was thinking about my party, indulging in nostalgia. Tell me, what's happening with you?"

Michael, as always, was happy to change the subject back to him. "Ah yes, the party. It was great. Nice earrings your husband gave you. You have a pair like them already, right? Anyway, you are absolutely not going to believe what happened! It has to do with Madame Pompidou. Just guess."

"How in the world can I guess? Just tell me." She did not miss the reference to the earrings.

"Okay, okay, don't get all persnickety on me. So, you know, La

Mama buys lottery tickets every week. I've always thought it is so *plebibian* of her and such a waste of money. She usually uses the winning card from her last bingo game to come up with the number, or a combination of our birthdays."

"It's plebeian, and … ?"

"And this time she won! Big time!"

"That's wonderful. How much did she win?" Elie smiled and felt the release of some tension.

"Are you ready for this? One hundred fucking thousand dollars." I am absolutely *plotzing* over this my dear, *plotzing*. Did I get that word right?"

"Oh my god, that's amazing! I never heard of anyone winning the lottery. What is she going to do with all that money?"

"Are you kidding me? She's already spent a chunk. First, she bought herself a Cadillac, a silver Cadillac. What the hell is my mother going to do with a Cadillac? All she drives to is the mall, the church and the bingo parlor. But wait, there's more …"

"That is so cool. I love it! What else?" Elie was feeling that this was exactly the dose of medicine she needed to get out of her blue mood.

"She bought new furniture. You would figure that since her son is a *primo* interior designer, he would have some good connections, right? Like even, Sands Furniture. I could certainly whip her up a gorgeous new living room, or maybe she could use the money as a down payment on a condo in Florida and finally leave her stupid little house in Lynbrook. But *no*, what does she do? She goes to Levitz and buys a three, two, oner!"

Elie had to control herself from spitting the drink out of her mouth. "Oh stop it. You're lying."

"Would I lie about such a tragedy? A goddamn three-seat sofa, two-seater and a matching club chair. And it gets worse. She tells me that the upholstery is a sort of red, purple and black velvet, some 'bee-yu-tee-ful fabric that has like fuzzy parts and flat parts'. And of course she wants to protect it, so she goes and buys *friggin* plastic slipcovers. Did you hear me? She's putting plastic slipcovers on her *deesgusting* new furniture. I am so dying over this."

Elie started to laugh and could not stop.

"Don't you dare laugh, because I still haven't told you everything. When I hassled her about the slipcovers, she tells me that they are not the old-fashioned plastic kind that make you sweat, but rather some new type that allows 'air in the *derrière*'. She actually repeated what the salesperson told her, 'air in the *derrière* for your heirs'."

Michael sighed and continued. "When I asked her why she went ahead and ordered all this without me, she answered that she didn't want to trouble me. Then, Madame Pompidou admitted that she really doesn't like my taste so much. It's too uppity high class and only good for those rich folks. Elie, I am so throwing up over this."

"Oh come on, Michael, this is hysterical. Good for her, she must be over the moon with all this. Think of what she can do with all that money."

"Yeah, if there's any left when she's through with her adventures. Are you ready for the *pièce de résistance?*"

"Don't tell me there's more. What else?"

"Madame has decided that it's time our whole family took a vacation together. Would you like to know what her brilliant idea of a vacation is? She, my homophobic brother, Kenny, his neurotic, anorexic second wife, Melanie, and those two little monstrous children of theirs, Shrek and Ogre, and of course *moi*, get into a van that she rents and we drive down to Pigeon Forge, Tennessee. Conveniently located 35 miles southeast of Knoxville, do you know what's there? *Dollywood!* We go to Miss Dolly Parton's amusement park!"

Elie could not hold it in anymore and howled with laughter. She had trouble catching her breath. Michael joined in, and they spent the next few minutes cackling hysterically. Every time either one of them tried to regain control, they lost it all over again.

"Eleanora, you simply do not understand. This is a major tragedy, of Shakespearean proportions. I am a descendant of that woman. Do you know how that makes me feel?"

She could not resist. "Well darling, if you like, why don't you convert and we will adopt you? My mother always wanted more children, I'm sure she will accept you as a son."

"Oh, sure. You guys cut off the thingy before it even has a chance to grow. And in my line of work, I can't afford that. No thanks, sweets, I'll stay a sinning Catholic and make believe all this isn't happening. Listen dolly girl, I really have to get off now. My call waiting has been beeping and you never know – maybe someone wants to make a movie about my life."

As she started to say goodbye Michael interrupted her.

"Ah, I almost forgot! Christmas Day, at our place, as usual. Open house, from four on. Let's speak again soon. Love ya!"

Elie hung up and felt recharged. So what if she was fifty? She had a feeling that the best was yet to come.

Three

On Tuesday morning, Elie drove Lexi to the airport, treasuring the last hour with her daughter. Because of security regulations, she was not allowed to accompany her into the terminal. She hugged and kissed her outside, checked once again that she had everything with her, and made her promise to call the minute she got home. Elie turned the car around, got back on the expressway and braced herself for the rush-hour trip back into Manhattan. She was driving the new Jaguar, which she hated, and struggled with the electronics to find her favorite radio station.

While driving, Elie had plenty of time to think. She felt very sad saying goodbye to Lexi. Her daughter was now a grown woman embarking on a new life. She had always imagined that this period would be a time of shared joy, but the geographical distance prevented that. As Elie reflected on the last few days, she let her mind drift to the last few decades. Before her birthday, she had not given much thought to the idea of turning fifty, but since then, she had thought of little else. She contemplated her accomplishments and wondered about her future.

She compartmentalized the aspects of her life. Her work was satisfying, although it was getting old. She felt jaded – interior design no longer thrilled her. Her marriage had settled into a comfortable spot that was neither overly satisfying nor awful. She was disappointed with many things about Philip, but she rationalized that every wife has complaints about her husband.

The tributes made by her friends and family had touched her deeply and gave her cause to consider how much each person meant to her. Devi's letter was particularly poignant. It related to a past that no one else knew about, including a significant period when she was transformed from girl to woman. Realizing that she did not want to deal with all those thoughts, she turned up the radio volume.

Driving through the Midtown Tunnel, Elie decided not to waste time returning the car to her building. She headed instead towards a parking lot near the office, rationalizing that the time saved was worth the cost.

The atmosphere around the Flat Iron District always cheered her. The neighborhood, a magnet for architects, designers, photographers and fashionistas, had a distinctly New York kind of buzz. Ever since the magazine relocated its headquarters there from staid midtown, she never tired of the surroundings.

As she passed the Armani Exchange store on Fifth Avenue, she had an idea. Suddenly, she knew what they could do as a substitute for the Montecristo story. It would not only solve that immediate problem, it might fix another lingering issue that was plaguing the magazine.

Lately, readers had been giving the magazine some flack, complaining that the issues were becoming too highbrow, overly devoted to grandiose projects. Features were also moving further away from strictly residential and leaning towards commercial ventures. The editorial department was receiving complaint letters and threats to cancel subscriptions.

The topic caused a debate among staff members. Some felt that the magazine had to head in the direction of more contract work rather than focusing on residential and purely decorative interiors. They believed there was too much competition in the home design field and if *Interior Design & Style* was going to continue to be a trendsetter, it needed to maintain its edge.

Apparently, the readership did not agree and Elie had predicted it; she believed that the magazine should never have steered away from its original focus. There was no doubt that it was a delicate balancing act – how to keep loyal readers happy while pushing the envelope with exciting work. When the subject was raised at editorial meetings, it always caused a heated discussion.

Elie thought that her idea would bridge the gap, at least temporarily. When she got to the office, she excitedly proposed it to Walter, who conferred his partial blessing. He suggested she discuss it with Leigh.

Leigh Fairchild was the archivist for the magazine and she had been with *Interior Design & Style* from the beginning, when Walter snatched her away from the library at Rhode Island School of Design. The myriad furniture catalogues, textile, wall and flooring samples were all kept under her lock and key.

Leigh understood style, she smelled trends before they happened and she was an authority on everything that had occurred in the world of interiors since the 1897 publication of Edith Wharton's *The Decoration of Houses*. She also had an amazing memory.

If someone needed to find the striped fabric used on a dining room chair in a West Hampton beach house featured in an issue several summers ago, Leigh's photographic memory could call it up. "Oh yes, I believe that was from the Robert Allen Thai Silk Collection." Her capacity for details was so remarkable that on more than one occasion she was able to help a reader track down a particular piece of furniture from years back.

Leigh was not a social person, even her look was severe and off-putting. She wore her jet-black hair in a bob, with bangs cut straight across her forehead. She dressed in designer clothes, always monotone, and she was rail thin. She did not engage in small talk, never joined the others for lunch or after work get-togethers, and she projected a dismissive air. Staff members tended to avoid her, but Elie found excuses to talk to her, eager to benefit from her knowledge.

She walked into Leigh's office hoping that she would share enthusiasm for the idea. Elie proposed running a feature about the similarities between fashion and interior design – how both could inspire and reflect on one another. The concept was to use some of the magazine's most extraordinary projects from past issues and compare them with the work of fashion designers, the classics to the moderns.

"I believe I understand." Leigh sat forward in her chair. "We display a black and white living room next to a Chanel black evening gown. Or we display a classic taupe worsted wool suit by Calvin Klein and juxtapose it next to that tailored bedroom we ran last year that was decorated in shades of ecru."

"Yes, exactly!" Elie said eagerly. "Expose the commonalities between fashion and interior design. Perhaps we could enlist the participation of current designers. Wow, that would be a knock-out!"

"Elie, I like it, and I know just how to go about it. I have my contacts at Vogue, I'm sure I can have access to anything I want there. Why don't we go a bit further and suggest to a few choice interior and fashion designers that we all work together as a team?"

"Yes! Yes! And you just gave me another idea!" Elie clapped her hands together. "We've been approached by the Fashion Institute of Technology to participate in their AIDS charity function. It's short notice, but if we could possibly combine this story with the FIT project, we may be onto something really unique."

She continued. "We get the top design students to create rooms that blend with clothes by known designers. We could get an organization to donate a house, or better yet a loft space, and build the rooms according to the specs. Open the show to the public and we'll make money for the charity, have a great article for the magazine, publicity for the school and good deed credit for the designers. It could be like the Kips Bay Showcase but with a focus on students, fashion and glorious interiors. What do you say?"

Leigh bowed her head and exclaimed, "*Chapeau*, my dear, *chapeau*."

Elie was all keyed up. She was certain that under Leigh's guidance, the project would be a great success. Walter was pleased and it was full speed ahead. There was a looming deadline and with all the ideas that were spilling out of their brains, they decided to set up a small team to work on it. Elie gave Keira an additional load of work, taking Walter's advice to delegate more, and cleared her desk of as much paperwork as she could.

When the two women started proposing fashion designers, they discovered a connection. It was a resounding yes to Armani, Chanel, Klein, Karan and Saint Laurent and a less than enthusiastic maybe to Gaultier and some others. As they were devising the short list, they got so carried away that Elie almost missed the lunch appointment she had with an important advertiser. She left Leigh with the ideas scribbled on a legal pad, grabbed a cab and got to the restaurant ten minutes late.

After lunch, Elie spent the remainder of the afternoon going through the papers on her desk and checking stories that were waiting for approval. She was in no rush to leave, since Philip was away and the empty apartment would remind her that Lexi was on her way home, six thousand miles away.

She stayed late at the office, and picked up sushi before driving home. Her plan was to relax in the den with her takeout feast, a glass of Chardonnay and an old movie.

When she arrived home, she caught a glimpse of the letter from Devi lying on the coffee table with all the presents, and her plans changed. She began reading and found herself transported back in time.

FOUR

They had been inseparable as youngsters, but that ended when Devi's parents upgraded to a home on Long Island. They tried to keep in touch by telephone and letters, but the distance took its toll. When both girls decided to spend their junior year together on an overseas program, the friendship was reignited.

The year in Israel left a very strong mark on both of them. Devi rebelled against her background and experimented with things she had never thought about, much less tried. Raised in an observant home, the sudden freedom from parental guidelines caused her to go slightly wild. She tasted pork, gave up fasting on Yom Kippur and went further than before with boys. By the end of the first semester, all observances were shed, as was her virginity.

When she returned home after the year, Devi insisted on transferring to an out-of-state university, rather than the local one she had previously attended. She convinced her parents that she could get a much better education there. They succumbed, unknowingly sealing the fate of her complete fall from Orthodox Judaism. At the university, she met Lawrence Young, a brilliant political science major who was Protestant. Their relationship became serious, despite the disapproval of Devi's parents. The couple married at the Young's summer residence in Rhode Island, and Devi's brother was the only member of her family in attendance.

Elie's year in Israel was marked by a serious romance. David Abarbanel was someone she met quite unexpectedly and she was struck by his good looks and commanding presence. He had a muscular tanned body, wavy dark brown hair and soft green eyes. He was a few years older, having completed his Israeli army service before enrolling in the university, and seemed to know exactly what he wanted from life. He returned Elie's strong feelings and their relationship blossomed. By the end of the school year, Elie dreamt about staying in Israel. She wrote to her parents asking for permission to continue her studies there and the response was unequivocal. No!

During the plane ride back to New York, she thought about David constantly. While her friends were carrying on, visiting each other in the aisles and getting scolded by the flight attendants, Elie sat in her seat and reminisced about the last few months. She touched his gift and looked at his note, repeatedly. She was so confused, furious at her parents for not allowing her to stay in Israel but missing them terribly. She felt certain she would be able to change their minds as soon as they had a chance to talk.

Her mother was there waiting in the arrivals hall at JFK airport, and as she ran into her arms all the tensions melted away. In the midst of all the excitement of saying goodbye to friends and promising to stay in touch, Elie did not ask why her father was not there. She talked incessantly as they exited the terminal and wheeled the luggage cart through the parking lot. Breathing in the muggy New York air of late June, she felt happy to be home.

They put the luggage in the trunk and settled in the front seat of the car. Her mother put the keys in the ignition, but then turned towards her.

"Eleanora, I need to tell you something."

Wound up and exhausted, Elie did not notice the severity of her mother's expression.

"It's about your father, why he's not here."

"Isn't he at work? I figured that's why he didn't come with you."

"No, *cara*, that's not why. I'm so sorry to spring it on you like this, but there was no other way. Your father has not been well. I'm afraid he's very sick. That's why he did not come with me to pick you up."

"What do you mean? How sick? Is it his heart? He's always so stressed at work." Elie felt panic. Her parents were her rocks, how could anything happen to one of them?

"No, it's not his heart. I'm afraid it's ... it's cancer. He has undergone many treatments but they don't help much anymore. We kept it from you because we didn't want it to ruin your time in Israel."

The words stung. Elie folded her arms across her chest and held them close. It took her a moment before she could reply. "Why didn't you let me know?" She felt a lump in her throat. "You should have told me. I would have come home."

"There was nothing you could do. Daddy and I agreed that you should finish your school year. But now, I hope you can understand why staying in Israel was out of the question. I guess we both need you here. I hope you can forgive us."

"Oh my God, forgive you? I feel so stupid, thinking of myself when you were both going through this. My poor daddy. How is he, really?" Tears streamed down her cheeks and she looked like a frightened child.

"You know your father. He's not complaining. Maybe you could try not to let your shock show when you see him. It would be better for him to feel like everything is normal and that he's not causing anyone stress. Do you think you can do that?"

"I'll try, Mommy. Oh, I feel just awful. I should have come home sooner." She wiped her eyes with the back of her hand.

Sophia reached out and gently held her daughter's chin. "Eleanora, you are not to think such thoughts. Your father and I were thrilled that you had this opportunity to study in Israel. We both believed it would be a wonderful experience for you and I think it has been. Especially after we heard about this boy David. You look wonderful and I know you've been happy. Please believe me, this is what we wanted for you."

They drove home in silence, each lost in thought. As they approached the driveway of the house, Elie became hopeful. Perhaps seeing her would make her father better.

She ran from the car into the house and straight up the stairs to her parents' bedroom. Her father was sitting up in bed. As she approached, she saw that his skin had a yellowish cast, his face was drawn and the body beneath the blanket was noticeably thinner.

"Oh Daddy, Daddy. I missed you so much." She hugged him

tenderly; alarmed to feel how much of him had disappeared.

"Hello my sweet girl! Let me take a look at you." He gently pushed her away. "You aren't my little princess anymore. You look like a queen!"

"Oh, cut it out. I'm still your little princess. Nothing's changed." She sat on the side of his bed, trying desperately to hide her sadness.

"No, nothing except that there's a new guy in your life. I understand that my position as the number one man in my daughter's life has been usurped. So, tell me all about my competition, this David of yours."

"He's great, the absolute greatest. You would love him and I hope you'll meet him. He's gorgeous, and smart and kind and ..."

Sophia walked into the room. "How about if I bring my two favorite people some snacks. Elie, Aaron, are you hungry?"

"No thanks sweetheart, I'd just like to talk to my girl for a while." He took Elie's hand in his.

"I'm fine, Mom."

They continued to talk until Elie noticed that her father was drifting in and out of sleep. She kissed him on the cheek and tiptoed out of the room.

She walked into her bedroom and, seeing that it was just as she had left it, felt a deep sense of comfort. She plopped down on the bed and immediately fell asleep. She was awakened by her mother gently touching her arm.

"Elie honey, you've slept for three hours and I'm afraid if you sleep any longer, you won't sleep tonight. Your dad has been asking for you. I'm going down to fix you both some lunch. Why don't you have a shower and change? I've laid out some clothes for you."

Elie rubbed her eyes and took a minute to establish her bearings. She followed her mother's suggestion and as she came out of the bathroom, she heard the telephone ringing and her mother calling up to her.

"Elie, you have a phone call. Hurry up, it's from Israel."

Her heart skipped a beat. She ran to the phone in the hallway and picked up the receiver. "Hello?"

"So, that's how much you miss me? You don't even call the minute you get home? Some girlfriend *you* turned out to be. I bet you forgot all about me already."

She could barely contain her excitement. "Oh, David. It's so great to hear your voice. I didn't sleep on the plane so I came home and collapsed. How are you? I miss you so much. Oh my God, this call must be costing you a fortune."

"It sure is! I can't talk long. I just wanted to check on you. You're okay? The flight?"

"Yes, yes, everything was fine."

"Did you open the gift?"

"Of course I did! I didn't let go of it. Oh my God – the earrings are so beautiful. I love them. And your note! I started to cry when I read it."

He laughed. "I'm sorry I made you cry but I'm glad you liked them. Listen, I better get off. I miss you, I send you a big kiss, say hi to your parents and write soon. Okay?"

"Yes, David, I will. I'm so glad you called."

"Bye, Elie Stein." He hung up.

She went back to her room and sat down on the bed. Everything was a blur. She was back home after a year, she had a boyfriend in Israel and he just phoned, she was no longer a virgin, she was in her beautiful pink and green bedroom, her dad was ill and she didn't tell David about him.

After a few minutes, Elie went downstairs and into the kitchen where her mother was preparing food. "That was him, Mom. Doesn't he sound so wonderful? I promised to phone him when I got home, but I guess with all the news and stuff, I forgot. Oh I love his voice."

Sophia smiled and hugged her daughter. "My *piccola bambina*. He sounds wonderful. I think we would like this David of yours. But before we talk anymore, I want you to eat something. Is tuna fish still your favorite or do I have to start making falafel?" She smiled as she touched her daughter's face. "Here, sit down, have this sandwich and then let's go up and talk to your father."

Elie ate the sandwich quickly, not realizing how hungry she was and how good it was to have a taste of home, especially tuna fish salad with Hellmann's mayonnaise. When she finished, she asked for a cup of coffee and Sophia looked at her quizzically, but she made it without question. She put a few chocolate chip cookies on the saucer.

"Oh Mom, I missed your food. It's so great to taste these again."

Elie was feeling optimistic; her dad would regain his health, her mother would stop worrying, and she would figure out a way to be with David. She was thrilled that he phoned. Oh yes, it will all be fine, she thought to herself as she bit into a cookie.

The chapel was packed for the funeral. Aaron Stein had been a very well liked man and dozens of people from his office, synagogue and community showed up. Elie was greatly touched by the tributes expressed. When Michael walked into the room she almost lost it; the emotion of seeing her friend again after a year brought a stream of tears to her eyes.

"Hey, Eleanora. This was not the way we were supposed to have our reunion." He hugged her, then took out his handkerchief and dabbed at her cheeks.

"Thank you for coming, Michael. I'm so glad you're here. You know, I didn't even know that my dad was ill. They kept it from me. I could have done something. I should have been here for him." Elie's guilt over not having been with her family during the last year came pouring out of her.

"Elie, sweets, what could you have done? You told me on the phone that your dad was happy you were in Israel. He thought it was a great experience for you. So don't put that guilt trip on yourself. Please don't."

Devi walked in and approached them. She had just returned from Israel and she and Elie hadn't yet had a chance to meet. Devi opened her arms and Elie fell into them. She was introduced to Michael and they immediately connected. Elie held onto both their hands.

Sophia held herself in a dignified manner and was gracious to all who came to pay their respects. Elie glanced at her and thought that her mother looked beautiful, but older and tired. Her lustrous thick black hair now had strands of gray, and her eyes were no longer shining.

During the ceremony, a close friend spoke about what a courageous and fine man Elie's dad had been. The rabbi referred to his kindnesses and sense of humor. The cantor sang the memorial prayers and then the simple pine casket was carried outside and placed in a hearse. With Sophia and Elie in the lead car, the procession drove slowly along the highway with lit headlights towards the cemetery, to bid a final farewell to Aaron Stein.

Five

Elie was surprised to see the number on her phone. Syd rarely called during the day, and almost never on the cell phone. She said hello and heard, "I'm doing paella tomorrow night and you're coming for dinner."

"Am I? It's New Year's Eve. Don't you have anything better to do than entertain me?"

"No. I know Philip is away and since you spent Christmas Day with that designer friend of yours who shall remain nameless, you owe me. Don't give me any lip and be here by eight. I'm trying out a new recipe and I need a lab rat. Bring wine. A good bottle! *Hasta la* whatever baby!"

Elie smiled. Her friend probably felt sorry for her that she would be alone on New Year's Eve. Philip did ask her to join him on this trip but she hadn't felt comfortable taking off more time from work.

She considered Syd's life, and admitted to herself that sometimes it seemed ideal. She was responsible only for herself. She had no cares in the world except two dogs and her clients. Her business was great, she made loads of money and she could afford to do whatever she pleased. If she wanted to run off to the Seychelles or Thailand, she could and she did.

Elie envied her friend's independence. In spite of the blow of Julian's illness and death, Syd continued to live life to the fullest. She had few friends, and expressed no need for them. She maintained a busy work schedule and went out whenever and wherever she wanted.

Elie wondered why she did not feel the same sense of freedom.

She arrived at Syd's apartment with two bottles of a Spanish wine that the shop owner recommended.

"Well, lookey-lookey. Not one bottle of wine, but two. And good ones, as well. Bravo girl, you did great." Syd ushered her in and took the bottles from her hands.

"Thank you, oh wise one. Coming from you, that certainly is a compliment."

"Hush up, you old crone, and get in here. Everything is ready and we're doing formal tonight, in honor of the occasion."

Syd had set up dinner in the dining room – with fine china, crystal wine goblets, candlesticks and a centerpiece of white roses. Everything was sparkling.

The drinks were poured and the two friends ate the paella and talked endlessly. They spoke about their past, their present, their business lives and Elie's daughters. When neither could eat another bite, Syd suggested that they move to the library. They walked down the corridor with their glasses and what was left of the second bottle of wine.

Whenever Elie walked into this room, the beauty of it overwhelmed her. It was semi-circular, with twelve foot high ceilings and built-in bookcases stocked with leather bound volumes. A polished mahogany ladder slid on a track on the floor, allowing access to the high shelves. The sofas were Biedermeier style, upholstered in hunter green leather and accessorized with tapestry pillows. An enormous antique desk sat at one end of the room, at the other end was a fireplace with a black marble mantelpiece. The crowning glory was a pair of windows majestically overlooking Central Park.

"Ah, my beloved library. I do so love this room." Syd placed her glass and the bottle on the coffee table.

"Do you remember the first time you invited me up here?" Elie started to reminisce. "*Jeez*, your apartment was so disgusting, yet this room was so exquisite. I could not believe it was all part of the same place."

"I know. It was quite a dump. I think if the co-op board had seen the way we lived, they would have evicted us. Remember my eternal quest to get the place furnished? I think I fired more decorators than you knew!"

"I do remember you having a bit of trouble with all of them. That's how we got around to talking about Michael. You were so delighted that I knew him and could put in a good word for you. Didn't you hire him almost immediately after that?"

"Yeah, don't remind me. I was desperate. What a clown. It was so unpleasant to see him at your party."

"Syd," Elie shook her head, "you're not still on that anti-Michael *shtick* of yours, are you? For God's sake, it's been two decades. Get over it!"

"It galls me that you're still friends with him. He left me with an unfinished mess here and never once did he apologize or try to correct the mistakes. Until I got it all fixed by the next designer, I thought I would have a coronary. I respect you, my dear, and shall now remain silent on the subject, but just know that it lingers."

"Like I couldn't figure that out? You certainly do carry a grudge. Shall we segue into another subject now?"

Syd squinted her eyes at Elie and smirked. She curled her feet under her, getting comfortable on the sofa. "I remember feeding you coffee and muffins the morning we first met. It had been one of those nights when I couldn't sleep so I was busy in the kitchen, baking as usual. Do you remember?"

"Who could forget? I was so impressed with you. Gorgeous, smart and a great baker. You had that nice house cleaner. What was her name?" Taking the lead from Syd, Elie took off her shoes and put her legs up on the other sofa.

"Juanita. You know, I still get holiday cards from her. She lives with her son in North Carolina. She was lovely. I remember how careful she was about cleaning this room, because she knew it was *Senor* Sorenstein's special place."

Syd took a sip of wine and continued. "He would sit in here for hours – reading, watching television, sometimes taking a nap. During his last few months, he spent all his time here."

"You still miss him, don't you?" Elie realized that Syd rarely mentioned him, and her first husband, never.

"I suppose I shall miss him forever. He rescued me. After my marriage to that *schmuck, How-weird,* I thought I would never marry again. I was fed up with all men, especially after a few very unpleasant affairs.

Then, Julian Sorenstein walked into my life, at a dinner party in Paris, of all places. And, in spite of the twenty-year age difference, I fell madly in love with him. That, my dear, is why I'm still alone. I weigh each man up against Julian and no one ever makes the grade."

"How long has it been now? About three years?"

"Three, in March."

"But don't you miss being with someone, having companionship? You have to do everything yourself, you don't have a partner to go to the opera, dinners, concerts ..." Elie was feeling the effects of the wine and did not refrain from blurting out her thoughts.

"Elie, really! Having a steady date is not a reason to get or stay married. I don't mind going out alone. Actually, I rather enjoy it. I prefer to be by myself at the opera, totally absorbed, rather than worry about my companion not enjoying it. Moreover, if someone hesitates to invite me to a dinner party because I'm an unattached single, then screw 'em. I mean it, who needs those kinds of people?"

"I know you're right, but still ..." Elie hesitated. "There must be times when it feels like there is no one around to share your dreams, to cheer you up or hold you when you feel sad. Even someone to sleep with. You know what I mean."

Syd stared at her intently. "Do you have that with Philip? Be honest."

Elie contemplated the question before responding. "The sharing my dreams with? No, not really. And if I was really upset about something, I'd rather talk to you or Michael."

"*Et voilà!* That's what I mean. I do not require a husband to validate my presence or make me feel whole. And I *certainly* do not want marriage just to have sex. If I feel that need, I'll find a partner. The emotional connection I felt to Julian was so intense that I would prefer to hold on to those precious memories, rather than cheapen them with a relationship of convenience. Can you understand that?"

"Yes. I admire you for it. I think you are a very strong woman and quite remarkable in the way you lead your life."

"Well, thank you. I shall keep that compliment in the treasury of nice things said about me, in case you forget." As she spoke, she stroked Luckshen, who had jumped up onto the sofa. Kugel, the older dog, was curled up on the rug.

"See what happens when you get to be my age and you have no kids? You treat your dogs like children. God help me if I become a crazy old woman walking the streets of the Upper West Side, pushing my poodles in a baby carriage. I've actually seen that and it horrified me."

"I don't think you have anything to worry about. You're so sharp and on top of things. I can't imagine you ever going cuckoo."

"Thanks for the vote of confidence. If they ever pack me away to a loony bin, I'll tell them to call you as my reference. Okay?"

"Absolutely, I'll protect you. Not to worry."

"Too bad you can't do that for me now. I could use some protection."

"What do you mean?" Elie's face showed concern. Her friend rarely complained or asked for help.

"It's about work. Some lousy things are happening. The authorities are conducting a fraud investigation against my colleague William. There are rumors that one or two others will be taken in for questioning, and one of those others could be me."

"Oh, no! That's awful. What did he do?" Elie's body tensed.

"Let's see. What didn't he do? According to rumor, it was raising money in the name of a bogus fund, channeling money overseas, insider trading; just name it – a whole litany of egregious and illegal acts. I helped bring in one of the clients that he's apparently conspiring with, so I could be accused as well, even though I knew nothing about it.

"What will you do?" Elie asked.

"Get myself a goddamn expensive lawyer. Then, hope to hell that he gets me out of this. I'm clean, but when the shit hits the fan, I may be in for a bucketful."

"Well that certainly sucks."

"Elie Stein Sands! Did I just hear you use the word *sucks*? What happened to you? Are you joining the human race?"

"Cut it out, Syd. I can use foul language on occasion. Although I must admit, it does sound funny coming out of my mouth."

"Well, drink up girl, and let's toast to foul language. There's nothing like it. It's *fuckin'* fabulous!" She grabbed the bottle and leaned over to pour wine into Elie's glass.

"Okay. Okay. You've made your point." Elie smiled and put up her hand to indicate she had enough wine. "Seriously Syd, there's something I've been meaning to ask you, on another topic. However, after what you just told me, I feel funny bringing it up. It's trite in comparison."

"My issues are being dealt with and there's nothing more to be said about the topic. Come on, talk. What's on your mind?"

"You said something when you phoned me after the party that has stuck with me. I've been meaning to ask you about it." Elie swept a few strands of hair off her face. "You mentioned, and you said it quite strongly, that you hoped Lexi did all the pre-natal and genetic tests. Why were you so adamant about it?"

"Because I adore her and I don't want anything bad to happen to her or the baby. It's much better to know in advance."

"And?"

"And what?"

"Well, the way you said it, I got the feeling there was more behind the comment. Like something you weren't telling me. Is there?"

Syd was silent for a moment and then spoke. "Yes, there is more. Or was more."

"I'm listening."

"I've never discussed this with anyone. Of course Julian, but only him."

"What Syd? What is it? Tell me."

She hesitated for another moment and then spoke. "I was pregnant and had an abortion. It was the most difficult decision of my life and I still think about it today, all these years later."

"I had no idea. When?"

"It was right before Chloe was born. Julian and I had tried for years and since nothing happened, I assumed that I was one of those unlucky infertile women. Then, out of the blue, I became pregnant. I was dying to tell you but I just couldn't. Surprisingly for someone so cynical about life, I was superstitious and wanted to keep quiet until I was sure everything was okay. But it wasn't okay. I found out that the baby had Down syndrome and I chose to abort."

"Oh how awful. What a horrible decision to be forced to make. How did Julian feel?"

"He was upset, but mostly for me. He had Raphael and Karine from his first marriage, so he didn't feel the need to start another family. He was in his fifties at the time; I can't say he was thrilled. Plus, he liked our relationship the way it was. But when he saw how ecstatic I was about being pregnant, he shared my joy. It was a very sad time for both of us; we just couldn't see ourselves caring for a Down syndrome child."

"You know what I'm remembering now?" Elie ran her fingers through her hair. "That when I was pregnant, there was a lull in our friendship. You were very distant; I hardly heard from you in those days. And you didn't even see Chloe until she was several weeks old. I always wondered what happened. Truthfully, I figured you were a bit jealous because you didn't have children of your own and that's why you stayed away. But I also thought that your not having kids was a deliberate decision, so I was confused."

"It was horrible for me. I was happy for you but miserably jealous and heartbroken. I couldn't bear looking at you with your swollen belly and me with my flat one."

As she listened to the story, Elie thought how strange it was that not a word had ever been said about it between the two of them. They had ignored the temporary lapse in the friendship and took up where they had left off.

"And after that, you couldn't get pregnant again?"

"I gave up trying. I was already way into my thirties, I figured my chances of having a healthy baby were not good, although that was just my *mishegoss;* my doctor said I could go through with it again. I just decided to close that part of my life. And you know, I did have a very good life with Julian until he got sick. I can't imagine how I ever could have done most of the things we did, traveling to all those marvelous places, if we had a child. Can you just see me dealing with a wailing baby as I made my way in and out of my favorite Parisian boutiques? Visiting the temples in India with a toddler throwing a temper tantrum? I guess it was all for the best. At least that's what I tell myself."

"I feel awful. I'm sorry I couldn't be there for you, Syd."

"Oh come on, let's not get morose. It was a lifetime ago. You were, and have been, a wonderful friend. And, you are just about my only friend, so don't get all sappy on me. But that's the reason I was concerned about Lexi. I don't want her to have any bad surprises when she gives birth. Since she married a religious man, I was fearful that they might not want to do all the exams."

"I spoke with Lexi and she assured me that she's taking all the necessary tests. She and Dovey are from different backgrounds so it's a good idea anyway to check for all the Ashkenazi and Sephardic heredity problems. And anyway, he's not fanatic religious, he wouldn't object."

"Excellent. That's all I was concerned about." Syd stroked the dog. "Now onto a lighter subject. I'm thinking back to when you first came up here. I believe I interrogated you. I don't know what came over me but I just had to know everything about you. Remember, I asked you all about contract furniture, because I didn't know that it meant office furniture?"

Elie was still reeling from Syd's admission. Feelings from the past were bubbling up to the surface and starting to make sense. Syd and her younger daughter had a very special relationship; there were knowing glances between them, almost as if they had a language all their own. She had often been jealous, but never discussed it with either one. Now she understood that there was another layer – Syd probably related to Chloe as the child she lost.

"Hello? Earth to Elie, come in please." Syd was clinking her glass with her fingernail to get Elie's attention.

"Oh, sorry. The difference between office and residential. Didn't I have to explain to you about open plan systems?"

"Yes! The ultimate office design of the time. And you told me about Philip's father building up the business from a mattress factory to a furniture empire. You spoke about the troubles you had with your mother-in-law. Tillie the T-Rex in Dior, you called her. I loved that. Wow, so many memories are flooding back. How drunk do you figure we are right now?" She moved her legs from underneath her and stretched out across the sofa, pushing the dog to the other side.

"Pretty drunk. I don't think I ever drank two bottles with just one other person before. Remember how much we talked that first time? Lexi fell asleep in her stroller and we just went on and on. I was so excited about meeting you – you seemed so exotic."

Suddenly, Luckshen jumped off the sofa and trotted across the room. Elie followed him with her eyes and caught sight of a framed photograph on a side table. It was of Syd and Julian, she dressed in a cream-colored tailored pantsuit and he in a suit and tie.

"What are you looking at?"

"The wedding photo of you and Julian. I was always mesmerized by it, I don't know why."

"Perhaps because we made such an odd couple. No hunk my Julian, shorter than me and a bit chunky. I always thought that he resembled Henry Kissinger.

You know, Elie girl, I was madly in love with that man. He put up with my big mouth, was amused by my quirks, and coped so well with my neurotic behavior. I was so incredibly fortunate to have had him in my life."

She stopped for a moment, and then continued. "Apparently, he adored his first wife and went through a very difficult period with her illness. We met two years after her death. His kids were away at boarding school so we really got to know one another. His friends used to tell me that I brought the sparkle back to his eyes. I don't know if it's true, but I loved hearing it."

"You really were very well suited for each other, weren't you? In spite of your differences."

"He was my absolute soul mate. It was an unimaginable relationship: Austrian intellectual and Brooklyn bitch. We could talk for hours about almost any subject. Sometimes we would lie in bed and he would hold me, and tell me stories about his years in Vienna, about medical school and becoming a psychiatrist. And boy did I give him grief about that – that he was Viennese and a shrink. Come in Freud!"

Elie laughed and Syd continued. "And man, was sex amazing with him! Believe it or not, he was a fantastic lover, he seemed to know instinctively what I needed and wanted. I can't describe in words what that man meant to me."

"I envy you. I don't think I've ever loved Philip the way you loved Julian."

"What do you mean?" Syd's face changed from looking dreamy to serious. "Don't you love Philip?"

"Yes, but not so intensely. Truthfully, lately, I'm wondering how much I really love him and why I married him."

"Whoa! Elie, you surprise me. I thought he was the love of your life."

"No. I let that one get away."

"What? You've been holding out on me! Who was he?"

"Someone in Israel, but never mind. Let's leave it for now."

"You sure?"

"Yes. I've been overdosing on nostalgia lately. I need to get back to reality." Elie finished the last of her wine.

Syd bore one of her older and wiser looks. "You know, my dear friend, sometimes bittersweet memories are best left in one's memory bank. One shouldn't attempt to change fate. Then you always have a lovely recollection instead of a nasty breakup or a disappointing fade-out to think back on."

"Maybe you're right. Nice thought."

"I didn't realize things weren't so great in paradise. Are you sure it's not just because you've hit the grand old age of fifty? Maybe it's menopause and your hormones causing havoc. Or the fact that Philip is away so much."

Elie played with the fringes of the decorative pillow. "No, I've gotten used to his traveling. There's an undercurrent of something. We've grown apart, not that we were ever great conversationalists. I always had a little feeling that Philip married me to check off that column in his life. You know, nice Jewish boy needs nice Jewish girl to fill position of devoted wife and mother. I guess I fit the bill."

Elie sat up, stretched her legs out in front of her and pushed her hair back behind her ears. "Maybe it's because the girls are out of the house, there just isn't much there anymore. We never had a lot to discuss, but now it seems that it's down to zero. I don't know what we share, Syd, or even if that's important."

She sighed and continued. "For example, my ideal Sunday would be reading *The Times* together, having a leisurely breakfast and then walking across the park to the Metropolitan to catch the latest exhibit. Philip would rather play a game of golf or watch sports on TV, anything but a joint activity. The only topics we share are which parties to attend, which parties to host and how much money to donate to the various charities. Even our mutual business interests don't come up anymore. I don't know, maybe I'm just getting old and cranky."

"And maybe you just need to do more for yourself."

"Do more for myself? I think I do a lot for myself. Maybe you are right, about my restlessness relating to menopause symptoms. They say everything changes – your body, your moods, your health. I suddenly feel my age, Syd."

"That's ridiculous. You should be shining now. This is your time, Elie. No kids at home to worry about, a rewarding career that you can feel secure about, a handsome husband who probably wouldn't object if you wanted to make changes in your life. You could dust off some old dream and go for it."

"What else would I do? I like my work. Why leave it? And in all my years of dabbling with different hobbies, nothing has really triggered a passion. As for Philip, I think we've just grown up and grown apart. But that doesn't mean I should leave him and start all over. Does it?" She looked at her friend and waited for her response.

"Oh, no. I'm not going there – I'm not touching the subject of your marriage. As for your career, I wouldn't hesitate to recommend starting over if there was a dream you wanted to pursue. This is certainly the time to do it. But not something casual and frivolous, something serious that touched your soul." Syd looked at her friend and waited.

Elie smiled. "Ah. Okay. So could you kindly find that thing that touches my soul and then let me know how to grab it?"

"Sure thing, darling."

Elie made movements to get up. "But until then, I think I shall return to my humble abode on the sixteenth floor. I am way beyond zonked. Time to fall into bed and start fresh tomorrow, hangover and all. It's been a lovely evening, my friend. Thank you. Hey! We forgot to make New Year's resolutions! Shouldn't we?"

"No ma'am, not my style. I never keep them, so why bother? Happy New Year, Elie girl. This has been a great way to start it. Good night sweetie." Syd kissed her friend and walked her to the door.

Six

Syd was feeling especially tense. There was volatility in the market, her business was down and William's arrest for securities violations was hanging over her head. She was off the hook for the moment, but she knew she could be called in for questioning and the uncertainty was gnawing at her. She decided that an afternoon dedicated to body and soul was what she needed.

She called the health club and scheduled a facial and a massage. Then she phoned Elie to see if she was up for a light dinner afterward. They agreed to meet at a local place at seven.

Syd got to the club and headed straight for the treadmill. After a warm-up, she decided to tackle the boxing bag. She donned her gloves and started punching. She loved this exercise, it met her need to be aggressive without directly impacting on anyone. She always picked a subject to focus on and this time it was Michael Delmonico.

She had been thinking of him during the last few weeks. Probably because she was forced to be in the same room with him at Elie's party, and because of the timing. Years ago, they spent the week after New Year's shopping the antique markets of Paris together. She discovered that besides her husband, Michael was her perfect travel partner. They explored out-of-the-way shops, dined in cute cafés and made fun of everyone around them.

"Yo, Syd, you're really on fire today. Take it easy!" Rahm was the head trainer at the gym. She had heard that he referred to her as the hot older babe, and she loved it.

"Not to worry, Rahm. I'm thinking of one particular person and it's helping me get rid of all my aggression."

"Okay, as long as that person is not me, you go girl."

Syd laughed and concentrated her thoughts on Michael.

The difficulties between them occurred many years ago, when she was just getting to know Elie. As soon as she had discovered that Michael Delmonico was a friend of Elie's, she insisted on an introduction. She had worked, unhappily, with several designers and was convinced that Michael Delmonico was the answer to her prayers.

Elie seemed reluctant to introduce them, but Syd was intent on discovering the cause of her friend's hesitation.

Elie finally spoke frankly. "Look Syd, he's a genius. Seriously, I think he's one of the most brilliant designers out there. He's knowledgeable about every style of furniture, a wizard with colors, brilliant with space planning. Moreover, he's hysterical, the funniest person ever. I adore him."

"And of course he's gay?" Syd looked at Elie with a glint in her eyes.

"And what exactly would make you assume that?" Elie said.

"Oh come on. With all the qualities you just mentioned and good-looking – I've seen his photo in that magazine article about him – how could this guy possibly be straight? He sounds just too divine. Now tell me, why are you playing coy with me? What's the problem?"

"Michael is my dearest friend. I adore him on a personal basis and I admire him greatly on a professional basis. However, being his best friend has given me certain insights. He can be arrogant and very inflexible. I would hate to see any problems develop between the two of you."

"Okay, got it. Why don't you let me worry about that? I'll decide if he's appropriate for the job and I'll keep you out of it. Please give me his telephone number. I'll speak to him and make a date. And we won't include you. That way you protect your friendship with him and your blossoming friendship with me. Deal?"

Elie agreed and the contact was made. Syd was convinced that Michael would succeed in transforming her huge and neglected apartment into a showcase. She also liked the idea of being among his patrons. With Julian's approval, she hired Michael to start with the kitchen and bedroom.

The kitchen was a major job to tackle. Syd decided to break down walls and incorporate the maid's room and bathroom so that it would become one huge space. She insisted on everything state-of-the-art, even though she knew the time spent in the room would be minimal.

The two met many times, to discuss the layout and review finish samples, but mostly for showroom visits, schmoozing, and high tea at the Plaza. Michael worked on the concept, with Syd's participation and enthusiasm, and when he presented the final plan, Syd bestowed her blessing.

The design included bird's eye maple cabinets, a farmhouse style white porcelain sink, gray pearl granite for the countertops and leaded glass for the pantry doors. The center island was to have a thick butcher-block top, a small round sink and an inlay of hand painted Deruta ceramic tiles.

Michael worked alone in those days, without a staff of draftsmen, and unfortunately, his carpentry detailing skills left something to be desired. On the final kitchen blueprints, he forgot to properly indicate the secondary sink on the island – there was a circle, but no description.

The contractor ripped apart the kitchen and installed new flooring – marble tiles imported from Italy. He brought in the cabinetry and when Syd got the bill for the leaded glass doors, she asked if Louis Comfort Tiffany had designed them. When the island arrived, she realized that there was a hole for the sink, but no plumbing had been installed on the floor. That's when the fireworks went off.

Michael blamed the contractor for being a moron and not paying attention to the drawings. The contractor blamed Michael for not providing professional plans or being on site to check. He also laid into the carpenter for not coordinating with him. Syd was in the middle, tearing her hair out. It did not end well. A second butcher-block counter had to be ordered, with new Deruta tiles and no sink.

Deciding to be magnanimous and overlook his error, Syd retained Michael for the bedroom design. She explained that they loved their custom king-sized bed frame and mattress, and wanted to keep them. However, everything else had to go – the room was to be transformed into a sleek and contemporary master suite. Michael designed a black lacquer wall unit that incorporated shelves, night tables and recessed lighting. It cost a fortune but Syd did not care – she thought it was worth the astronomical price.

Michael had measured the mattress, but neglected to measure the bed frame. That mistake cost him his job, his reputation and his remaining fee.

When the wall unit arrived, the elevator ceiling had to be removed and a team of three came along to assemble it. It fit perfectly against the bedroom wall, and they all breathed a sigh of relief. The drama occurred when they attempted to slip bed frame and mattress into the wall unit – the frame was four inches wider than the recess designed to accommodate it. Michael's solution was simple.

"No *problemo*. Dump the bed. We'll have a new one made."

Syd's reaction was also simple. "Over my dead body! You knew I wanted that bed frame and mattress. I made it clear to you a thousand times. Now you expect me not only to get rid of the set, but to pay for a custom-made one? You'd better think again!"

Syd rejected the entire wall unit, had it removed from her apartment and sent back the invoice, unpaid. She went to a carpenter on her own, had another unit made, and never forgave Michael for his mistakes. He, on the other hand, believed he was right and that it was the fault of others, so he accepted none of the blame. He also got stuck with the bills.

Neither Syd nor Michael ever let go of the anger. Perhaps because each was friendly with Elie, the hostilities festered.

Focusing on her ex-designer must have helped, because Syd felt great when her punching session was over. Her pulse was up, her adrenalin was flowing and she was ready to take on the world. She took a quick shower and then treated herself to a twenty-minute break in the café area by drinking a power shake and reading *The Wall Street Journal*. When the cosmetician called her in for the facial, Syd was so relaxed that she gave no directives as to which creams to avoid or how many minutes to leave her under the lights. After that, she felt renewed and eager for her pampering massage.

Sean was a new masseur that she had used only once before. There was something sexy, yet shy, about him. He was short and muscular, with a blond crew cut, a Marine tattoo on his left bicep and enormous hands. He did not have much of a sense of humor – actually, he rarely spoke – which was just fine with Syd. When she entered the massage room, he was putting out the towels and warming up the oils.

"Hi, Sean. Today's my day for *me*. I did the treadmill, forty on the bag and got a facial." She tossed her robe on the chair and got on the table, face down.

"Good for you, Ms. Sorenstein." He covered her back with a soft white towel and started his routine.

He lowered the towel to right above her buttocks and methodically moved his hands over her back, palpating to sense the areas of tension.

"You're wound up, your muscles are so tense. Is it okay if I do it strong?"

"You can definitely do it strong, as strong as you want."

New age music was playing in the background and she insisted that he turn it off. Syd hated the sounds of rippling streams, gushing winds and other manufactured sounds of nature. She preferred silence to help her slip away to pleasant thoughts.

Sean poured the oil into his hands and rubbed them together. He started to slowly work them over her skin, moving up and down her spine, sometimes with strokes and sometimes kneading deeply into the muscle tissue. He commented on the knots in her back, and pressed into those areas with an intensity that caused her pain, but she said nothing. His hands moved up to her shoulders and dug into her flesh, making her wince.

"I'm sorry. I have to do some deep tissue work."

Syd mumbled a response.

He removed the towel from her backside and advanced towards her legs and upper thighs. As his hands massaged the cheeks of her buttocks, Syd felt a jolt of desire sweep through her, an uncontrollable sexual craving. She spread her legs apart and Sean's fingers slipped down between them. He stopped, and apologized. He seemed embarrassed.

"Why are you stopping? Keep going, it feels amazing."

He didn't move for a moment, and Syd noticed his hesitation. She had a feeling he would comply with her wishes, she sensed it about him. It did not take more than a second to decide what to do. "Come on Sean, give me all you've got. You see I'm tight, I really need to let go."

She turned her body halfway around, exposing her breasts, stretched out her arm and grabbed the inside of his leg. She moved her hand up his inner thigh until it reached his crotch. She moved it under his gym shorts and she touched him, gently playing with her fingers. She turned over on the table, totally uncovered.

"I want this," she said matter-of-factly, and pulled him towards her.

He didn't say a word. He took off his shorts and got on top of her. He tried to kiss her but she moved her face away. He caressed her body and as he entered her, she contracted her muscles and held him tightly within. He started moving slowly and she moaned in delight.

After they both climaxed, Sean got off the table and Syd lay still for a moment. Then she reached for the towel and covered herself. "That was amazing."

"I should not have done that. I could be fired if anyone found out." He was tying the string of his shorts and looked upset.

"Well then, we'll just have to make sure they don't find out. Won't we?"

"But we're not done. I didn't even massage your front."

She controlled her urge to burst out laughing. "Don't worry, you did more than enough. Thank you, Sean. See you next time."

As she walked out of the room, she felt a rush. Now *this* was what she needed to keep her spirits up, she thought. She showered again, dressed, and wondered if she should acknowledge Sean for the extra treatment. She hoped he would not think it insulting if she gave him money. She asked for an envelope at the reception desk, put in a one hundred dollar bill and sealed it. On the outside, she wrote *For Sean. Thanks. S.S.* She left it at the desk and walked out beaming.

Seven

At the age of fifty-one, Michael Delmonico finally felt settled. He was forty-six when he met Daniel, and it took him a while to open up and share his world. Once he did, he knew he had found his partner. Daniel moved into Michael's Grammercy Park apartment and they began life as a couple.

Michael was raised in a working class environment and had been subjected to a tough childhood. Daniel Keane came from a wealthy New England family and was given every possible privilege in life.

Michael was egotistical and prone to theatrics, Daniel was selfless and calm. Michael was tall and well turned out, Daniel was shorter and had a bit of a paunch, which Michael never ceased to tease him about. Michael was a well-known interior designer with a flair for making the ordinary, extraordinary. Daniel was a former high-end lawyer who now worked mostly on pro-bono and legal aide cases. He was six years older than Michael, and had a reassuring, fatherly manner about him.

Both men loved fine dining, but Michael had a tendency to fuss over every aspect of a dinner party to the point of nearly ruining it. While Daniel treasured a quiet evening at home reading or doing a crossword puzzle, Michael loved going out and making a splash. He always had to be the center of attention, while Daniel took a back seat and enjoyed his partner's shenanigans. They were faithful and devoted to each other, and their relationship was solid.

It was a Sunday evening and both men were home, relaxing. The thunderstorms of the past two days had subsided and the post rain fresh air wafted through the open windows of the apartment. Michael was propped up on the bed, covered with an afghan, scanning the latest issue of *Architectural Digest*. Surveying the photos, he could tell instantly whose work was featured and whether or not he approved. As he was flipping through the pages, the phone rang. Daniel had a separate number, so Michael knew it was either for him or one of their mutual friends. In a million years, he could not have guessed who was on the other end of the line.

"Michael?" The voice was female and unfamiliar.

"Yes?" He answered suspiciously, assuming it was a telemarketer.

"Michael, this is Pat. Pat Cullen Smith."

It took a moment for the name to sink in. Pat Cullen was his best friend in high school and he had not spoken to her since.

"Pat? As in my Pretty Pattie?"

"Yes. It's me. How are you?"

"In shock! What a surprise! How are you, Pattie? How did you find me?"

"I took a chance that your mother still lived on Long Island. I got her number, phoned, and she gave me yours. I hope that's okay."

"Yes, of course it is. What a nice surprise." He made a mental note to scold his mother for not telling him and for giving out his number without asking. "So, are you arranging a reunion or something?"

"No, Michael, no reunion. Something very different. I need to see you. It's very important. Can we meet soon? I can come to the city."

He was taken aback by her abruptness. No chit chat, just right to the point. "Pat, what is this all about? Where do you live, by the way?" The last he had heard she had moved out of New York, but he had no idea to where.

"Near Philadelphia. But it's no problem, I can get to the city by train. I'd rather not get into this on the phone. Could we meet, maybe in the next few days?"

He thought for a moment. He had a crazy schedule all week, and taking time off to meet an old friend would be the last item on his to-do list. But she sounded desperate, and he was curious.

"Of course, Pat. How's Thursday? Why don't we meet at the Brooklyn Diner on West Fifty-Seventh Street and Broadway, around one o'clock. Do you know the place? It's near Carnegie Hall."

"No, I don't know it, but I'll find it. Brooklyn Diner, West Fifty-Seventh and Broadway. Thanks Michael, I'll see you Thursday at one."

Michael hung up and thought about how odd the call was. He and Pat had been best friends in high school, but the friendship faded when she got married. He had tried to keep in touch but realized it was hopeless and gave up.

Michael got off the bed and went to the study. Daniel was sitting at his desk reviewing papers. As he saw Michael enter, he took off his reading glasses and looked up.

"D., you are not going to believe who just called me." Michael sat down on the sofa opposite the desk.

"Let me guess. Your mother has another winning lottery ticket and this time she wants to take us both to Atlantic City."

"Not even close. You're never going to get it so I'll just tell you. It was Pat – the Pat who was my friend in junior high and high school. She was my best friend before Elie came into my life."

"Isn't that the girl that you slept with?"

"Yikes! You really do remember everything I tell you. Yes, she's the one. I can't believe she called me."

"What did she want?"

"I haven't the faintest idea. I'm still trying to figure it out. It's so weird." He put his feet up on the small coffee table, making sure to put a newspaper underneath them.

"She was my very best *amiga* and we were inseparable. Then it all fell apart after that one night when it happened. It was New Year's Eve and she had just broken up with her boyfriend. I, of course, had nothing to do, so we went to her house and hung out while her parents were out. We got stoned and drunk, took some Quaaludes and the next thing I knew, we were doing it."

"How did you feel about it, then?"

"Well, I can't say I really enjoyed it. Although, I really don't remember much. I woke up in a stupor, she had this funny look on her face that sort of said oops, and we forgot about it."

"Really forgot about it?" Daniel was looking at him questioningly.

"Yes, Daniel. Really. I wasn't turned on by her if that's what you're hinting at, nor was she turned on by me, or at least I don't think she was. I felt I was gay and that night sealed it for me. Very soon after that, she got back together with her boyfriend, married him and dumped me because he was kind of a redneck, not a strong supporter of the homosexual community."

"So what brings her back into your life?"

"Jealous, darling?"

"Maybe. Come on Michael, be serious."

"Okay, okay. Absolutely no idea. She wants to see me. She said it's very important. She lives near Philly but is willing to come to the city to meet me. We're having lunch on Thursday. Totally *bizarro*, no?"

"Perhaps not. Maybe she just wants to reconnect with her past. You know, some people when they get to a certain age, want to track down lost friends. They're looking back and taking stock."

"Oh my God, sweetness, she's exactly my age and I'm not looking back. I'm thinking maybe she needs money. I'm sure she hasn't made much of herself; her big dream in high school was to get married and have kids. Do you think she could be after me for my money?"

"I have no idea. Why don't you just relax and look forward to Thursday. It will probably be a nice experience for you. Think positive!"

"Ah, you are indeed wise. And, always so optimistic. Imagine, I get a shrink, best friend and lover all wrapped up in one!" He walked over to the desk and bent down to kiss Daniel.

Michael was very busy during the following days, but thoughts of Pat kept popping into his head. When Thursday arrived, he made an extra effort to be at the restaurant on time. As he was sitting in the booth looking out at all the people and traffic on West Fifty-Seventh Street, he realized he did not know what she looked like. A woman of fifty could look considerably different than she did at seventeen.

When Pat walked in, he recognized her immediately, and saw that she had aged quite ungracefully. She was still blond, but the cut was shaggy and the color was dull. Her face was drawn and she looked ragged. She had on a faux leather jacket with a synthetic fur collar over a blue polyester pantsuit. He felt annoyed with himself that he had chosen such a public place to meet.

Pat scanned the restaurant nervously and looked relieved when he came up to her. "Oh my, how wonderful you look! You're so handsome and stylish, Michael."

He smiled, kissed her and guided her to the booth, helping her off with her jacket.

After the initial awkward moments, Michael suggested they review the menus. When the waitress came by, he asked for the chef salad, with the dressing on the side, and a Diet Coke in a tall glass with a separate glass of ice. Pat ordered a cup of coffee.

"Oh no, you're not going to just drink coffee if I'm eating lunch. Order something!"

"No Michael, it's okay. I don't usually eat lunch."

"Well, I don't eat alone. So choose something for yourself or I will. As a matter of fact, I'm ordering you the Reuben sandwich. Its one of their specialties." He hated dining alone and was not willing to make an exception, even for an old friend.

Pat smiled sheepishly at the waitress.

As she walked away, Michael looked at Pat. "So?"

Pat was fidgeting, and pulled a pack of cigarettes out of her purse. She searched for an ashtray, as Michael looked on in horror. He refrained from making a rude comment, feeling uncommonly kind towards this person sitting opposite him.

"Pat, there's no smoking here. Actually, not in any restaurant in Manhattan."

"Oh. I thought maybe because this was a diner it would be okay. All right, I can manage without." She slipped the cigarette back in the pack and placed it on the table.

Michael looked at her hands. They were thin, with dark spots. Overall, she looked much older than her age. Seeing that she was nervous, he asked if she would like a glass of wine, but she declined. He decided to let the next move be up to her.

"You know, I've seen your work. You've really made a name for yourself. I've even told people I know you, can you believe that?"

"Really? Have you been to any of my installations?" He couldn't imagine her knowing what was happening in the interior design world.

"Me?" She pointed to herself. "No, of course not. How would I come to be in such places? No, I meant I saw your projects in the magazines. One day, I was waiting on line in the supermarket, flipping through this magazine and I saw your name. That was such a hoot. So I started looking at designer magazines all the time and whenever I saw a Michael Delmonico project in the issue, I bought the magazine. You've gone so far Michael. I knew you would make something great of yourself."

"Thank you. You're very kind. And I'm glad to know I have a fan out there who is buying the magazines only to see my work. Good for you!"

They chatted about his work for several minutes until the food came. They continued to talk about the old days and reminisce between bites. After they finished eating and the plates were taken away, Pat cleared her throat and, once again, started to fiddle with the cigarette pack.

"Pat, if it's that big a deal you can go outside to smoke. They don't forbid it on the street, you know."

"Sorry. I didn't realize it was that obvious. No, let me try this without it. I guess you're wondering why I asked to meet you."

"Yes. It's nice to catch up with you, but I am curious."

"I'll come right out with it. I need your help, Michael."

His suspicions were right. She needed money. He felt anger, and pity. He could certainly help an old friend but something did not feel right. "Pat, whatever you need, tell me. How much money do you want?"

"Oh my God, no. It's not about money. Sweet Jesus, Michael, how could you think that? I would never come to you for money." She looked indignant.

"Well, I just assumed that if you needed something from me, it would be financial. How else could I be of help to you?" He motioned to the waitress to bring them refills.

As she was pouring the coffee, Michael looked out the window and noticed the people on the street. There was a Sabrett hot dog vendor, a businessman talking on a cell phone, a messenger whizzing by on roller skates and a woman walking two Shih Tzus in matching leopard skin coats. For a moment, he escaped what was becoming a very uncomfortable scene at the table.

Pat spoke again. "Oh gosh. This is going to be so hard to explain. It's a long story, Michael, and I have to start where you and I left off. Very soon after you and I were together … I assume you remember that night?"

"Yes. Kind of hard not to. My first and only time with a woman."

"Really? Never since then? I was your only?" She smiled a bit.

"Yes. I knew forever that I was into boys, men. Whatever. So?"

"Well, I ran into Jimmy afterwards and I told him what happened between us, just to make him jealous. It was kind of stupid but it worked, because he wanted to get back together with me. I was seventeen. I didn't have much confidence in myself, or in my ability to find another boyfriend. So we went together again and then I discovered I was pregnant so we got married."

"Oh. I didn't know that. I mean I knew you got married, actually, I was hurt that you didn't invite me. But I didn't know about the pregnant thing."

"Yeah, well, it wasn't exactly the kind of wedding I imagined for myself. I was visibly pregnant with a furious mother and father. We had a small church ceremony with only the family and that was that. Jimmy's parents were divorced, his father had a garage and body shop outside of Philly and he offered him a job. He gave us the apartment above the garage and we moved in there."

Pat seemed to sense Michael's reaction. "Actually it wasn't so bad. Jimmy was a good husband and I was glad to get away from my parents. He helped his father build up the business; they specialized in souping up cars for races and stuff. They did quite good and we were able to move into a nice three-bedroom house not far from the garage. It was a good life. I was happy being at home and playing house."

"And the baby?"

Pat was fingering the coffee cup as she spoke and Michael sat back in the booth, listening and watching. He felt as if he were in a movie, the busy world of the city only inches away but he was here, engrossed in the life this woman was describing. It sounded horrid, yet she seemed content in the retelling, even smiling once or twice.

"The baby was a girl. Miranda. What an angel! She was beautiful and happy and brought us a lot of joy. Jimmy was a real macho sort of guy. I was sure he would ignore her because she was not a boy. But he was amazing. He adored that child and was such a wonderful father. I actually felt quite lucky."

Michael knew something was coming. For one of the rare times in his life, he kept his mouth shut and waited patiently for the rest of the story to unfold.

"Unfortunately, Miranda didn't stay the happy-go-lucky child. She hung around with the wrong kind of crowd in high school and got into trouble."

"What kind of trouble?"

"Every kind – detention, smoking, drugs, gangs. It was awful. Then, she got pregnant. Funny, huh? Like mother like daughter. I figured I was pretty stupid when we were young. With all the fooling around I did with Jimmy before we were married, I never thought I'd get pregnant. But Miranda was smarter than me, actually, she was a really bright kid who took a bad turn. She said that the father was someone she didn't even know. Eighteen, barely making it through her last year of high school, and pregnant. Sounds like a real white trash story doesn't it?"

"No Pat, don't say that. These things can happen to anyone. Believe me, I hear stories. My partner, Daniel, works with lots of unfortunate cases. Even kids from upper class homes get into terrible trouble."

"Yeah, whatever. Anyway, the truth is I wasn't all that miserable about my daughter being pregnant. I had desperately wanted more kids but couldn't have them. I had cancer in my twenties and I had to have a hysterectomy and that took care of that."

"Jeez Pat! That's awful." He felt genuinely sad for this woman, thinking that life had certainly not been very kind to her.

"I know. But I handled it okay. Anyway, they said everything was fine, but obviously, I would never be able to have more kids. I thought Jimmy would just about die over that. But he was great. He said we had other blessings to be thankful for and when Miranda decided not to have an abortion, which anyway we were opposed to, we decided to raise the baby with her. It worked out good in the end. She had the baby, a boy, straightened herself out, went back to school, graduated, met a nice young man and got married. Could have been a happy ending."

"So, why wasn't it?" Michael didn't want to push her but it was getting late. He glanced at his watch wondering if he should cancel the appointment he had later in the afternoon.

"Oh, I'm sorry. I know I'm going on and on. I bet you must be really busy. I didn't mean to take up so much of your time." She looked nervous.

"No Pat, it's okay. Really. It's just that I have a meeting later. Maybe I'll cancel it and then I won't be worried. Why don't I do that, I'll phone the person now." He took out his cell phone and as he did, Pat got up.

"Then I'll go out for a smoke. I'm just about dying here."

Michael made the call and postponed the appointment to another day. Then, he looked out the window at the woman who used to be his best friend, and he felt a rush of emotions. She repulsed him, for she represented everything he had struggled to leave behind, and yet he was drawn to her, as if reconnecting with a past that he longed to touch. He also ached for her – her life seemed so wretched. Pat stomped out the cigarette on the sidewalk and walked back into the restaurant.

"Ooh, chilly out there." She rubbed her arms and left the jacket over her shoulders. "Are you okay with your person? Is he mad at you?"

"No doll, no one gets mad at Michael Delmonico. I'm a big star you know, and I call the shots. Cancellations are just part of life, aren't they? How about dessert? They have the best pies here."

"No Michael, I've already eaten more than I usually do. I have to be going soon. I need to tell you the rest of the story."

"Okay, I'm all ears."

"Where was I? Oh yeah, Miranda getting married. So she gets married to Gary and he adopted Jimmy Junior, or J.J., as we called him, as his own. They lived nearby and everything was going along fine. Miranda was working as a secretary at a real estate office, she had a real nice boss, a Jewish man, and Gary was the manager of the Home Depot over by them.

So anyway, after several years of trying, Miranda got pregnant again, this time on purpose. I have to tell you, I thought she was cursed like me, like she wouldn't be able to have any more children. But she had a beautiful baby girl – Isabel. And this Isabel is the absolute light of my life."

"So? Happy ending after all?"

"I wish. I was at home with Isabel one night while Miranda and Gary were at a basketball game that J.J. was in. They're in the car on their way home, and are hit head-on by a drunk driver. Gary and J.J. were killed instantly, Miranda was in a coma for a couple of days and then she just couldn't hold out. She died, too."

Michael felt a chill throughout his body. "Oh my God, Pat. I'm so sorry. How did you ever pull through?"

"I don't know. Obviously, God had some grand plan for me, because he gave me strength to get through all this. The story gets worse."

She took a breath and continued. "Jimmy and I got custody of Isabel and we managed, somehow. But two years ago, Jimmy died. He had a heart attack and just went. He was fifty-two. Pretty damn lousy, huh? I figure he never got over losing his daughter and grandson. He was a changed man after that. He was a good soul, Michael, I'm sorry you didn't get to know him."

Michael sat there, looking at Pat, unable to digest all that she was saying. He put his hand to his head and ran his fingers through his hair.

She continued. "I was beyond all pain at this point but I had to cope. I had to raise Isabel. She was just three when we got her. She's almost ten years old now."

Michael was at a loss as to what he could possibly say. "I am so sorry, Pat. It sounds like way more than anyone should ever have to go through in a lifetime. Truly, I am so sorry, but I'm still not sure ..."

"I know, I know. I'm getting there. Look Michael, to put it straight, I need your help and only you can help me."

"Whatever it is, just name it." At least now, she was getting to the point, he thought.

"Isabel is sick and needs a bone marrow transplant."

Michael heard the words but did not understand. Pat saw his look of confusion and continued.

"Isabel has cancer, leukemia. Probably from my lousy genes. She needs a bone marrow transplant to survive and the sooner the better. It's best to come from a relative. I've tried with whoever is left in the family, but no one is a match. Even Gary's parents, who live in Tennessee and were never very involved with the kids, agreed to be tested. The results were negative. I'm desperate Michael."

"I don't get it. Why me? How can I possibly help Isabel?"

She took a deep breath. "Because ... oh sweet Jesus, this is so hard to say. Because, Michael, I think you are Isabel's grandfather."

"*Excuse me?*"

"I didn't mean to blurt it out. I rehearsed it so many times in my head." Her fingers played nervously with the cigarette pack on the table. "Michael, I think you were Miranda's biological father. Her blood type didn't match mine or Jimmy's and, I don't know, it's just something I always felt."

"What are you saying?" Michael's hands gripped the edge of his seat. He felt a wave of dizziness come over him.

Pat swept strands of hair off her face with a shaky movement of her hand. She took a sip of water, the first since she had started to talk. She spoke again.

"When you and I had sex that time, obviously we didn't use protection, we were so out of it. I had made it with Jimmy so many times before, that when I found out I was pregnant, I just figured it was his.

The truth is, the minute Miranda was born, I had my suspicions. She had your eyes – those amazing, bright blue, shining eyes. And there was something about her personality. She was fussy, and insistent on doing things her way. There was an elegance about her, a grace that she sure didn't get from us."

"Pat, are you telling me that for all these years you suspected that she was my daughter and you never once tried to contact me? It never occurred to you that I might have wanted to know that I fathered a child?" He thought about how desperately he would have liked to have a child, but by the time he was with Daniel, it was late and the conditions for a gay couple were too complicated. He felt a rising storm of anger.

"Michael, I had to convince myself that she wasn't yours. Jimmy was such a good daddy; it would have killed him to know she wasn't his biological daughter. When she died, I think I hurt more for Jimmy than for myself. His pain was so great. After he died, what was the point? What should I have done, find you and tell you that you might have had a daughter but she was dead?" Pat squirmed in her seat and continued.

"Now her daughter is sick. I've tried everyone I know. But so far, no donor has been found. That's why I'm here, Michael. I'm begging you to save my granddaughter." For the first time since she arrived, she started to cry. She wiped her eyes with a tissue and apologized for the outburst.

Michael felt a migraine coming on. He took a small pillbox out of his pocket and swallowed a capsule with his Diet Coke. He was shaken by the news and unable to speak.

"What is that? What kind of drugs are you taking?" Pat looked concerned and suspicious.

"Excedrin. I'm getting a migraine."

"Oh yeah, I remember that. You used to get those awful headaches as a kid."

He had forgotten. He wondered what else about his past he might have blocked out.

"Michael? You haven't said anything."

"Pat, I am in shock. I've heard some pretty wild stories in my life but this is beyond it all."

"You don't believe me?" She looked horrified.

"No. I mean yes, I believe you. It's just so much for me to take in. You're telling me that I had a daughter, and a grandson. And now, I have a granddaughter who is very ill. This is not exactly news you get every day. Especially when you're a gay man. Right now, I'm feeling a whole slew of emotions."

"I am really so sorry to spring this on you. I just couldn't figure out what else to do. Isabel is such a charming child, everyone in the hospital has fallen in love with her. She's cute and funny, and she's so smart, Michael. Like a whip. I'm desperate and you are my last hope. Will you help me? At least, would you just get tested to see if you are a match?"

Her pleading made him very uncomfortable. His instinct was to say yes, but he felt that he needed to process all this information. He had no idea what it meant to be a bone marrow donor. He was also feeling a range of emotions: anger, resentment, sadness. He needed time.

Pat went on. "Look, Michael. I know this is a shock. You don't have to give me an answer now. But I beg you, please consider it. The doctor said he would be glad to speak to you and explain everything. Here, I have his number for you. If you want more information you could call him." She took a folded piece of paper out of her purse and pushed it across the table towards Michael.

Michael stared at the paper but did not move.

"Or maybe you would like to meet Isabel first? If you would come to Philadelphia, I'm sure you will fall in love with her. Whatever you want, Michael. But please, tell me you'll consider it. You're my only hope."

She stopped sniffling and looked at Michael with the saddest eyes he had ever seen. He was so touched by her appeal on behalf of her granddaughter that he almost let go of his fury at not having known he had possibly fathered a child.

"Pat, this is more than I can handle right now. I would like to think about all this. I need some time to digest this story."

"Of course. Isabel can wait a bit, but not too much longer. My number is also on the paper. You can call me anytime, day or night. I guess I better be going now."

She started to gather her things and look around for the waitress. Michael told her to leave it, the lunch was on him. He got up, gave her a hug and said goodbye. He sat down again and remained frozen in his seat as Pat walked out the door.

After several minutes Michael left the restaurant and headed towards Central Park. He walked aimlessly for an hour, until he could no longer bear the pressure inside his head. He phoned Daniel.

"D., you must come home immediately. It's urgent."

"Hi, Michael. What's up? I'm in the middle of an important brief. Let's talk about whatever it is over dinner tonight."

"No, Daniel. Now! I'm not kidding. This is a matter of extreme importance, and I don't care what you're in the middle of. Please meet me at home."

"Okay. I'll be there within the hour. Try to calm down."

Michael went home, poured himself a scotch, and lay down on the bed. When Daniel walked in, he was more than concerned to find his lover in the bedroom, in a state.

"You're lying on the brocade spread with your clothes on? Now I know something is very wrong! What happened?" Daniel leaned down to kiss him and Michael hardly responded. He sat down on the edge of the bed. "Michael, what's going on? You're scaring me."

Michael began to tell the story he had been going over repeatedly in his head. He told it in a non-stop monologue and Daniel did not interrupt. When he finished, he looked at Daniel with questioning eyes. Daniel put his arms around him and held him close, saying nothing. They stayed like that for several minutes.

Finally, Daniel took action. "Okay, we need to have a serious talk about this. Get up, we're moving into the living room." He knew that Michael considered the bedroom his sanctuary, where he loved to dream and fantasize. He understood that he needed to get him out of the room, to bring him back into the present. He pulled him up by both hands and guided him through the corridor.

"Daniel, I am absolutely desiccated by this. I have absolutely no idea of what to do." He walked with Daniel half holding him up.

"Well the first thing you will do is stop using words like 'desiccated'. You have no idea what it means, have you?" He laughed, hoping to get Michael to do the same. He understood his mistake when he saw the look on his partner's face. He was glad he had not made any cracks about the drama queen performance.

"I don't get enough of this from Elie? I need criticism from you too? Do you really think now is the time to correct my vocabulary? How cruel can you be?"

"I'm sorry, Michael, really I am. I was just hoping to lighten the mood a bit. Come on, we'll figure this out. Let me bring you something to eat. What would you like?" He guided him to the sofa, helped him down and fluffed the pillows behind his back.

"Are you serious? How can you think I would even consider eating right now? Do I need this in my life? First, all my overly demanding clients, then, late deliveries on the Peyser estate in East Hampton, and the totally mangled cabinetry on the Kerrigan library job. Now this? A family I knew nothing about, two out of three of them are dead, and the one who is living needs my bone marrow. Do you understand what has happened to me?"

"Yes Michael, I do. And I promise, I will help you solve this. I know this is serious. I came home, didn't I? Now please, relax. I'm going to bring you a drink. I think you need a strong cup of coffee. Or, perhaps another scotch?"

"No. Bring me a Diet Coke, with a lot of ice. Make that a whole lot of ice. Maybe you had better bring me the whole bottle. And one of those little rum cakes we picked up yesterday. To hell with my waistline."

"Coming right up!"

Daniel's concern worked its magic and Michael was able to calm down. For the remainder of the afternoon, they discussed all the options and possibilities. They decided that Michael would go to Philadelphia, speak to the doctor in charge, and find out if a DNA test was possible to prove his relationship to the girl. Daniel assured him that he would look into the legal and medical ramifications. And he promised Michael that until they knew more, friends and family would not be told.

Eight

Elie was already waiting at the table when Syd entered the restaurant. "Wow! You look great. That must have been some massage."

"You have no idea! No idea at all!" Syd grinned.

"Gee, maybe I should book one. I haven't had a massage in ages."

Syd could not contain herself. "Honey, I got a massage like you'd never agree to. Believe me, what I had you don't need. Although, then again, maybe you do. Let's sit down, and I'll tell you all about it."

After receiving the menus, Elie put hers down and looked Syd directly in the eye. "Explain yourself."

"I didn't just get a massage. I got laid." Syd smirked and waited for Elie's response.

"Excuse me? I don't think I heard you correctly."

Syd leaned in towards Elie. "Yeah, you did. We fucked. And it felt great. And I feel great." She leaned back and folded her arms across her chest.

Elie stared at her, unable to believe what she was hearing.

"Oh, stop being such a prude. Really, Elie, you'd think you never heard of people screwing around." Syd looked annoyed.

"In the gym? With a masseur? Are you out of your mind?"

"No. Not at all. I think it was one of the wiser things I've done lately."

"You're an absolute maniac."

"Yeah, I know. Of the nympho variety!"

"You never cease to amaze me Sydell Cohen Sorenstein. Never!"

"Listen, I know it was a bit irregular, maybe I even took advantage of the poor boy. But let's face it, I'm a single woman and I have my needs. I figured he's a body builder, he can't have any diseases and I'm way too old to get pregnant, so why not?"

"Oh, this is really more than I can handle. Not even with a condom? Have you totally lost it?"

"Maybe. Think I'm playing God? Taking chances? Maybe it's a suicide wish, what do you think?"

"Syd, cut it out. It was unwise and very risky of you."

"Elie, do me a favor, stop being so priggish. Not everyone lives their life according to the Elie Sands code of ethics." She picked up her menu and read it, purposely ignoring her friend.

The waiter came by and asked if they were ready to order. When he walked away, Syd put down her menu and continued. "I know this is hard for you to understand. You have a husband, and I assume you can have sex whenever you want. But I don't. And I've been feeling very uptight these days. Too much shit is happening. I told you about the Feds picking up William. And if you must know the whole truth, I'm feeling my age lately. I'm not as on top of it all, as I once was."

"And screwing your masseur helps?" Elie immediately regretted her reaction, because she realized that she should be toning it down.

"You really like saying that word *masseur*, don't you?" Syd replied. "Yes, to tell you the truth, in a way it does help. First of all, I was horny. I had worked out, and then had a facial and I was feeling somewhat oozy. He started to massage my legs, and I don't know, things just happened. I didn't plan it. Immediately afterwards, I felt revived, like I had recharged all my batteries. I used him for my purpose and got what I wanted. I know that sounds egocentric, but that's how it was. I wish you could try to understand." She reached over to touch Elie's hand and continued.

"Sometimes you are so prudish, Elie. It seems as if you have no idea what life is like beyond the hallowed walls of your home and office."

Elie sat silently for a moment. "Do you think I'm naïve, Syd? Seriously, because Philip tells me that all the time. Am I such a prude?"

"No, I don't think you're a prude. Well, in a way, maybe yes, about certain things." She did not want to relate to Philip. She knew if she revealed her thoughts about her friend's husband, she would regret it.

Elie went on. "He teases me a lot. Tells me I have no idea what the real world is all about. That I think too highly of everyone. Maybe he's right, but I don't want to become arrogant like him, thinking everyone is beneath me, that I'm better than most of the people I meet."

"Philip is intolerant. You are not. And it's one of your nicest qualities. You think well of everyone, until they prove you wrong. I think that's sweet. Sometimes I wish I could relate to people that way. I'm much too cynical and judgmental. You know what my opinion is of the world."

"Yes, but at least you don't really show it. I've never seen you be purposely cruel to anyone. You're not a snob. You're very different from Philip."

"Thank you, if you meant that as a compliment."

"I don't like that quality in Philip. I find it rather disturbing."

The comment surprised Syd. It was the first time that Elie had criticized her husband so strongly. She wanted to be gentle in her response.

"I guess everyone has some negative qualities. If we could custom design our partners, it would be an ideal world. No one is perfect, as they say. Ooh, I can't believe I just said that. I'm usually such an anti-cliché creature." Syd laughed, hoping that she could get Elie to laugh with her.

"Seriously, Syd. Sometimes I wonder why I ever married Philip. He's so different from me." It was out.

"Elie? What are you saying?" Syd's face showed concern.

"Just that, lately, I've been doing a lot of thinking. I thought it's the being fifty thing or menopause causing my moods to be all over the place. I don't know ... there is just so much about Philip that annoys me. Sometimes I wonder if I was right to have married him."

"Why, Elie? I know we discussed this recently, but I thought you were basically happy."

"Oh come on. Now who's being naive? Do you know anyone

who is really happy?"

"Ah, so there is a thinking brain behind that pretty face. You actually do philosophize about life in not-so-rosy terms."

"Too bad I finished my glass of water. Otherwise I would throw it at you!" Elie snickered.

"Here, would you like mine?" Syd offered Elie her glass. "Okay, so let's get a drink and keep going. Why don't we get sloshed, like we did on New Year's Eve?"

"Okay, but only if we can go back to talking about how you just seduced a young man, a total stranger!" She smirked at her friend.

"Oh, you mean my *masseur*? We don't need to keep rehashing that, do we?"

"Are you kidding me? I'm going to use it the rest of my life. I have one on you now for eternity!"

Syd shook her head in exasperation. They called over the waiter and ordered their salads.

"Okay, so now talk. What's on your mind? What has Philip done that has gotten to you so?" Syd reverted to being serious.

"Nothing in particular. Well, a bit of everything, I suppose. His behavior is often condescending and dismissive. He ignores important things and tells me I have no interests beyond my work and our girls."

"That is certainly a crock of shit. I don't know anyone who is involved in as many charity projects as you, who has taken so many courses at the 92nd Street Y, who has tried to avail herself of all that is out there. While I'm thinking of it, how many of those horrid parties have you made for him out at your house in the Hamptons? How many years have you hosted that bullshit design crowd while he prances around like some tsar of the furniture world? It is unkind what he said, and untrue. Your husband, if I may say so, is dead wrong."

"I know that he exaggerates, but his attitude really bugs me. He's a lot more distracted these days, more than usual. You know what he gave me for my birthday?"

"Those gorgeous diamond earrings, no?"

"Yes. And you know what he gave me for our twenty-fifth anniversary? Almost the exact same pair. The first pair was round, these new ones are square and a little larger. Do I need two pairs of diamond earrings, two years apart?"

"A woman always needs diamonds, Elie." She tried to make a joke out of it, but she understood her friend.

"Syd, really. It was so without thought. They are exquisite, but I was hurt."

"I can understand."

"And that's not all. Lately I just feel like he's different. More callous, uncaring."

"Elie, forgive me, but Philip was never one of the most caring people around. That shouldn't be news to you." She wondered if her friend was totally blind when it came to her husband.

"I know, but it never bothered me so much. No, actually it did. I don't know why I've let it go. Philip has other qualities that I like. He's usually fun to be with. He's bright and interesting. He can be the life of the party when he wants to. And he's handsome, I'm still very turned on by the way he looks."

"So maybe you just need to ignore his less than noble side. Just brush it off when he gets into a lousy mood." Syd refrained from saying what she was really thinking. She played with the napkin on her lap.

"I have tried to ignore his *shtick*. More often than I care to admit to you. But lately I don't want to play that game anymore, Syd." She looked at her friend, but stopped herself from saying anything else.

The restaurant was getting noisy and Syd moved in closer towards the center of the table. "So what are you saying? You want a divorce?"

"No, of course not. I would be crazy to divorce Philip." Elie looked around, and lowered her voice. "He provides for me in a way I could never do for myself. I like being married. I don't think I could be like you, content living alone. And what reason would I have to justify a divorce? That I got bored? That I decided he's just a bit nasty and I don't like it anymore? I've participated in this relationship for a long time, why all of a sudden would I jump ship now?"

"Maybe to create another life for yourself? Maybe to discover who Elie Stein Sands really is, without a husband by her side?"

"I couldn't. He's self-centered and neglectful, but he's not a monster. He doesn't cheat on me, he's not abusive. He's very generous. Let's face it, I live a pretty nice life."

"Elie, abuse is not just of the physical kind. Philip is not exactly building up your ego most of the time. And regarding cheating, you never know what another person is up to, or what's really on their mind. Look at me, not that I wanted to bring this up again, but I just did something that made me feel great and you just about fainted from it. Would you ever have imagined that I'd go for a zipless fuck like that? Sorry to be so crude."

"It's different. I know Philip. At least I think I do." Elie hesitated. "What are you trying to tell me? Do you know something that I don't?"

Syd wondered how she should answer the question. "No, no. Don't get me wrong. I'm just saying, you never know. People do all kinds of stupid things. And usually it's not because their partner pushed them to it. It's because of some need of theirs."

Elie was quiet for a minute and she had a strange look on her face. "You know what, Syd? This conversation is starting to make me uncomfortable. Would you mind if we changed the subject? I'd like the remainder of this dinner to be enjoyable. I've had so much stress at work."

"Yes ma'am, no problem. So how about politics? Religion? I know! How about those Mets? Oops sorry, no baseball in the winter. Got any good gossip?"

Elie slapped the side of her head. "Yikes! I didn't even ask you about William and all that's going on at your office. I've been so wrapped up in my own world lately. I'm sorry, Syd, what's the latest?"

"Leave it. We said the remainder of the dinner should be fun, didn't we? I don't want to think about all that now."

The women ate their dinner and spoke about other subjects, but the undercurrents lingered.

Nine

The dinner with Elie left Syd feeling uneasy, especially because of a recent talk she had with Chloe. It caused her to wonder whether she should have revealed that conversation to her friend.

She was surprised when the young woman phoned and asked to see her. They had a standing date about once a month, but it was usually Syd who initiated it.

Chloe was working in the marketing department of Sands Furniture and spent most of her time in the company's offices at the New York Design Center on Lexington Avenue. She asked Syd to meet her at a place downtown after work, before she headed home to Brooklyn Heights.

Syd, ever the fashion statement, walked in wearing a charcoal cashmere cape, a lustrous, deep purple blouse with upturned collar, charcoal wool pants and lots of bold silver jewelry. She found Chloe perched on a bar stool, sipping a glass of wine.

"Hello, my darling."

"Hi, Aunt Syd. Wow, you look great! Why can't you get my mom to dress more like that?"

"Because, if she dressed like me, then I wouldn't be so special anymore. Let your mom, the great Elie Sands, dress like a Coco Chanel wannabe, and I'll continue to stand out. Agreed?"

"Agreed." They kissed each other and headed for a table near the window.

"So, my dear, here I am. And you don't look bad yourself. That's quite a mini skirt you have on there. I love the look with the striped tights." She surveyed the restaurant. "Jeez Chloe, you couldn't pick out a darker place? I always get suspicious when the lights are low, I assume it means the food is inedible.

Chloe laughed. "You don't think I know better than to ask you to a cheesy place? They're known for their drinks here, not the food. And thanks for coming, I really appreciate it."

"For you? Anything, anytime, anywhere. I'm delighted you called. And to what do I owe this charming rendezvous?"

"I need your advice. I want to talk to you about something very personal."

"Okay, shoot."

"Wait until you get your drink."

"Uh oh, sounds serious. I need a drink to hear it?"

"No, I just want you to be relaxed and at your sharpest. Umm, that seems like an oxymoron."

The waitress came by and while Syd ordered her vodka tonic, Chloe played with something in her lap.

"What are you doing there?" Syd peered over the table to see Chloe fiddling with her cell phone.

"Oh, sorry. A friend sent me a message about a guy she's been seeing. Just wanted to give her the high five sign."

"Oh man, am I glad I'm not of your generation. Twittering and texting! Next you'll be carrying on complete relationships by computer."

"Yeah, that's already happening."

Syd shrugged. "Let's go back to why I'm here tonight. What's the big secret that I was summoned for?"

"I'm having an affair. And I shouldn't be."

"*Mazel tov!* Why shouldn't you be?"

"Because, he's married."

"Oh."

"Is that all you have to say?"

"What do you expect me to say, Chloe? That it's wrong and you're a bad girl? Okay, it's wrong and you're a bad girl." She slapped Chloe's wrist three times. "Seriously, I don't know any of the details, how could I possibly comment?"

"I met him through work, at a furniture show. I had *way* too many cocktails that night. Dad knows him and would kill the guy if he found out. He's older and really sexy. And I've had the hots for him ever since we met. I've never done anything like this. I know it's stupid, but I really like him."

"Do you love him, Chloe?"

"No, but I could. I'm smart enough to know that although I'm overwhelmed by him, I don't think it's love. He takes me to fabulous places – no one my age would go there, or could afford to. He's knowledgeable about food and wine and he likes to eat and drink and laugh. He is seriously cool. Not like the losers I know. I hate the guys I've been going out with, each time I get fixed up I swear I'll never do it again. This man is different. He's totally smooth."

"So what's the problem?"

"Aunt Syd!"

"Yes?"

"He's married!"

"And?" Syd took a sip of her drink and wiped her mouth with the cocktail napkin.

"Isn't that enough? It's wrong. He belongs to another woman. It's a sin."

"Oh God, Chloe, please don't get all moralistic on me. If you want to talk Ten Commandments, then I'm not the address. We're not going to explore that topic, are we?"

"No. I guess not."

"So what exactly is bothering you? Do you know his wife?"

"No! I'd die if I met her. The guilt alone would kill me."

"So, it's guilt about her that's troubling you?"

"You're not supposed to talk to me like this. You're supposed to tell me it's absolutely wrong; to end it and go back to guys my own age."

Syd motioned to the server to refill Chloe's drink. "Is that what you want me to say? I should scold you and give you a motherly lecture?"

"No. I don't know. Yes, maybe. But without the repercussions of telling my mother."

"So, let me get this straight. I have to play the pseudo aunt role, as well as the wise, older friend? *Oy*, this is tough. Chloe baby, I have to tell you – you came to the wrong person. I'm not in the scolding business. You're a big girl, you're twenty-four now, right?

You apparently know what you're doing and I have no doubt that you also know all the reasons why not to get involved with a married man. It always spells trouble."

"Have you ever fooled around with a married man?"

"Define fooled around."

"Had an affair. More than a one night stand."

"Yes."

"And?"

"And?" Syd was not sure she wanted to share this part of her life with Chloe.

"What happened?"

"It ended. It was painful. I knew in my heart that he wouldn't leave his wife, but I kept hoping he would. I finally had the guts to leave him, after some heavy duty therapy sessions."

"It must have hurt very badly. How long until you got over it?"

"I don't remember. Why, Chloe? Are you really at that point where you think you are going to be in a lot of pain if you break up with this guy?"

Chloe was silent and sipped at her drink.

"Chloe, what do you really want to hear from me?"

"I guess I just needed to touch base, to tell someone about Steven. I don't know what to do. I was hoping you'd guide me."

Syd studied the freckled face with the big brown eyes, the perfect nose, the long auburn hair with the feathered bangs, and for the first time, saw a cross between an adorable girl and a sexy woman.

"I can tell you this. Having an affair with a married man leads to trouble. At best, he leaves his wife, but the mistress gets the wounded leftover, sometimes along with kids and other unwanted baggage. At worst, he uses his mistress as an outlet, with no intention of ever leaving his wife. In my experience, it never results in a happy ending. I think that it's something you have to figure out for yourself, whether or not you want to face the consequences of what will be."

Syd took Chloe's hands in hers. "Chloe, I would turn the world over for you. I hope you will always trust me enough to come to me with whatever ails you. However, I will never judge you or scold you. I can't tell you what to do honey, just to be very careful."

"I guess you're right. I knew it would be good to talk to you. Even if you didn't exactly tell me what I wanted to hear."

"That's probably why you love me so. Now, how about having dinner with me? And not in this place. I need to see what I'm ingesting."

"Okay, it's a deal. Dinner sounds great."

They walked out arm in arm as a light snow flurry began to fall.

Ten

Elie was not sure why she had opened the can of worms with Syd, revealing doubts about her marriage. Once the words were out though, she could not stop thinking about them.

When Philip walked into the classroom that day, he had a look that radiated 'I'm late and I don't care'. How conceited, she thought, and how gorgeous. He seemed older than most of the students, perhaps he was auditing. He had a tan, brown shaggy hair and an athletic body.

When he sat down in the empty chair in front of her and she got a whiff of his cologne, that was it! She had already started negotiating with God – besides straight, could he also please be Jewish?

Eventually she summoned up every ounce of courage and started to joke around with him. That led to coffee, which led to a date. Thus began the romance between Eleanora Stein and Philip Sands.

After they had been dating for about a year, and Elie had finally met his family, Philip invited her for a Sunday drive. It was Labor Day weekend, the last official weekend of summer, and the weather was perfect.

He kept the destination a secret, telling her only to dress nicely and be ready by ten-thirty. She complied, and had her long hair pulled up so that she could enjoy riding in the convertible. They headed north out of the city and after two hours on the road, Philip turned onto a tree-lined path that led to a stately stone mansion. He announced that they had lunch reservations there.

The Manor was a splendid Tudor-style estate that had been the vacation home of a wealthy New York couple during the last century. It had recently been converted into an inn and restaurant.

The lobby was decorated with French antiques, floral print sofas and bronze urns filled with masses of colorful flowers. Philip approached the clerk at the reception desk and asked for the Garden Room. They were pointed in the direction and as they walked in, Elie gasped.

The octagon shaped room, a conservatory in its previous life, had a skylight, leaded glass walls and an aging black and white marble floor. The round dining tables, far enough away from each other to preserve privacy, were draped in deep pink tablecloths and each held a small glass vase of white tea roses. Around the perimeter of the room were potted plants: ferns, palms and philodendrons. The restaurant looked like a botanical garden.

After they were seated, Philip looked at Elie and said, "I take it you're pleased?"

"It's perfect. Absolutely divine. How in the world did you find this place?"

"Never mind that. I'm glad you're happy. I want to make you happy forever, Eleanora Stein."

Just then the waiter appeared. He placed the napkins on their laps and presented them with menus. The bus boy came by to fill their water glasses and they spent the next few minutes looking over the menu options. They finally settled on their choices and ordered.

Philip's New England clam chowder arrived, as did Elie's shrimp cocktail. They shared a bottle of wine and commented on how delicious everything was. The service was superb, with attentive waiters hovering in the background. After their plates were cleared, their water glasses refilled and their napkins refolded, the main courses were served: Steak au Poivre for him and Sole Véronique for her.

They took their first bites and Philip remarked that the steak was done to perfection and Elie made cooing sounds over her fish. She insisted that he taste hers, putting a piece of fish on her fork and carefully scooping up some of the cream sauce and grapes. An easy, relaxed conversation flowed between them. Not used to drinking wine during the day, Elie got a bit light-headed.

The dreamy atmosphere made her nostalgic, and she thought about the significant events of the last few years. The magical time in Israel was a memory, the relationship with David a suppressed fantasy, and her father no longer alive. She had graduated from design school and was working for *Interior Design & Style*. She shared an apartment in the Village with a roommate and had this gorgeous boyfriend, while most of her friends were complaining about the lack of good guys around. Philip had entered her life after a very emotional period, and she felt grateful and content.

As the dishes were cleared away, Philip reached for his glass and drank the water in one gulp. When the waiter arrived with the dessert menus, he shooed him away. He reached over and took Elie's hand.

"Elie, I want to talk to you about a serious matter."

She looked at him and suddenly felt a sense of dread.

"I think you're aware that I've gone out with a lot of girls, and you're the first one I took home to meet my family."

Panic. Oh no, here it comes, she thought, he's dumping me. I must have gotten bad ratings from the July Fourth gathering.

"I know you really well and I've never met anyone like you. You're sweet, and smart and pretty. You have your head on straight, you're not silly like so many of the girls I know. And then there's the matter of your fabulous ass."

"Ugh, you had to mention that?" She hated when he referred to her backside; it embarrassed her. Even though he claimed to love it, she was sensitive and thought it was too big.

"I'm sorry. Let me start over. I think you're sweet, and smart and beautiful. *And*, my family had rave reviews about you. You were a big hit at the barbecue."

"Really? I'm sure your mother didn't have such great things to say. I think she wanted to eat me alive."

"Well, she's a story by herself, but she's come around. Elie, I'm getting close to thirty and I feel it's time to make some serious decisions about my life. What I'm trying to say is that I'm crazy about you and would like to spend the rest of my life with you. Eleanora Stein, will you marry me?"

Elie was shocked. While she was trying to digest his words,

Philip took his hand off hers and reached into his pocket. He pulled out a small purple and gold box, put it on the table, and flipped open the top.

"I hope you like this ring, I wasn't sure if it will fit, but the family jeweler will size it for you. So, what do you say?" He looked at her and smiled.

Elie sat back. She had not seen this coming. She thought she loved Philip, and did not want to date anyone else, but she had not considered marriage for the time being. Her mind was on her career, her future with the magazine, finding an apartment that she would not have to share and a million other things.

"Elie?" Philip looked concerned.

She understood that she had to speak. "Philip, I'm overwhelmed. You never hinted at this. I'm really, really in shock." The answer volleyed back and forth in her head. Yes or no, yes or no?

"Aw, come on. It can't come as that much of a shock, we've been dating for over a year now. Why wait any longer? I've decided you're the one, Eleanora Stein, so how about it? You know you're never going to find a better catch than me. I want to hear a great big 'Yes Philip!' for a response.

Impulsively and timidly, she responded, "Yes, Philip. I will marry you."

Eleven

While he was in Atlanta, Philip sent Elie a text message regarding "The Bash", the yearly party at their house in the Hamptons. When he arrived home, they had a dinner discussion about his plans for the guest list, the theme and the food. She understood that she could no longer postpone her involvement.

A few years after they were married, Philip decided that they should have a weekend house. Elie did not see the point, since most weekends were packed with activities in the city. When she finally conceded, she thought that the quiet country atmosphere of upstate New York or a place in New England would provide a welcome change. She envisioned a lovely old house with a wrap-around porch on a lake, perhaps in Woodstock or the Berkshires, a throwback to her childhood vacations.

Philip wouldn't hear of it. He insisted on East Hampton, the Long Island haven for wealthy Manhattanites who maintained their competitive lifestyle by spending fortunes on rarely used summer homes. When he heard that a house was available on Georgica Pond, and that the owners needed cash immediately, he bought it sight unseen. Elie was beside herself.

It was ultra modern, made of exposed concrete and towering sheets of glass. Most of the floors were huge squares of black slate, the walls were glazed in a pearlescent white and the furnishings were minimalist in style. It was very child-unfriendly, meant mostly to impress. Elie thought it was out of their league and too showy. She detested it.

The only place she felt comfortable in was a loft Philip "let" her have upstairs – which she furnished with an overstuffed sofa slipcovered in a cabbage rose chintz, needlepoint throw pillows, oak side tables and piles of books and magazines. The space provided a glaring counterpoint to the downstairs, and it was her refuge.

Philip expected her to do major entertaining in the house, to make it a gathering place for the who's who of the design and architecture crowd. But Elie detested the Hamptons scene, finding it glaringly pretentious. When she had to be out there, she preferred playing with the girls, lying on the beach, or disappearing upstairs, curled up with a book. Her only joy was when family or good friends came out. When her mother took over in the kitchen and prepared her delicious Middle Eastern and Italian specialties, Elie felt that the house served its purpose, with the sounds of children laughing, wonderful aromas and a relaxed, happy atmosphere prevailing.

"The Bash" was Philip's annual salute to the design industry. He wanted to acknowledge the community that kept his company flourishing by providing them with a spectacular time. Elie thought that a discount on the high priced Sands Furniture collections might have been a more appropriate recognition, but she kept her mouth shut. Syd baptized the event Prince Philip's Royal Assembly of Ass Kissing.

This year's party would take place the last Sunday of May, during the Memorial Day weekend. It would also be a celebration of Max and Tillie Sands' sixtieth wedding anniversary – a tribute to the couple who founded and built Sands Furniture, and to their remarkable devotion to one another for six decades. For that, Elie was willing to make the effort, although not without mixed emotions.

She was not fond of her mother-in-law. She disliked the way Tillie took every opportunity to pump up her image and present herself as the world's authority on everything. She also resented the woman's interference in her life; her status as Philip's mother seemed to confer upon her supreme dominance over her children's lives. However, Elie also respected the woman for her accomplishments and her fierce devotion to the family. Over the years, she learned to accept her, without feeling the need to like her.

By contrast, Max Sands was unassuming and down to earth. He did not have an easy beginning in life, yet he felt that there was much to be thankful for – that God had granted him much *mazel*. It was because of his genius, along with Tillie's *chutzpah*, that the small mattress factory in Brooklyn grew into an international furniture conglomerate. He was kind and sweet, and Elie adored him.

She knew that her lack of enthusiasm about the party annoyed Philip, but she could not work up excitement for something she felt was so artificial. She had wanted to take the whole family on a trip to celebrate the milestone anniversary, and suggested a two-week vacation in Israel. She thought that they could observe Passover there, but Philip would not hear of it. Instead, they had their usual Seder at Tillie and Max's apartment and Philip spent most of it talking about his plans for the party.

Philip chose The Farmstead, on Newton Lane, to handle the catering. The Farmstead was anything but its modest name. It was a pretentious culinary boutique offering organic fruits and vegetables, free-range meats, artisan breads, and delicacies from all over the world, all at exorbitant prices. Hand painted marbleized walls, solid mahogany shelves, thick granite countertops and terra cotta floor tiles all contributed to the luxurious atmosphere. Syd referred to it as a Harrods Food Hall wannabe and joked that it was probably cheaper to fly to London and shop for groceries there.

Philip had them email a list of catering options, then he insisted on meeting with the owner. Elie participated in the discussions, hoping that her husband would not demand extravagant foods like white asparagus, truffles and Russian caviar.

As the big day approached, Elie tried to stay focused on her work. She even experimented with meditation exercises to keep her stress level under control. A telephone call caught her off guard.

"Mom, it's going to happen soon!"

"Hello Lexi! What did you say, darling?" Her thoughts were on a layout she was reviewing.

"I've had pains, big ones. I went to the doctor and he said they're preterm contractions, meaning I could give birth this week! I was supposed to have another month!"

"Oh my goodness! Wow! How did that happen?" Her mind suddenly snapped to attention and she forgot all about the English country manor spread out on her desk.

"I don't know. I'm scared, Mommy. The doctor said there is no reason to panic. I'm in my 36th week and he says the baby is fine. Apparently, this little person wants to come out soon and doesn't want to wait until the proper time. But if the contractions continue, it's any day. Mom, could you come? I would so love you to be here. I know you're busy and all but …"

"Are you kidding? Of course I'll be there, honey." Elie's mind was already on plane tickets, assigning stories to Keira and shopping for baby clothes.

"He said I could give birth in the next few days. The baby is in position, it's all happening so soon!"

"It sure is! Okay, sweetie, I'll make the arrangements. You take it easy, try to relax. I'll phone you back with the details."

"Thanks Mom. I love you, you're the greatest."

"I love you too, Lexi. Take good care now and hold on until I get there. Just kidding. Speak to you soon."

Elie hung up and immediately called Philip to tell him the news. His reaction was not what she expected.

"What do you mean she's giving birth any minute? She told us early June. How can this be?"

"Apparently she has early contractions. It happens. I'm going to leave immediately. Do you want to come with me?" She hoped he would say yes.

"No babe, how can I? With all that's going on here? But is Lexi okay? The baby?"

"Yes. Her doctor assured her that she and the baby are fine."

"El, you know how busy I am, especially with this party. Shit, I hope you'll get back in time for it. Look, you go and I'll come later. She doesn't need me around anyway. What can I possibly do, boil water?" He waited for a response.

"Okay, I'll go myself. Talk to you later." She hung up.

She called Chloe and gave her the exciting news. Her younger daughter asked if she should come and Elie suggested she wait until after the baby was born and perhaps be of some help to her sister then.

She called the travel agent and told her to book a ticket to Israel immediately. She made notes for Keira on the important files and then thought about the things Lexi would need and realized she hadn't the faintest idea of what to buy. What do babies require these days?

She called her expert on all things, Syd. She knew that Syd's stepdaughter, Karine, owned a baby boutique and would doubtless be up on all the modern paraphernalia. She asked her for Karine's telephone number.

"Forget it," was Syd's reaction when Elie told her she wanted to bring an extra suitcase full of baby clothes.

"What do you mean? I'm leaving pronto and Lexi needs everything. How can I forget it?"

"Elie, calm down. Here's the thing. Didn't you tell me her husband is religious?"

"Yes, so?"

"So, religious people don't buy layettes before the baby is born. *Kine-ahora* or something like that. That's why they don't have baby showers before the birth. It's bad luck."

"Oh my God! Of course, you're right. I should have remembered that. My mother's family is religious, both of my cousin's daughters didn't have baby showers. How could I have forgotten?"

"Because you're about to become a grandmother, that's how. But listen, buy stuff for her two little stepchildren. Go to FAO Schwarz, open your wallet, and let some cute salesperson there spend your money. You can get it done in fifteen minutes. And I can FedEx you the layette Lexi needs after she gives birth."

"Syd, you're a genius. I'm so glad you're my dearest friend. Okay, gotta go. I'm off to Schwarz. Love you a zillion. And if I don't have a chance to say goodbye – goodbye!"

Syd laughed. "Elie, remember your camera and be calm. And you don't need a lot of clothes; you know they never dress up for anything in Israel. Have a great time, good luck and send my love to Lexi. Ah wait, do you want to stay in my apartment?"

"You are such a dear. Thanks, but I'll stay in Jerusalem to be near the kids. Being in Tel Aviv would be too much of a *schlep*."

"Okay, Elie girl. *Bon voyage*, keep in touch."

Twelve

Elie wrapped the cashmere shawl around her shoulders and tried to get comfortable in the airplane seat. She thought back to Lexi's birth, and the memories were returning with perfect clarity.

She discovered she was pregnant soon after their first anniversary. Philip had hoped for a boy, she secretly rooted for a girl. She had proudly strutted around as if she were the first person on the planet to create a living being inside her. She was determined to devote her life to this baby, who would be unspoiled, brilliant and beautiful.

Elie loved every part of being pregnant, never minding the swollen ankles and varicose veins. The only tension that existed was generated by her mother-in-law, who gave her opinion, often and aggressively, on every aspect of birth and child rearing. Elie was still learning how to cope with Tillie Sands and it was difficult to stand her ground. The naming of the baby was a perfect example.

Elie was in love with the name Alexis. From the moment she first heard it, she fantasized about it as a name for a daughter. If the baby was a boy, the name would be Aaron Alexander. Philip was fine with both and they decided to keep the names to themselves until the baby was born.

Tillie let her have it right in the hospital room. "What kind of name is Alexis for a Jewish child? I really do not understand how you can consider it. My mother, may God rest her soul, was named Rachel – now *that* would be a lovely name for your first child. Don't you agree, Sofia?" Pulling Elie's mother into the fray was a new and desperate tactic.

Sofia Stein was no fool, and her priority was to defend her daughter. "Why don't we just let the matter rest a bit, I'm sure Elie and Philip will make the right decision."

The experience of giving birth instilled in Elie courage she did not know she possessed. Her gorgeous new daughter would indeed be named Alexis, and she did not care that it aggravated Philip's mother. The name represented a break from the old world and it sounded lovely to her.

She chose Avigayil for the baby's Hebrew name when she learned that it meant 'father rejoices'. It would be a tribute to her father.

Shortly after her arrival in the world Alexis was nicknamed Lexi. The child was a delight – she was happy, unfussy and easy to care for. Elie was totally in love, as was Philip, and the baby brought much joy into their lives. Two years later, when Chloe was born, Elie felt like their perfect little family was complete.

Her older daughter showed great promise throughout her school years. When she was accepted into Cornell University, Elie was sure that she would become a brilliant career woman. She earned a Master's degree in psychology and Elie imagined her as an illustrious therapist, giving lectures worldwide and consulting on difficult cases. Lexi, however, chose a more conventional path, becoming a psychologist in a public school. She was not built for a life of stardom – her sweet nature didn't include drive and ambition.

She was devoted to her students, committed to her work, and spent her free time participating in events for Jewish singles. Her younger sister teased her about "those hopeless attempts at matrimony with equally hopeless Jewish nerds," but Lexi didn't care. Judaism was important to her – as a teenager she belonged to youth groups, attended Jewish sleep-away camps and went to Israel several times on organized tours. It was during one of those trips that she met Dovey.

Dov Nissim was a sweet, sincere man whose wife was killed in a terrorist explosion while waiting in line at a Jerusalem pizza shop. Her death left him devastated, and in charge of their two small children. When it became apparent that he could barely cope, his wife's mother, Miriam, stepped in and helped with the household.

Lexi and Dovey were casually fixed up by a mutual acquaintance. Her nurturing instincts kicked in and she poured all her attention and kindness onto this lost man. He slowly came out of his shell and permitted an American woman to give him back his soul. The fact that she loved spending time with his children also helped. She became his Avigayil.

Since his loss, Dovey had turned to religion, finding a source of comfort there. This suited Lexi, as it was a tempting direction for her as well. The relationship quickly became serious and Lexi resigned from her job in New York and moved to Israel. They were married in a modest ceremony a few months later.

Elie had mixed feelings about the marriage. Dovey was nice, but not the husband she would have selected for her daughter. Among other things, she was not comfortable with his born again attitude towards Judaism, but she felt she had no right to judge, considering the traumatic circumstances he had lived through. It was also very difficult to accept the fact that her daughter would be living across an ocean – she was close to Lexi and this would be a painful adjustment. She made peace with the situation when she saw how happy her daughter was.

As the plane approached the airport near Tel Aviv, Elie realized that Lexi was leading the life she had once envisioned for herself. A long forgotten dream was coming to fruition via her daughter. She felt comforted, and looked forward to welcoming her first grandchild.

It was morning when the plane touched down, and the sun was shining brightly in a cloudless sky. Elie had requested that Dovey not pick her up at the airport, fearing that Lexi might need to be rushed to the hospital. She took a taxi to the King David Hotel in Jerusalem and checked in.

"*Shalom* and welcome, Mrs. Sands. Your husband has upgraded you to the Royal Suite. I hope you will be happy there. It has a magnificent view of the Old City. Please let us know how we can make your stay as comfortable as possible."

Leave it to Philip, she thought. I'd never have the guts to treat myself to a suite, at least my husband knows how to enjoy wealth. She fumbled with her phone to send him a thank you and realized that texting had advantages after all.

The luxurious suite and the expansive view it offered of Jerusalem was breathtaking; the sunlight reflecting off the rooftops, the imposing walls of the Old City, all the stone buildings in varying shades of white. The scenery touched her, as it always did. Although badly in need of sleep, she avoided the temptation to climb into the king-sized bed. Not bothering to unpack, she took a quick shower, put on some fresh clothes and headed out to see her daughter.

The taxi zigzagged in and out of city traffic and meandered through the hills of Jerusalem, which were awash with the pink blossoms of almond trees. The scenery and the smell of pine in the air were exhilarating, and Elie relished being back in one of her favorite places on earth.

When they arrived at the entrance of the *moshav*, Elie realized that she did not remember how to get to the house. There were no street signs or paved sidewalks and every block of the little village looked the same. As they drove around, she finally recognized the synagogue, and directed the driver from there. As they pulled up to the driveway, Elie caught a glimpse of her daughter in the backyard, hanging laundry.

"This is how I find my overly pregnant daughter? Doing laundry?" She opened her arms.

"Mom! You're here!" Lexi rushed towards her mother. "And wow, you look great!"

"Me? Look at you, my big, fat, gorgeous Lexi. You look fabulous. And like you're about to pop!"

"*Oy*, you don't know how much I want this to happen already. I'm doing everything I can to encourage it. Miriam nearly had a fit when she saw me taking out the laundry, but maybe the stretching will help get things moving. First, I had contractions, then they stopped, then they started again. Ooh, it's so good to see you. My mom is here! Yes! Come on, let's go into the house. Everyone is waiting for you."

The house was abuzz with activity. The children were chasing each other around the kitchen table, while their grandmother was scolding them and trying to get their food ready. Elie received a warm welcome from Miriam and shy greetings from the little boy and girl.

She spent the next few hours with Lexi's family, getting acquainted with Miriam and the children, and meeting some of the neighbors. When she finally left back for the hotel, she was overcome with exhaustion. She ordered room service, checked her emails, and promptly fell asleep by seven in the evening.

On her third day in Israel, the phone awakened her early in the morning. It was Dovey saying that they were heading to the hospital, and asking if she would like to meet them there. Elie could barely contain her excitement and was touched that they wanted her with them.

The couple reached the maternity entrance of Hadassah Hospital just as Elie's taxi pulled up. She helped her daughter out of the car and as Dovey went off to park, she guided Lexi towards the admittance desk.

"No! It is not Lexus. My name is Alexis, A-l-e-x-i-s. Alexis Nissim."

"Yes, yes, that's what I say, Lexus. What, you got a name like a car?" The clerk was chewing gum and looked up at Lexi in all seriousness.

Elie was tempted to get tough but instead, started chuckling. She'd been to Israel enough times to know that serious situations could often become absurd. And it was always the receptionist, secretary or clerk who had the power to create or alleviate problems.

When she saw how uncomfortable her daughter was, her maternal instincts kicked in. "Listen," she said in a loud voice, "this girl is about to give birth, her name is Alexis, just as she spelled it for you. That's what needs to go on the form, now just do it. Please." It worked.

A nurse's aid came to the desk with a wheelchair just as Dovey was running in. They all headed up in the elevator and then down the corridor to the Labor Suite, where Elie hesitated at the door. She felt that this was an experience Lexi and Dovey should share privately. She kissed her daughter on the forehead, squeezed her hand and reassured her that it would all be okay.

As Elie entered the waiting room, she was struck by its drabness. The walls were gray white, the floor was speckled beige terrazzo and the furniture was gray metal with blue vinyl upholstery. The artwork consisted of one sunset, two smiling babies and an instructional poster detailing procedures in case of a missile attack. In contrast to the depressing decoration, people were laughing, eating, playing cards and talking on cell phones. Elie thought about what a melting pot this scene this was – every layer of Israeli society in one place at one time – Jewish, Arab, wealthy, poor, orthodox, secular – all awaiting a joyful event in their family.

As she settled into a chair, she wondered about how to keep occupied. She dug into her tote, pulled out her laptop and a book, but realized she would need neither. She was too excited, her baby was about to have a baby.

For some reason, her immediate thoughts went to Michael, and she imagined the rolling of his eyes as he reacted to the environment. She heard his voice complaining about the decor, insisting on replacing the paint with wallpaper, the floor tiles with carpet and the posters with framed art. She could even envision the waving of his arms as he explained how lovely a periwinkle and lemon yellow scheme would be. Umm, Grammercy Park meets the Levant. The battle of the superpowers: the great Hadassah Hospital versus Michael Delmonico, reigning chief of interior design.

She smiled to herself as she went in search of a vending machine. She drank watery coffee, typed some notes, glanced at old magazines, dozed on and off, and felt someone gently touching her shoulder.

"Elie, Elie. It's a boy! We have a son! Come, Avigayil wants to see you." Dovey looked exhausted but jubilant.

The small, but healthy, infant was the most beautiful baby Elie had ever seen. She wrapped her arms around her daughter, who was cooing over her newborn son, and she felt tears falling.

The circumcision took place seven days later at the couple's home. Grandfather Philip held the baby in his arms, carrying out the ritual honor of *sandak*, while grandmother Elie and aunt Chloe stood off to the side, comforting the nervous mother. Great grandparents Tillie, Max and Sophia were there, as were Devi, who came from Tel Aviv, members of Dovey's family and a few close friends. The moment the baby's name was announced, Lexi's hand tightened over her mother's. As the sound of his cry was heard, everyone yelled out *mazal tov,* and Aaron Gabriel Nissim was welcomed into the Jewish nation.

Thirteen

For four straight days before the event, the Sands' property was filled with workers. They erected a tent in the garden, created and anchored down huge arrangements of tropical flowers, brought in tables and draped them with blue and white striped cloths, and tied blue grosgrain bows around the legs of the more than three hundred white wicker chairs. A stage was built to span the pool, and a top lighting designer and his crew worked non-stop on the lighting and audio-visual set up.

Philip insisted on a private tasting before the event. He was not satisfied with the hors d'oeuvres, and over Elie's objections, made changes to the menu, claiming that the food was banal. He rudely told the caterer to think again and when he left the room to take a call, Elie had to calm a furious chef who was ready to quit.

Elie had left the seating arrangements to Philip, insisting only that her in-laws not be forced to sit on a dais. She knew that Max would feel uncomfortable with that. She was grateful that Philip had asked Chloe to co-host the evening. Their daughter was taking on a bigger responsibility in the company and this would be her first major event. It would also relieve Elie of a duty she no longer wished to perform.

On the evening of the party, their street was closed off to traffic and a private security company was hired to ensure safety. Cars were valet parked and guests were driven to the house in Packards, Desotos, Studebakers and Hudsons – all from the year that the senior Sands couple was married. A tuxedoed waiter greeted each person at the door with a flute of champagne, and wraps and gifts were whisked away to another room.

The front doors of the house opened onto a rotunda, the showpiece of which was an enormous Calder-like steel and crystal chandelier. On the opposite side of the room was a set of doors leading out to the garden. The landscaping was illuminated and the impression it gave was dazzling. The reactions from the guests reaffirmed Philip's ever-present pride in his house.

Elie, wearing a close-fitting bronze tunic over a diaphanous copper-colored long skirt, greeted guests while standing next to Philip and Chloe. After an hour of air kissing, she floated into the crowd, leaving the remainder of the hosting in the capable hands of her husband and daughter.

As she glanced at Chloe from a distance, she was amazed – her daughter was striking. She looked so radiant that Elie wondered if there was a man in her life. No mention had been made, Elie assumed Chloe was just happy and excited in this new role. She would have preferred to see her in a less revealing dress than the lime green, backless, Lycra number she was in, but Elie knew better than to say anything. Since her fifth birthday party, when she insisted on wearing a red kimono that Syd had brought her from Japan, Chloe's wardrobe decisions were final and irreversible. She also had a temper like her father's, which was to be avoided at all costs.

The weather was perfect – it was a warm, star-filled evening and the garden looked like a fairyland. Drinks and appetizers were served by courteous waiters and open buffets were set up along the perimeter of the property. The instruction given to the wait staff was that no guest was to be empty-handed – Philip was not taking any chances that someone would have to search for food or drink.

After two hours of eating, drinking and dancing, Philip asked the guests to take their seats. He motioned for the band to stop playing and the lights to be dimmed, and then he introduced the video made in his parents' honor. It was projected on a huge screen and included interviews with the couple themselves, friends, family and business associates.

Everyone learned that Max Solomon arrived in the United States alone, with nothing more than a single bag of belongings and hope for a better life. As money for only one ticket could be raised, the rest of his family stayed behind in Poland and he never saw them again.

The steamship that carried him to the *goldeneh medina* docked at the pier and he was transported by ferry to Ellis Island. He was put through various examinations, given a stamp of approval and claimed by a distant cousin who had arrived in New York some years earlier. Max was provided with a place to sleep and a job.

The interview with him took place in the boardroom of Sands headquarters. He wore a gray and white striped shirt with white collar and cuffs, gold cufflinks and red suspenders. At eighty plus, he was still a dapper and handsome man.

"I owe it all to my cousin Lenny. He gave me a place to live and a way to earn a living. I was lucky to learn a skill from him – he taught me how to make quilts, how to fill them with down feathers and stitch them. We made the best you know, not like the *chazerai* you buy in the stores today. Bonwit Teller used to buy from us!"

When Max started Sands Furniture in Williamsburg, Brooklyn, he sold mattresses and comforters. He took a loan from his cousin and paid back every penny, "with interest".

"But Lenny also gave me advice that maybe I shouldn't have taken. He said Solomon was too Jewish a name, and if I wanted to be a real American, I had to change it to something like Sands. So, what, like I didn't want to be a real American? Of course I did! My name was good enough for my father, it should have been good enough for me. I was the end of the line of Solomons. I was such a greenhorn." He slapped the side of his head.

When the interviewer asked him how he met his wife, his face lit up. "Ah, this is a story! My friend, Seymour, and I were invited to a couple's house for Sabbath dinner. This couple was always trying to make a *shidach* among the singles in the neighborhood. You know, a match. It's a *mitzvah* to do such a thing, it guarantees your place in heaven.

We got to this couple's home and, all of a sudden, I see a vision. There, before me, was a beautiful woman with jet-black hair pulled back into a long braid. Like a gypsy she looked, with those piercing dark eyes. I just knew she was my *bashert*, my destiny. The funny thing is, I think they wanted to fix her up with Seymour, not me. Did I care? No sir! I didn't know then that she would aggravate me for the rest of my life, but what could a poor boy from Poland do? Such a prize!"

The guests at the party laughed and commented to each other. Elie noticed that everyone seemed to be enjoying the video, getting to know the personalities behind the company.

Max went on to talk about his wife and children, and how when he saw that he could trust the company to Philip and Sandra, he began to spend more time in Palm Beach. Philip invited him up to New York for board meetings, which Max found unnecessary.

"I told Philip, 'Why do I have to sit there with a bunch of strangers? I'm sure they're all very nice people, but what does it have to do with me? I built this company myself and if you want to make decisions with a bunch of consultants, go right ahead. But it's not for me. Don't *hock* me a *chineck* to come up there.' I just wanted to stay down in Florida where it's warm – with my cigar, my Jacuzzi, my pinochle buddies and my glass of tea."

Max's reluctance to stay involved was a bit of a performance. He was a crackerjack at all aspects of the business and could have run circles around the team of accountants and advisors that Philip had amassed. Leaving the decisions to Philip, and not interfering, was his way of showing his son that he loved and trusted him.

Max continued to speak for a few more minutes, and then it was his wife's turn. The camera zeroed in on Tillie sitting on the living room sofa in their Park Avenue apartment, as if she were posing for a formal portrait. She looked considerably less than her eighty years, wearing an elegant suit and heavy gold jewelry.

The family of Tillie Abramoff Sands immigrated to the United States in the early part of the twentieth century. The few relatives left in Russia disappeared, due to the Holocaust or Stalin, no one ever knew for sure. Tillie's father sent them what money he could, until he no longer received replies to his letters.

When describing her family, Tillie had a tendency to go overboard. She conveniently forgot that they were Russian immigrants, and she beefed up the story to make it sound like they descended from aristocracy and socialized with the Romanovs.

According to her version, she took one look at Max Sands and decided he would be her husband. "I can't say that my parents were thrilled. They had dreams of me marrying a Rothschild, nothing less. So what do I do? I come home with a mattress maker! But my Max was such a looker, I couldn't resist. Okay, so he wasn't from a background like mine, what can you do? I should leave him out there for some *yenta* to grab? No, of course not. And you know what? He's still got it! Believe me, I see how some of those women look at him. I'm not blind."

As they watched the movie, Max leaned over and kissed Tillie and she laughingly pushed him away.

The movie went on to talk about the company. Philip had been employed there from a young age, spending his summers working in the warehouse. He developed exceptional business instincts and built up the non-residential side of the business. Sands Contract became one of the most successful office furniture firms in the field, going head to head with competitors like Knoll and Herman Miller. There was also a division in Milan.

Sandy joined as manager of the New York showroom and her son, Eric, together with Chloe, were now the third generation to work for the family empire.

As the presentation and tributes continued, Elie reflected on her early days in the Sands family. Thanks to Philip's insensitive admissions, she knew more than she cared to about how her future mother-in-law had presented obstacles to their marriage.

Tillie had conceded that Elie was pretty and sweet, but she was from a "mixed family" and that couldn't possibly do. Mixed didn't mean, *God forbid,* a Jew and a non-Jew. In this case, it meant an Ashkenazi father and a Sephardic mother. She told Philip that their children would be half-breeds.

Philip related one particular conversation, in which he had tried to defend her. "Mom, Elie is wonderful and I adore her. She's kind and clever and she's talented. Plus, she's gorgeous. You know how many women I've been out with. You always say I'm too much of a playboy. Now I bring you a wonderful Jewish girl and you're giving me a hard time?"

"Yeah, and you're giving me a heart attack," she answered.

He didn't give up. "Look, her father was a serious guy, an

accountant with a good job in the city, who died a few years ago. Her mother, Sophia, is a lovely woman and even though she's widowed, she's managed to cope. She's a teacher, and has made a fine home for her daughter."

"So? Because she's a widow, I have to be nice to her daughter? And anyway, why didn't she have more children? What Jewish woman has only one child?"

"Mama, enough! Elie's mom is a real *guteh neshuma*. I've met her and I like her. She has a nice home, she's a good cook, what more could you want?"

"What, and like you weren't raised by an excellent cook? You want to tell me that her mother cooks better than me?"

Philip admitted to Elie that he knew it had been a mistake to mention the cooking. Tillie took great pride in her culinary capabilities, even though she had not been in the kitchen for years. They had Jessie for that, their Jamaican maid who had been with the family since Philip and Sandy were children. Jessie learned all about Eastern European cooking from Mrs. S. and made a great *brisket* and *tzimmes*. They were a lot better than Tillie's, but no one dared say it.

Tillie finally relented and gave her blessing for Philip to marry Elie. The whole family celebrated and when Philip retold the story, he expected Elie to be delighted. On the contrary, she was hurt. She never got over the fact that she wasn't good enough for Philip's mother.

It took Elie years to overcome her feelings of inadequacy. She eventually learned to respect Tillie for who she was, with all the arrogance and butting in. She found that as soon as she did, the tension evaporated. She no longer worried about her mother-in-law's opinions.

When the movie ended, several people got up to make speeches. Then, both Max and Tillie expressed their gratitude. Elie felt the urge to escape, she was tired of smiling and playing the happy hostess. She went into the house, climbed up to her loft with a glass of wine, and intended to stay there for a while to unwind. Her moments of reverie were interrupted by the sound of footsteps on the staircase.

"Elsinore? Are you up here? May I have a private audience?"

She was happy to see it was Michael coming up the stairs. She had not been able to say more than two words to him the whole evening.

"Of course you can, my sweet. I just needed to get away for a while."

"Well, it's no wonder. What a crowd down there. If someone plants a bomb here, the design world collapses on its *tush*. I mean everyone, but everyone, is here. Impressive! Very impressive! So, how are you, my darling Miss E.?"

"Me? Little, old me? I'm fine. Not thrilled about this party, but you know that about me already. I'm managing."

"Okay, enough about you. I have amazing news that I couldn't tell you on the phone. Jeez, we've both been so busy lately – this is definitely a chat we had to have in person."

Elie laughed, loving the way Michael always had a dramatic story to tell. "Okay, shoot. I'm all ears." She scooted over on the sofa and fluffed the pillow next to her.

"Girlfriend, this is the most amazing story you are ever going to hear. I've been bursting to tell you but I had to verify facts first, and it took a while."

"A story better than your mother winning the lottery?"

"Oh doll face, this is much, much better than that. I swear to God this is the story of the century. Are you ready, Elzie?"

"Michael dearest, I have a party downstairs and I really do have to get back there eventually. So start talking!"

"Screw the party. You know you can't stand those *pretentioso* people. Now hush up and listen to me."

Michael told the Pat story in its entirety, starting from the high school friendship. He included every detail, never knowing how to abbreviate. Elie had learned long ago not to interrupt, because he would get insulted and it would take even longer for him to finish.

As he got more into the retelling, Elie was transfixed. The sounds of the music and noise downstairs faded away as Michael revealed everything about Pat and Miranda and Isabel. When he finished the part about the restaurant meeting, he stopped to catch his breath.

"Michael, this is unbelievable. I cannot imagine how you must feel. Oh my God, you had a daughter, grandchildren! But how do you know it's for real, what will you do? Don't you have to prove that she is really your flesh and blood? I am absolutely stunned."

"I know! I know! But wait, there's so much more. Let me go on." He took a sip of wine from her glass, and then continued.

"So, I talk it out with Daniel and we decide that I should go to Philadelphia and insist on getting a paternity test."

"Isn't a paternity test only to determine whether or not you are the father?"

"Oh dear lord, could you just hold on for a sec? I'm getting to it. Paternity *schmaternity*, I needed to see that child and get this thing settled once and for all." He took a deep breath.

"So, I get to the hospital. Oh my word, that was so unpleasant! I have such an aversion to those places. Hate them! Hate them! And the design there, *oy!* Why can't they do something about the decoration in those places?"

"Could you please stay on track with this story and stop getting carried away?"

"Okay, okay, don't be such a *nudnikita*."

Elie smiled at his creative use of Yiddish, and waited for the rest of the tale to unfold.

"Eleanora Stein Sands, as I live and breathe, you will not believe what I saw when I entered that little girl's hospital room. I came in with Pat, whom I met in the lobby. I wasn't sure exactly what the child knew about me, apparently Pat had not told her the whole truth, so I didn't know how I would be introduced. I think Pat told her that I was a distant relative."

Michael put his hand on the back of the sofa and took a deep breath, adding to the drama of the moment. "So, I'll admit I'm kind of nervous. I mean, after all, it's not every day that you get to meet a little girl who could be your granddaughter. The room has two beds in it and the minute I looked at the child in the first bed, I nearly fainted. Elie, I could have picked that child out of a line-up. She is the spitting image of my mother! I mean *spitting!*

Can you believe this?"

Michael didn't give Elie a chance to respond. "I have a photograph of Mom when she was about the same age, it's the one in the gilt frame sitting on the Louis IV console table, you know, on the right side of my entry foyer. It's a picture of my mother sitting on the stoop of her house, waiting for someone or something. She has this rag doll in her hand and she's holding it upside down by the ankle – she never was any good with girly stuff – and she has this inquisitive expression on her face. This precious child in the hospital bed had the same exact face and expression. I almost died."

"Unbelievable. So what did you do?" Elie was fascinated.

"Well, this darling Isabel looks up at me with the biggest, bluest eyes I have ever seen and says 'Hi', just like that. As if we've been friends forever. Can I tell you that I just fell in love with her right then? I mean, here I am, talking to someone with my coloring, my blue eyes, and my mother's ten-year-old face. I just couldn't stop staring at her." Michael reached again for Elie's wine and she just gave him the glass.

"Darling, you cannot believe how charming and clever she is. I mean we're talking genius here. I knew I had smarts in me, this kid has them all."

"Okay, down boy. Stop taking credit for this child's wisdom and get back to the story. *Nu,* what did you do?"

"Get this ... we're chatting for several minutes and then she looks me straight in the face and says, 'my granny says you're a relative and you came all the way from New York City, and that maybe you can help me. I think I *kinda* look like you.' Now, what do you think of that? Tell me this kid is not one-hundred percent on the ball?"

"Amazing! How did you answer her?"

"What could I say? I didn't answer her, I just sort of mumbled or I think Pat said something. As for me, of course I'm going to give her whatever she needs, there's absolutely no doubt that she's my blood. I met with her doctor, took some tests and we're waiting to see if it's a match. It all happened in the last month. Man, with you being in Israel and all, I was so dying to talk to you and couldn't. Amazing story, no?"

"Michael, it is extraordinary. And I think it's wonderful that you're willing to give your bone marrow. That's no easy task, from what I understand."

"I don't want to know the details. I haven't dealt with the nitty gritty yet. You know me, just to get me to do a blood test is a major *gedilla*. I usually insist that Daniel go with me to the doctor, I'm such a hypochondriac and all. But if my bone marrow can help this precious little girl to live ... Elie, I don't know what I would do if something bad were to happen to her. I'm already so totally in love."

Michael could not stop gushing. "She's chatty and cute, she had her hair in pigtails and she has bangs and she's *sooooooo* pretty. I could just see taking her to the children's department at Bloomies and buying her a new wardrobe. Gee, I had better find out who makes designer kids' clothes. On the other hand, maybe we'll go to Paris together when she's well. I'll take her to all the wonderful places there, and in New York, we'll eat ice cream at Serendipity and I'll teach her about the finer things in life – she's never going to get any of that from her grandmother. I mean really, Pat is so, how can I say this ... working class, if you know what I mean. She has the kid in public school! And if that wasn't bad enough, no ballet! No music lessons! Can you imagine? My granddaughter should be in the finest private school, getting the best education money can buy. And I'll see to it. I absolutely will!"

"Michael sweetness, please be careful. Your friend has raised this little girl and if the child is as charming as you say, then Pat has done a fine job. Don't start fantasizing about snatching her away and remaking her in your image. You'll risk losing contact with her, Pat may feel threatened."

"Well, to hell with her then! And don't go raining on my parade. You always try to bring me down. That child has a wonderful future to look forward to and I will see to it! And no one will tell me otherwise!" Michael pouted.

"Michael, I love you to pieces and would never try to bring you down, especially after hearing such wonderful news. I just think you should be careful and go slowly, that's all. One step at a time. What does Daniel say?"

"He's pretty amazed by the whole story and wants to meet

her. Oh Elie, I just know he'll love her as much as I already do. Maybe we'll adopt her and raise her as our own. Wouldn't that be so *fabuloso?*"

Elie understood that there would be no point in continuing the conversation. Michael was off on a tangent and logical thinking had no place in the discussion. She also realized she had been up in the loft too long, and needed to show her face downstairs. She gave him a hug, told him she was happy and excited for him, hoped that Isabel would pull through with flying colors, and to please say the word if she could help in any way. They went downstairs and rejoined the party.

When she saw Philip, Elie was sure he would be furious that she had disappeared. On the contrary, he seemed happy, with a cigar in one hand and a whiskey in the other.

"Hey, babe! Where have you been? Look at what a great time they're all having. We did it, didn't we? Another perfect party at the Sands' place. Mom and Pop are living it up and Chloe's handling the crowd like a pro. I'm so proud. Come here and give me a kiss." He threw his arm around his wife and kissed her.

Elie refrained from commenting about Philip's alcohol and tobacco scented breath. She felt relieved that he was pleased.

Chloe was surrounded by a group of men and seemed to be reveling in the spotlight. She projected a very sophisticated air, a bit too sophisticated for a twenty-four-year old. As Elie watched her, she felt uncomfortable, and wondered about the appropriateness of this business environment for her daughter.

Elie's final act of the night was a telephone call to Syd. Although her friend had politely declined the invitation to attend, she wanted to be filled in on all the details.

Elie related that Max and Tillie were thrilled with all the attention, Philip had been on a high all night and Chloe was the belle of the ball. She admitted her discomfort watching Chloe behave in such a sexy manner, and she wondered aloud whether there could be someone in her daughter's life.

Syd expressed her delight, made a few wise cracks about the crowd and congratulated her on surviving the ordeal.

Elie went to bed feeling relieved that she would not have to think about "The Bash" for another year.

Fourteen

Elie was feeling relaxed. The stress of the Hamptons party was over, the office was relatively calm and Lexi reported that all was well with the baby. Philip was on his way to Milan, and she was looking forward to a quiet Sunday evening.

Deciding to snuggle in bed with a book she had just picked up, she put on her nightgown, slipped on her robe, and went to wash up. Before settling in for the night, she remembered the dry cleaning and decided to get it ready, instead of hassling with it in the morning.

As he was leaving for the airport that afternoon, she asked Philip if he had anything for the dry cleaners.

"Take the Armani tux and the Brooks Brothers blue suit," he said. He kissed her goodbye, promised to bring home a piece of Murano, and walked out of the apartment.

She thought about the Murano comment. She had once admired the handmade Italian glass in a shop window, and Philip walked in and bought the vase for her. Ever since then, he returned from every trip to Italy with a new piece, making a big deal about adding "to her collection". They were beautiful pieces, but obscenely expensive and practically useless – owning so many lost its appeal and made her uncomfortable. She gently asked him not to buy anymore, explaining that she loved what she had but didn't need any more. Philip ignored her request. He enjoyed telling people that his wife collected Murano.

She took the clothes out of the closet and checked the pockets. Philip always left stuff there – boarding passes, restaurant matchbooks, taxi receipts – the bits and pieces of his everyday business life. This detritus, unintentionally saved, was proof of his other existence, the one he did not share with her. She pulled out a few Italian business cards and then her hand felt something unfamiliar.

It was a pair of earrings. She held them up and dangled them between her fingers. They were long threads of liquid silver, studded with tiny fresh water pearls. They were expensive looking, and flashy. Definitely not her style.

There was a familiarity about them, but she could not place it. Why were these sexy earrings in her husband's pocket? Whose were they? Why wouldn't he have given them back?

Suddenly her mind raced to one thought – Philip was cheating on her! Could this very feminine symbol represent such an ugly reality? Her intuition said yes.

She stumbled backwards from the closet towards the bed. While her head said to calm down and not make such a big deal out of nothing, her stomach was doing flip-flops.

She needed to think. She scooted up to the top of the bed, arranged the pillows against the headboard and laid back. She stared ahead blankly and a rush of images swarmed in her head.

Philip was a sexy man, no doubt. He took care of his body, and was proud of it. He would often strut around the bedroom naked, commenting on how virile he still looked. Elie noticed that women of all ages were attracted to him, one smile or twinkle of his eyes and they were like puppies scampering around his feet.

She imagined him with another woman: naked in bed together, making love, whispering, giggling, touching. Each image made her sick, yet she continued to create them.

She pulled the robe tightly around her body and knotted the belt. She covered herself with the blanket and then kicked it off. She tried desperately to make herself comfortable, but couldn't. She started to cry.

She had never been jealous, because she thought that in spite of all his charisma, Philip was immune to the attention he received. He made fun of people who flocked around him, and once they were out of earshot, he was condescending and critical. She did not think he had it in him to fall victim to someone's charms.

As Elie lay there, wiping away the tears with her sleeve, her eye caught the framed photograph on the wall. She had taken it a few summers before, while visiting friends in Vermont.

It was of two red Adirondack chairs under an oak tree, in an open expanse of lush green lawn. In the background was a large Victorian house with a sweeping wrap-around porch. The picture had always intrigued her, for some reason beyond the visual composition. The stately chairs so classic in their design, the welcoming porch just calling out for visitors – it projected a message that said we've been here forever and we will continue to be. Come join us, or don't, but know that we will always be here.

The chairs reminded Elie of an aging married couple, content to sit quietly by each other's side.

That was it!

The photograph represented something she longed for – a partner to grow old with, a companion to sit by her side. It was a symbol of what she would never have. Philip and I are together, she thought, but we have practically no use for one another. We could sit by each other's side from now until eternity, but we will never fit. We will never sense what the other is thinking, we will never grow old happily in each other's company.

She was overcome with a feeling of sadness, and all she could think about was her past.

Fifteen

Their engagement had been a short one, and the period right before the wedding was packed with tasks. Elie worked at the magazine during the day, made lists at night, and tried to accomplish everything that had to be done during lunchtime breaks and on weekends. Philip was traveling, and left all the details to her.

She began to feel like she was losing control, as if she were on a runaway wagon. She realized that she needed to slow down and take stock. One evening, when her roommate was out, she allowed herself to stop and think.

She sat on the window seat with her knees up, balancing a bowl of macaroni and cheese. She looked down at the Greenwich Street traffic – buses shooting out exhaust, taxis swerving, and people rushing around.

She wondered about a life with Philip. Would he be a good husband? Up until now he had been very attentive; but she knew he had a tendency to get excited and go after things, and then lose interest. Would it be the same with her?

Since David Abarbanel, no one had touched her heart. She dated on and off, but nothing serious. When Philip Sands entered her life, she felt sexy and smart, desirable as a woman. He was popular and handsome, the ultimate catch, and his wanting her made her feel good about herself.

They had not yet resolved any of the important issues, like where they would live, how many children they wanted, and when to start having them. She wondered if she could juggle a career and parenthood at the same time, or if she would give up her job in order to become a full time mother.

The whole situation seemed like a dream, and she began to

wonder whether she had fallen in love with Philip, or with the idea of being in love with him. She wanted to talk to someone, but could not bring herself to admit the doubts. In the end, she blocked out the uncertainties, convincing herself that it was just jitters.

Once Philip's mother started interfering in the plans, Elie became more frustrated. Tillie Sands had very definite ideas about how her only son was going to get married, and she was not willing to consider any of Elie's concepts.

"A Gatsby-theme wedding? What are you, *mishugah?* Who has an all-white wedding? What are we, the Kennedys? And what exactly is this nonsense about a ceremony in a chapel? We're not poor! For what did we work so hard? That my son should marry with just a few relatives and friends? No, that is definitely not possible."

Tillie wanted a grand wedding in one of New York's top hotels. Moreover, she insisted that she and Max pay for it. Max, ever the diplomat, called Elie's mother and made the offer. Sophia would not hear of it, but Max finally convinced her to let them cover some of the expenses.

Elie had not realized that planning the wedding of her dreams included a mother-in-law of her nightmares. Tillie nixed every idea she had for an intimate wedding. It was becoming unbearable.

Having no one else to hash out her frustrations with, Elie finally confided in her mother.

Sophia responded without hesitation. "Elie, *cara*, don't you worry. This is Philip's and your wedding, and since it's up to the family of the bride to plan and pay for the event, we will do as we want. His mother is not going to hijack this from you. Over my dead body!"

Elie was shocked – her mother rarely got angry and never used such strong expressions. It occurred to her that perhaps this was more than her mother should have to handle.

"Mom," she said gently, "maybe I should just let Mrs. Sands take over. It seems to matter so much to her and I guess they can easily afford to pay for a wedding. I don't want it to become a burden on you."

"Darling, your wedding could never be a burden to me." Sophia was gentle, but definitive. "It's a day I've imagined for a long time and other than your dad not being with us, it will be perfect. Please don't worry about expenses, Daddy and I planned ahead and put money away for this day. No fretting, you understand?" She waited for a response, but then continued.

"You know what? It's time the two families got together. Why don't I call Mrs. Sands and arrange something?"

"I don't know. I guess we could, but ..."

"Rosh Hashanah is coming up. I could invite Philip's family for a lunch on one of the days. Do you think they would come? We could have them over when Uncle Simon and his family are here – that way everyone meets and it won't be awkward at the wedding."

Elie was touched that her mother was willing to share the day usually reserved for her brother's family. "I don't know, Mom. It sounds like a good idea, but maybe they have their own traditions."

"Well honey, they're adding to their family now so we might as well test this out. I'll phone Mrs. Sands and invite them. Let's see what happens."

Elie began to worry about how her demure and diplomatic mother would handle Tillie the Titanic. She hoped she could stand up to her, something she herself had been unable to do.

Less than an hour later, her mother called back. "Okay Eleanora, it's all done. I spoke to Tillie and she was very nice. She said she had to call her daughter, Sandra, to make sure she didn't have to go to her husband's family and then she phoned me back to say they would be delighted. They're all coming for lunch the first day of Rosh Hashanah. You can relax now."

Elie definitely did not relax.

Rosh Hashanah arrived and Sophia went to great lengths to make it perfect.

Silver name cards were set in front of each place setting, and the table displayed the seven foods that are part of the Rosh Hashanah custom in Sephardic families. There were round *challahs* laden with raisins, goblets of sweet wine; bowls of pomegranate seeds, a whole cooked fish, apples with honey, figs, dates, black-eyed peas, beetroot leaves, chick peas, and a variety of pumpkin dishes. Sophia's older brother, Simon, explained the symbolism for each of the foods, and recited the blessings.

Sophia outdid herself with the main meal. There was a beef and vegetable soup, chicken with apricots and prunes, brisket, a lamb and dried fruit tangine, sweet carrot *tzimmes*, couscous with pumpkin and sweet potatoes, spinach with pine nuts and currants, and okra in a pomegranate and onion sauce. To encourage a sweet new year, no salty or piquant foods were served.

Everyone helped themselves to seconds and thirds, and a lively conversation took place around the table. Even the less familiar foods were gobbled up by the Sands family. After the meal, Sandy's children and Simon's grandchildren went off to play in the basement.

With only the adults remaining at the table, Tillie tapped her glass and asked for attention. Philip winked at Elie, but she was too nervous to respond.

"Well Sophia, it looks like you have charmed everyone. Even my grandchildren ate, and that's no small feat to accomplish. It's obvious that you worked very hard and I would like to compliment you. Your food is delicious. I suppose I should get some of your secret recipes."

"Oh come on, Ma, you know you're not going to make any of this," Sandy piped up. "Why not just have Jessie phone Sophia directly for the recipes?"

"My dear daughter Sandra, I did not always have help in the kitchen, you know."

"Tillie, you are most welcome to any recipe you like. With pleasure, there are no secrets in my kitchen.

"Thank you. Perhaps you know where I can get better-behaved children. Wasn't like that in our day, was it Sophia? I could never open up a mouth to my mother. My parents never would have tolerated such conduct!"

Sandy wasn't letting up. "Yeah, yeah, ma. We know. You would have gotten a *zetz*, right across your face. Are we really going to go there now? Start talking about your aristocratic roots? Come on, we'll all relaxed here, admit that Jessie is one of the best cooks in the world and we're lucky to still have her."

Tillie looked at her husband. "Max, do something."

Max shook his head, eyes twinkling, and put his arm around his wife's shoulders.

Tillie pushed him away, waved her diamond-studded fingers dismissively and stood up. "Why don't I help you with the dishes, Sophia? Let's get away from this wise-guy family of mine."

Sophia accepted her offer and the two women cleared the table and headed for the kitchen. Once they were alone, Sophia brought up the subject of the wedding. She quietly explained that her daughter's dream was to have a small wedding with only the closest of family and friends. She also said that although she was sure a wedding in a hotel would be magnificent, it was not their style.

In her dignified way, Sophia Stein told Tillie Sands exactly what the score was and the message was relayed – her daughter would have her dream wedding. She asked Tillie to help her bring out the desserts, closing the subject to further discussion.

When Sophia and Tillie returned to the dining room, Max stood up and raised his glass. "Besides toasting the young couple, I think we have another reason to celebrate today. It is obvious to me that we are adding a most talented cook to our family. Sophia Stein, it is an honor to dine at your table and I look forward to many more such occasions. Will you all please join me in a *L'chayim?*"

By the end of the afternoon, everyone was happy, full and feeling a connection. When the Sands family left, they did so with promises to host the next get-together, and soon. As Elie kissed Philip goodbye, he whispered in her ear that it had been perfect. She closed the front door and walked into the kitchen, beaming.

"Mom, it was amazing! They all loved it, I could tell they had a great time. Philip said so. I'm so happy, and so relieved. What do you think? Did you talk to his mother?"

"One question at a time, *cara*. I also think it went very well, better than I anticipated." Sophia was washing the dishes.

"You were great. Really. I can't thank you enough for doing this. Everyone seemed to have such a good time, even the kids got along. And your food was delicious. Can you believe Mrs. Sands ate the okra with the pomegranate sauce? You did it!" She hugged her mother.

"You see honey, I told you there was nothing to worry about. Your mother-in-law seemed nice."

"Don't let her good behavior fool you, Mom. She's bossy and overbearing. But Mr. Sands is a doll, isn't he?"

"Yes, he's a lovely man. What a gentleman, I see where Philip gets it from."

"So? What about my wedding? Did you talk to her? Were you able to bring up the subject?" She feared that her mother might say no.

"Yes, darling I did. It's settled. Your wedding will be exactly as you want it."

"Are you serious?" Elie's face lit up. "She really agreed to what we, I, want?"

"Yes, sweetheart. Where you want it, and as you want it. Didn't I tell you not to worry?"

All of Elie's fears, frustrations and worries poured out of her. "Oh Mommy, it's going to be okay, isn't it? I mean my marriage and everything?"

"Eleanora, you're just getting those pre-wedding butterflies. You do love Philip, don't you?" She turned from the sink, wiped her hands on her apron and examined her daughter's face.

"Yes, Mom, I do love him. I guess I'm just tired and overwhelmed. I was very nervous about today and I'm glad it's over and it went well.

She helped her mother with the clean-up and felt better than she had for weeks.

Shortly before the wedding, Philip called from North Carolina, but Elie could hardly understand him. "You're talking too fast and it's not a good connection. What did you say about your parents?"

Philip slowed down. "My parents have decided on a gift they want to give us. I can't tell you what it is because my mother made me promise that she could be the one to tell you, but it's big! They want us to join them for brunch on Sunday. I told them okay. Okay?"

"Sure Philip. But can't you give me a hint? And why are they giving us a gift? They're doing enough already."

"Never mind, babe. They can afford it and it gives them *naches*. We're meeting them at one on Sunday at Café des Artistes. I'll try to get back by Saturday afternoon so that we can spend the rest of the weekend together but I can't promise. Everything okay with you?"

"Yes, sure. Great. I'm working on the seating plans for the wedding and ..."

"Sorry, babe, have to get off. Love you. See you Saturday or at the latest Sunday morning. Love me?" Without waiting for an answer, he hung up.

When Philip arrived at Elie's apartment on Sunday morning, her roommate, Donna, was walking around in a robe, coffee cup in one hand, *The New York Times* in the other, with hair dangling in her eyes. Elie was already showered, made-up, dressed and ready for the date with her future in-laws.

"Hey Donna, you're going to catch some hell of a guy with that get-up. Let me use the phone and call all my buddies so that they can come over and line up for you."

"Screw you, Philip. I see you haven't gained any charm during your myriad attempts to sell sofas to suckers."

"Okay, you two, knock it off. Hi Philip, how about some coffee?" Elie kissed him while Donna walked into her room.

The coffee was accompanied by a full description of Philip's adventures in North Carolina, where one of the factories was located. "You know El, I used to think this would be a temporary step for me, that I'd choose another direction. But what we're doing is a real turn-on, and I think my dad is digging my part in the business."

"I'm really happy for you, Philip, although I'm getting a bit nervous about all this travel. What will happen after we're married?" Elie decided to share her worries with her future husband. "It seems you'll be away more than you'll be home."

"El, we've spoken about this. I have to be willing to travel, I'm second in command. I can't let my dad down. I have to be available to do what he wants if we're going to push Sands Furniture forward. Maybe you'll come with me on some business trips. That would be cool – I'll do my thing during the day and we'll do our thing at night, in great hotel rooms. What do you say?" He winked at her.

On the cab ride uptown, Philip turned to Elie as they passed Macy's department store, and took her hand in his. "You know what my dream is, Elie? That one day we'll have a Sands Furniture store right here on this corner. No one will go to Macy's for furniture anymore, they'll come to us. We'll be able to advertise – '34th & Broadway – the home of Sands Furniture … and Macy's too'."

She laughed. She loved his determination, although she was concerned about his drive and methods. She put the thought out of her mind as they approached the restaurant.

Elie had been to Café des Artistes once before and was totally taken with the place. It had colorful murals of frolicking wood nymphs, leather banquette seats and a highly polished mahogany bar. The restaurant radiated elegance and class, and was frequented by an upscale clientele. Elie felt uncomfortable, as if she didn't belong among such well-heeled people.

The Maitre d' escorted them to their table. Max and Tillie were already seated, waiting for them.

"Eleanora, you get prettier each time I see you. How are you, my soon-to-be favorite daughter-in-law?" Max stood up to kiss her.

Elie loved that he called her Eleanora, just like her dad. Before she had a chance to respond, Tillie took over.

"Okay, Max, enough. Elie knows your *shtick* already. By the way, she'll be your only daughter-in-law. You really do look lovely dear; pink is definitely your color. Looks like my son is making you very happy. You're a lucky girl."

"Mom, I think Elie is pretty wonderful and I'm a lucky guy to have her." Philip held the chair out for Elie.

"I'm getting embarrassed here," Elie said, smiling meekly.

"I say we discuss brunch." Max came to the rescue. "In my opinion, the Eggs Benedict are the best dish in the place. Have you ever tried them here, Eleanora?"

"No. Actually, I've only been here once, and it was for an evening cocktail party. I've always wanted to come back,"

"Well then," Tillie said, "we'll just have to make this our restaurant. Why don't we have a standing date with you two every Sunday? Our treat, of course."

"Don't get carried away, Mom," Philip answered. "Do you think that once I marry this gorgeous girl, we're going to want to spend our precious weekends with my parents? Sorry folks, but I don't think so. How about if you make us that offer in another year or two? No, make that three."

Elie lovingly punched him in the arm and they all laughed.

The waiter came by and took their orders and Max asked for a bottle of champagne. When it was popped open and poured into each glass, Tillie said she had an announcement. Her gold and diamond charm bracelet clanked as she raised her glass with a flourish.

"Elie, I don't know if Philip told you, but we would like to give the two of you a special present for your wedding. We told him what it is and we hope you like it as much as he did."

Max interrupted Tillie's dramatic presentation. "Yeah, and if you don't like it sweetheart, please tell us because it cost a fortune and I could open another damn store with the money."

"Oh Max, be quiet. You should not say things like that. Elie will take you seriously." Tillie shook her head and looked annoyed.

Elie responded, "Philip did tell me you had a special gift for us, but he didn't give me any details. Truthfully, I feel like you're doing enough already. You're being so generous, helping with the wedding and all. I don't feel comfortable about accepting any more presents from you."

"Look dear, it's our pleasure to give you things." Tillie reached for Elie's hand. "You are just starting out in life and we would like to make it easier for you. We are fortunate that we've done well for ourselves and we have more than enough. We worked very hard, now we want to share what we have with our children." She glanced at her husband, got his nod of approval, and took a small turquoise box out of her handbag.

Elie immediately recognized the signature Tiffany packaging

and panicked, thinking that the box might contain a wedding ring. Philip hadn't had time to look for rings with her. She would be furious if that's what the gift was.

Tillie passed it across the table towards Elie and Philip.

"It's from Tiffany, I already think it's too extravagant." She felt awkward and didn't really know how to react.

"Never mind dear, just open it." Tillie's eyes sparkled as she spoke.

Elie looked at Philip as she untied the white satin ribbon. She made a nervous remark, wondering aloud how they always managed to tie the bows so perfectly. Inside the box was a black velvet bag. She opened the drawstring of the bag and a silver horseshoe-shaped key ring slipped out. It held a single key.

"Umm. Well, the key ring is lovely. I must say, I never owned a Tiffany key ring. And the key is to ...?" Elie held it up.

Tillie leaned forward. "That's the surprise, dear. We bought you an apartment!"

"*Excuse me?*" Elie was not sure she had heard correctly.

Philip put his arm around Elie and kissed her on the cheek. "I knew about the apartment, babe, but I haven't seen it. I told them I wanted to see it for the first time with you."

Elie sat there stunned. She realized her mouth was open so she closed it. "I don't know what to say – I'm speechless."

Max reached across the table and took Elie's hands in his. "Sweetheart, I know this is a shock for you and I have a feeling that you're not going to be such an easy sell. If I'm right, you might feel it's too extravagant. However, it's true what Tillie said. We love you both, we want you to be happy and we'd like you to start your life together in an apartment you can raise a family in. Anyway, I was joking about what I said before, I got a deal on the place."

Elie started to stutter. "I ... I cannot believe what I'm hearing. It's impossible. How could we accept such a gift?" She looked at Philip to corroborate what she was saying, but she understood that he saw nothing wrong with it, he was in on the deal. She felt shocked and trapped. And, very excited.

The meal was served, but Elie could barely eat a bite. She always had an appetite, but today it was non-existent. She played with the food on her plate, unable to swallow it.

Tillie noticed. "Is something wrong dear? If you don't like your food we can order something else."

"No, it's fine. I'm sorry. I'm just so taken by all this that I don't feel much like eating. I have butterflies in my stomach. And I thought only the wedding could make me jittery!" She giggled nervously.

"No need to be jittery. The apartment is empty so why don't we go over there after brunch. I hope you two don't have any plans." Tillie looked at Philip for confirmation.

"No Mom, we're free. Of course we can go."

Elie sensed Philip's enthusiasm; she just wished she could have had a private moment with him.

When they finished eating, Max paid the bill and the four of them left the restaurant. On the way out he pressed a bill into the hand of the Maitre d', saying, "Jacques, it was perfect as always."

The Maitre d' refused the money and responded, "And as always, it was our pleasure, Mr. Sands."

Once outside, Tillie rebuked her husband. "Max, I told you a million times not to do that. This is not that kind of place, it's insulting to them. Really, why do you have to do it here?" Tillie rarely criticized Max in public, but this time she was adamant.

Suddenly, Elie realized she was going to be part of this family, and that she was about to be taken to a place that would become her home. A full range of emotions ran through her head. "I don't even know where this apartment is. Does anyone want to tell me?"

"We'll grab a taxi and surprise you." Tillie looped her arm through Elie's and they walked to the curb.

In the ride up Central Park West, Elie calmed down. Her shock was wearing off and her excitement was building. The taxi approached the Museum of Natural History and Max told the driver to pull over on the far corner of West Eighty-First Street. Elie recognized the building – she had learned about The Beresford in her History of New York Architecture course.

She loved the Upper West Side. Some thought it too seedy a

place to live, since there were pockets of less than desirable areas. However, it had a very homey atmosphere and was not snobby, like so many other Manhattan locations. Visiting Philip's parents in their Park Avenue apartment, for instance, always made her feel like she needed to provide pedigree papers upon entry.

Elie assumed that the apartment was on one of the side streets in the West Eighties, perhaps one of the old townhouses.

"Well kids, let's go say hello to your new home." Max led them inside the doors of The Beresford.

Elie felt her heart stop. She looked at Philip, but got no reaction. The doorman tipped his hat as they walked in, Max waved his key, and they headed through the lobby.

The elevator was the old-fashioned kind, with a metal gate that closed from within. After greeting them and asking for their floor, the operator pulled the gate closed, pushed down the lever and guided the elevator up.

"Here you go, sixteenth floor, please watch your step." He held the gate open with his gloved hand as they piled out.

Max turned left and led them down the corridor. As they reached the apartment, he turned to Elie. "Eleanora, would you like to use your key to open the door to your new home?"

Elie turned to face Philip, who said, "Go ahead, let's see our apartment."

As she unlocked the door and opened it widely, both she and Philip said in unison, "Oh my God!"

Tillie and Max looked at each other and smiled, knowingly.

The small foyer fronted an enormous living room. The three windows on the opposite wall were floor-to-ceiling and faced Central Park. The apartment was in a corner and the windows on the right side provided views of the Natural History Museum and West Eighty-First Street. Elie and Philip stepped in and looked around, silently.

Tillie stood in the center of the empty room, her handbag dangling from her folded arm. "Will someone please say something?"

Philip walked over to his mother and grabbed her in a bear hug. "Mom, this is spectacular. Really amazing. Elie's right, I'm not sure we can accept it."

"Oh bull." Max slapped his son on the back. "Of course you're going to accept it. Now, what about Eleanora? My dear, do you have anything to say?" He turned and looked at her.

"I'm catatonic. I need a few minutes." She stood with her arms limp at her sides.

Tillie clapped her hands. "Okay, all of you. Enough! We bought you an apartment, not a kingdom. You haven't even seen it yet. Let me show you around."

She took the lead and the others followed. It was a spacious three bedroom with an eat-in kitchen, separate dining room, two and a half bathrooms and a maid's quarters off the kitchen. The floors were herringbone parquet, all the ceilings had plaster moldings and the doors and door frames were solid wood.

When they returned to the living room, Elie rummaged through her bag for tissues. She used one to wipe away her tears and ended up smearing her mascara. "I'm sorry. I guess I'm a bit emotional. I feel like I'm dreaming." She took a deep breath. "This is the most beautiful apartment I have ever seen. This is the most extraordinary gift I have ever received. And you two are the most wonderful parents-in-law a girl could ever hope for. I just can't believe it, Mr. and Mrs. Sands, I don't know what to say."

Tillie once again took the reins. "Look Elie, I know you're a modest girl from a fine family and you don't have ambitions to be wealthy. That's one of the reasons we approve of you. How about, we say that we bought this more for us, than for you. We want you to be happy. We want you to raise our grandchildren in a lovely home. I know the East Side is not your style; we figured that the Upper West Side would be more to your liking. You once mentioned to me how much you liked it here. And Max really did get a great buy on this place. Someone changed his mind about living here and he had to sell fast. It is a co-op, and you will have to pass the board's inspection, but I don't suppose there will be any problem with that. Please don't think too much about this. Just tell me you love it."

"I more than love it. Can we move in right now?"

They all laughed. "Okay, good, I'm glad that's settled. Now, another thing. This Mr. and Mrs. Sands business is ridiculous.

We're Tillie and Max. No, better yet, I want you to call me mom. After all, I will be like your mother soon."

Elie smiled, but did not respond.

The wedding took place in November, in the synagogue that Elie grew up in. With its long aisle up to the *bema*, the mahogany pews upholstered in navy blue velvet, and the beautiful stained glass windows flanking both sides of the sanctuary, she felt at home.

As she stood under the flower-draped *chupah*, the rabbi and cantor chanted the blessings. Philip placed a simple gold band on Elie's finger, recited the Hebrew words that consecrated her to him, and stomped on the glass on the floor. Eleanora Stein and Philip Sands were joined as husband and wife.

Sixteen

Elie wallowed in the past all night. The discovery of the earrings triggered an onslaught of memories. The early days of their marriage had been glorious. They went out often, partied until late and thoroughly enjoyed Manhattan life. Elie worked at the magazine, decorated their apartment and took pride in preparing gourmet dinners. She loved performing the roles of junior editor and fashionable wife.

The insecurity she had felt when she first knew Philip was dissipating. There was no doubt that the lavishing of his attention on her boosted her self-esteem. Being his wife made her feel good about herself, and gave her confidence.

Life changed dramatically when Lexi was born. With Philip's encouragement, Elie gave up work and became a full time mother. Then Chloe arrived. Everything was proceeding according to plan, Philip's plan. A son might have been the jewel in the crown, but Philip seemed so happy with his girls that Elie doubted that it was a sore point.

He was not a very involved father, but most men in those days were not. He rarely made it home in time to see the girls in the evenings and he never offered to help with homework or attend school functions. He made up for his absences by spoiling them with gifts.

Philip was an excellent provider, generous to a fault. He never hassled Elie about money, on the contrary, he had always been a bit frivolous, extravagant in the gifts he gave her and overindulgent of their daughters. At times, when she thought they should prudently save for the future, Philip disregarded her fears and told her not to worry. She always acquiesced, choosing to give in rather than argue with him. It became a pattern of their life together.

Elie's thoughts returned to the present, and she wondered if she had really made significant changes since those days. She questioned if she would marry her husband today, if given the chance to do it all over again. She felt a sense of guilt, as she acknowledged that she would probably not.

She had known for some time that Philip was not the most principled of men, and in truth, over the years she had gradually been losing respect for him. She long ago gave up any hope of him becoming a different person, yet she stayed in the marriage. Why?

It was convenient to use the girls as an excuse, not wanting to disturb their childhood. But they were grown now. Financial worries? She knew deep down that she would never starve, she earned a good salary at the magazine and Philip would not allow her to suffer financially, she was certain of that.

She dug into her soul to understand why she was still with Philip if the relationship was not right, and she didn't like the answers she came up with. Because I'm weak, she thought. Because I don't have the guts to make a change in my life. Because I'm afraid to be on my own – I don't want to be a divorced woman.

She recognized the look of divorced women, it radiated wounded and desperate. Their eyes were always searching for the next man, the hero who would rescue them and allow them to breathe easy once more. But then again, she knew divorced women who were doing absolutely fine.

She still desired Philip, although their lovemaking had become less frequent and routine. During those occasional intimate moments when he held her, she felt tenderness and the sense of security she longed for. However, that sense of security had been slowly evaporating.

After Lexi and Chloe left home, Elie was sure that her marriage would spring back to life, that a spark would be ignited. She hoped that she and Philip would be able to recapture what had faded. But quite the opposite took place. Philip became distant and callous. He traveled more frequently and brushed off dates that she had made for them, claiming he had more important matters to deal with. He would refuse, often at the last minute, to go to a concert or ballet they had tickets for.

He became intolerant and easily irritated. She recalled an incident when he found a package of moldy cheese in the refrigerator. He blew up, accusing her of not caring about him or the household. She witnessed his being rude to strangers and curt with his family. It was not like the Philip she knew.

He was definitely in good health; his recent annual physical had shown that. She was also aware that the company was having a banner year, so it could not be business related problems. Eliminating those two possibilities, Elie came to the unpleasant conclusion that Philip's recent behavior was probably some warped way of justifying himself. If he indeed had been unfaithful, wouldn't it make sense to assuage his guilt by finding fault with his wife?

As to her part in the situation, she had been aware of the changing dynamics – why did she not say anything? Why had she not confronted him?

Elie began to realize that the earrings were just a symptom, physical proof of a crumbling marriage. They were a sign of a relationship that had lost its vitality. Philip may have betrayed her, which was a very tough pill to swallow, but she shared some of the responsibility. Although she had never been unfaithful, she certainly no longer felt an intimate bond with him. Maybe this token of infidelity, if that's what it was, was the dose of reality she had been waiting for. Perhaps this was the proof she needed that their life together was not worth salvaging.

The phone rang the next morning and woke her up. She glanced at the clock on the bedside table – it was past eleven.

"Elie, are you okay? You didn't make it to the editorial meeting this morning and I was starting to worry. And Leigh was looking for you, to finalize some details of the designer party."

She recognized the voice as Heather's. She remembered why she was still in bed and thought fast.

"Hi, Heather. I'm not feeling very well, I must have overslept this morning. Please tell them that I'm not coming in today."

"Yes, of course. I hope you feel better."

"Thanks. And Heather?"

"Yes?"

"Is Keira there?" She wondered why the call came from Heather and not from her assistant.

"Yes, she's in the office, but I believe she's in that editorial meeting. Do you want me to call her out?"

"No, that's okay. Hope to see you tomorrow. Bye now and thanks." She hung up.

Elie was annoyed. Why was Keira sitting in on the Monday morning meeting, which was for editors only? Who authorized that? She decided to worry about it some other time, having more pressing issues to deal with now.

She sat up, and took a minute to focus. Then she reached for the phone. "Oh, thank God, you're home. I need to talk to you, it's urgent. Can you? Are you free?"

Syd did not hesitate. "I'll be right down."

Elie felt relieved, and grateful. Living in the same building as her best friend had benefits way beyond borrowing the proverbial cup of sugar. It included an emergency babysitter, the perfect accessory for an important dinner or, on occasion, a shoulder to cry on. Syd was Elie's on-site shrink.

She managed to brush her teeth and run a comb through her hair, but she was still in her robe when Syd knocked on the door. She opened it and hugged her friend, who gently pushed her away at arm's distance and looked her up and down with serious concern on her face.

"What happened, Elie? Speak to me."

Elie couldn't quite get it out. "Come into the kitchen. We need a cup of coffee for this. If it wasn't so early, I'd pour us a drink."

Syd was respectfully quiet and followed her into the kitchen.

Elie made the coffee and took a few homemade cookies out of the cookie jar, a habit she held onto from when the girls lived at home. She put them on a brightly colored Italian ceramic plate, part of the set she had bought in Lake Como. She opened a drawer and ruffled through the linens, looking for two matching napkins.

Syd exploded. "For God's sake Elie, stop with the damn cookies and napkins! Tell me what's going on!"

Elie sat down. "Here, look at this. What do you have to say?"

She dropped the earrings in Syd's hand, realizing that they were still in the pocket of the robe she had been wearing since last night.

"Nice earrings. But aren't they a bit young looking for you?" Syd laughed, but she knew something was amiss. "Where did you find them?"

"In Philip's pocket. I was getting clothes ready for the dry cleaners. Ironically, he told me to take the suit. I found them last night and I've been obsessing about it ever since. I feel sick, Syd. I don't know what to do."

"I'll tell you what to do. You rip a new asshole into him."

"Be serious. I'm so lost. I'm not even sure it means what I think it means."

"Well, that's your first mission, to determine if this is what you think it is. Maybe it's innocent and you're just getting carried away." Syd stopped for a moment, and took a sip of coffee. "It is possible, you know, that he's not guilty of anything, that he just happened to find the earrings and put them in his pocket." She was trying to be levelheaded, but her expression belied her words.

Elie didn't seem to notice. "Doubtful. He would have handed them right over, not wanting to be bothered with a lost-and-found item. I know that finding these earrings is not cause for indictment but I've had a bad feeling for some time now. Things haven't been right between us. He's been short-tempered and mean. I really think he could be cheating on me."

Elie pushed her coffee cup away, rested her elbows on the table and supported her chin in her palms.

Syd put her hand on her friend's arm. "Elie, first you need to think about how, and even if, you want to approach this. Once you expose your suspicions to Philip, you could be opening a Pandora's Box. I don't mean to be dramatic, but ... I think you must determine for yourself if you really want to know the truth.

And if you do want to know the truth, you have to be clever about it. You can't just accuse him with the earrings in your hand as he walks in the door. We both know that Philip is a smart man and if he has to be, I am sure he can be sly. You do not want to put him in a corner. I think we should hatch a plan."

"Okay, now you're scaring me." Elie picked her head up. "This is not going to be an episode of *The Bold and the Beautiful*."

"No, it's more like *The Good, the Bad and the Ugly*." Syd smirked while stroking Elie's hand. "Sorry, couldn't resist."

Elie knew that she could tell Syd anything. She trusted her implicitly. She poured more coffee and talked to Syd about Philip's behavior of late. She was, however, less than open about her own personal feelings. She had not yet sorted them out.

Syd glanced at the clock on the wall and jumped up. "Damn! It's late. Look Elie, I have to get to the office. I have an important meeting. It's this on-going investigation. They opened a second case and I have to be the perfect cooperative girl if I want to stay far away from the mess. However, I can cancel the rest of my day and come back here. Maybe we need a spa afternoon, or a spree at *Bloomies?* What do you say?"

"No Syd, thanks, I'll be fine. I just needed to talk a bit. You're right; I have to think about what I want. I think I need to know the truth, because I don't see how I can live with the uncertainty. On the other hand, maybe I'm better off not knowing. In any case, I'll be okay today. Thank you so much for coming down. It did calm me." Elie walked her to the door.

Syd seemed unconvinced. "Elie, I'm serious. I can blow off the rest of the day, there's nothing urgent after this meeting. I'm ready to come back later and kidnap you. How about we mosey over to Bergdorf and treat ourselves to a Gotham salad?"

"Thank you, but no. I have to go into the office for a few hours, which will be good for me. I hope that it will take my mind off all this. Philip is in Italy again, so I have time to think things through before he gets back. Bye, sweetie, and thank you."

Elie kissed her friend. "And good luck – I hope everything is okay at the office. Be strong." She closed the door behind her.

She lied about going to the office. She just didn't want Syd to think that she was going to mope at home all day. But that was exactly what she intended to do. She walked back into the kitchen, threw the earrings in the junk drawer, slammed it shut and decided to make herself a tuna melt.

When the sandwich was ready, she put it on a tray, along with a bottle of Pellegrino and a piece of bittersweet chocolate. She carried her meal back to the bedroom and placed it on her night table, nearly shoving the clock and telephone off the edge. She did not intend to leave the room for the remainder of the day.

She sat cross-legged on her bed, ate the sandwich and sipped the water. When she finished, she started to feel a little better. She reached over to the drawer of the night table and pulled out the bottle of Valium, her emergency stash when she absolutely could not sleep. Half a pill usually did the trick, she took a whole one and washed it down with a swig of water.

Syd walked out of Elie's apartment steaming. Of course Philip was cheating, she was certain of it. The problem was whether or not to tell her friend what she knew. She felt the weight of being just a little too close to two of the Sands women.

Elie meant the world to Syd. She knew that most other women were threatened by her dominant personality, but Elie had accepted her, as is, from the start. She did not judge her, compete with her, or expect her to meet some set of standards. Syd considered Elie the sister she would have liked to have.

But, there was the Chloe complication. She loved the girl very much, and she was astute enough to realize that her feelings had to do with displaced love for the child she had aborted. She knew it caused Elie pain to realize that her daughter was confiding in her best friend, but Elie was usually big about it, making a few nervous jokes and moving on.

Now Syd was burdened by two major stories, and she could not tell one protagonist about the other. Her recent talks with Chloe had been very disturbing. First, there was the married lover episode. Then, on a recent visit home, Chloe popped in upstairs and dropped another bombshell.

She had been surprised by the knock on the door, but delighted to see her young friend through the peephole. She invited her in and they sat in the kitchen sipping margaritas and downing a fresh batch of guacamole.

"Syd, does my mother fool around?"

Syd spit the drink out of her mouth. She picked up the napkin to wipe her lips and looked at Chloe incredulously. "Chloe, what in the world has come over you?"

"Nothing. I just want to know if my mother has fooled around."

"That is not something you should be asking me. And what makes you think I would even consider answering such a question?"

"I think my father is cheating. I'm pretty certain of it. I just wanted to know if she does it too. I don't think they have a very good marriage. Maybe they're both fooling around and I'm just a naive kid who doesn't know anything." She loaded the guacamole onto a chip and put the whole thing into her mouth.

There was no uncertainty in Syd's response. "Chloe, I don't mean to be rude or put you off, but I will not speak with you about your mother. She is my dearest friend and anything I would say about her would feel like a betrayal. I do not tell her what you and I discuss, and I certainly would not share with you what she and I discuss. But I will say this: I don't think there's a chance in hell that your mother is cheating."

She hesitated and then spoke again. "Why do you suspect your father?" Syd broke her own code, knowing that her question would involve her in something she was not sure she wanted to be a part of.

"I've seen the way he behaves around women, especially attractive women. He acts like such a fool, he gets all flirty and stuff. It makes me want to throw up. He goes out to lots of lunches, sometimes dinners. You know how much he travels. It's all out in public, but I'm not fooled by it."

"Your dad is very friendly, maybe a little too friendly when it comes to business contacts, but that does not mean he's guilty of cheating." Syd waited for a response.

"I'm telling you – you should see how women are around him. He's like so old, what's the deal with that? I've also heard whispers and rumors from people who didn't know I was his daughter. There was an incident recently that I saw. Anyway, I have no proof, just a feeling. What should I do?"

"Nothing. You should do absolutely nothing."

"Why? If he's cheating on her, shouldn't my mother know? He's making a fool out of her."

"I will tell you a lesson I learned years ago. I was certain a friend's husband was cheating, so I told her. She confronted him and he denied it. She accused me of jealousy, and was quite the bitch about it, and she terminated her friendship with me. Later, she found out that he was a cheating bastard and she wanted to get back together, but I was no longer interested in renewing the relationship." Syd fingered the glass, but did not drink.

"I thought a lot about that incident and I realized that I was wrong. It was too much for my friend to accept. It was easier to find fault with me, rather than with her husband. I learned it's best to stay out of these things."

"But these people are my parents!"

"So? Does that make them any different? Do you think they're impervious to human frailties? They're normal like anyone else, and if something is going on, I would guess it's best to keep quiet. You're a big girl, Chloe. For God's sake, you're fooling around yourself. Who are you to judge your father or mother?"

"Hey! I'm not cheating on anyone. I'm not married!"

"Ah, but you are cheating on another woman, by sleeping with her husband. Instead of going for a man who could be all yours, you're giving yourself half a relationship, accepting much less than you deserve. You're not being honest with yourself, my dear."

Chloe was silent.

"And while we're on the subject, what exactly is happening with the man? Steven, if I recall correctly?"

"We're still involved. He calls the shots. I don't like the situation, but I'm really stuck on him. I'm hoping he'll leave his wife."

"Oh Chloe, you're not."

"Why? Would it be so bad? Just because he's older? I'm mature for my age."

Syd suddenly realized how delicate this situation was. She did not want to lose the trust of this young woman, but she also wanted to get a strong message across. "Honey, you are mature, but you're still young and you deserve a lot better. Your whole life is ahead of you, why hook up with someone with so much baggage?"

"Because he's so cool. He makes me feel like a woman, not a girl. Do you know what I mean, Aunt Syd? I'm a mess, huh? No better than my dad. Guess I got the cheating gene from him."

Syd saw that Chloe was not as sure of herself as she pretended to be, guilt and confusion simmered beneath the bravado. She smiled and put her arm around the girl.

"I think you are the greatest, Chloe Sands, and the guy who wins your love has to be really spectacular. You are going to do remarkable things in life, and only a man of the highest character will earn the right to share your world. He's out there waiting for you, I'm certain of it."

Chloe leaned towards Syd and hugged her. "I love you, Aunt Syd."

"And I love you too, my darling. As for your father, that's a slippery slope. I think you should not get involved in it. If the situation becomes unbearable, then maybe you should consider talking to your dad. Or come talk to me, anytime. Okay? Do we have a deal?"

Chloe mumbled "Okay."

Seventeen

The test results came back positive, Michael was a perfect donor match. He felt a huge sense of relief, and for once, did not care how much pain was involved, or what would be required. He had the proof he needed that Isabel was his granddaughter, and he would provide whatever she needed.

Daniel had done the research and planned to discuss it with Michael. They had just finished dinner, when he brought up the subject.

Michael raised his hand, as if to block out Daniel's words. "I don't want to know. If you tell me, I'll get faint and I might chicken out. I have to do this for her. You understand, don't you?"

"I do, of course. However, I think you should be aware of what's involved. Admittedly, it isn't much on your part, but you should know."

"Daniel darling, I have the feeling that it will include needles, hypodermics, whatever you call them. And you know how I feel about those. Why did I consistently refuse to give blood to the AIDS Center? Why have I been willing to donate time, money and anything else they need from me, as long as it didn't involve puncturing any part of my body? I just cannot bear the thought of it. So please do not, I repeat, do not, give me the details. Going for the tests to determine my eligibility was enough to nearly wipe me out. Just tell me I won't die over this."

"You won't die over this. You are a brave man, my love. I'm very proud of you. I'll go with you to Philadelphia and I'll be there with you throughout. And really, from what I understand, it's no big deal on your part. Isabel though, will go through a rough period."

Michael placed his hand over his heart. "Oh, that poor little angel. We must do everything we can to make her comfortable,

Daniel. I want her in a private room, with round-the-clock nurses of course. Let's do this right."

"Michael, I know you want to do everything you can for Isabel and it's admirable." Daniel looked concerned. "But you must remember that you cannot make those decisions. Her grandmother is the one responsible for her."

"Oh, please. Now you sound like Elie. That little girl is my flesh and blood, and that woman kept her from me. I will insist on a private room and anything else I want, and if Pat doesn't like it, she can kiss my butt in Macy's window." He threw his napkin onto the table.

"Michael, listen to me. I'm being very serious now." Daniel reached over and touched his lover's hand. "You cannot interfere in that little girl's life. I'm sorry to be so blunt about this, but I want you to understand the situation. No court in the land will give you any rights to her, and don't tell me you haven't already thought of adopting her. I know you, and I am telling you to calm down."

"You are being unnecessarily cruel to me." Dinner was obviously over. Michael pushed back his chair and turned his head away.

Daniel swept up a few crumbs from the table and put them on his plate. "No, I'm being necessarily honest. You need to hear this and I want you to stop playing the petulant boy routine with me. A child's life is at stake. If you are willing to do this transplant for Isabel, it's noble of you. I respect and admire you for it. However, if you think that it gives you rights to that child, then you had better think again. I will not have you fantasizing about starting a new life with her. You will get your heart broken. Please hear me on this."

Michael turned back to face him and raised his voice. "You don't understand what's going on there. That child plays hockey for God's sake! What kind of game is that for a young lady? Pat made her into a tomboy! She should have ballet and piano lessons, at the least. The situation is totally unacceptable. You must be on my side on this. If not, then you're horrid. And a traitor!"

"Well, maybe I am. And you are dear. Very dear to me. I think I know you pretty well, and I want to protect you. Isn't that my job?" Daniel smiled. "You've been dreaming of making her over in your image, haven't you? I'm sure you were already redecorating our guest room into a princess palace. Was it going to be all pink or pink and periwinkle?" He crossed his legs, folded his hands and waited for a response.

Michael smiled sheepishly. "It was going to be pink with white stripes, with periwinkle accents. With a pink marble ice cream sundae table against the window and two white wrought iron chairs. And a full canopy over her bed with frilly French lace flowing down from the top and on the sides."

Daniel reached for Michael's hand. "I'll tell you what. After she recovers and can travel, if Pat agrees, why don't we invite her here for a weekend? And, if she likes it, we'll convert the guest bedroom for her and the two of you can have a ball decorating it. How does that sound?"

"What about for the whole summer? I want her with us."

"Michael, my love, let's take this one step at a time. First, let's get over this bone marrow procedure. Let's pray for her good health and then move on. Okay?"

"Fine," said Michael, looking annoyed.

The date for the procedure was set. Daniel drove them to Philadelphia and Michael was unusually quiet during the ride. He was thinking about the little girl – a bond had developed between them, thanks to calls and email, and she had become quite significant in his life.

They stopped at the hotel to drop off their things and then headed for the hospital. Isabel already had undergone a battery of tests to establish that she was in good enough condition to receive the transplant and to determine a baseline for the post-operative period. She had begun chemotherapy and her long hair was now short and thinned out.

She was watching television when the two men entered her room.

"Hello Queen Isabel, how are you doing?" Michael bent down to kiss her but then pulled back, realizing that he could pass on germs. He turned to Daniel.

"Isabel, I would like to introduce to you Daniel Keane. He is a very special person in my life."

Isabel looked up at him and smiled. "Hi! You're his light partner, right?"

Both men giggled. "No darling, that's life partner. Daniel is my life partner. We live together."

"My friend Janey, at school, has two moms. Her biological mom, and another one. Only one works, and the other stays home. And the one that works is a photographer for the *Philadelphia Inquirer*. Pretty cool, huh?" Isabel straightened the edges of her blanket. "Wanna watch *The Young & the Restless* with me? I think Victor is going to get married again."

"Darlin', that man has been married more times and has more ex-wives that I have silk scarves. And I have a lot of silk scarves! Oh, here, I brought you one. What do you think of that?" He handed her a beautifully wrapped present.

"Ooh, I love presents. But why did you tell me what it is? Now it's not a surprise." She pouted.

Michael started to respond, but Daniel interrupted him. "I'll tell you why, Isabel. Because, Michael can never keep a secret. And also, because he wants to give you time to prepare a nice response, in case you don't like it."

Michael rolled his eyes and was about to say something, when Pat walked in.

"Well, hello." She looked surprised. "I thought you'd be here only tonight. Hi honey." She bent down to kiss the girl. "What's this?"

"Hey, Gran! I got a present! And I already know what it is!" She fumbled with the paper and ribbons.

"How kind, thank you." She smiled at Michael and shook Daniel's hand, meeting him for the first time.

As Isabel opened the box, she exclaimed with glee, "Oh, it's so cool. I never had nothing like this before." It was pink and white striped silk, with long white fringes on the ends.

Michael corrected her. "It's, 'I never had anything like this before.' Here, let's put it on you." He caught Daniel's scolding glance.

He draped it around her neck and pulled his own scarf out of his jacket. "See, we're twins. How's that, my Queen Isabel?"

"I shall never take it off. Thank you, Sir Michael."

Pat walked over to the window, giving the men space to be with her granddaughter.

Daniel looked from Isabel to Michael. "What's with this sir business?"

"Well, I decided that since Michael calls me his Queen, I have to call him something. I can't call him a knight or whatever, so I just decided on sir. I can call you Sir Daniel if you like."

"Thanks, Isabel, but plain old Daniel is just fine with me."

"Okay, if you say so, Plain Old Daniel." Isabel giggled.

Michael looked at his partner. "Hey! Plain Old D. – I like that! Now, how about if you leave me and my queen alone for a while to have a little talk?"

"No problem. Pat, can I treat you to coffee in the cafeteria?" He looked at Pat, who smiled in agreement, and they walked out together.

Left alone in the room, Michael turned to Isabel.

"You know, sweetheart, this operation is going to be a big success and you're going to get well and be able to do all kinds of things."

"I know. But I look so ugly now. My hair fell out because of the chemotherapy." She touched her head.

"You certainly do not look ugly! Why, you are the prettiest girl I have ever seen! And you know what? When this is all over, I'll take you to a top hair stylist in New York and we'll have a bob designed just for you. My friend Elie has her hair done at The Cutting Room in the Village. I'll take you to Lisa and we'll get the royal treatment there. "

"Oh, man. That would be major *coolio*." She stopped for a moment. "I'm not scared, you know." She motioned for him to join her on the bed.

"Really not?" He sat down and fussed with her blanket, straightening out the edge.

"Uh uh. They explained everything to me – it's not so bad. I'm glad it's you giving me the bone marrow. You'll be okay, too."

"I sure hope so. I don't even know what they're going to do to me."

"Want me to explain? I can, you know."

"Yes, but maybe not so much about the needle part." Michael made a face and shivered.

"Oh, you're such a baby." She put both her hands out in the air, as if to conduct an orchestra. "Okay, here goes. First, they check me and make sure that everything is okay. Then, they harvest your bone marrow."

"What do you mean harvest? Like what a farmer does?"

"You're so silly. No, they stick a you-know-what in some place in your hip and draw out the goop, and that's what they harvest. And don't complain, because guess what they have to do to me? They have to make a little hole here, right near my heart," she pointed to her chest, "and put a tube in. Then they vacuum out my bad cells, and give me more chemo to get rid of all the junk and then, when there's none of the bad stuff left, I get your good bone marrow. And that's it!"

"Isabel, honey, maybe you'd better not give me any more details. Between the harvesting and vacuuming, I'm getting queasy." He put his hand on his stomach.

"Well, it's not real vacuuming. It's just that the chemo gets rid of all the nasty cells that are making me sick. Get it?"

"I think so."

"And then, I have to stay here for a while. And when I'm better, I can go home and *recupterate*. And they said that my friends can bring my homework over, so I don't have to miss school."

"It's recuperate, precious. Tell me, what do you think of coming to visit Daniel and me in Manhattan when this is all over? A trip to New York to celebrate your recovery?"

"Oh yes, please. Can I?" Isabel put her hands together in a begging motion. "Did you ask Granny? I've only been to New York City once, when she and Grandpa took me to Radio City Music Hall. That was amazing. I think New York is just about the most beautiful city in the whole wide world."

"And how many cities have you been to, exactly?"

"Philadelphia, Scranton and Lancaster, Pennsylvania, where they have all those Pennsylvania Dutch apple people."

"Do you mean Dutch Amish?"

"Oh yeah, that's it. But I don't think those cities are as fun as New York. Right?"

Michael controlled himself from comparing Scranton to New York. He knew he would have to watch his sarcasm with her. "Yes, you are right. And I hope that one day I'll be able to take you to many wonderful cities, if your Gran says it's okay. Now, there's another matter I would like to bring up with you."

"Okay, shoot." She made a motion with her fingers imitating a gun.

"We're going to have to do away with this Sir Michael stuff. It is a bit silly. I think you should call me something else. I don't know what though."

"Well, I had a Grandpa, but he's dead now. So, I can't call you Grandpa. Do you want me to call you Gramps or Uncle Mikey?"

Michael instinctively put his hand to his forehead. "Oh no, dear. That won't do at all. I'll have to think of something appropriate. You leave it to me."

Isabel yawned and leaned back. "Okay. And you can call me Izzy if you want. I like that name."

Michael understood that she was getting tired. He moved the blanket up on her, brushed the wispy bangs off her face and suggested that she try to sleep. As she closed her eyes, he felt an overwhelming rush of love.

The procedure of extracting Michael's bone marrow was successful. He stayed overnight at the hospital and was kept comfortable with painkillers. Isabel was given high doses of chemotherapy, to deplete her body of its bone marrow, and her immune system was crippled. She was pumped with antibiotics to fight infection, and deemed ready for the transplant.

The next day, Michael, Daniel and Pat huddled together in the waiting area as Michael's healthy bone marrow was injected through a tube in Isabel's chest. When the doctor came out of the room and assured them that everything went according to procedure, there was a collective sigh of relief. It was now up to Isabel's body to accept the donor marrow and begin producing normal blood cells.

Michael received calls from his mother and Elie, both asking if they could visit. He explained that this was not the right time. Anyone who entered Isabel's room had to wear a protective mask, gown and gloves, and no items from the outside were allowed in. Every effort was made to keep the environment free from unwanted organisms. He reassured them that all went well, and promised to keep in touch.

The weeks following the procedure proved to be very difficult. Isabel went home, but was uncomfortable most of the time. Her grandmother stayed by her bedside and when the child was receptive, one or two friends were allowed to visit. Michael called every day and sent presents.

When given the green light by Pat, Michael and Daniel drove down to visit. As they entered the small wooden frame house, they found Isabel seated in the living room wearing a sweat suit and baseball cap, watching a game on television.

"This is how you recover? By watching silly sports? Oh my word, didn't I send you the most wonderful videos? Why aren't you watching *The Princess Diaries* and *National Velvet* and *Beauty & The Beast?*" Michael was beside himself.

"*Hellooooo?* Who watches that stuff? I mean, thanks and all, but I'm not a little kid, you know. And anyway, I love baseball – the Phillies have been having a really good season – maybe they're *gonna* win the World Series this year!" Isabel barely took her eyes off the screen.

Daniel laughed and handed Isabel a box containing a chemistry set, knowing that she liked science. Michael sat down on the sofa next to her and presented her with two shopping bags full of clothes from The Gap. He pulled each piece out individually and made comments about it, while Isabel nodded her approval and tried desperately to continue watching the game.

Eighteen

Philip returned from his trip with a vintage Murano piece that he "got for a steal". It was a multi-colored glass vase, which reminded him of "that painter Klimt". It reminded Elie of a pillar of Allsorts licorice candies, and she hated it.

After a few days of having him home, the uncertainty of whether or not he was having an affair was driving her mad. She could no longer live with the doubts, it was time to ask the question. Regardless of what his response would be she needed to confront him about the earrings. She planned a dinner at home, reasoning that she could not bring up the topic in a restaurant.

When Philip arrived that evening, he put his keys and wallet on the foyer table, called out, "Hey babe, I'm home," and glanced at the mail as he headed towards the bedroom to take off his jacket and tie.

"I'm in the kitchen, Philip, dinner is almost ready."

"Great. I'm starving."

He came into the kitchen and kissed her. "Smells great in here. What have you cooked up for us tonight?"

He seemed to be in a good mood. She wondered, for a moment, if it was worth bringing up the subject. She decided to stick with her original plan and turned from stirring the sauce to face him.

"Grilled lamb chops in a rosemary cream sauce and lemon soufflé for dessert."

"Wow, that's major! What's the occasion? Are you buttering me up, before you tell me about an expensive trinket you bought? A home upstate? A new car?"

"No Philip. I made no large purchases. You need not worry." She made an effort to disguise her attitude, but there was a sarcastic tone to her voice.

He seemed not to notice. "I see you're breaking out the Amarone, now I *know* something is happening." Rather than pick up the simple waiter's corkscrew she had placed on the counter, he walked over to the wall-mounted, antique, brass wine bottle opener, another "steal" he got at Christie's. "So, what's the occasion, Elie? Did you total the Jag?"

"I don't think so, Philip." Her hostility was mounting. She placed wine glasses on the table and Philip poured.

He twirled the wine around in the glass, took a sip, kept it in his mouth for a moment and then swallowed.

"Umm, not bad. I thought this was a good bottle when I spotted it. Paid a bloody fortune for it, but I managed to convince Albert to sell me the last case."

Elie ladled out New England clam chowder for the first course. It was Philip's favorite and one of her specialties. If she was going to commence with an interrogation, she knew it would have to be while his mood was good and his stomach full.

When they finished, she removed the soup bowls and served the lamb chops. Philip, talking about business between bites, was complimentary about the food. Finally, when the table was cleared and he was describing a new office system they were designing, she poured the espresso and served the lemon soufflé. Now, she thought. Do it now!

"Philip, I'd like to talk to you about something."

"Sure babe, what is it?" He mumbled as he dug into the dessert.

She opened the kitchen drawer and took out the earrings. She put them on the table in front of Philip and sat down facing him. "Can you explain these? I found them in the pocket of your blue suit, the one you told me to take to the cleaners."

He was stone-faced. It took him a few seconds to respond. "Ah. I forgot about those. I found them in the showroom and put them in my pocket, thinking I would ask around to see who lost them. Good thing you found them, I had forgotten all about it." He was looking at the earrings.

Elie had trouble reading his face and could not figure out what to do next. Make a big stink or let it go? She did not want to sound like a jealous, insecure wife, but she also wanted an explanation for his rotten attitude lately. She wondered which approach to take and her silence was palpable.

"Why, Elie? Were you worried? Did you think I was cheating on you?" He half smiled.

"I wasn't sure, Philip. I did consider it a possibility." She could not look at him, her fingers played with the edge of the placemat.

"You're joshing me. You really think I could do that? What, like sneak around behind your back? Have a secret mistress stashed away somewhere? You've got to be kidding me. What's come over you?" He started out smirking, but his mood quickly changed to annoyance.

Take it easy, she told herself, he's testing you. Don't overreact.

Philip pushed the soufflé away and looked at Elie directly in the eyes. "Well, Elie? I'm waiting for an answer. I want to know why you think I'm cheating on you. I am really hurt by your suspicions, and I do not like the implications."

She took a deep breath. "Philip, I found a pair of earrings in your pocket. If you found them in the showroom, why didn't you just give them to the receptionist? Wouldn't someone have claimed them? My suspicions were raised, not just because of the earrings, but because you have not been yourself for some time now."

"What are you talking about? *Of course,* I am myself. You're getting paranoid. Maybe you should take one of those Valiums of yours." He pushed his chair back and it made a scrapping sound on the floor.

Her blood was starting to boil, but she was determined to face him down. She folded her hands together on the table and moved closer to him.

"I am not paranoid, nor do I need a Valium. Perhaps you would like to explain to me why you have been such a shit lately."

Obviously, he was shocked by her choice of words. "*A shit? Me?* You really don't know what you're talking about. I think I'm a damn good husband. Just ask all your girlfriends, see what their husbands are like."

She sat there, staring at him. She was cringing inside, struggling to maintain a cool appearance.

"Philip, you have not been yourself for quite some time. I don't know why you are behaving so badly, I've tried to figure it out, but nothing makes sense. You've been speaking rudely, barking orders, complaining that I neglect the house. You've been callous and insensitive. I'm sorry to say it, but you're different lately, and not in a good way."

This time he screeched his chair all the way back, nearly flipping it over, and stood up with an air of self-righteousness. "And you, Elie, don't know what the hell you're talking about. I don't have to take this crap from you anymore." He stormed out of the kitchen.

She heard the front door slam. Elie sat still for a few minutes, trying to process what had just happened. She felt her heart beating. She never imagined that her carefully planned evening would end like this.

She reviewed her words. She had not been angry or vicious, she had been calm. But he totally lost it. She had never seen him so furious. If Philip were innocent, wouldn't he have put his arms around her in an attempt to reassure her? Wouldn't he have tried to make her feel better? Could his aggressive reaction be caused by exactly what she suspected, that he was lying to her and guilt ridden?

She got up and walked to the foyer, to see if his keys and wallet were still there. They were not. She was tempted to call Syd, but then reconsidered. Maybe Philip would come back and apologize. If so, she should not be on the telephone. Even if he did not come back, she needed time to think, without outside influences.

She went into the den, dimmed the lights and lay down on the sofa. She stayed there for a long time, feeling sad and frustrated. The truth she had been afraid to face was staring her in the face. Philip had a secret, and she felt certain she knew what the secret was.

She began to think about the couples in their circle, and she wondered what their marriages were like below the surface. Were people as happy as they seemed, or was there a conspiracy of silence? Her mind focused on a proverb from a wedding card they had received. *May your life together be like a pair of scissors – each blade going in its own direction, but coming together to destroy anything that gets between them.* Elie had treasured that sentiment and kept the card. She had hoped that her marriage would be such an example.

Memories were seeping into her consciousness. She covered herself with the afghan and let her mind drift.

Philip Sands had not been the love of her life. She loved him, but with reservations. He seemed like he could be the right partner in so many ways that she subjugated her doubts and allowed herself to be swept off her feet.

David Abarbanel was her first love, the man with whom she became a woman. She loved him with all her heart, but the end of her year in Israel foretold the end of the relationship. Overcoming the pain of losing him had been tortuous.

Philip entered her life at just the right time. He was nothing like David, but he possessed such a sure sense of himself that she was drawn to him. She admitted to herself that perhaps she married him for less than the noblest of reasons – life with Philip meant security, comfort and a close family. In truth, she adored being married in the beginning, and she was determined to be the best wife ever. At some point though, it started to crumble.

Philip was probably aware of her dissatisfaction. Perhaps through her behavior, her way of speaking, her commitment to her work – there could have been so many means by which she transmitted her unhappiness. He was not ignorant. Maybe he got the message and took revenge, or solace, in the arms of another woman. Had she sent him there?

She snapped out of her reverie to recall that the remains of dinner were still on the table. She did not like leaving a mess for Gloria to face in the morning, so she returned to the kitchen. When she spied the earrings on the table, she fingered them for a moment, then threw them back in the drawer and slammed it shut.

When Elie awoke in the morning, Philip was there. He was showered, shaved and getting dressed. It was seven, earlier than usual for him. She recalled him coming home late last night, but she had feigned sleep. She sat up in bed and looked at him, not sure of what to say. He spoke first.

"Elie, we need to talk. I'm sorry about last night – that I stormed off – but you really pissed me off. I didn't like the position you put me in, as if you were setting a trap. I'm scheduled to fly to Chicago today, but I'll try to cancel. If I can, let's go out for dinner. I promise not to get angry again. All right?"

She was surprised by his apology, although she sensed that he was playing Philip the Prince Charming card. Her antennae were on alert, but she saw no reason not to accept his invitation.

"Okay. Why don't you call my cell and tell me if your trip has been cancelled."

"Will do. See you later." He leaned down, kissed her goodbye and walked out of the room.

She heard the front door close as she got up out of bed.

When she entered the kitchen to make coffee, she opened the drawer and saw that the earrings were gone. She had a bad feeling. Was he running off to see his mistress? Was he really going to cancel Chicago and come home, or was that just a ruse? Was he even really supposed to go to Chicago?

She hated herself for all her doubts. Why couldn't she just believe his explanation and go back to living her life, *happily ever after?*

Elie found it difficult to concentrate at work. She decided to discuss her situation with Walter, hoping for a man's perspective. She looked through the glass office wall and saw some men talking to him.

She stopped at his secretary's desk. "Hi, Denise. Something going on there?"

"Yes, but no idea what. My orders are no interruptions and no calls."

She asked her to leave a message that she would like to speak with Walter as soon as possible.

The mounds of work on her desk helped her get through the

morning. Besides the regular magazine features, the AIDS benefit was approaching and there were still many details to be worked out. At a few minutes past twelve, her intercom rang.

"Hey kid, heard you were looking for me."

She took a deep breath and began. "Walter, I have a problem and I need an objective ear. It's a personal matter, so if you want to back off, I understand. But I hope you won't."

"I see. Sounds serious, want to join me for lunch?"

"I'd love to. Give me two seconds." She was relieved.

"Meet me at the elevators. I'll tell Denise to change the reservation to two."

They walked to Union Square Café, where Walter had a regular table. They got settled and Elie asked about the meeting in his office.

"Nothing you need to know about for the time being. I'll fill you in later. What's on your mind, Elie?"

"Walter, I think you know how much I respect your opinion and how much you mean to me. I …" She hesitated.

"Oh no, you're not going to tell me you need more time off, are you? You get me nervous when you start with how much you respect me. Last time we had such a serious beginning, you told me you were pregnant and needed an indefinite leave. Get to the main topic."

Elie smiled. "No pregnancy and no time off required. This topic is that I think my husband is having an affair and I don't know how to handle it."

"*Holy mackerel!* I certainly did not see that coming. Why in the world do you want to talk to me about this? What good could an old geezer like me be to you?" Walter gulped down his martini, which had just arrived.

Elie had never initiated such an intimate talk with her boss, he was not a touchy-feely kind of guy. On the contrary, Walter Lavigne was a man's man, tough talking, cigar smoking and straight-shooting. She desperately wanted to hear what he had to say.

"Walter, look, I know this is beyond what usually passes

for discussions between us. But I've been haunted by what has happened and I would like a man's perspective. I want you to give me your honest opinion."

"You will owe me big time for this, Eleanora Sands." He motioned to the waiter to bring him another drink.

"I know. I will owe you for ever and ever. Anyway I owe you so much, just add it to the list."

"Yeah, big talk. So what's happening?" He looked ready to take on her issues.

Elie related the story, starting from when she began to notice a change in Philip's attitude. She told him about the earrings, Philip's behavior the night before and his apology that morning. She laid the whole story out and waited for him to comment.

"You really want my honest opinion? From what you've just described, I think you behaved inappropriately and unfairly. There was no justification for the manner in which you confronted Philip."

Elie was taken aback, but she did not interrupt.

"Look Elie, this is a delicate matter. A wife discovers what she thinks is proof that her husband is cheating and all hell breaks loose. She challenges him, he becomes defensive. Pretty typical scenario if you ask me. But the problem is that the wife has no actual evidence and the husband is so incensed, he doesn't read his wife's insecurities. Big mess for nothing."

He continued. "Basically, you accused Philip without giving him a chance to explain. Or rather, he did explain and you did not accept it. You already convicted him of a crime and refused to listen to his defense. That was unfair."

As Walter was talking, the waiter came by and recited the specials. In spite of Elie's tension, she loved the food at the restaurant and enjoyed hearing the descriptions. They both ordered and continued to talk.

"Look at me, even with all this *tsouris* on my mind, I still get excited about food."

"That's why you're okay in my book. You have a healthy appetite for life. I can't stand women who pick at their food and drive wait staff crazy. They want to diet, they should do it at home."

Elie smiled. "Okay, so let's get back to the topic. I believe you were telling me off."

"No, not telling you off. Telling you what I think. There's a difference."

"But Walter, Philip became really angry. He made *me* the guilty party and he stormed out in a huff. Maybe I can understand his indignation, but wouldn't he try to redeem himself? And what about me? The end of my marriage may be staring me in the face. Why Walter? Why would he do it? I could not live with myself if I cheated on Philip."

"Elie, I cannot speak from experience, because I have never been unfaithful to Katherine. However, I know plenty of people, women too by the way, who betray their spouses. There are dozens of reasons. They don't love their wife or husband anymore, but are afraid to leave. They feel unattractive or unloved, and seek reassurance from another. They're angry about something and do it as revenge, to feel in control. I'm no shrink, but it looks to me like it's a way of dealing with dissatisfaction with one's life. It's cheaper than therapy, I suppose. No, on second thought, maybe it's not."

He leaned forward in his chair. "Elie, I think what's most important is to determine what you want, regardless of what you think Philip is up to. You mentioned that you two have been going through a rough patch lately. So maybe the timing is right to take a good, hard look at your relationship. Only you can determine what you want from your marriage."

"What do you mean?" Elie asked.

"What I mean is that you need to decide what *you* want, and then take it from there. If you love Philip and want to stay married to him, fight for him, no matter whether he's cheating or not. Find a way to demonstrate your love and make your marriage work. Make him forget the other woman, if she even exists. *But*, if you decide that you do not love Philip and do not want to share the rest of your life with him, then get out. You're a strong woman, I have always believed that you are much more capable than you believe yourself to be. You can manage without him. You don't have to stay in a loveless relationship. Set yourself free."

Elie listened intently.

"And that is the catch ... the hardest part." Walter leaned back.

"You don't need the excuse of his cheating to decide what to do. You do not need anything from him. You must talk to yourself, understand what it is you really want and then, go get it. You want Philip? Then fight for him. You want out? Then leave, and do it as cleanly as you can. But be fair to him. Be a *mensch*, don't be an avenging bitch. It's not your style, kid."

Walter put the napkin on his lap as the first course arrived. "I think that's about all I want to say on the subject. Now, can I enjoy my carpaccio?"

Elie was not sure how she felt. She needed time to think. "Thank you, Walter. I really appreciate your input. I'm very grateful."

"Don't be so grateful. You know, in the end, we all do things that are good for us. You need to find out what's best for you, and I don't mean just in your marriage. In work, too. It's always good to look around and check options and see what's happening in the world."

Elie wondered what he meant, as if there was a hidden meaning. But with all that she had on her mind, she brushed it off. They started eating and the subject was closed.

When Elie got back to the office, Heather handed her a message, which made her realize that she had forgotten to take her cell phone. It was from Philip and said to call him back immediately.

She tried to sound nice on the phone. "Hi, Philip. Sorry, I forgot my cell."

"Hi, El. I cancelled Chicago. I'll go tomorrow instead. Why don't we have dinner at Il Divino tonight? I'll book our usual table?"

"Sure. What time?"

"Let's meet at the restaurant at eight. Is that okay?"

"Yes, that's fine. See you then."

Good, Elie thought. That would provide enough time to go home, shower and change before meeting him. She started to feel better.

Elie arrived at the restaurant a little after eight, and was delighted to be greeted by Claudia, the owner's beautiful daughter. She had just come back from a year in Florence and was now running the family business. They chatted for a few minutes, until the young woman had to acknowledge other guests. As Elie got settled at the table, she wondered if Philip would show up. It was not unlike him to cancel at the last moment. To her relief, he walked in two minutes later.

"Sorry I'm late. It was hell catching a cab." He bent down and kissed her on the cheek.

"No problem," Elie answered, "I chatted with Claudia for a while. Looks like our young friend has stepped into her father's shoes. Remember when she was such a cute little girl, hanging around here?"

"Sure do. So ... a bottle of wine or a drink to start with? Which do you prefer?"

He wasn't wasting any time, she thought. "I'd like a spritzer." It was unusual for her to order a watered down drink but tonight she wanted to be relaxed, but in control. Her mood was good, but cautious.

Philip suggested that they order immediately, to avoid being interrupted later.

Although very familiar with the dishes, they looked over the menu, as if to stall for time. Elie chose the Sword Fish Putanesca and Philip opted for the Veal Scaloppini. He ordered the antipasti and concurred with Claudia's suggestion for a matching wine.

"So Elie, what's happening with work these days? You haven't told me much lately." He placed the napkin on his lap.

She was caught off guard, but liked the fact that he was asking. At least he was making an effort. She went into details about the AIDS event, that it was becoming the talk of the industry and it all started because Anthony Montecristo's project was axed. Philip made a few comments about Montecristo being another temperamental designer and related some problems his company had had with the man.

They were both laughing when the antipasti arrived. They continued to chat casually as they ate.

Philip reminded Elie that it had been some time since Sands Furniture got publicity in the magazine, and she reminded him that they had not advertised for a while. They spoke about Philip's competition in the market, and which companies were big advertisers.

It was not until they were almost finished with their main courses that Philip brought up the subject of the mysterious earrings.

"Elie, I have not forgotten what I promised you this morning, that we would talk about what happened. I guess now is as good a time as any."

"I'm all ears, Philip." She put down her fork.

"I wasn't exactly truthful with you last night. You caught me off guard, and I got really angry."

"I noticed."

"I do know the owner of the earrings." He swallowed hard.

Elie's heart started to pound and she had to remind herself to breathe in and out. Stay calm, stay calm, she kept thinking. "I'm listening."

"They belong to a girl I met in Milan."

Wow. Just like that. It was not her imagination. It had really happened. Girl? This was how he was going to describe the woman in his life? Was she really a girl, meaning less than thirty in Elie's eyes? Or was this his demeaning way of describing a female?

"And?" Her skin was beginning to itch.

"Elie, it meant nothing. She means nothing to me. It was just a stupid, silly ..."

Elie interrupted him. "Philip, are you telling me you had an affair with this *girl?*"

"No, not exactly. I would say it was more of a quick thing. I met her in the showroom in Milan. She was coming on to me, we went out to dinner, I got sloshed, and it just happened. I found the earrings after she left. I don't love her or anything like that. Truthfully, I've hated lying to you about it. I've been feeling really guilty. I'm glad we can get this on the table now."

Elie could not believe what she was hearing. She felt like hurling her wine at him.

Philip continued. "Elie, I'm so sorry. I don't want to hurt you. I never intended it to happen. I know this sounds like a line, I know I've been a heel, I just didn't know how to handle it. I didn't know how to tell you. I don't know, maybe leaving the earrings in my pocket was Freudian, like maybe I wanted you to find them."

Now he was talking Freud? This man who refused to go for couples counseling because he said the problems were all in her head? This was the same man who laughed at people who were in therapy, saying they were weak? *He* was talking psychology to *her*?

"Elie, please say something. You haven't said a word. That's not like you."

"I've never had a man tell me he's been cheating on me before, Philip. I'm not sure what the proper protocol is here. What does one say when confronted with a husband's betrayal?" She was moving from nervous to furious, fast.

"I don't expect you to forgive me right away or even to understand this. I admit I did something bad, but it's not as if we've had such a perfect marriage lately. Things have not been right for a long time, I needed a place to rest my head, so to speak."

"So rather than discuss it with me, or seek the advice of a professional, you chose to *shtup* some girl you met on a business trip? That's what you're telling me?"

"It wasn't a *shtup*, Elie, and you shouldn't talk like that. It doesn't suit you."

"Being cheated on also doesn't suit me, Philip. Wouldn't you agree?" She couldn't believe his nerve. But then again, she could. This was the new Philip talking, the Philip she had begun to dislike.

"Look, we shouldn't get into all this here. You wanted to know, I made the gesture to come clean. I'm not feeling good about what I did. However, there are issues that you are not aware of. When something like this happens in a marriage, it's an indication that something is not right. I am not saying that to justify my behavior, but you have to look at the whole picture."

"Philip, the picture I see is of a man who has been married to a woman for almost twenty-eight years and decided to ignore what that stood for and sleep around. I think you have pissed on our marriage, our children and everything that we hold sacred."

"Elie, don't make a tsunami out of this. It happened and it's over. We can get through it. I still love you and I don't want to destroy our marriage. We can fix things."

They hadn't touched the food on their plates for several minutes and the waiter was standing off to the side waiting to clear the table. Philip motioned to him and they both sat silently as he removed the dishes. He offered them the dessert menu, which Philip rejected.

Elie desperately wanted to keep her cool. She was shocked by Philip's words, she had not expected a confession. Then she realized how stupid that was. She had indeed expected a confession. She had been sure he was cheating, now it was out in the open. She surprised herself by what she did next, not knowing where the courage came from.

She removed the napkin from her lap, folded it and put it on the table. "Philip, I think you have said quite enough. I don't want to hear another word. Right now, I need to process what you have told me. I would like you to stay at a hotel or your corporate apartment from now on. I want to be alone." She was calm as she spoke, her voice did not break even once.

"You can't be serious. You cannot kick me out of my own home. We have to talk about this." His eyes grew large and he looked furious.

"Yes, I am serious. We do need to talk about this, and about other things, but not tonight. I can't anymore. I'm leaving." She stood up and walked out of the restaurant.

She went home in a daze. She realized that she was returning to reality when she closed the front door, and in addition to locking it, left the key in.

Nineteen

When Elie went to work the next day, she realized that it was the first time since the discovery of the earrings, that she did not have a knot in her stomach. She knew the feeling was temporary, that it would eventually hit her what all this meant, but for the time being, she felt unburdened.

She did not telephone Philip, nor did he call her. She wondered where he had spent the night and how he had managed without his things. Then, she decided that her days of worrying about Philip were over.

It was especially busy at the office, with important calls, review meetings and time set aside to work with Leigh. One of the major designers had a medical emergency and pulled out of the show. A decision had to be made about his space, since the designs were already in progress. Elie was also aware that Walter had had a meeting with the executive editor of a competing magazine. That publication was closing down and Elie wondered if the woman was trying to get a job at *Interior Design & Style* – her job!

She picked up the intercom to call him, but reconsidered and walked over to his office. He was outside the room, talking to Denise and she caught him just before he went back in.

"Hi, Elie. Come on in." He waved her into his office as he signed papers that Denise held out to him. He followed her in and closed the door behind him.

"How are you?"

"I'm okay, considering." She replied. "How did it go with Dee Grant?"

"Cost me an expensive dinner last night. She tried to convince me how good she is and why she should be working here. Your turn."

"Hold on there! Not so fast. So she is trying to take over my position?" Elie knew she shouldn't be paranoid, but she started to feel uncomfortable.

"No, she didn't express herself as wanting to take over your position. But she probably would love to. She dominated the conversation with her take on the current state of the publishing industry. She tried to convince me how she could position *Interior Design & Style* above its competition, or what's left of the competition."

"And?"

"What do you mean 'and'? Are you nervous? Get over it. The woman is a piranha. I wouldn't trust her with polishing my left Bally, never mind my magazine. Can we please get back to you now?"

She breathed a sigh of relief and told Walter what had happened with Philip. "I know I'll have to face him again and make a decision about what to do. But right now I feel relieved to know the truth, and reassured that I was not losing my mind. I'm also sad and quite angry."

"I'm sorry, kid. I was hoping you were mistaken about your suspicions. I'd say you should trust your instincts on this one. And good luck."

"Thanks, Walter."

They chatted for a few more minutes, mostly about the upcoming design show. Elie told him she wanted Michael Delmonico to act as Master of Ceremonies and Walter agreed. She then recalled the strange comment of the other day, about keeping options open, and was tempted to ask him about it, but let it go.

Elie found it increasingly difficult to concentrate on work. The repercussions of what had happened with Philip were settling in. At the end of what seemed like an eternity, she headed home.

When she entered the apartment, she checked to see if Philip had been there. He had. His overnight bag was missing from the closet and his toiletries kit was gone. She looked around for a note and checked the answering machine. Nothing. She phoned Syd.

Her friend had been away and they had not spoken for several days. "That's it, Syd, I'm doing it!"

"Hello to you too. Doing what, Elie?"

"I'm going to divorce Philip. I've had it."

"Oh my God! Will you just take it easy? When did this happen? Last I knew, you were obsessing about whether or not he had an affair."

Elie understood that she not only sounded crazy, she also just verbalized a decision she had not yet realized she made. "We had a talk. He admitted it. She was someone he met through work. I don't know if it's a fling or an affair and I don't care. I don't want to be with this man anymore!"

"Oh Jeez, how can you dump this on me by phone? I have to leave soon for a dinner that I can't cancel. Shit. Shit. Shit. I need to see you. You cannot make these kinds of decisions like that. I'm coming down. Stay put!"

Ten minutes later, Syd was at the door. She walked in, sat down on the sofa, and made Elie go over the main points of her decision. Elie ran through the last days, describing her anxieties and the talk with Walter. She ended with the dinner in the restaurant and kicking Philip out of the apartment. She spoke non-stop, and then sighed.

Syd took her hand. "Good for you, for kicking him out. But why the decision to divorce? I'm not saying he doesn't deserve some major punishment for cheating on you, but you're ready to discard your marriage over this? Isn't that a bit drastic?"

Elie updated Syd, admitting that for the first time in a long time, she felt a weight lifted from her shoulders. She said she knew she would be dooming herself to become like some of the divorced women she knew, but she did not care.

"Hey, take it easy. I know plenty of divorced women, and they're damn happy. To tell you the truth, I've always thought marriage is overrated. I think there should be compulsory divorce at age forty or fifty. Then, if you want to get back together with your ex-spouse, you can. But if not, you've been handed a get-out-of-jail card. For free!"

"Syd, be serious."

"Okay, here's serious. Two things need to happen. First, you must get a lawyer, a good divorce lawyer. Just to have a chat and find out what your options are. What do you think?" Syd looked at her and waited for a reaction.

"I guess you're right." Elie sighed and ran her fingers through her hair. "But I don't know any lawyers who are not tied to Philip and his business. Do you?"

"*Hellooooo?* I'm Jewish and well connected. Of course, I know lawyers. As for divorce lawyers, hmm, it must be a very good one. Give me a day or two. Don't make any rash decisions until then. Can I trust you? Man, I so don't want to go out now and leave you alone."

"You can relax, Syd. I just had to tell you, to hear myself say it. Not to worry, I'm not going to make any sudden moves. What's the second thing that needs to happen?"

"What?"

"You said there are two things that need to happen."

"Oh, that. Have sex. Find a lover and have a quickie." She winked and smiled mischievously.

"*Excuse me?*"

"Oh relax, it's just a joke. No, actually it's not. You know, to get yourself back in the saddle. You're a beautiful, vibrant woman—you need to be reminded of that. In addition, I can personally recommend doing it with a younger man. They are so sweet and grateful for the attention."

"Syd Sorenstein, you have totally lost your mind." Elie laughed. "By what stroke of luck did the gods of fortune position you here in my building?"

"You got that right! It was a pure stroke of luck and don't you forget it! Seriously, Elie, I feel so uncomfortable leaving you right now. Will you be okay?" Syd got up from the sofa.

"Yes, I'm fine. Really. As a matter of fact, I'm going to call Michael, I wanted to share the news with the two of you first. I'll be fine. Please, don't baby me. Just do what you have to do and we'll talk later. I'm okay, really."

"You're absolutely sure?"

"Yes. I'm sure. " As Elie closed the door behind her friend, she wondered how true that was.

She could not predict how Michael would react. He was not a huge fan of Philip's, but then again, he hardly tolerated most people. He had never really spoken his mind about her husband. Now would be his chance.

"Hi, Michael. You're home! Not off to Katmandu or Tahiti on some exciting new design project?"

"Hey doll face! How're ya doing? Nope, poor me, I'm stuck here in the good ole USA. By the way, I got your message the other day, but I was *inorbintantly* busy so I couldn't phone back. Yes, of course I'll emcee the opening of the AIDS soiree. I'm sorry I couldn't volunteer to do a room, but you know what my schedule has been like, with Isabel and all. Anyway, hosting it will be my pleasure."

"Great. I'm glad. Tell me about Isabel. How is she?"

"She's wonderful. Improving daily and we're making plans to bring her to New York soon. You have to get to know her, you are so going to adore her."

"I'm sure I will. And I'm so happy to hear that she's well."

"Okay, so what's the deal? Did you call to ask about hosting the party or do you have some other news to share with your favorite person in the whole wide world?"

"Well, there is very big news actually. Are you sitting down?"

"Elie sweets, don't play theatrics with me. You know it so doesn't suit you. If there has to be a Sarah Bernhardt in our relationship, it's me honey, only me. Now, go ahead darlin', tell me your big fat news."

She sensed the cynicism in his voice, as if nothing exciting could ever happen to her. He had a tendency to tease her about her life and work, except when he wanted something from the magazine – then he remembered that she had a powerful job there.

"Well, my big fat news is that I'm asking Philip for a divorce."

"*Excuse me?* Say that again."

"I'm going to ask Philip for a divorce. I've thought about it endlessly and I finally made the decision. Our marriage is over."

"You're right. I should have sat down. I am now. And girl, you really got me with this one. Man, you could knock me over with a feather. I am in major shock. *Major.*"

"No need to become melodramatic. It's not the end of the world. I intend to have a very good life after this is all settled."

"And I am sure you will have, I will see to it. But Elie, this is really *gigondo*. May I ask what happened? You don't have a lover do you? No, of course not. You would never. Philip does. *That's it!* Philip has a lover and you found out. You're leaving him before he leaves you. Wow. What a son of a bitch. I hate him. I absolutely hate that man. Didn't I tell you straight men are not to be trusted?"

"Michael, calm down. It's not that at all. Look, there is a lot to this story and it's ridiculous to try to dissect my marital problems over the phone. Why don't we meet? When are you free?"

"Are you kidding? For this mega telenovela? Tomorrow! You're meeting me for lunch. How's that place Flo's near your office? Let's meet there at one."

"Okay, sounds good."

"And El?"

"Yes, Michael?"

"All kidding aside, I'm here for you. I love you, Elzie."

"I know you do, my sweet. Thanks."

Elie got to the restaurant on time, and as expected, Michael had yet to arrive. She settled into a booth and ordered a drink. The restaurant was a retro fifties place with vinyl booths, mini jukeboxes at every table, lots of chrome and very non-fifties prices. She ordered a glass of Chardonnay and asked the waiter to leave the menus on the table.

Michael strolled in ten minutes later. "Sorry, doll. I actually took the subway, would you believe it? Of course I got lost. I can never figure out what they're saying. Who can read those maps they have on board? The print is so tiny. The whole system is just so primitive. It's much more sophisticated in Paris. I swear, New York needs a major transformation, nothing works here anymore." He finished his monologue, took off his jacket and scarf, bent down and kissed Elie on both cheeks.

"Nice to see you too, Michael." Elie laughed, as she usually did, when he came in like a tornado.

"I absolutely must have a Diet Coke. Where's the waiter?" Michael glanced around the restaurant. "Oh, there he is. *Yoo hoo*, over here please!" He looked from the waiter, back to Elie. "Ooh, look Elie, he's gorgeous. I wonder how old he is. My type, don't you think?"

The waiter arrived as summoned. "Hi, I'm Jeff. I'll be your server this afternoon. May I offer you a drink, sir?"

"Ooh, you're so formal, Jeffrey. No need to call me sir. Michael will do just fine. Yes, you can indeed bring me a drink. I would like a Diet Coke in a tall glass. Please make sure it is tall. I don't want any ice in it, but bring me another glass with just ice. Got that, sweetie?"

The waiter looked slightly embarrassed, smiled, and walked off with Michael's order.

Elie rolled her eyes.

"Oh please, don't give me that look. This is New York City, the gay capital of the world. If he can't take the heat, he should get out of the kitchen. No, better yet, he should get into my kitchen! Daniel would never know."

"You are absolutely incorrigible, Michael Delmonico. Hopelessly, incurably wicked."

"Yeah, yeah. But you adore me. Now let's get back to the topic at hand. No, better yet, order first. Our usual in times of stress? Tuna melt for one, with a large side of fries and coleslaw?"

Nothing had changed. They had shared their first over thirty years ago, and it was still their favorite sandwich.

"You bet," Elie smiled and felt content to be sitting with her old friend.

Once they ordered their lunch, Michael asked for all the details. Elie began to explain the reasons behind her decision. She had never exposed her true feelings about Philip to her close friends, thinking that it was a betrayal to verbalize her doubts. They knew only bits and pieces of her dissatisfaction.

The food arrived and they spoke and ate. Michael complained that the sandwich was greasy and pushed his plate aside.

"Forget the tuna melt, Michael, I'm talking the end of my

marriage here!"

"Sorry. Go ahead, continue."

She told him that she had felt unfulfilled for years. That she believed her marriage had become one of convenience, and very little else. How Philip's betrayal was just a symptom to her, and didn't make her furious anymore, just sad.

"You're joking aren't you? How could you be so *cavaliery* about his cheating on you? It's low down, that's what it is. He should be hung up by his scrawny little balls."

"The word is cavalier and what makes you think he has scrawny little balls?"

"He doesn't? Oh, do tell, come on, now you can really tell me how the guy is hung. You're divorcing him anyway, I must know."

"You are disgusting, you know that? Don't ask me questions like that, you pervert."

He waved his finger at her. "Okay, you might refuse to tell me now. But, one day you'll tell me, Eleanora Stein. You'll confess everything to me, even your love making with that man. Oops, I just called you Eleanora Stein instead of Sands. Do you think it means something? Maybe I've been hoping for this ever since I met you. Maybe now you and I should tie the knot and live happily ever after. With Daniel, of course. And my precious Isabel."

"Michael, I think we had better let me live alone for a while first. You know, I never have. Lived alone that is. From my parents' home, to a dorm in Israel with roommates, to an apartment in New York with a roommate, and then with Philip. It's about time, don't you think?"

"You know what you're going to have to do? I'm serious now. What you really need to do?"

"What?"

"Get laid."

"Pardon me?"

"My dear, don't play that innocent little girl routine on me. I'm not kidding about this. You need to go and screw your brains out." He saw the look on her face. "Okay, I'll put it more gently. You need to have sex. Is that plain enough? I'm not kidding. You need to go out and play. To discover yourself through men. Believe me, I know what I'm talking about. I know you've been faithful to Philip. I would bet on it. I assume you haven't had another lover since you were married. I'm telling you girl, the sooner you get this over with, the better. You will blossom from getting out there. I can just tell."

"Funny you say that. Syd told me the same exact thing. That I need to go out, get back on that horse again."

"Well! Far be it for me to be in total agreement with Her Serene Royal Highness Syd Sorenstein, the Duchess of Delancey Street who made it all the way to Central Park West. Maybe I'm mistaken then."

"Oh Michael, get off of it. Are you still on that anti-Syd *shtick* of yours?"

"Am and always will be. Quite frankly, I don't see how you are not on my side. You know how she screwed me. She never finished paying me for designing her apartment and I think she's a perfect bitch. How can you stay so friendly with her?"

"Michael, I will not discuss this subject with you. You are both my dear friends. I made the connection between you because I thought it was a good thing. If you remember, you both loved each other at the beginning. You were having such a romance with her, her money and her good taste that you almost forgot about me. It was all going perfectly well until you came to those disagreements. Please, let's drop this."

"Okay, we'll drop it. But you're making a mistake for keeping her as a friend. She's a barracuda."

"I know what you think. You've been telling me that for way too many years. Can we please go back to our original subject? I believe you were trying to convince me to get out more?"

"Right. Elzie listen, you've been with your husband forever. I remember there was some other guy you found in Israel, during that year that you deserted me. What was his name?"

"Never mind. What are you getting at?"

"I know there was no one significant between him and Philip. And no doubt, no one since Philip. If that is the case, you really do need to find yourself again. I don't mean you have to become a slut, although the idea of it does intrigue me, but you should put yourself out on the market."

"Michael, I just want a divorce."

He rambled on. "And I can help you. I may be of another persuasion, but I certainly know how to attract men – it can't be that different from homo to hetero. I shall give you lessons, you will be my Eliza Doolittle and I shall be your Professor Higgins."

"And once again you are turning my life into a Broadway musical. This is serious, Michael Delmonico!"

"I know, Elie, I know. I am quite serious, you just don't believe me. Try to see this from my perspective. You will get out there, you will meet men and let them take you to wonderful dinners. They'll be impressed by your pretty face, your surprisingly well-kept body, your *savoir-faire*. Of course, they'll want to bed you, that's just how guys are. And, oh my God, I can see it now – you'll become a sex goddess!"

Elie laughed and shook her head. "You're out of your mind."

"Elie?"

"Yes?"

"A lawyer. You have to have a lawyer. A good one. And I bet you don't have one."

"Syd also mentioned that. No. I don't have one."

"Oh lord. That's of *primo* importance. Okay, I'll talk to Daniel; he knows the entire collection of shark lawyers, the ones who know how to take a chunk out of a cheating husband's ass. We'll get him to recommend a few."

"No, Michael, I definitely do not want to take advantage of Philip. I think we can do this amicably. I just want out of my marriage and maybe pursue a new direction in life. Keeping my old friends, of course."

"You'll keep your old friends, but hon, I insist you rethink the lawyer part. I bet your ex-hubby-to-be will find himself a bastard."

"*Oy.* Maybe we should change the subject. I'm starting to feel queasy. I just wanted to tell you my news and hear that you'll be there for me."

"Sweetie, I am here for you. I was there when you met Philip and I will be there when you're no longer with him. I really mean this, if I can lend an ear, a shoulder to cry on, whatever you need, you just call me. Wow, I think I just ripped off the lyrics to three songs. Anyway, you know how much I love you, right?"

"I do know." She put her hands across the table and took his.

"But don't spread the word. I must maintain my image. Okay?"

Twenty

Michael relayed Elie's news to Daniel, who was surprised and saddened. He listened quietly, knowing enough to sift through Michael's exaggerations in order to get to the core of the story.

"D., I'm really nervous about something. Elie says she does not want to screw Philip, she thinks she can end it all pretty like. You and I both know that's *crapola*. But how do we convince her? I know Philip from my business dealings with him and that man has a heart of stone. He'll rake her over the coals. We have to convince Elie to get a good lawyer."

"You might be right." Daniel looked concerned.

"Well, what do you know? For once, you don't think I'm being hysterical and over-reacting. I must write this day down in my diary for *prosterity*."

"It's posterity, and calm yourself. I may have an idea how to convince her, but you are not going to like it."

"What? I'll do anything. Really, I love Elie like a sister and I want to protect her. She can be just a wee bit naive at times. Maybe a lot naive. Tell me."

"You need to coordinate with Syd and have an intervention with Elie."

"With who, and a what?"

"You need to combine forces with Syd. You and she are the closest people to Elie, outside her family. I think if you are going to have any chance of convincing her to sharpen her claws, you will need all the help you can get. You have a pow-wow, sit her down, gang up on her, whatever you want to call it. You do it as a team and convince her."

"But Daniel, you know how I hate that woman. Syd Sorenstein

is a she-wolf. How could I possibly? Do you know how she …"

"Michael, enough! That screw-up over her apartment happened two decades ago. Do you know how much time that is? The money you lost on that job you make in a day now. Be the bigger person, get off your high horse, call her and arrange it. You told me you had great times with her at first, so maybe you'll even be able to rekindle the friendship. She's Elie's friend, that means she can't be that bad. Do it, if you really love your friend. You have to."

Michael pouted, but he considered Daniel's advice.

Syd was amazed to hear who was on the other end of the phone line.

"Hello, Michael. This is certainly unexpected."

"Syd Sorenstein, as of this phone call, I am willing to put aside all our differences. Elie needs us. I want an intervention with her."

"You're joking."

"No, I am not. She's in trouble, Syd. I know you know about the divorce. That girl doesn't even have an attorney yet! She's talking about going soft on Philip and not taking him for all he's worth. Listen, I know this takes *chutzpah* on my part, and you and I certainly have our issues, but I'm trying to be the bigger man here, if you know what I mean. This is strictly for Elie. I don't want her getting ripped apart by some vulture that I'm sure Philip will hire. I've spoken to Daniel, my partner, and he knows the right people. I want to meet with Elie, Daniel, and you, and have a sit down. Are you in?"

Syd was silent for a moment and then responded. "I'm in and I think it's great. You're a good friend, Michael, and I really appreciate what you're doing. Definitely, let's do this."

"Okay, I'll be in touch. I want to do it soon, before she finds some *shyster* lawyer on her own. I'll be in touch. Bye, Syd. And thanks."

"No, thank you, Michael. Really. Speak to you soon."

A dinner at the men's apartment was arranged. Elie assumed it would be a get-together with Michael and Daniel, in an effort to show their support.

When she arrived, she noticed that the table was set for four. She was disappointed that they had invited someone else, she'd been hoping for an intimate evening.

The doorman buzzed and announced the guest and Elie was sure she had misheard the name. When Michael opened the front door, she nearly fell off the sofa. She saw Syd give him a peck on the cheek as if they had been friends forever. They both walked into the living room and faced Elie.

Michael was the first to speak. "Yes, I know darling. This is an unbelievable occurrence and it will only happen once in a millennium, so burn it into the hard drive of your brain. I've asked Syd to join us because we both love you and we are worried, well let's say, concerned. We figured that if we cornered you, and knocked some sense into you, we'd have a better chance of convincing you. Daniel doesn't know all the sordid details but he's in on this. Actually, it was his idea."

"Convince me of what?"

"Elie, may I participate in this discussion?" Daniel waited for Elie's response.

Elie kissed Syd, who joined her on the sofa. Michael brought over drinks and sat down on the other side of Elie.

"Yes, of course Daniel. But, I don't understand. What is this about?" She was confused, but touched. "I can't believe that you two have made up, on my behalf. But convince me of what? I appreciate your concern, but why are you all so worried, other than I'm totally screwing up my life?" She laughed nervously.

Without waiting for a response, she looked directly at Daniel and continued. "I guess I should explain. I found out that Philip was unfaithful, and that forced me to do some serious introspection. I realized that things have not been right for a long time and I came to the conclusion that the best path for me is divorce. Both Syd and Michael recommended that before I do anything, I see a lawyer. They also both recommended that I have sex with a stranger, but that bit of advice I thought was excessive."

"I agree with them one hundred percent, I mean about the lawyer, not the sex part." They all laughed. "But Elie, you are very certain that you want to take this route?" He glanced at Michael and then back to Elie.

Elie always loved listening to Daniel. His New England accent and his dignified manner radiated wisdom and composure. "Yes, Daniel. I'm afraid so."

Syd joined in. "Daniel, I told Elie that no matter what she decides, and parenthetically, I think this decision to divorce is a bit rash, that she must seek out the guidance of a good divorce lawyer. She needs to ascertain her rights."

"I think that's wise."

Syd apparently decided to be the bad cop. She turned from Daniel to her friend. "Elie, we are very worried that you are being too naive about this divorce. You don't seem to realize what can really go on. I'm sorry darling, but the truth is you have a tendency to believe the best in people, even when that belief is not warranted."

"Okay, so what? Why does that have anything to do with me getting a divorce?" Elie was starting to feel uncomfortable.

"Because we, Michael and I, think that Philip will eat you alive. He won't take this divorce sitting down. He'll find the best damn attorney in New York and go after you." Syd folded her arms across her chest.

Michael reached over to touch his friend's hand. "Elie sweets, I've done business with your husband. That man can be heartless. I don't trust him."

Feeling trapped, Elie started to squirm. "I know you all mean well, but you're being unfair. Philip is not a monster. He may have cheated on me, but he won't try to ruin me. You don't know him as I do."

Michael and Syd exchanged glances.

"And Daniel, I really appreciate your concern. Truly, I do. But I think this whole thing is unnecessary. I can work it out with my husband. I don't want to go the vicious lawyer route. Why should I? I'm initiating this divorce, I don't have to do it cruelly. I just want a peaceful and fair end to my marriage. I'm sure we can be civilized about it."

"You're being ludicrous, Elie. Your thinking is warped if you really believe that Philip will take this lying down." Syd's irritation was obvious in her tone.

Elie looked at her, then at Michael. "You're both treating me like a child, and you're making me very uncomfortable. Is this why you invited me here tonight? To bully me?" Tears started to fall from Elie's eyes and everyone understood that they had better tone it down.

Michael put his arm around her, Daniel came over with a tissue and Syd remained silent.

Elie took a deep breath. "I'm sorry about getting emotional. I know you're doing this for me and you're all concerned, and I love you for it. I feel so conflicted now. Perhaps you're right, but I don't want to go the route you're suggesting. Then there will be no chance that Philip and I can ever be friends. Don't you see? I want out of my marriage, because of *me*, not him. He's exactly who he's always been, maybe a bit meaner these days, but Philip hasn't changed significantly. It's that I finally woke up. I admitted to myself that I don't want this life anymore. I'm not being naive or simplistic, I'm just trying to be fair." She looked at all three of them, hoping for acknowledgment.

"You know what, Elie? Let's take a different path." Daniel had her attention. "You don't need someone ferocious, you need someone wise. Michael asked me to check out divorce attorneys and I have a few names. Just think about going to see one or two. Ascertain what your rights are, then have a good long think on it and decide what you want to do. How does that sound? May I give you the list?"

Syd spoke, more softly now. "I also did some research and got the name of a man from a few people. It's Joshua Strauss and he's supposed to be very smart, but not brutal. Do you know him Daniel?"

"As a matter of fact, I do know him. He specializes in divorce and he has a sterling reputation. He was one of the men on my list, and he would be an excellent person to talk to."

The name rang a bell for Elie. "That's funny. I also know a Joshua Strauss. At least I did know one. My friend Devi's older brother became a rabbi and then a lawyer. I wonder if it could be the same one."

"I would not be able to verify that for you, but I do believe he has a strong Jewish background. Why don't I phone him and open the door for you?"

"Okay Daniel, that would be nice." She smiled, while crumpling the tissue in her hand

"Consider it done. Still, I hope you won't require his services. Perhaps you and Philip can work things out satisfactorily."

"That's very kind of you to say. Thank you."

The intervention seemed to work. The difficult part was over and the rest of the evening was spent enjoying a lovely dinner. Michael told Syd about Isabel, and gave everyone the latest update on her improving health. The talk veered towards babies and children and how ironic it was that both Elie and Michael had become grandparents in the last few months. The air between Michael and Syd seemed to be clearing, although Elie could not be sure that they would return to their previous love fest. As she watched them rediscover their mutual intolerance for the rest of the world, Eli felt hopeful.

Twenty-One

As promised, Daniel made the call to Joshua Strauss. He telephoned Elie and relayed that the lawyer was awaiting a call from her.

Elie put it off. Her excuse to herself was that she was too busy with arrangements for the design event, but she knew she was procrastinating in order to avoid taking the step. She felt that the moment she made that move, she would be putting everything into irreversible motion. Meeting with him was the first step to ending her marriage. Fortunately, her mind was kept busy with other matters.

The office was buzzing with talk of the event. Word had gotten out about it and the requests for opening night tickets were flooding in. Designers Ditch AIDS was going to take place in a downtown loft. In the past, the Temple of Dendur at the Metropolitan Museum of Art was hired for such occasions, always resplendent and regal. But this time the atmosphere had to be chic yet cool, meaning black tie to jeans. Every major fashion designer, interior designer, architect and furniture company representative would be there, as well as fashionistas from every level of society.

Each team of students from the Fashion Institute of Technology was supervised by a fashion designer, and assigned a space in the loft. Sketches had been submitted to a judges' committee and the best room designs were chosen. The work was inspiring.

Among the problems cropping up, one totally unsettled Elie. Philip's company was among the project's major sponsors. He had barely listened to her when she had described it to him, but apparently perked up when he heard about it through industry talk. He wanted Sands Furniture to have a strong presence there.

Since the fight in the restaurant, Philip had been living in the corporate apartment. He had been back to their apartment to collect his things, but Elie had not been present. No one outside her tight circle was aware of the situation, or if they were, they were not talking. Chloe knew something was wrong, but when she asked, neither of her parents were willing to speak about it.

At parties thrown by Sands Furniture, Elie had always played the role of elegant, smiling wife of the owner. This time it would be different. She would be attending as Elie Sands, executive editor of *Interior Design & Style*. The evening belonged to her, Leigh Fairchild and the hardworking team they had put together. She was excited and proud, but nervous about a confrontation with Philip.

Giving in to an impulse, she decided to wear a dress she had purchased on sale but never had the guts to put on. It was a bright red, strapless chiffon gown that had "sexy, strong woman" written all over it. As she pulled it out of its protective bag, Elie felt exhilarated. Tonight would be her defining moment. Along with the gown, a new Elie Sands was coming out of the closet.

She used a heavy hand with her makeup, going for an evening look. Being a bit daring, she slid a comb with a red silk flower in her hair, pulling back the curls that fell on the side of her face. She put on a strapless bra and a pair of diamond earrings – the first pair that Philip had given her. She carefully slipped on the dress and held her breath. One of the disadvantages of divorcing your husband, she realized, is that there will be no one to zip you up. A small price to pay, she decided. She adjusted the bra, straightened out the lines of the dress and took a good look in the mirror. She did not recognize herself.

She wrapped herself in the matching red chiffon stole and left the apartment. As she walked out of her building, she saw that the car she had ordered was waiting for her. The driver, someone she knew, gave out a wolf whistle as he held open the door. She laughed, and thought that it was exactly the reaction she was hoping for.

"Oh man, do you look hot! Ms. Sands, forgive me for being so forward, but I never saw an older woman that I wanted to be with until right this moment. Damn, you look good!" It was one of the students from the project.

"Thanks, Kevin. You needn't apologize, I take that as a giant compliment." Elie couldn't wipe the smile off her face.

The loft was transformed. The rooms were exquisite, the models gorgeous, and the fiber optic lighting, which was designed by a Broadway set designer, had the place absolutely glowing. A band played in the background, drinks and canapés were served, and the evening was off to a great start.

Elie was delighted to see Michael there early. He looked strikingly handsome in a black tuxedo and purple silk cummerbund. He seemed to be relishing every moment in the spotlight – he welcomed the crowd, thanked the participants and gave credit to each team. He was charming and warm, and Elie could not have been any prouder.

For the Chanel living room, the model wore a black and white herringbone cropped jacket over black wool crepe sailor pants. The stark white background of the walls was set off by two Le Corbusier sofas in black leather, Eileen Gray steel and glass side tables and a few Bauhaus-inspired accessories.

A man wearing a Dolce & Gabbana chocolate brown velvet suit with a suede vest was seen relaxing in an cherry wood library, surrounded by old books, a time-worn globe twirling atop a wooden pedestal and a bear rug beneath his cranberry leather high back arm chair.

A young woman in shimmering gold harem pants, a fuchsia blouson top and multiple strands of colorful beads represented Dior's cruise wear collection. Her surrounding was the recreation of a ship's deck.

There was an Art Deco dining room inspired by the geometrically infused fashions of Mark Jacobs, a modern day office suite filled with models wearing Donna Karan for women and men, and a state of the art music room with wild fashions by Gaultier.

Perhaps the most dramatic of all was an all white conservatory space with stained glass windows, wicker furniture, Kentia palms, and dramatic lighting to compliment a woman posing in a wedding gown reminiscent of the 1940's. It was a Vera Wang white silk charmeuse sheath with a halter-top.

At the beginning of the evening, Elie stood with Walter, Leigh and the school's dignitaries, greeting the guests. As expected, Walter was surrounded by admirers – sycophants to respected colleagues. Leigh seemed uncomfortable in the spotlight, but she played the role expected of her. Elie spent a lot of time thanking those who came to see the show, and then wandered off on her own and mingled within the crowd. She received dozens of compliments, for the brilliant exhibit and for how gorgeous she looked. She was soaring.

"Elie, is that really you?" Philip's face was lit up and his reaction was exactly what she would have hoped for.

"Yes, it's me."

"You look stunning. I mean *wow!* New dress?"

"No, just something I had in the closet." She couldn't believe she uttered those words.

"Well, it does wonders for you. I've been watching how everyone is looking at you. You're a big hit – the belle of the ball tonight."

"Thanks, Philip, kind of you to say." She certainly was not going to be effusive in her gratitude.

"El, listen." He moved closer towards her. "I know this is not the time and place, but we really do have to talk. I respected your wishes and moved out, but it's time to stop this nonsense. We cannot go on like this."

"I agree Philip, we cannot."

"So, how about we get together. When can we meet?" He stood there looking very serious.

"Look, Philip, things are very hectic for me now. Would you mind phoning me at the office and I'll check my calendar? Then we'll set something up."

"Okay, sure."

Before he could say another word, she saw some people she wanted to say hello to; she excused herself and left Philip standing there with his drink.

Twenty-Two

It was time to call the lawyer. Elie closed the door to her office, took a deep breath, picked up the receiver and pressed the numbers.

She gave her name to the secretary, and was put through immediately. A male voice came on. "Hello, this is Joshua Strauss."

"Hello, Mr. Strauss. Daniel Keane was kind enough to refer me to you. I am contemplating divorce and he recommended that I speak with you."

"Yes, Ms. Sands, Daniel told me about you. Might I suggest that we meet and talk in person? I don't think the telephone is a very good means of communication for this sort of thing."

Elie was caught off guard. Her mind was floating back in time, and she was overwhelmed with a feeling that this was the Joshua she knew.

"Ms. Sands?"

"Mr. Strauss, I must ask you something. I realize that this will sound ridiculous, but you could always chalk it up to the ramblings of a crazed woman facing divorce. Are you, by any chance, the brother of Devi, I mean, Devorah Strauss Young?"

There was a moment of silence on the other end of the phone. She immediately regretted her question.

"Yes. As a matter of fact, I am. Now, how would you know that?"

She couldn't contain her excitement and her voice showed it. "Because, I'm Elie! Elie Stein, your sister's childhood friend!"

"Elie? As in Elie-Belly?"

There was only one person in the world who had ever called her that. She hated it now, as she hated it then, but she was thrilled to realize the voice on the other end of the line belonged to the Joshua of her youth.

"I don't believe it. The one and only Josh the Nosh? Is that really you?"

He laughed. "The one and only. And I suggest that we both stop using the nicknames immediately. I never want to hear Josh the Nosh again and I promise not to inflict Elie-Belly on you again. Deal?"

"Deal. Wow! What an amazing coincidence. I had a feeling the moment I heard your voice. You know it hasn't changed in … better not to think of how many years it's been. I can't believe it. You're the wonder boy that Daniel spoke so highly of?" Elie was smiling from ear to ear.

"I would not exactly refer to myself as a boy, considering I'm heading towards the end of my sixth decade on this planet. And as for wonder, that should be taken under advisement. What a nice surprise – I didn't recognize your name. So, you need advice from a nice friendly lawyer?"

"I do indeed, Josh or Joshua, which do you prefer? Actually, I thought it was Rabbi Strauss. Weren't you ordained?"

"I was. I am a full-fledged Rabbi with *smicha* papers to prove it. However, I was also interested in law and once I started studying, I decided to head in this direction. Let's meet. Can you come to my office one day this week?"

"Yes, of course. Whenever you say."

"Okay, Elie, we'll meet and catch up. I expect a full report on everything you've been up to. Hang on, I'll get my secretary back on the line, and you can arrange a time with her. I'm looking forward to seeing you again, Elie."

Elie awaited the meeting with great anticipation. It would be a reunion with the first boy she had a crush on, a case of unrequited love at the tender age of twelve. He was Devi's older brother and she had known him for as long as she had known Devi. He had been on the chubby side, hence Josh the Nosh, but Elie had always thought he was cute. He didn't look down at her, or tease her, as other friends' brothers did. There was the Elie-Belly thing, but that was payback for Josh the Nosh.

Arriving ten minutes early and looking around the office, she saw that a professional had designed it – elegant, yet inviting, with muted colors, traditional furniture and highly polished parquet floors. Elie had heard that they were a top law firm, and it showed.

At exactly five minutes past the appointed time, a medium-height, gray-haired man with silver framed glasses walked down the corridor. As he approached Elie, the smile on his face grew. She stood up to greet him and he embraced her warmly. She was struck by how good he looked – conservative, yet sexy, and he smelled great.

"They say time takes it toll, but it certainly hasn't on you. Elie, you look absolutely gorgeous. You haven't aged at all, how is that possible?"

She was embarrassed, and flattered. "Lots of aggravation actually. That's how I keep my girlish figure." She immediately regretted how lame that sounded.

Joshua laughed and escorted her into his office. "I've cleared my schedule for an hour and I want a complete recap of your life. Tell me everything. First, can I offer you coffee or tea, a cold drink perhaps? I can even have a cappuccino whipped up for you." He motioned for her to sit on the sofa.

"I'd love a cappuccino, if it's not too much trouble."

"No, of course it's not." He pressed the intercom on his phone. "Carol, can we have two cappuccinos please?" He looked again at Elie. "That's one of the benefits of owning a big, fancy law firm. You can have a big, fancy coffee machine. Look at me, drinking cappuccino. I bet your parents drank Sanka, like mine did."

Elie laughed. "My father drank it. My mother was, and still is, strictly an espresso person. She never got used to American coffee."

Joshua smiled. "So, tell me about your life. You have two daughters, if I recall correctly?"

"I do. Alexis, we call her Lexi, lives in Israel and just had a baby boy. Her husband was a widower with very small children, so Lexi took on quite a load. I can hardly believe it, but I'm the proud grandmother of three now."

"That's wonderful!"

"Yes, it sure is. Except that they live outside of Jerusalem. I wish they were here, but she's very happy, so how can I complain? And my other daughter, Chloe, lives in Brooklyn Heights, has an MBA and is working in PR and marketing in the family business."

Elie continued to speak, but was interrupted by the arrival of the coffee. When the secretary left the room, she answered Joshua's questions and spoke about her work. "Okay, that's it in a nutshell for me. Now, your turn. Last I heard you had lost your wife and I believe I sent you a note." As soon as the words were out of her mouth, she felt idiotic for saying something so inane.

"I did receive your note, and I was touched by it. It was a very difficult period for me. My wife was sick for several years. We had a wonderful life together, but she was diagnosed with breast cancer and that was that."

"Devi told me a little about it. How did you and the children manage?"

"The children were almost grown, so I believe they took it better than had it happened when they were young. Nonetheless, it was quite a loss. Becca was a remarkable woman, an immense presence in all of our lives. It's a pity you never met her."

"Yes, it is. I would have liked to know her. How are you doing since?"

"I keep very busy. This law practice is demanding. I could devote all my time to it, so I have to make a concerted effort not to."

"But you were a rabbi. Why did you give it up, and how did your parents react to the decision?"

"I gave it up because I couldn't see myself leading a congregation. I'm good at making decisions and cutting to the core of issues, but dealing with psychology and counseling and giving sermons, that's not for me. It's funny, because often in this field I end up being a therapist to my clients." He smiled and went on.

"As for my family, I think they handled it quite well. After the aggravation my sister put them through, they let me off easy. You know how traditional they are. Well, once they got used to the idea that Devi married a non-Jew and they accepted Lawrence, well sort of accepted him, the fact that I left the rabbinate was not such a big issue. After all, aren't doctors and lawyers the quintessential choices for a Jewish mother's son?"

"I don't know. I think there are more important qualities to look for. At least, I hope so for the sake of my daughters."

The conversation flowed to Devi and how content she seemed. The life she led with Lawrence, as an ambassador's wife, had an enormous impact on her. She had turned into a woman of intellect and humor, and was as popular and well-respected as her husband. They agreed that if times had been different, Devi would no doubt also bear the title of ambassador, and not just her husband.

"What about your personal life? Is someone taking good care of you?" Elie knew she was stalling, but she was truly curious about Joshua.

He laughed. "Not to worry. Do I look like I'm starving? I may no longer be chubby, but does this look like I'm not being taken care of?" He patted his stomach. "I go out once in a while, but I'm not seeing anyone in particular. My kids are always trying to fix me up, but it's not my thing."

"Wouldn't you like to be in a relationship? Don't you miss it? I would imagine that within the religious community it's awkward to be older and single." She stopped for a moment and considered her comment. "Gee, that was insensitive of me. Excuse me, Joshua, I should not have been so forward."

"You are not being forward, and I appreciate your concern. And you're right – it is odd in the observant community to be single. I stick out and every time I go to services on *Shabbos*, someone has someone they want me to meet. It makes me stay away sometimes. It's so annoying.

There was actually a woman I was interested in, but she had elderly parents in Miami and wanted to be near them. She turned out to be of the g.u. variety."

"How's that again?"

"Aha! Now I know you don't prowl the singles scene. It's used to denote a 'geographically undesirable' person."

Elie laughed and thanked Joshua for updating her on the lingo. There was a moment's silence.

"So, Elie, why don't you tell me why you're here. How can I help you?"

She took a deep breath and began to speak about Philip's

betrayal, her own lingering doubts, her feeling that the marriage had long ago taken a downturn. There was something comforting about Joshua, and it made her want to tell him everything.

He took notes while she spoke. When she finished, he put down the pad and looked directly at her. "Okay, so now let's discuss how I can help you. Do you know what you would like to do?"

"Not exactly."

"Would you like me to give you some basic information?" He smiled kindly.

"Yes. Look, Joshua, this is all very fresh for me, but my friends pushed me to meet with you. I guess I need to know what my options are, and what to expect. That's why I'm here."

"Well, I am sorry for the reason, but I am very happy to see you. Let me review some facts for you."

He proceeded to explain the New York divorce laws. He detailed what her rights were after twenty-eight years of marriage, what she could expect and what she would have to fight for. He told her that no two cases are alike, that when there is animosity, the process of divorce usually takes longer and causes more stress and unhappiness. He told her about cases that started simply and got bitter as time wore on, as the parties started to build resentment.

"Oh God, Joshua. I don't want a battle with Philip. I've heard divorce horror stories and I would hope ours would not be like that. I'm not the type of woman who would take her husband for all he's worth. There will be no mud slinging."

"Elie, I don't want to scare you, but you must be aware of the fact that going through a divorce can be ugly. I try to keep my clients on an even keel, to make them realize that at some point they loved the person they are now divorcing and that they should try to keep *shalom bayit*, you know, a peaceful atmosphere in the home. I will admit to you though, that it rarely succeeds."

He pushed his glasses up onto his forehead, rubbed his eyes and continued. "I believe a good divorce settlement means that both parties make compromises, neither gets everything he or she wants, but no one has to forfeit everything either. Let me ask you as a starting point, do you think your husband will agree to the divorce or will he object?"

"I'm really not sure. I assume he will be surprised and will not want it. However, I think he has too much pride to fight me on this. I don't think he'll make the effort."

"Have you been to counseling together?"

Elie thought that Joshua was asking all the right questions, and she liked the fact that he was gentle. She had heard many stories about aggressive lawyers who manipulated their clients.

"I certainly considered it and suggested it to Philip. He refused, saying he thought that whatever problems I referred to were mine, not his. I never pushed it, because basically, I think he's right. I don't want to change Philip's behavior in our marriage, I want him to be a different man – and that's not possible. I'm feeling that I can live a fuller life on my own, or with someone who is more in tune with who I am."

Elie continued. "Joshua, I know this may sound strange, especially since I'm expressing it to you as a lawyer, and not on an analyst's couch. But I just feel that Philip and I are no longer right for each other. Don't think I'm not terrified of what I am about to do. It's not that I'm dying to be a divorced woman. I just think I will be better off in the long run. I feel myself becoming hostile to my husband, and I don't want to grow old detesting him. Can you understand that?"

"Yes, I can." He moved towards the edge of the sofa, as if to end the meeting. "The good thing is that no one is holding a gun to your head. You do not have to make this decision now. You can do it at your own pace, when you are ready. Perhaps you will decide that divorce is not the right solution for you. Why don't you think about what we discussed?" He waited for a moment, as if to see whether Elie was absorbing what he said.

"I'm here if you need me. I want you to feel free to call anytime, don't hesitate. Carol will have instructions to always put you through. That is, as long as I don't have a tall, leggy blonde in here with me. Then I may not take the call." He smiled as he got up from the sofa.

They had been talking for over an hour, and Elie assumed that he must have juggled a lot of work in order to set aside this time for her. She felt grateful, and a little embarrassed to ask him the next question.

"Joshua, I can't thank you enough. It's been great seeing you and catching up. And, I'm very grateful for your time and patience. I will think about everything you've said, and I'll be in touch. Now, what about your fee? Can I settle with your secretary?"

"No, you may not. And don't even think of such a thing. There is no fee for this and I don't want to hear another word about it."

"But that's ridiculous. I must pay you for your time. I would not have come here if I understood that you would not let me pay you."

"Elie, don't you dare say another word, or I will be insulted. I can certainly afford to meet an old friend, especially one so lovely, and offer her some pointers without being paid for it. If you decide to go ahead with the divorce, and you would like me to represent you, then we will revisit the issue. Agreed?"

"Agreed, but under duress. Thank you again." With that, she reached out to shake his hand and he leaned over and kissed her on the cheek. She got a whiff of his cologne again, and for a very brief moment, she felt a twinge of something. She walked out of the office smiling.

Twenty-Three

Elie spent several fitful nights wondering if she was making the right decision. She made lists, reviewed the highs and lows of her marriage and always found the bad times outweighing the good. Every instinct she had told her to go forward with the divorce. She finally felt at peace with the decision, but dreaded the inevitable encounter with Philip.

He had phoned after the event, but she wasn't able to see him on the night he suggested. He had to leave on a business trip but promised to call when he returned. She phoned first and Philip seemed happy to hear from her. He mentioned a new tapas bar that neither was familiar with and they agreed on a day and time.

Elie practiced her lines. Philip, I want a divorce. Philip, I think it's time we spoke about divorce. Philip, I've been thinking a lot about our situation and I believe that we need to make a very significant change. Our marriage cannot go on any longer. Philip, it's over. I have a lawyer. I suggest you get one, too.

Her words never sounded natural, and although she kept rehearsing, she was filled with anxiety about the confrontation. She prayed that he would not make a scene.

They were seated in the restaurant, their drinks had been served, and Philip started the conversation.

"I know I told you that night, but you really looked stunning at the designer benefit. You were a knock-out."

"Thanks Philip. Nice to hear."

"Did the evening do well? Raise lots of money?"

"Yes, wonderful. A very respectable amount was raised, everyone involved is thrilled and the loft is still open to the public and getting great coverage. By the way, that was a very generous contribution Sands made. Thank you."

"You're welcome. No problem. Good cause."

Several plates of tapas arrived and Philip dug in, while continuing to talk. "So, Elie? What about us? Umm, this caponata is great. Here, try some." He scooped some of the eggplant dip onto a cracker and offered it to her. "Can we stop this charade and go back to the way things were?"

She had not expected a full frontal assault. It took her a minute and a gulp of wine before she could respond.

"I'm afraid not, Philip. We can never go back to the way things were before."

"Okay, I guess I realize that. I know it's been hard for you to understand what I did. But it's over Elie, we can move on. It doesn't have to change everything."

"But it has, Philip. It has highlighted the gap between us. More like a chasm." She could not even look at the food, and wondered how Philip was able to keep eating it.

"Aw, come on, babe. You don't have to make a federal case out of this. I admitted my wrongdoing and you've had your say by not letting me come home. I think you've made your point." He looked annoyed and the concerned, sweet Philip was fading away.

"Philip, do you really think I should not be angry at you. Do you think betrayal is something I take lightly? That I should just forget it and let it go?"

"No, I didn't say that. But I've been punished enough. This can't go on."

"What do you mean, you've been punished enough? Because you're living in a penthouse apartment across town, instead of our home? That's punishment?"

"Come on Elie, don't be childish. You know what I mean."

Suddenly she got it. He had no idea what she was going through. He simply had not paid attention to the collapse of their marriage. While she was struggling with the pieces, examining and analyzing them, he hadn't even noticed that something broke.

Elie looked away, because she could not look at Philip's face anymore. She noticed the restaurant's all-white interior, the exposed brick kitchen, the pretentious servers and the tiny plates of food that cost a fortune. The whole scene seemed ridiculous to her, especially the conversation she was having with her husband. She erupted.

"Philip, there is no gentle way to put this, so I'll just come right out with it. I want a divorce."

He choked on his food. Then he laughed.

"Oh, Jesus. You can't be serious. Are you drunk or something? What are you, into bad jokes now?"

"No, I am not drunk and I am quite serious." Elie told herself to stay calm. "This is something I have been thinking about for a while. To put it frankly, I believe there is nothing left of our marriage to salvage. We are no longer friends, we are hardly lovers and it's obvious to me now that things have not been right for you as well. I think it's time to move on. We should each structure a new life for ourselves, which hopefully will bring us happiness." She felt a huge sense of relief as she completed the sentence.

"El, you don't know what you're talking about. I had an affair. It was wrong and I admitted it. It won't happen again. But you don't break up a marriage of so many years over that."

"Philip, your affair is not the reason, it's a symptom. I don't want a divorce because you fooled around. Although, your betrayal hurt. It hurt me a lot."

"But Elie, we're a couple. We have a history together. We share an important bond. We have two daughters, for God's sake, and a grandchild!"

"Philip, tell me something. When is the last time you said you loved me?"

He snickered. "Oh come on, Elie. Don't be juvenile. We're not newlyweds. We're beyond stuff like that."

"No, we are not beyond stuff like that. I think telling your wife you love her is to be expected, no matter how many years one is married. We married young, at least I was, and I think we grew in opposite directions. We are different people now, and I believe we are no longer suited to one another. I am sorry, but that is how I feel."

"I know where this is coming from." Philip started to get angry.

"From that bitch friend of yours. Syd is poisoning your mind. She's always hated me and now she's convincing you to move on. Isn't that what's happening here, Elie?"

The food on the table was no longer touched.

He continued. "She's had it in for me from the beginning. And when Chloe was born, you remember how horrible she was to you? She completely deserted you. And why? Because she was jealous – you had two kids and she had none. You call that a friend?"

Elie bit her lip and tried to compose herself. "Philip, the decision is mine and mine alone. I have not discussed this at length with anyone, Syd included. You are free to think what you want, but I can assure you that I am quite capable of making up my own mind. And if you intend to keep dredging up the past, please know that it will no longer have an effect on me. I am beyond falling for your declarations; that I don't understand situations as you do, that my perceptions of life are skewed, that only you have an accurate view of the way things really are. Believe it or not, Philip, I have finally come to the conclusion that I am quite okay."

"Oh come on, Elie. Now you're talking like an abused wife. Get real. I know you. I've known you since you were twenty-one, and probably better than you know yourself. You have no idea what you're asking for. Divorce? You really want a divorce? I can't figure out the game you're playing, but I tell you it's not going to work. If you want to get revenge on me, so be it. But don't pull this. It's beneath you."

She wondered if his arrogance could get any more glaring. If she was harboring any doubts at all about her decision, he was doing a great job of dispelling them. Through his arguments, Philip was actually supporting hers. Now that he was belittling and disrespectful, she felt even more determined.

"Philip, this is not a joke and I am definitely not playing a game with you. I will not stand for your rude behavior or your condescending attitude. I have made up my mind. I simply do not want to spend whatever years I have left with you as my husband. This marriage does not work anymore, and if you're honest with yourself, you will agree with me." She felt tension throughout her body, but was determined not to lose her cool.

"You know what your problem is, Elie? You're spoiled! You've had everything a woman could want. Is there anything you asked for that I didn't give you? Is there anything you've craved that I didn't say yes to?"

"As a matter of fact, there is." Elie was actually feeling stronger as the argument continued.

"What? What have I ever denied you?" Looking like he was ready to pounce on her, he gulped down the rest of his wine and slammed the glass on the table.

"You've denied me a full partnership in this marriage. It's true that you've been very generous, I don't deny that. When it came to money or material things, you've always thrown caution to the wind and gone for it. I don't think there's any particular object that I have wanted that I did not get."

"So?" He put his hands out, palms up, as if to say that Elie had just proven his point for him.

"So, you may have been generous with material things. But when it came to matters of the heart, you were quite stingy. Most of the time I felt like I was in our marriage alone."

"What are you talking about? And by the way, I have so told you I've loved you."

Elie smiled. "Oh Philip, I wish it were so easy. Saying 'Babe, I love ya' is not exactly, 'You are my soul mate and I treasure you.' You know, I can't remember any time when you just wanted to be with me, to share something that the two of us could enjoy."

She went on. "When I asked you to spend a romantic weekend with me at Tanglewood, where we could picnic and listen to a concert, you told me to buy the CD and you were off on a business trip. When I asked you about joining a book club, you said you had no time to read and don't like *schmoozing* with pseudo-intellectuals. When I talked to you about my work at the magazine, you always managed to throw in a negative comment about the project or the designer. All you wanted to know is why Sands Furniture isn't in the picture more, why we don't encourage people to buy your furniture."

"Well, would it have killed you to put in a plug once in a while?"

"Philip, you don't get it. I married Philip Sands, not Sands

Furniture. I thought we were building a legacy of our own, but I realized that the only legacy you were interested in was that of your company. You didn't build a life with me and the girls – we built our life according to yours. As your company grew, we had more and more access to wealth, and what it could buy. But with each new showroom that opened, I felt that I lost another part of you. I can list my disappointments by geographical location."

Elie was on a roll. "When I was pregnant the second time and not feeling well, I asked you not to travel to Houston, but you said you had to. I had a miscarriage and who was with me in the hospital? Your sister and Syd. Who stayed with Lexi? My mother. When we had plans to go to Israel for our tenth anniversary, you cancelled because you had to fire the manager of the Florida showroom and you said the timing was bad. When they promoted me to executive editor and made a dinner in my honor, you managed to fly in from Boston and join me in time for dessert. Shall I continue?"

He just stared at her.

"When Chloe was a little girl and had her ballet recital, she asked you to be there. You promised you would, but at the last minute, you had to fly off to San Francisco. You broke your promise to her and you tried to make it up by buying her a Barbie Ballerina doll. Do you think she ever wanted to look at that doll? She guessed that you bought it at the airport. She was eight years old and she had sized you up already.

Remember Lexi's spelling bee contest? She was the top in her class and was invited to participate in a city-wide competition. You said you'd be there, but were you? No, it was business once again. Even your parents managed to come. And what did you do to make it up to her? You bought her a Mont Blanc pen. A Mont Blanc pen for a ten-year-old!"

"Enough! So that's it, Elie? You're getting back at me for those times? You want to cut off my balls because I was busy building up a business, which, by the way, you very much benefited from? I know what this is, it's all part of some menopause mania. You're acting crazy because your hormones are all of whack."

She tried to ignore the last comment. "No Philip, I don't want to punish you. Those days are over. I finally understand that I am not a priority for you, I am merely an ornament, an accessory of your life. I don't know if you would be different with a different wife. Perhaps if I were someone else, you would have made more of an effort. Perhaps not. I do know that your business is everything to you, and you just never took the time to realize that there are other essential things in life."

She took a deep breath and went on. "I'm not content and I haven't been for a while. I finally realized that I have different priorities than you and I no longer want to be part of your business plan. I want to create something for myself, and I cannot do that with you."

"Why? I wouldn't stop you. Go do whatever you want. Change careers and become a shrink for all I care. You went back to work. I didn't stop you. And what about the girls? Don't you care about what you'd be doing to them? Don't you care about how this will upset them? My parents? Your mother?"

She leaned back and realized, sadly, that there was no more talking to him. He really did not get it. She understood that he was not being stubborn or malicious, he just could not comprehend what she was talking about. He had lived for so many years doing exactly what he wanted, that catering to or even understanding someone else's needs was totally foreign to him. He simply could not absorb the meaning of what she was saying.

"Did you hear me, Elie? I asked you about our daughters. Don't you care how they will feel if their parents divorce? Have you no compassion?"

"I hear you. I'm sure they will be upset, maybe even devastated a little. But they will get over it. As will everyone else. This is about you and me, Philip, only you and me. Our life as husband and wife is over. I've already seen a lawyer, I suggest you do the same. I hope we can do this civilly, without battles. I would very much like for this to be resolved peacefully."

"You're crazy, Elie. Absolutely crazy. You need a good doctor." He dismissed her by brandishing his hand in the air.

The restaurant was packed. There was a line at the door and they hadn't ordered anything since the first tapas arrived. She needed to get out.

"Philip, you know what? You don't agree with my decision, okay, so be it. But you really ought not to insult me along the way. Right now I am tired, and I have had enough. I suggest we forget about the rest of dinner tonight. I'm no longer hungry."

She made movements to get up.

"So, Elie ... that's it? You're doing this to do your own thing, to pursue your own goals? What should I say when people ask me why we divorced? Because my wife wanted a life of her own?"

"Yes, Philip, that's exactly what you should say. That your wife wanted a life of her own."

Twenty-Four

Elie phoned Joshua and told him she had made her decision. She was going through with the divorce. He advised her to consider their assets, make a list of what she wanted and photocopy all deeds, titles, bank accounts, et cetera. He told her to send it to his office, and once he had a chance to review all the paperwork, they would meet.

She took out a legal pad and a pen, and sat down at the kitchen table. So this is how I'm going to divide up the years of my life with Philip, she thought, a list of stuff defining almost twenty-eight years of marriage.

The apartment was her first thought. It was the home she had lived in the longest. Her children were raised there, she had always loved it and she could not consider giving it up. Philip would have to move out. Taking into account how many times he had pushed to live in a newer building, she assumed he would not object.

The house in East Hampton. She hated it. He can keep it.

The car. She laughed to herself. When it came time to lease the latest car, Elie had asked for something with four-wheel drive. She had had a couple of near accidents on the ice and wanted a car that could handle wintry roads. Philip had insisted on a Jaguar, which she hated driving. He gets the car, she would ask for a new one.

Regarding assets in the apartment, she assumed she would keep the furniture. He could easily furnish several apartments by borrowing some pieces from the Sands New York showroom floor. If there was anything he wanted, no problem.

Artwork – she didn't care. She was aware that it was worth a small fortune, but she didn't feel a bond with most of it. Primarily they were pieces Philip had chosen for their investment potential. She thought about the Murano collection, and decided to keep only the first piece he had bought for her.

Elie continued this process with everything she could remember they had accumulated over the years. It was a very revealing exercise, enabling her to grasp in material terms how much of her life had been determined by Philip.

She saved the most important decisions for last. She decided to make no claims on Philip's business. His family had founded it, and although she had been his wife the whole time it was expanding, she felt she had no right to demand a part of it. Matter settled. Sands Furniture is all Philip's.

Then she considered the joint bank accounts, which were sizable. She kept a separate account for her earnings, and Philip had several accounts of his own. She was never certain of his financial dealings, he kept her out of that loop. She would request the accounts that were in both their names, after ascertaining that no withdrawals had been made.

Her final consideration was that of her daughters and their financial situation. Although they were both independent and living fine on their own, they knew that their parents would always help out, in any situation. Elie wondered how she would manage if an emergency arose requiring a great deal of money. She decided she would ask Philip to take responsibility for that.

She gathered up the papers and made copies on the scanner. Assembling it all into a neat package, she put it in a manila envelope, addressed it, and laid it on the foyer table to messenger over to Joshua's office. She poured herself a glass of wine and went into the den to relax. She wanted to think, as if she hadn't done enough of that over the last few weeks.

She fretted over the inevitable reactions of family and friends, especially that of her daughters. Although they were adults, it would not be easy to hear that their parents were splitting. She knew that she was shaking their foundation and it unsettled her.

She felt sad regarding her mother and Philip's parents. Her decision would cause pain to many people and she regretted that deeply. The enormity of what she was about to do overwhelmed her. She sat on the sofa with the lights low, sipping her wine and looking out at the night sky over the city.

Elie heard from Joshua a few days later and they arranged an appointment. She was surprised at how much she was looking forward to the meeting, and not just because of legal matters.

When she arrived at his office, Joshua greeted her warmly. He complimented her on how she looked and without asking if she would like something to drink, he buzzed his secretary and asked her to bring in two cappuccinos and soda water.

"So Elie, that's it? You've reached a decision?"

She was thinking about how handsome he looked. Well-tailored white shirt, beautiful silk tie – he radiated a mix of professionalism and masculinity. Sitting next to him on the sofa, Elie could not help but notice the cologne, again. It took her a minute to focus.

"Yes, Joshua, I have. I'm pretty sure of what I want in terms of settlement. I need to know if I'm within my rights." She went over the list she had made. She was organized and precise.

Joshua listened and when she finished, he spoke. "How will you maintain your standard of living? Isn't Philip paying the monthly bills now?" His glasses were perched on the bridge of his nose and he leafed through the papers on the coffee table in front of him.

"I earn a very decent salary at the magazine. I'll be fine. The amount in the joint accounts is significant, although mostly tied up in long-term bonds. But I can manage on the interest earned."

"I see. Elie, it's my job to inform my clients of their rights and help them get fair settlements. Without knowing what your husband's assets are, your proposal does not sit well with me. I think you are being unfair to yourself. You deserve more after such a lengthy marriage, and you are certainly entitled to a portion of his business."

"No. Joshua, this divorce is at my instigation. The success of Philip's company has enabled us to enjoy a good lifestyle, and I'm not saying I want to forfeit that lifestyle. However, I don't need to interfere with his business. I don't feel that I have any right to that and I believe I'll be just fine without it."

"Besides what you have given me here, can you provide me with his papers, titles to other properties he might have, and whatever else you can get your hands on?"

"I guess I could, but I don't want to. I don't want him to feel that I am interfering in any way in his affairs, so to speak." She smiled, acknowledging the ironic choice of words.

Joshua responded. "The sad reality is that most men hide financial matters from their spouses. They open bank accounts without informing the wife. They make real estate investments without the wife's consent or knowledge. Philip could be sitting on millions of dollars that he has accumulated during your marriage. You are within your rights to expect a part of that. I don't want to scare you, nor discourage you, but you should be fully aware of what the actual financial situation is before you make such an important decision. On the other hand, he may have great debts and you could be liable for them. It would help if you knew about his other accounts."

He waited for a response, which was not forthcoming, and spoke again.

"And Elie, what about the apartment? You're insisting on keeping it, but it's not yours."

"What do you mean? Of course it is. The apartment belongs to both of us." She looked at him strangely.

"I am very sorry, Elie, but according to what you have given me, if these papers are correct and have not been amended, then Philip is the sole owner of the apartment on Central Park West and in case of his demise, it reverts to his parents. It is stated quite clearly in black and white."

Elie felt her throat tightening. A very bad memory was floating up to the surface.

It was right before their wedding. Elie realized that they had not completed the co-op application papers – it was another one of the many tasks left until the last minute. She reminded Philip and he brushed her off. He said he had business contacts that would vouch for them, and told her not to worry.

"But I am worried, Philip. According to these papers, you are the sole owner of this apartment and in case of non-payment, the responsibility is on your parents. Is it an oversight or am I misunderstanding something? My name is not even mentioned."

"It's just a formality, Elie. Since my folks bought it, I guess they wanted their name on the deed in case there's a problem. Like if we can't pay the maintenance costs, the board is obligated to go to them before they approach the courts to extract payment. It's nothing, really."

They had a small argument. Elie felt insecure that her name was not on the title, it made her feel as if she would be a guest in her own home. Philip told her to relax, and that he would take care of it.

She did not want to make a big fuss over the issue, the wedding was coming up, and there was so much to do. In the end, Elie did exactly what she did most of the time, she let it go. She dropped something she felt strongly about, because she thought that maybe, deep down, she was wrong. Maybe it was greedy and selfish of her to insist that her name be on the deed. Once again, she did not listen to her gut.

Joshua noticed her mood. "I see I've touched a nerve. I'm sorry, I understand now that you didn't know." He put his hand on the back of the sofa, behind her.

"I am such an idiot. In all these years I never asked Philip if he took care of it." Her voice cracked. "I just assumed, or hoped, that he had. I suppose, unconsciously, I didn't want to know if he had not resolved it. It would hurt too badly."

"Well, it doesn't really harm your case, so not to worry. You've lived in it all these years, it's been your only home. Whether or not your name is on the deed, you're entitled to at least half of it. And if it's true, as you say, that Philip doesn't have a strong bond with it, and he wants to be a *mensch*, it will be yours."

"And if he doesn't want to be a *mensch?* One trait that has never been used to describe my husband is noble or kind."

"Not to worry, that's my problem."

"Okay Joshua, I trust you. Let's leave it at what I mentioned and if I have second thoughts, I will call you. Please start to draw up papers or do whatever has to be done. This divorce must get underway. I want to breathe again."

Twenty-Five

It was finally going to happen. Isabel was coming to New York and Michael planned every hour of their time together. Pat had been nervous about allowing the child to go to the big city, not just about letting her out of her sight for the first time but about her health – she was still within the six-month recovery period. It took the doctor's blessing and a good deal of skilled persuasion from Michael and Daniel to convince her.

Isabel was chirping to anyone who would listen that she was going to visit her "uncles" in the Big Apple. She packed and re-packed her little suitcase several times.

It was a crisp and sunny Friday afternoon when the men drove to Philadelphia, one of those perfect late autumn days. Michael could hardly contain himself; he was so looking forward to the visit. During a telephone conversation with Isabel, he had even agreed to let her try skate boarding in Central Park. Daniel had to convince him that it might not be such a wise idea, and that a trip to Tiffany would probably not be on the child's wish list.

When they arrived at the house, Isabel was waiting, wearing her favorite jeans, a light jacket and the ever-present baseball cap. Michael stopped himself from making a crack about the cap, hearing Daniel's words in his head. "Don't try to make her over, just love and accept her for who she is. Go easy on all the girly stuff."

Pat was emotional saying goodbye. Even though it was only for a weekend, she couldn't contain her tears. She hugged her granddaughter, who told her not to miss her too much and could she please have meat loaf for dinner Sunday night.

On the ride back to the city, Isabel recited all the things she would like to do in New York, including attending a baseball game, visiting Central Park Zoo, the Statue of Liberty, Radio City Music

Hall and The Gap. Upon hearing mention of The Gap, Michael knew that not all was lost – at least the child liked to shop! Daniel reminded them both that Isabel still had to take it easy and that perhaps for this first visit, the itinerary should be less ambitious.

Friday evening was spent at home. After devouring bowls of pasta, the two men and their young guest settled down in the library for a night of movies. As the hour got late, Isabel happily snuggled into the queen-sized bed in the guest room, which was the "biggest and prettiest" she had ever seen, and with a pile of *Eloise* books next to her, drifted off to sleep.

When Michael and Daniel finally retired to their bedroom, they were quiet. Isabel had not only penetrated Michael's heart, but Daniel's as well. This experience of hosting Michael's granddaughter touched them deeply, as if, at last, they shared the treasured bond of parenthood. They tenderly kissed goodnight, and fell asleep in each other's arms.

Early the next morning, Michael tiptoed out of his bedroom and peeked in on Isabel, who was sleeping soundly. He headed into the kitchen and got busy squeezing fresh orange juice and preparing breakfast. Although Saturday was usually a lounging day, and he never emerged from the bedroom before ten, today he was too excited to sleep in.

Isabel entered the kitchen in flowered pajamas, with hotel slippers flopping on her feet and her small hands rubbing her eyes.

"Good morning, my darling Queen Isabel! How was your first night sleeping in Manhattan?" He motioned for her to sit at the table, but she chose to climb up on the stool at the counter and watch him.

"Not bad, but what about all those car alarms and fire engine trucks? It sure is noisy here. Don't they have like rules, no noise between the hours of when kids are sleeping?" She placed her elbows on the counter and rested her chin in her palms.

"Oh my goodness. I forgot to inform the authorities that Queen Isabel would be spending the weekend here, and that her beauty sleep must not be disturbed! I left your window open, so that there would be a breeze, but tonight I'll put on the fan. You won't hear a thing, just a nice melodious hum. Would that be better for you, m'lady?"

"We'll see. What's for breakfast? Gran makes me French toast or pancakes on Saturdays."

Michael had no idea how to make either, he had planned on bagels and eggs. He panicked, thinking that she would not like what he had prepared. "Uh-oh, I hope you will accept something else. I bought fresh bagels yesterday and I thought we'd eat breakfast here now, and then have a big, yummy lunch out later. Is that okay?"

He surprised himself by how solicitous he was with the little girl. His brother's kids had been over a few times and they were brats. They wouldn't eat anything but fish sticks, and iceberg lettuce drowned in Ranch dressing. He prayed that Isabel had a more refined palate.

"Sure. I like bagels. Gran buys the frozen kind, I never had fresh ones. Do you want me to set the table? Where's Daniel?"

"You know what? I have an idea. Let's go check on him. I'm sure he'd love that – to wake up to you and me saying good morning."

"And can we jump on the bed? That would really wake him up!" Isabel hopped off the stool and looked at Michael with big shining eyes.

He laughed, and said maybe they had better not. She held Michael's hand as they walked down the hall towards the master bedroom. At the touch of her fingers, Michael took a deep breath.

Daniel, just waking up, was delighted to welcome visitors. He motioned for Isabel to climb in next to him, and Michael got in on the other side. The three lay there, tickling each other, talking nonsense and planning their day.

After breakfast, the men took Isabel for a tour of their Grammercy Park neighborhood, explaining the history of the area. She was excited when they whipped out the key and opened the gate of the private park for residents only. Later, as they headed into the lobby of the Grammercy Park Hotel, Isabel's mouth and eyes popped open. She stood under the crystal chandelier and told them she wanted to stay there forever.

It took considerable effort to get her to leave the hotel. But

Michael had a plan, which meant next stop Serendipity, the home of the Frozen Hot Chocolate. According to the law of Michael Delmonico, no little girl's visit to New York would be complete without a visit to the East Sixtieth Street bastion of delightful desserts. They took a cab to the restaurant, greeted the receptionist and were escorted to a table against the wall. The long narrow space with its white iron chairs, coffered ceiling and Tiffany lamps created an enchanted atmosphere. Isabel's blue eyes opened wide and she covered her cheeks with her hands.

When handed the menu, the little girl looked it over. She responded to Daniel, who had asked if she found anything she liked. "Could I please just have a hamburger?"

The enormous hamburger arrived, and Michael and Daniel enjoyed watching her tackle it as they ate their salads. When it came to desserts, she was once again dazed. Both men told her the Frozen Hot Chocolate was a must.

"But it costs a lot of money. Gran doesn't let me get the most expensive thing in a restaurant. I could have just one scoop of ice cream maybe."

"That's ridiculous! Of course you can have the Frozen Chocolate and anything else you want. You're not with Gran now." Michael looked horrified.

"Honey, your Gran is right. One should be aware of prices and one needn't always go for the most expensive item." Daniel, ever the more sensible of the two, knew that it was not their place to question the way the child was raised. "But it's fine for today. We want you to have a really special experience and we're not considering the cost of things, okay?"

The delightful lunch was followed by a bus trip up Madison Avenue and a walk over to Fifth Avenue to visit the Metropolitan Museum of Art. Michael sensed that Isabel's patience might be limited, but he wanted to expose her to at least some of the magnificent collection. It was part of his plan to inculcate a sense of culture and beauty into her.

After visiting several galleries and showing genuine interest in the paintings, Isabel seemed tired. They had planned to take her to Dylan's Candy Bar – the East Side sweets emporium that was

Mecca for kids and to FAO Schwarz, but after a brief negotiation, it was decided to save those activities for Sunday. As they walked past the museum gift shop on their way out, Isabel mentioned that she would like to buy something for her grandmother. They helped her pick out a calendar with photos of old New York.

By the end of the weekend, Daniel and Michael were totally enamored with their protégé. She had absorbed the city like a sponge, and could not seem to get enough of it. She learned the street grid, understood the subway maps, insisted on a ride on the Lexington Avenue line, and gleefully enjoyed a trip around Central Park in a horse-drawn buggy. By late Sunday afternoon, all three were sad that the activities had to end. Michael helped her pack up her things, including the gifts the men had bought her, and they reluctantly drove to Philadelphia.

When she arrived home, Isabel was greeted by a very relieved grandmother, and the smell of meat loaf wafting out of the kitchen. Michael and Daniel stayed for dinner, and it was agreed that Isabel would visit again in a few weeks.

Michael, not usually prone to sentimentality, had been strongly affected by the weekend. He was subdued on the way home, and he admitted to Daniel that Isabel's visit had done more for him than all the accolades and awards he had received for his design projects over the span of his career. He decided that spending more time with the little girl, if Pat would allow it, would become his priority.

Twenty-Six

Elie's life went into automatic pilot. Months later, she would say she was not at all sure where she got her energy and determination from, but it was there.

At a meeting with Joshua, she learned that Philip's lawyer had been a bit overwhelmed, or rather underwhelmed, by Elie's demands.

Joshua explained. "He was surprised. He took a second or two on the phone and said to me, 'Really? That's all she wants? This isn't a tactic, is it Joshua? She's not going to come back and knock us over the head? We both know she could get more if she fought for it.' I had to put his mind at rest that you were serious and not playing games."

Joshua related that he reassured the opposing attorney that Elie would not seek additional funds in the future, that she wanted a clean break and no further financial ties to Philip. A complete and final settlement would provide her with the emotional freedom and sense of independence that she craved. Joshua said he hoped Philip had been apprised of Elie's fairness.

Joshua then asked Elie about a Jewish divorce. He explained the benefit of having a *get,* which would be necessary if she wanted to remarry in a Jewish ceremony.

"I realize that you are not observant. And maybe you don't see the benefit now of obtaining a Jewish divorce. Nevertheless, if I may be so bold and take a step outside my jurisdiction as your lawyer and wear my former hat as rabbi, establishing yourself as a free woman according to *halacha,* the Jewish law, is important. Your status will never come under question and it will allow you to be free to remarry, or just to be single without the noose of the title *agunah*. Do you know what that is?"

"No."

"It refers to a chained woman, someone whose husband has not granted her a divorce. If he withholds his consent, the wife is prevented from marrying in the future."

"Well isn't that lovely and fair." She grimaced.

"Yes, I agree, but let's not get into that. You should not have to go through anything like that. Obtaining a *get* is a simple ceremony in a rabbi's study. I can arrange it for you. Will Philip agree?"

"I don't know, but I can't imagine he'd have any problem with it. Okay, let's go for it. What else?"

"You tell me. What are your plans after the divorce?"

"To get my life back. No, I'm going to start a new one. And I plan to take a lot of deep breaths. I'm still just enjoying the fact that when I open the medicine cabinet, only my things are in there."

Joshua laughed. "That's an odd reaction."

"I know. I guess this divorce thing affects us all in different ways. Anyway, I'm a little scared, but I'm really looking forward to starting over. I think I'll be happy."

"I am certain of it. You seem to have your head on straight and you're in control. You're a fine person, Elie Sands. I hope you know that about yourself." He seemed to want to say more, but reconsidered and stopped.

As Elie had predicted, Philip agreed to the divorce. At first he balked about her requests, he didn't want to give up ownership of the apartment, nor of their joint accounts. Eventually he conceded. Apparently his lawyer made it clear to him that the arrangements Elie was asking for were modest, as she was entitled to a lot more.

Philip decided to stay in the corporate apartment until he found a place of his own, and he made plans to empty their apartment of all his belongings. He wanted the majority of artwork and some of the furniture – which Elie was quite willing to part with. The couple agreed that further communication between them would be conducted via their attorneys. It was also decided that Elie would be the one to inform their daughters. She dreaded this, but agreed that it should be her responsibility.

Lexi had always been close to her mother, and she was a trouble-free child to raise. She was easygoing, relaxed and always concerned for others. Elie assumed that she would be understanding of the situation, and compassionate. She sent her daughter an email saying she had something serious to discuss, and asked for a good time to phone.

Chloe was another matter. From the time she was a little girl, she had been determined and opinionated. As a teenager, she was rebellious, strong-willed, and insistent on doing things her way. By now, her defiant nature had calmed down and she had turned into an impressive young woman. She and Elie were developing a bond of friendship that went beyond mother and daughter, and Elie hoped that the news would not damage that. She invited Chloe to dinner at the apartment.

In preparation, Elie debated with herself what to say. Should she talk about Philip's betrayal? She was loathe to do so, but on the other hand, not mentioning that fact might make her children rebel against her. How could they understand her leaving their father if he did nothing wrong? She decided to play it by ear.

Chloe arrived, walked into the kitchen and wasted no time before launching the interrogation. "So, what's the deal Mom? It's Tuesday, not the usual Friday night dinner. Why the urgency? You're finally going to tell me what's going on between you and Daddy?"

"Yes, honey, I will. Come sit down. Let's start eating." Elie delayed the discussion by asking about Chloe's work.

Her daughter was eating and talking at the same time. Elie could never figure out how the girl managed to stay so thin, when she ate like a truck driver. Not my genes, she thought. Finally, it was time to break the news.

"Chloe, I've got something really important to talk to you about. It's not good news, but I'm hoping you will be able to understand where it's coming from."

"Oh my God! Is someone sick or dying or something?" She stopped eating and looked nervous.

"No, nothing like that."

"So what? Are you and Daddy like getting a divorce?" She smirked.

Just like that, she said it. Elie thought she might have meant it as a joke, but as long as Chloe dropped the grenade, Elie would handle the explosion.

"Well, as a matter of fact, Chloe, we are."

"Are you kidding me? You're not serious, are you?" She looked astonished.

"I'm afraid I do mean it. There are a lot of reasons, faults on both sides. I just really believe, after a great deal of soul searching, that this is the right thing to do, for both of us. I expect it will be difficult for all of us, maybe even the most for your dad, but it's for the best. I am truly sorry, Chloe."

"No sweat, Mom. I figured it would happen one of these days."

"You what?" She stared at Chloe from across the table, unable to fathom what she had just said.

"Mom, I'm not an idiot. I know that you guys don't have a good marriage. I know Daddy is a charmer and probably fools around. I mean, I don't know for sure, but I kind of figured he did. And I assumed you put up with it for whatever reason. I thought that maybe one day you'd get sick and tired of it and wake up. And if you had the strength I hoped you had, you'd finally fight back. I even talked to Aunt Syd about it. So it's not like I couldn't figure this out."

"Chloe, you absolutely shock me. I had no idea you were aware of anything going on between your dad and me. If you thought he was having an affair, why didn't you ask him, or me? And you discussed this with Syd, and not me? I can't believe that!"

"Are you kidding me? I'm going to ask my father if he has some chick stashed away? I don't think so. I figured if he was doing it, he's a slime ball and doesn't deserve you. And that sooner or later he'd get caught and you'd get up the courage to move on. That's the reason, isn't it? He's been cheating? Anyway, Syd advised me to stay out of it. I mean, it's not that I have proof of anything."

"Chloe, this is very uncomfortable for me. I'm still reeling from the fact that you claim you were onto this, and that you suspected Daddy was fooling around. And that you spoke to Syd about it.

Boy this is weird, speaking with you about all this."

"Mom, I spoke to Syd because we're close, you know that. And we talk about stuff. It wasn't the major topic, it just came up. I love Daddy, but I don't think he's very nice to you. Truthfully, a lot of times I get pissed off at the way he rags on you. I also don't like that you take it from him."

"This is sure not the scenario I imagined. I'm feeling like you're the mother and I'm the little girl." She reached over and took Chloe's hand in hers.

"Yeah, but you'll still make me chocolate chip cookies and carrot cake, little girl or not, right?"

"Honey, you have that promise from me for life. I will always make you your favorite cookies and cakes and I'll do the same for your children."

"Oh yeah, like I'm running off to get married and have kids. Don't you think I learned anything from this example?"

"Chloe, the fact that Daddy and I are splitting does not take away anything from the family life we've always had. We've tried very hard to give both you girls a good upbringing. I don't think you have any legitimate complaints in that area, do you?"

"No, Mom. It's been great. Except that you wouldn't let me have a pet snake, you refused to let me pierce my tongue and *Dislexi* was always your favorite."

Elie hated when Chloe used that nickname for her sister, but right now she was not going to scold her. She laughed.

"Talking about *Dislexi*, does she know? Have you spoken to her yet?" Chloe put down her fork.

"No. I sent her an email and asked her to tell me a good time to call. Please don't mention it to her, if you speak to her first."

"Mom, get real. If I speak to her, of course I'll want to blab it. Tell her soon, and good luck. I bet she'll freak."

The dinner with Chloe turned out better than Elie had predicted. Although she was flabbergasted at Chloe's take on the situation, she was relieved that her daughter was not in shock. The business of Syd's involvement, however, was another matter. She was very unsettled by the knowledge that Syd had shared this with her daughter. She would have to figure out how to handle it.

Later that night, Elie phoned her older daughter. It was early morning in Israel.

"Hi sweetheart, how is everything?" She started calmly, wanting to ease into it.

"Great, Mom. Everything is wonderful. Gavri is an angel, and Miriam comes over a lot to help. I hope you don't mind that we're calling him by his middle name, Aaron seemed so serious for a baby."

"Of course not, darling. It was lovely that you named him after my father, but you should definitely call him what you're comfortable with. I'm so happy about Miriam. I saw during my visit, what a wonderful homemaker she is. You're lucky, sweetheart, that she has been so accepting, considering the circumstances. She lost her daughter in such a tragic way, yet she clearly accepts you as the new woman in her son-in-law's life. And boy, can that woman cook!"

"I know. I am very fortunate. And you're not kidding about her cooking. Her food reminds me a lot of Nonna's – it's mostly Sephardic. Anyway, she doesn't let me walk into the kitchen. She's been doing everything. When I'm not breast-feeding and Gavri is asleep, she makes me lie down, so I can catch up on my rest. I couldn't ask for a better situation. Well, maybe if my own mother was here ..."

"Ah, how I wish I could be there with you, honey. It was so difficult for me to leave you.

"Difficult for you? I couldn't stop crying when you left. I wanted my mommy to stay here with me."

"Oh Lexi, now I feel bad. I'm so sorry that I couldn't stay longer. It's just that with all the magazine work, and that big AIDS party and the company party at the Hamptons ..."

"Oh, Mom, it's fine. I'm just teasing you. I mean, I did cry but I got over it. I know you'd like to be here more. And I know that if I really need you, you'll come. So don't worry. I am, no we, are doing really well. So what's this phone call about? Your email sounded very serious."

"It is. Honey, I'm afraid I have unpleasant news. I've thought of a million ways to break this to you, but there is no simple way. I wish I could be there in person to tell you, but that's not possible."

"Mom, you're scaring me. What happened? Is someone sick, in the hospital? Oh no, is it Nonna or Grandpa or Grandma?"

"No, no. Everyone is fine. No one died. It's about me and Daddy."

"What about you and Daddy?" There was an uncertainty in her voice.

"Honey, Daddy and I have not been getting along. Not for a long time. And after much soul searching, I've decided that I want a divorce. I just feel that both Daddy and I will be happier people away from each other."

There was silence at the other end of the telephone.

"Lexi, did you hear me?"

"I heard you, but it's not true. You can't mean this." Her voice cracked.

Elie felt stung by the pain she was inflicting on her daughter. "Sweetheart, I am so very sorry. I know this is difficult to hear. But you're an adult now, with children of your own. Perhaps you will be able to see marriage from a different perspective. There is so much to say, but the bottom line is that Daddy and I don't belong together anymore."

"You don't love him?"

"No, not in the way I once did. I care about him, he will always be very special to me and of course, because we have you and Chloe, we will always be connected. I truly hope that your Dad and I will be able to maintain a good relationship. That is my dream, but at this point I am not sure if that will happen."

"Mom, this is a nightmare. I'm in shock and I don't understand. You didn't say anything when you were here. Why all of a sudden? I thought you guys were happy. I always felt that we were an example of a model family. My friends were jealous that I had such wonderful parents. You and Daddy breaking up sort of makes all that a lie."

"No, it does not. We had a wonderful family. We still do. You girls got everything we could give you in terms of love and attention. You were our priority, on that Daddy and I agreed. My focus was always on making a wonderful home for the two of you. And perhaps along the way, I forgot to carve out a piece of happiness for myself."

"Mom, forgive me, but that sounds rather trivial. Too me, me, me. Are you saying you resented raising us? You've had a career. Haven't you been happy?"

Elie was taken aback by the question. "Oh God, Lexi, it's not like that. It's not that I wasn't happy, I loved being at home with you girls. It's just that for a long time I had no place in the world other than as your mother and Daddy's wife. I do not blame anyone for that situation, or if I do, I can only blame myself. I got so caught up in my roles as wife and mother, that even with all that I've accomplished at work, I don't feel satisfied." She stopped, but before giving Lexi a chance to respond, continued.

"I went from being a full time mom to being the absolute best editor I could be. It never even occurred to me to ascertain whether I really wanted that. I felt so grateful to Walter for letting me come back to the magazine, that I've been trying to prove myself there ever since. I know I'm talented and smart, but I need to explore other sides of me. I need to get back to the person I once was. Or perhaps discover her for the first time. Can you understand any of what I am saying?"

"I think I can. But why can't you do that and stay married to Daddy? Surely he doesn't care if you change careers or do what you want. He supported you going back to work, didn't he? I never noticed that he was hostile or jealous."

Elie was feeling uncomfortable that all this had to be discussed by phone. She walked to the kitchen with the cordless to take a glass of water while she listened to her daughter.

"There are some layers to his acceptance, Lexi. He was not very supportive of me, but darling, that's not the only issue. He and I have personal problems between us and they cannot be solved. We're very different and I don't think we belong together. Oh Lexi, I wish you were here so that I could give you a hug and explain all this better. I'm afraid this is not coming out right."

"Mom, this doesn't make sense to me. It's seems so all of a sudden. I think you're making a mistake. You've shared more than half your life with him. If you haven't loved each other then what was all that about? Why did you invest so many years in this marriage?"

Lexi's questions were a little too direct, in both approach and content. She knew her daughter was right. Why did she stay so long in the marriage if the love had gone? Why had she waited until she was almost fifty-one years old, before waking up to the fact that she was not fulfilled? How could she explain that?

She did not want to mention Philip's affair. Lexi adored her father, he had always been a hero in her eyes. How could she add this to Lexi's burden? Elie decided that there would be no more smashing of fantasies. And that she needed to end the discussion before it unraveled her.

"Darling, I think we had better just leave it at this for now. I will explain more later. It's still all very new for me too, and difficult to talk about. Will you please try to trust me, and believe that I know what I'm doing? I need you to tell me you'll consider that."

"Mom, you've hit me with heavy news. I'll try to think about what you said, but I am going to ask you to do the same. Reconsider your decision. I think it's a mistake what you're doing."

Elie understood that her daughter was hurting, and she chose not to argue with her. "Okay sweetheart, we'll both think about it. I'll call you again soon. In the meantime, I love you. Please give a kiss to Dovey and those precious little children of yours."

Elie hung up and felt wretched. The conversation with Lexi brought up suppressed feelings, that she hadn't really dealt with. Obviously, there was more beneath the surface than she had realized. She had trouble falling asleep that night, worrying about how the rest of the family would react to the news.

Sophia Stein was next. Elie drove out to Queens to see her. Her mother was obviously not prepared for the news and was noticeably stunned. Her face reflected concern and sorrow. She accepted Elie's explanations quietly, without pumping her for details. She promised to be there for her daughter in any way she could.

Max and Tillie heard the news from their son and were shocked. They asked for a meeting with Elie and Philip. Elie rejected the idea out of hand, but Philip insisted that it was the least she could do for them. She reluctantly agreed.

They met at the Sands' apartment. Max sat silently and looked sad. Of all the people she knew she was hurting, Elie felt especially bad about Max. She loved him very much – he had always been a wonderful father-in-law and she felt a special kindness and warmth from him that she missed so much since her own father's death.

Tillie had a speech prepared in advance. She said it did not matter who did what, they must think of themselves as having an unbreakable bond and fix the problems and move on. Yes, she was aware that Philip had an affair and she thought it was outrageous and unacceptable. She told Elie she must get over it and forgive Philip.

It was difficult to listen to her mother-in-law's monologue. Elie was not prepared to tell her that she had lost the feeling of love. It would just be too hurtful to everyone. She did her best to explain that they had grown far apart, they had nothing left in common and their lives were no longer on the same path.

Philip sat on the sofa dejected and told his mother to give it up – there was no convincing his wife. He told her that Elie's mind was made up and that was that. The discussion ended when Tillie instructed her daughter-in-law to think again and reconsider. Elie smiled at Tillie, without committing herself, and left the apartment feeling exasperated.

The dissolution of the marriage between Elie Stein Sands and Philip Sands took place in early November, the month that would have marked their twenty-eighth anniversary. The couple, along with their respective attorneys, sat on opposite sides of a large conference table in Joshua's office. Greetings and small talk were made, while a secretary offered coffee and pastries that had been set up on a credenza. It was all very civilized, as if a board meeting was taking place.

Joshua reviewed the documents and reiterated what Elie would receive: ownership of the Central Park apartment, a check to cover the cost of a new car, and the joint savings accounts – with verification of the current amounts to be conducted by telephone with the bank at precisely eleven. Philip committed to pay all miscellaneous expenses for one year, such as health and apartment insurance.

It was also confirmed in writing that any significant financial needs of their daughters would be covered by Philip. Elie felt a bit dodgey about that, but she was forfeiting access to a large sum of money and therefore insistent. The document also stated that Elie would be reverting to her maiden name, and that the couple agreed to obtain a Jewish divorce, which would be arranged by Joshua.

The papers were signed by both parties and Philip's lawyer presented Elie with a check. The two attorneys witnessed the signatures and Joshua's secretary notarized the agreement. The papers still had to be submitted to the court, but with the simple signing of her name, Elie Stein Sands ended her marriage and the life she had known for the last twenty-eight years.

Elie had assumed that she and Philip would go out to lunch after the meeting. Only later, did she realize how silly that assumption was.

When the formalities were over, Philip got up and declared, "Well, I guess that wraps everything up. I have a meeting to run to. Elie, I hope you're happy. Goodbye all." He walked out of the room.

She sat there for a minute, dazed. Then she thanked Joshua, shook hands with Philip's lawyer and left the office. It was over.

Twenty-Seven

After the divorce, Elie took a week off from work. Although for the most part she was feeling good, it was an odd time for her. The tension was gone, she felt hopeful and looked forward to a good future. Nevertheless, the fact that she was no longer married to the man she had been with for so many years left her with a void. She was certain that she had made the right decision, but at low points, she wondered what she was doing.

She understood that it would take a while to get used to her new situation. There were still moments when she expected Philip to walk in the door, or call out to her and ask if she wanted to grab some sushi around the corner. She expected his nightly phone calls from whatever city he happened to be in. Even the act of telling people about the change in status felt bizarre, so she avoided it. She was aware that she and Philip had some prominence in their circles, she assumed the word was already spreading.

She made a point of spending a day with Michael in Philadelphia and got to know Isabel, whom she fell in love with. When she returned home, she got down to the task of fixing her apartment: reorganizing, painting, and shopping for furniture and artwork.

A firm hand needed to be taken with the apartment's contents, it was time to purge. She asked Syd to help, knowing her friend could be ruthless when it came to saving or tossing.

The uncomfortable matter of Chloe and Syd being in on the secret of Philip's affair also had to be resolved. She felt betrayed that both her daughter and her best friend had suspected it, and not told her. Rather than let the matter fester, she brought it up with Syd as they sat on the floor of the living room, surrounded by boxes.

"Syd, there's been something bugging me and I don't want it

to interfere with our friendship. I have to talk to you about it."

"Sounds serious. What did I do wrong?" Syd said.

"Chloe told me that you and she discussed the possibility of Philip having an affair. That was a very strange thing to hear from my daughter. I was shocked. You never said a word to me about it."

"Oh." Syd stopped what she was doing. "I'm sorry, Elie. Actually, it was a hard call. If I told you, I would be betraying Chloe. And since she had no proof, what would have been the point? To torture you?"

"You should not have kept something so important from me. I think this goes beyond the friendship you have with Chloe, your allegiance to me ranks higher. And besides that, even if it was only a suspicion, did you really think it was possible that Chloe was right? You believed that my husband could have been cheating on me?"

"The truth? Yes. I did think Philip capable of being unfaithful. Even now, admitting it to you, I feel slightly guilty. But it's out. I just never fully trusted him, Elie. Sorry, but that's how I felt."

"You must have thought I was a total fool for staying with him." Elie's insecurities were floating up to the surface.

"Whoa. Slow down. I thought no such thing. Don't jump to that conclusion. I was just never very fond of Philip, but Elie, you know me – I dislike most people. Hell, how many friends, besides you, do I have? Real friends? I would never judge you for being with Philip. Who am I to take a stand on that?" Syd looked at her friend with a sincere, questioning look on her face.

"It felt weird and very uncomfortable. I really didn't like the Syd Chloe link this time. I'm sure you know that I have some bouts of jealousy when it comes to your relationship with my daughter."

"I do know. And perhaps I overdo it at times, trying to impress her as the cool, older woman. It's not an excuse, because I love both your girls, but with Chloe there's something special for me. I guess it doesn't take a shrink to figure out the reason – transference for the child I lost. But you know how much she loves you, don't you?"

"Oh thanks, so glad to hear that from you." Elie made a face.

"Oops. That did sound rather patronizing. Sorry again. Look, I know I've overstepped boundaries a few times, and I apologize. But you know me, I can be such a witch. I'll probably do it again."

She laughed and reached over to touch her friend.

"Aw gee, that makes me feel so much better." It was impossible for Elie to stay annoyed at Syd, and she realized that her resentment had a lot to do with her own insecurities. "Is there anything else I should know, my dear, devoted, loyal friend? Any other secrets you've kept from me?"

Syd thought about Chloe and the relationship with Steven. She did not want to reveal it to Elie, but how could she conceal it any longer?

Apparently Elie read her mind. "I know about Chloe's affair, so if that's what's going through your head, don't worry. You don't have to tell me a thing. Chloe did."

"Oh, thank God. I did not want to be in that position. So what happened? How did you get her to tell you?"

"I didn't. We were together one evening, just the two of us, and she brought it up. I was shocked, but I think I handled it rather well. Even you would have been proud of me. I listened, I didn't judge or make comments, and I just comforted her. Apparently, the guy dumped her."

"What? He dumped Chloe Sands? That son of a bitch! Is he some kind of moron?"

"Syd Sorenstein, whose side are you on? The moron was married! It's a good ending, she's fine now."

"So we're good? All of us?" Syd held out her hand and Elie took it.

"That we are. Now let's dig. I have to get rid of this stuff and your job is to be heartless and force me to do it."

The two women went through boxes of old clothes, shoes, accessories, children's things and unused gifts. Syd teased Elie about how much junk she had acquired over the years, and Elie accepted it in good humor.

Syd was assigned the cartons stored in the maid's room. When she found a cloisonné tin at the bottom of a box with skates and ski boots, she called Elie over. "What's this? It's so pretty."

"Oh my God, it's my treasure box! Hand it over!"

"Your what?" She gave Elie the box.

It was something Elie had kept since her childhood. It held all the mementos that had significance in her life, like her Girls Scouts Badge, her first Valentine's Day card and her school ring.

Elie was visibly excited to go through the contents and as she opened a small jewelry box, she let out a gasp.

"What is it? What did you find there?" Syd peered over, trying to see what got her friend so excited.

It was the pair of earrings that she received from David when they parted in Israel so many years ago. Each earring was a small, ancient Roman coin secured within a thin silver rim, with two delicate silver threads hanging down, ending in a fresh water pearl. Suddenly she understood why the earrings in Philip's jacket pocket had been familiar. They reminded her of a gift she had received a lifetime ago.

Elie put the box back inside the tin. She smiled, as she thought back to those days, and she spoke to Syd about her experiences. She had lived through her first taste of independence, the bliss of young love, and the tragedy of losing a parent. She had not recognized it then, but the period was a turning point in her life.

It occurred to her that finding the gift from David was a sign, once again her life was entering a new phase. One chapter had closed, but another was just about to open.

Soon after, when Elie went back to work, she sensed something funny in the atmosphere. People were congregating, and speaking in whispered tones. A few unfamiliar people were walking around the corridors. Denise buzzed her on the intercom and said Walter wanted to see her.

She hesitated at the entrance to his office, seeing that he was speaking to two men she did not recognize. Walter noticed her and waved her in.

"Elie, come in, come in. I want you to meet some people. This is John Anderson and Darren Gilmont. Gentlemen, Eleanora Sands, executive editor, and the best damn magazine woman in the business."

Elie shook their hands. "Nice to meet you." She looked at Walter, waiting for an explanation.

"Gentlemen, would you excuse us, please?"

"Certainly. Ms. Sands, it was a pleasure meeting you. I'm sure we'll meet again." John, the more vocal of the two, tipped his head towards her as he walked out of the office.

Walter closed the door and faced Elie. "Sit down. I have some news." He looked somber.

"You're making me nervous, Walter. What's going on?" He had introduced her as Elie Sands and she thought about telling him that she was back to using her maiden name, but she kept quiet.

"Something important."

"I'm listening." She squirmed in her seat.

"First, I have to say, this is about the worst timing that could possibly be. I would have preferred to give you a breather, before dumping this on you, since it's so close to your divorce and all."

Elie's mind was racing but she sat frozen.

"You know, of course, that this magazine means the world to me. I started and nurtured it and now it's become the standard-bearer in the industry. I'm very proud of it, and of what our whole team has accomplished."

"As you have every right to be. But why are you talking in the past?"

"Because, it's time to move on. I love this magazine with all my heart. Perhaps because Katherine and I never had children, this publication became my baby."

"And ...?"

"There is only one thing I love more than this magazine, and that's my wife. She has been a remarkable partner to me."

Elie sensed that Walter was heading towards something not good.

"You are aware that she has been sick for quite some time now. Some days she's lucid and almost her old self. Other days ... well, it's been difficult. I've decided, Elie, that it's time to devote myself to Katherine. She deserves it — actually, she deserved it a long time ago."

Elie tried to react, but Walter kept talking.

"I told you that I was planning to move her upstate. Well, I did, and it seems to have helped. But the traveling back and forth is hell and I can't keep up this routine. I'm getting old, Elie. Katherine is my priority now, not the magazine. Whatever clear moments she has left, I want to share them with her. I want to see her smiling, enjoying a boat ride, swimming, riding the horses. I don't know if we have weeks or months or years left together, but I'm determined to make the best of them with her. Can you see where I'm heading with this?" He stopped and looked at her.

"I think I'm getting the picture." She crossed her legs, and then uncrossed them. She waited for the bomb to drop.

"The magazine is mine. I've had offers to sell many times, but never accepted. This time I did. The men you've seen walking around are from the company buying the magazine. You've been out lately – I know it's because of the divorce – I wanted to tell you sooner, but I just didn't have the heart. I figured you had enough *tsouris* to deal with."

"So tell me now. What exactly is going to happen?" Elie tried to stop the tapping of her foot.

Walter sat down in the chair next to her. "The firm taking over the magazine is a conglomerate out of Chicago. They have no experience in the media field, but they are very anxious to get their fingers into the pie. Apparently, the owner made millions in real estate and he's looking to expand into other fields. He found us, and hasn't let go. I don't have to tell you, Elie, the publishing industry is going to hell in a hand basket. I'm lucky to have gotten this offer."

"Why didn't you let me know, Walter?" She felt hurt.

"I was under obligation to remain silent. Those who guessed at what was going on, so be it. But I could not come out and say anything during the negotiations. I am truly sorry. If there was anyone I felt I owed an explanation to, it was you. I hope you can understand."

"I guess I do. Okay, so now give me the final bad news. Am I being canned?" The panic was beginning to set in. What great timing she thought – this coming on top of the divorce.

"No, you are definitely not being canned. However, the alternative might not be to your liking. The powers that be are leaning towards offering the position of editor-in-chief to Keira. They want to change the magazine, to go after a younger demographic. They think she will be able to achieve that."

Elie felt slapped across the face. Keira? Her assistant, whom she had discovered barely out of college? The girl she took in and trained? That job should have been Elie's, it was always assumed that when Walter retired, she would step into his shoes.

"I see." She straightened the pleats of her skirt. "Not great news for the older generation, is it? I guess I'm antiquated here." Her attempt to squelch an indulgence in self-pity was failing.

"No, Elie, it's not that. They admire your work and they think very highly of you. I've gone head to head with them on this, because I think the position belongs to you. On the other hand, I cannot tell them how to run the magazine. They want to keep the feel of the magazine, but broaden the readership. Maybe they're right, that we've become too static, staid. I don't know. They believe that the circulation numbers could go up substantially with a different content.

I can't fight them. It will be their decision and I've made my stand very clear: what I think the magazine is all about, who our audience is, why it should maintain a high standard and an emphasis on residential work. But in the end, I'm walking away with a big package of money and they get my baby. They are entitled to do with it as they please. That's just the way it is."

Elie tried to absorb what she was hearing. She took a deep breath. "Okay, Walter. I understand, kind of. I guess I have some decisions to make. And to think, I was sure that my life would be clear sailing from now on."

"Elie, listen. Things don't have to change. You can continue here of course, but I guess you would be working for Keira. I can only imagine what that would feel like. Please don't make any hasty decisions. We should meet again and discuss this. Tell me you will consider all options before reaching a decision."

"I promise, Walter. Not to worry." She got up from the chair and touched his shoulder as she headed towards the door. She felt an urge to comfort him, as if his distress was greater than hers.

Elie finished her urgent work and left the office. Outside the building, she pulled out her phone and called Syd.

"Hi, friend. What are you doing tonight?"

"Hi, Elie. No plans. What do you have in mind?"

"I have in mind treating us to a yummy dinner, getting drunk on an excellent bottle of wine and then ranting and raving. Calories don't count. How does that sound?"

"Excellent. You want me to meet you somewhere?"

"No. I'm on my way home. I need a hot shower. How about I call you in an hour and we head out together?"

"Great. Speak to you then. I'll be ready. Are we dressing for gorgeous girls' night out, or is it an elastic waist band kind of evening?"

Elie laughed. "A bit of both. See you soon."

As Elie entered her apartment, she felt secure, protected. The redecorating she had done contributed to the feeling that this was, at last, her sanctuary. There were no massive pieces of furniture, or giant abstract paintings overwhelming the space. All the hard-edged pieces were gone. Now the apartment conveyed a sense of serenity, with soft colors, comfortable sofas, and artwork that held significance for her. She had gone a little over the top by painting the guest bathroom glossy black and hanging a crystal chandelier in there. Philip would have thrown a fit, she loved it.

It was a cold evening and when the women met in the lobby, they saw that they were dressed the same: black sweater, black stretch pants and black leather jacket. They laughed at their shared taste in wardrobe and walked arm in arm to a place on Columbus Avenue.

They chose to sit by the window, where they could watch all the street action. When presented with the menu, Elie scanned the dinner choices and made a declaration. "Sirloin with Smashed Potatoes! I especially want the *smashed* part!"

"Oh boy. Now I know you're in trouble. Not your usual Caesar salad?" Syd ordered fish and when the waitress walked away, she looked back at Elie. "So? What's the deal? Why did you want to treat me to dinner and then rant and rave?"

"Because, I got axed today. Made redundant. Laid off. Canned. Well, sort of anyway."

"You are not serious! Don't tell me they're letting you go. Have they gone crazy over there?"

As Elie started to tell the story of Walter retiring, the manager came by with margaritas on the house.

Syd grinned. "Man, I do so love this place. It sure pays to be a loyal customer here. Okay, a toast and then tell me why Walter's departure means your elimination." Syd clinked her glass to Elie's.

"Because I learned that the new owners are considering Keira for the position of editor-in-chief. *Keira, my loyal assistant.*"

"That's absurd! What a totally asinine idea." Syd looked indignant.

"I know. Maybe Keira has even been vying for the position. Her attitude towards me has gotten weird, even a bit hostile, and she's been working like crazy. Or maybe that's just my paranoia speaking. The point is, Walter said that the whole format of the magazine will be overhauled – the works. They want to create something that will appeal to a younger crowd. Does that sound like a scenario I want to be a part of?"

"No, of course you wouldn't want that. What will you do?"

"Would I have invited you to dinner if I knew the answer to that?" She folded her arms across her chest. "That's your job here, tell me what to do."

"You got me, Elie girl. This is really a tough one. I don't see how you can possibly work for Keira. Anyway, the direction of the magazine sounds like something you would not want to be affiliated with. Hmm, who would have thought, a divorce *and* losing your job at the same time."

"Do you want to cheer me up or encourage my suicide?" Elie leaned in. "Syd, this is serious. *Interior Design & Style* is the only job I ever had. I started working for them right after graduating and the only break was when I was at home with the girls. What else would I do? At my age, who would hire me? And talking about my age, I'll be fifty-one very soon. Man, who would have thought? My husband cheating, a divorce and losing my job, all in the year between fifty and fifty-one."

Syd put her palm up to signal stop. "Give me a break. Don't get so melodramatic. Obviously, I have to remind you that in the past year you also became a grandmother to a beautiful baby boy, created an amazing Designers Ditch AIDS event, transformed your apartment into the home you've always wanted, you're healthy and you look gorgeous – even though you don't come to the gym with me. And well, take tonight for instance. Two friends having a lovely dinner, in this wonderful restaurant, in this wonderful city, and it's a beautiful November night, and we were given free margaritas."

Just at that moment, their doorman walked by, apparently he had just finished his shift. They knocked on the window and waved.

Syd continued. "See? We even know the people on the street in this crazy town. Come on, admit it, life isn't so bad. And regarding your future, there has to be something else you've wanted to do. Wouldn't this be the perfect time to pursue a dream, something new and adventurous?" She kept talking, without giving Elie a chance to respond.

"You know, now that I think of it, finding the earrings was the push you needed to ask Philip for a divorce. You probably knew for a long time that you wanted to do it, but you gathered up the courage only when you found proof of his cheating. So, maybe, this bad news is another sign – that it's time to move on."

"You think? But did it have to come right after I forfeited my rights to alimony – because I thought I made good money?" Elie waved her bread stick in the air.

Syd laughed. "Oh come on. You have enough money to live on and I'm sure you'll get a good package out of the magazine. By the way, if you want me to check out the new owners, with my contacts and all, no problem, I will."

"No, who cares about them? It really doesn't matter."

"Elie, listen. This may sound hokey, knowing my level of cynicism and all, but I have always been a big believer that bad news begets good. You know the drill, if you are stuck with a batch of lemons, make lemonade!

I swear to you, that every time I have been faced with a bad surprise, I was able to turn it around to something positive. Ninety-five percent of the time anyway. I'm not kidding, this could be your chance."

"Yeah, I'm on a new path now. I dumped my husband, I painted my apartment, so what's a little losing my job? I can handle it. I am woman! I am strong!" She raised her glass to Syd's and they both laughed.

Syd responded, "Indeed! To strong women! *L'chayim!*"

Elie suddenly looked serious and lowered her voice. "Jeez Syd, here I am running on and on about myself. What about you, with all the stuff at your office? Now that William has finally been indicted, what's going to happen? Update me."

"I'm fine, but there's going to be quite a price to pay at some of the companies he was involved with. What a snake, you would not believe the crap he pulled. I had no idea. Anyway, I'm free and clear, but to tell you the truth, I'm fed up. This episode has taken a chunk out of me and I'm tired of the rat race. I have plenty of money. My clients have made plenty of money off me. I'm thinking that maybe it's time to stop and smell the coffee. Or the roses and make the coffee. Whatever that saying is."

"So maybe we both need a new direction. Let's open up a boutique for tired, old women – tired, old women who are still very chic, of course."

"Yeah. Two women who have lived so long in the same building that they start to wear the same clothes. No thanks, I'll keep doing what I'm doing until I can figure out something else. Thank you for the vote of confidence, but believe me, you don't want to go into business with me, I'm way too neurotic."

Syd changed the subject back to her friend again. "Elie seriously, I'm sure you'll land on your feet. I'm damn positive of it. You need to stop thinking negatively, you do way too much of that. Just start dreaming. I have a feeling that you have lots of ideas tucked away in that lovely head of yours – now is the time to let them come out and play."

Elie listened to her friend and tried to concentrate on what she was saying, and not drown in despair.

After a full evening of talk, laughter, food and drink, Elie went home feeling better. Later, when she was lying in bed, she wondered if her bout of optimism had not been alcohol-induced.

Twenty-Eight

A few weeks later, the phone rang at two am, waking Elie out of a deep sleep. She panicked, thinking something had happened to one of the girls. She said hello in a groggy voice.

"El, it's me. I think my dad had a heart attack. You have to get over there. I'm in Singapore and Sandy is on her way down from Vermont, but she won't be able to get there for a few hours. I don't know what to do. It's awful." He was talking quickly and she barely understood him.

She shot up in bed. "Philip, calm down. Tell me what happened, but not so fast."

"My dad had chest pains. My mother called an ambulance and they took him to Mt. Sinai. I'm here at this damn furniture show. I'll get the next flight out. Please, Elie, can you go over there and be with my mom?"

"Of course, I'm on my way. I'll speak with you later."

"I have my cell phone on. Call me as soon as you can, okay?"

"Yes, Philip, of course, don't worry."

"Elie?"

"Yes?"

"Thanks. Thanks a lot."

"You don't have to thank me. Talk to you later." She hung up.

Elie threw on some clothes, grabbed her coat and purse and headed out the door. She hailed a taxi outside her building and got to Mt. Sinai Hospital on Fifth Avenue in what seemed like five minutes. After checking his computer screen, a bored-looking reception clerk gave her the room number for Max Sands.

She found Tillie sitting by his bedside and Max asleep, surrounded by tubes, IV poles and monitors. Tillie looked frail, and a lot older since Elie had last seen her. It was a shock, more so than seeing Max in the hospital bed. This dynamo of a woman looked frightened and terribly small. Elie's heart went out to her. Tillie glanced up and smiled as Elie walked in.

"Oh, Elie dear, you came. I'm so glad. Philip mentioned he would call you, but I wasn't sure you would want to come."

Elie leaned down and kissed her. "What do you mean? Of course I would come. Have you spoken to the doctors?"

"Yes, but only right after we got here. Apparently, it's a heart attack, but a minor one. They say it's lucky I called when I did. We could have lost him. Oh God, what would I do without my Max?"

Tillie took Elie's hand and didn't let go. Her cheeks became stained with tears, but she did not weep out loud. Elie had difficulty witnessing this, she thought of Tillie as stronger than all of them.

"Elie, if something should happen to Max, I'll go crazy. I can't survive without him. He's so strong, he carries all of us on his shoulders. How could this have happened to him? What will I do? What will I do?"

Elie sat down next to Tillie and took both her hands. "You're talking nonsense. Max is going to be fine. He'll be out of here and back to smoking his cigars very soon." Elie hoped that her words would comfort Tillie.

"I swear to God, if that man picks up even just one cigar after this, I'll kill him myself. Don't even joke about that, Elie. No more cigars, do you hear me, Max Sands?" She pointed her finger at her husband.

"Tillie, you look exhausted. How about I bring you a cup of coffee or something to eat?"

"Who could eat? You should have seen him. What he looked like at home, and then in the ambulance. It was so horrible. No, I can't eat a thing." She took a tissue out of her purse and wiped her eyes.

"It looks like he will be sleeping for a while. How about if we take you downstairs to get a bite? Or perhaps I can bring you something up here?" Elie did not know what else to offer, but she wanted to distract Tillie.

"No sweetheart, I don't want to leave him. Maybe, just some water. That would be nice."

"Okay. I'll be right back." She left the room in search of a water fountain.

She returned with a plastic cup of water and handed it to Tillie. She watched her drink as if she were supervising one of her girls finishing all her medicine. "Good. Now maybe we can get some food into you?"

"Elie, whatever food they have here, I'm sure will be *dreck*. I'm not so desperate yet that I'm reduced to eating hospital food. I can wait until later."

Elie smiled. Even in the hospital, Tillie maintained her standards.

"Elie, sit down please and tell me what's happening with you. We haven't seen you in a long time." She used the universal "we", reiterating that everything was in partnership with Max.

"I'm fine. It's been a difficult process, but I'm doing okay." Elie realized that this was the first time that she'd had a chance to talk with Tillie since she and Philip split.

"You had a good marriage, you raised two beautiful girls together. This never should have happened, it was wrong." Tillie faced her and looked serious.

"Tillie, the marriage could not be saved. We grew apart. It wasn't either one's fault." Elie did not want to have this conversation with her, especially not here and now.

"*Nurishkeit*. You know what that means, Elie?" Before Elie had a chance to respond, Tillie continued.

"It means nonsense. It was a good marriage. You shared something special and it should not have ended."

Elie could not believe what she was hearing. Was the woman really going to use this opportunity to blame her for the breakup of her son's marriage?

"Don't think I don't know. I may be old, but I'm not old-fashioned. I am well aware of what goes on around me, and I know damn well that my son loused up. I know that it was his fault."

Elie thought she might have heard incorrectly, but she did not want to belabor the point. Regardless of Tillie's current thinking, she wanted to end the conversation. "You know what Tillie? Let's not get into this. I'm going to go out and see if I can find some food for you. You really need to keep up your strength."

As she left the room, her mind was racing. She knew that Tillie had been against their marriage, that the matriarch thought she was not good enough for Philip. The hostility she sensed from Tillie over the years was cleverly cloaked, but it simmered below the surface, and Elie could never get over the feeling that she was not Tillie's first choice. Now she comes out with this? Where was she for all those years?

She found a vending machine, settled on a coffee cake and forced herself to stop thinking about Tillie's comments. When she got back to the room, Tillie was in the same position.

Elie removed the cake from the package and handed it to her. "Here you go. It's not your delicious cinnamon coffee *kuchen*, but it's something. Please have a bite."

Tillie ate it. "Thank you, dear. I guess I was rather hungry. I just don't feel right about leaving his bedside."

Elie began to think that Tillie might not be able to stand all the stress, that she needed to keep an eye on her. "You know, I think maybe you should come home with me, get some rest and then we'll come back here later. What do you say?"

"Oh no, I wouldn't think of it. We can't leave him alone, Elie, we must stay with him. I'm sure Sandy will be here soon. Philip told me that he would get the first flight out. I promised to call him but I haven't." She looked even more worried.

Elie understood that Tillie would feel better when one of her children was with her. "We can call Philip on my mobile. I promised to phone him." She tried but there was no answer.

"Why doesn't he answer? What could have happened to him?"

"Nothing at all happened to him. I'm sure he's either at the airport or already on a flight home. Let's just relax and wait for Sandy. She'll be here soon."

"That was the other reason, wasn't it Elie? That Philip traveled so much and left you alone. He cared about his business too much. I knew it wasn't good for your marriage. I knew it would do harm. I told Max not to let him go away all the time. You should not have had to raise those girls by yourself."

"It wasn't so bad. Philip was there when he could be, and the girls adore him. I don't think his trips harmed them." She refrained from agreeing with Tillie, but the woman was right.

"Elie, don't make excuses. You cannot build a family when the man is always away. Maybe that's what gave him the idea that it's okay to be unfaithful. Maybe he was lonely and felt the need for someone. I'm sure it meant nothing. I know he loved you, Elie."

"Tillie, I really don't feel comfortable with this discussion."

The night turned into morning and they spent it sitting in the room, mostly silently, watching Max's breathing and waiting for him to open his eyes. Elie called the office and explained that she wouldn't be in. She phoned Chloe, who said she'd be right over, and asked her to call Lexi.

When Sandy finally walked into the room, Tillie started to cry. The relief of seeing her daughter released the tension that she had been holding in. As Sandy held and comforted her, she glanced at Elie with a nod and grateful smile.

Sandy said that Richard was parking the car and asked if anyone had met with the doctor yet. Tillie explained that she had been waiting for her to arrive before calling for him. Elie began to feel like an outsider.

When Richard walked in, the doctor was right behind him. He explained that Max had minor damage to his heart, but he appeared to be strong and should recover well. He was out of danger, the worst was over and they could look forward to getting him back home within a few days. There was a collective sigh of relief.

As Elie got ready to leave, she turned to Tillie. "Tillie, why don't you come home with me for a while? Or let me take you to your apartment. You must get some rest."

Sandy jumped in. "Oh Elie, that's a wonderful idea. Mom, you should go and rest a bit. Richard and I are here, Amy and Eric will be here soon. How about it, Mom, why don't you go home with Elie?"

"Absolutely not. I have been by this man's side for over sixty years, and I am not going to leave him now!" Tillie was not about to let anyone tell her what to do.

"Mom, don't get so dramatic. Pop is going to be fine. You heard what the doctor said. However, if *you* don't take care of yourself, we'll have to order another bed next to him. Come on, you're not such a young chicken anymore, even if your Pilates teacher says you are. I think Elie is right. Relax for a while and then come back here refreshed. Pop should wake up and see you looking perfect."

Richard piped in. "Okay, I'm taking charge. All the women in this family are now going to listen to me. Finally! Tillie, you're going home with Elie. Elie, please make her eat something, put her to bed and then come back here when you've both had a chance to rest. I assume you've been here for several hours, too." He stopped for a second. "Gee, that felt good. I finally have a say in this family."

They all laughed. Sandy touched him on the shoulder. "Don't get too used to the situation dear, my dad will be on his feet again soon and I'm sure my mother will be back to telling us all what to do. Your reign will be short lived. Right, Mom?"

"I've had enough of all of you telling me what to do. I will agree to go to my own apartment to change clothes. I'll eat, rest for a maximum of one hour and then come back here. Those are my conditions." With that, she walked over to her sleeping husband, kissed him on the cheek and said to Elie, "Let's go."

The crisis of Max's heart attack passed. He was sent home to recuperate and a live-in nurse was hired. Tillie nearly had a fit over the arrangement, but the rest of the family insisted. Elie went to visit a few times and played scrabble with him. The subject of the divorce was never raised again.

Philip was grateful to Elie for her involvement with his family and invited her to dinner as a thank you. For the first time since their divorce, they had a nice evening. With her defenses down, and her wine consumption up, she told Philip about the changes at work.

"El, are you kidding me? That's lousy. After you've been there so many years. I always assumed that you would be the next head of that magazine. Do you want me to make some calls? I bet tons of companies would grab you in a second. You could run any department with your eyes closed."

Elie could not believe she was hearing these words from her ex-husband. Was this the same man who had denigrated her, who told her she was wasting her time with that magazine? She was touched and told him so, kindly turning down his offer. She left the restaurant thinking that maybe it was possible to have a friendship with Philip after all.

Twenty-Nine

A few days later, Elie got a message from Joshua, asking her to phone him. What could he want? Was Philip up to something? They had just had such a lovely evening, all the divorce issues were over by now. The checks were paid, the bank transfers made, even the *get* was finalized. She panicked, aware that she was being ridiculous, but concerned nonetheless. She phoned him back immediately.

"Hello, Joshua. I got your message. What's up?"

"Hi, Elie. How are you?"

"I'm fine." She was too nervous to make small talk.

"Elie, I hope I'm not overstepping my bounds here, but there's something I'd like to talk to you about. Or rather ask you."

"Yes?" She took a breath. It didn't sound too serious.

"I'd like to ask you out on a date."

"What?"

"I said I'd like to ask you out on a date. It's been a while since your divorce, I wanted to give you some time. Now that the professional relationship between us is over, and you're a single woman again and I'm a not-so-confirmed bachelor, I thought we could try something more personal. What do you say?"

She had a big smile on her face. "I don't know what to say. I was so not expecting this." Her mind raced. *A date!* Michael would be so proud.

"Let's not make a big deal out of it. *La Traviata* is playing at the Met on Thursday. I'll try to get two tickets and we'll grab a bite to eat first. What do you say?"

Elie was tempted. She found Joshua attractive, and comforting to be with, and she loved opera ...

"Are you sure you can get tickets? Wouldn't they be sold out by now?"

"I'll do my best. Agreed?"

"I'd love to Joshua. Sounds terrific."

"Good. How about if I pick you up at six and we head over to Lincoln Center? There's a little kosher restaurant I like nearby."

"Okay, great. But I can meet you there."

"No. A gentleman picks up his date. At least, they did in my day."

Thursday night arrived and Elie was nervous. Although she had been relaxed with Joshua during the legal proceedings, now the circumstances were different. She realized that this would be her first date in almost thirty years. She fussed over her outfit and finally decided on a red wool suit with a nipped-in-the-waist jacket, a straight skirt and a white body suit underneath.

Joshua arrived at exactly three minutes to six, proudly bearing a single red rose. He wore a camel jacket and charcoal pants, and Elie thought he looked especially handsome. He was freshly shaven and his hair looked just cut. She recognized that cologne of his, and felt a fluttering inside of her.

"Why, kind sir, is that for me?" She reached out to take the flower.

"Yes, unless you have a mother living here that I need to bribe."

"Nope. No one here but me. Thank you for the rose, that was so sweet of you. Come on in, I'll just put this in water." She couldn't believe how nervous she felt. As she walked into the kitchen, she wondered if Joshua felt the same. She kept hearing Syd and Michael's voices in her head, teasing her about taking a lover. She returned to the living room, and placed the bud vase on a side table.

"Here we go. Would you like a drink, Joshua?"

"I'd love one, but I think we better get going if we want some time to *schmooze* over dinner. Elie, this apartment is lovely. What a magnificent view of the park!"

"I know. I never get tired of it. Now you see why I wasn't willing to give it up?"

"Absolutely." He moved to help her with her coat, but her arm missed the sleeve. It was an awkward moment, and they both laughed. "I guess I better let you do this yourself."

While they waited for the elevator, he turned to her. "You look beautiful, Elie."

"Thank you." She felt embarrassed. "You look quite handsome yourself." She changed the subject and kept talking, hoping to camouflage her nervousness. "You know, I haven't been to the Met for a while, but I love it, and dressing up for it. Philip and I used to have a subscription, but he was away so much, I cancelled it."

"Couldn't you have taken someone else?"

"Yes, but he often cancelled at the last minute. It's not easy to find a substitute date in Manhattan, even for the Metropolitan Opera. But let's not talk about that."

"So then you've probably seen *La Traviata* many times." He looked disappointed.

"I can see it again and again. I adore it. I'll admit that I don't feel that way about all operas. German ones, for instance, I don't get. I guess I'm pretty simple in my music tastes, if the composition is not melodious, I can't relate."

"I know what you mean. German opera, modern symphonies, I also don't know how to properly enjoy them. I guess my palate is not sophisticated enough."

As they got to the restaurant, Joshua held open the door just as Elie was about to open it for him. Another awkward moment passed and Elie sensed that they were both feeling self-conscious. Their behavior seemed unnatural to her, and their conversation contrived.

During dinner, they spoke about recent events and Elie began to feel less edgy. As the wine had its effect, and the tension dissolved, she started to fantasize about Joshua as a potential lover. She was imagining scenes in her head when he mentioned that they should get going.

The opera was mesmerizing – the gorgeous sets, the richly decorated costumes and, of course, the incredible voices. Both Elie and Joshua thoroughly enjoyed it. After the last curtain call, he escorted her out of the row, guiding her through the throng of people leaving the hall. They walked across the Lincoln Center plaza, lingered by the fountain and spoke about the tenor, whose voice was thrilling. As they headed to the street, Joshua steered her towards a crowd of people waiting for a cab.

Elie protested. "Why don't we walk? These heels aren't so bad, and it's such a lovely night."

"Yes, let's. I could use the walk, it's a good break for me. I'm in the office all day and usually they're long days. Actually, this whole evening has been a very special break for me, Elie."

"Well, it's not over yet. Walking up Columbus Avenue is one of my favorite activities. Even at this late hour, it's full of people. We've had such a nice bout of weather lately, we should take advantage of it."

They walked uptown, sometimes in silence, sometimes commenting on a shop or restaurant that they passed. A few times, they admired something in a window, often pointing to the same object. As they approached the corner of West Seventy-Seventh Street, Joshua stopped and pulled Elie toward him. He kissed her on the lips.

He moved slightly away. "I just had an irresistible urge to do that. I'm not sure what the etiquette is. Do I apologize?"

"You're asking me? I'm the freshly divorced one here. I have no idea of how this game is played."

"Elie, I'm not playing a game. I've been thinking of doing this since the day you walked into my office. To tell you the truth, I even had a crush on you when you came over to play with my sister."

Elie was shaken. It had been so many years since a man kissed her like that. She felt young, and excited.

"Elie, are you with me?" He touched her chin lightly. "It seems like you're off in another world. Tell me, will you grant this besotted man another date?"

"Well, since you put it that way ..." She smiled. "Joshua, I don't know where I'm at right now. I'm not sure I should get involved. It feels too soon. Does that make sense?" She tried to sort out her feelings, whether she was really ready for a relationship.

"Yes, of course. I'm not asking for a commitment. I would just like to see you again. And if you want to keep it purely platonic, I can do that."

"You make me laugh. I think the last time I used the term

platonic was with a guy I met in summer camp. I didn't want to French kiss and he thought I was a tease, so he went off to the waitresses' bunk and apparently found his solace there."

"Ah yes, those waitresses at summer camps – the stuff of Jewish boys' dreams. Look, let's keep it casual for now. I know you're brand new at this. We'll take it slow."

"Brand new? How about infantile? You know when was the last time a strange man kissed me? That is, I mean, not a strange man, but a guy who wasn't my husband?"

He laughed. "I know what you mean, no need to explain." He took her arm and they started walking again.

"It's been three decades, Joshua. I'm very rusty." She felt a warmth in her cheeks and she suspected she was blushing.

"Not to worry. Come on, let's forget it for now. I don't want you to be uncomfortable. This has been a perfect evening and I want to hold on to all the good memories."

They continued to walk up Columbus Avenue and turned right at the Natural History Museum. Joshua took Elie's arm as they stepped off the curb, guiding her as they cut diagonally across the street and headed towards her building. Outside the lobby entrance, he turned and gave her a peck on the cheek.

"I guess I should say good night here, we don't want people in your building getting any ideas."

"It's been a great evening, Joshua. As far as first dates go, after a hiatus of so long, I'd say it was perfect. Thank you." She returned the kiss and they parted at the door as the doorman held it open for her.

Thirty

The date with Joshua set off a spark inside Elie. She liked him, and wondered if she should let the relationship develop. She found herself daydreaming about him and indulging in tame fantasies.

Her attitude about work changed. She kept busy, but the enthusiasm and commitment were gone. She felt betrayed, even though she understood that the situation had nothing to do with her. Knowing that the magazine was sold, and realizing that she would probably be working for Keira, left her with an emptiness inside. Elie finally admitted to herself that she could not envision continuing at *Interior Design & Style*.

She was at the office, checking layouts, when her mind wandered to her evening plans, there were none. Ever since she and Philip separated, she felt a blissful freedom from schedules, planned dates, and most of all, his business commitments. She could now do whatever she liked. She picked up the phone and called Michael, hoping that he would be up for an impromptu sushi dinner. He accepted, and they decided on a new place in Grammercy Park.

Elie arrived at the restaurant first. Michael arrived a few minutes later, with the usual flourish.

"Hello, my darling Eleanora. You look ravishing. Divorce absolutely agrees with you!" He leaned down and kissed her.

"And hello to you too, my dear Michael. Thank you for being spontaneous and accepting my offer."

"Ah yes, well you know, us royals must be human and meet with the common folk once in a while. It is our sacred duty. Anyway, Daniel is staying late at the office tonight."

"Sit down, you old fool, and order your Diet Coke."

The menus were presented to them and after a few minutes

of scanning, Michael called back the waiter and started a cross-examination. How was the sea bass prepared, olive oil or butter? Was the steak top grade sirloin, or something of lesser quality? Was the salad dressed? What was in the dressing, lemon juice or vinegar? If vinegar, balsamic or white wine? Did they use peanuts in any of the preparations?

Elie could not contain herself. "Michael, for God's sake, we're in a Japanese restaurant! Their specialty is sushi! Why are you asking about steaks and salads?"

"Because my dear, I wouldn't dream of eating raw fish, you know – mercury, PCBs and all that. Oh my God, never. I heard that this is *the* restaurant, that's why we're here." He looked back at the waiter. "I shall have the steak on your recommendation, done medium, sauce on the side. Please make sure they handle my order with special care, won't you?"

The waiter turned to Elie and she gave her order.

Michael turned to Elie. "So my precious, now that our ordering is taken care of and you've scolded me in public, bad girl, bad girl, you go first. Are you enjoying your new life? Are you getting laid yet? Oh, I'm sure not, you're such a virginal princess. So, talk! No wait, first tell me, what do we think of this place?"

The design of the restaurant was sleek, ultra modern. The surfaces were black, steel and exposed concrete. The materials were cold, but there were towering flower arrangements throughout the space that contributed to an elegant atmosphere. Jazz was playing in the background.

Without giving her a chance to respond, he pronounced his verdict. "I give it an eight. I like it. Not too fussy, not too icy, just right. Yes, it's fine. I think I'll come back. Now, on to your news, then mine. Speak! Family, work, sex, what's happening? How's your darling mother? Ah, the lovely Sophia – the classiest woman I know. Is she well?"

"She's amazing." Elie knew that with his ability to keep talking, she had better jump in quickly. "She just got back from a trip to Italy and Israel. She spent time with her cousins in Rome and then with Lexi and her family. She loves the children, got on beautifully with Miriam, the previous mother-in-law, and what can I say? She takes good care of herself and looks wonderful. The woman is a wonder."

"And those girls of yours, my darling Alexis and Chloe? And all the grandchildren?"

Elie filled Michael in on their news, then hers. Life without Philip was fine, and she loved living alone. She updated him on Max's condition and Philip being nice afterwards. Then she dumped the news of the magazine and the new reign.

"Oh, I just hate that bitch Keira." Michael's eyes narrowed. "I could rip the skin off her face!"

Elie chuckled. "Thank you for that show of support, but it's not necessary. It's not her fault. She may have wanted the job, but she wasn't the one to sell the magazine. Once Walter made his decision, the writing was on the wall. I'm weighing my options now."

When the food arrived, they ate slowly, continuing to talk about Elie's work situation. Then she told Michael about her date with Joshua. She spoke about her confused feelings, that she was attracted to him, but there were obstacles. For one, his being religious.

"You mean like, he wears a beanie on his head? And if you marry him, you'd have to shave yours and wear some *schmateh*?" He stared at her in disbelief.

"No, he does not wear a *yarmulke* and I'm not marrying him and if I did, I wouldn't shave my head nor wear a *schmateh*." She shook her head and made a *tsk* sound.

"Well, what do you want from me? I'm not Jewish, I don't know what religious people do."

"Relax, Michael. He's just a nice person who wants to see me again, and I think I'd like that. I find him kind of sexy. But I'm holding off."

"Why? You should go for it. You remember my advice, don't you?"

She put her hand on her forehead and lowered her voice. "Yes, but please don't remind me of it here."

Michael started to pontificate on why she needed to "get on the horse again," but he stopped mid-sentence. He leaned forward, and in a hushed tone, instructed her to look across the room. A well-known celebrity had just sat down.

"This, I really don't get. Why do people wear sunglasses at night? And in the middle of winter yet! Is he for real? Shall I tell him that it's not very correct? Doesn't he know? He'll just attract more attention that way."

After a short discourse on the vanity of celebrities, Michael changed the subject to his work, mostly the problems. There were demanding clients, late deliveries, mistaken measurements, wrong materials, on and on. It was a litany of what could go wrong in the interior design field. Although he was extraordinarily talented, he never seemed to enjoy a flawless project from start to finish; there was always some disaster waiting to happen.

He segued into his personal life, which apparently could not be any better. The relationship with Daniel was stronger than ever, and since Isabel entered their lives, Michael felt that they had been blessed with a gift. He and Daniel traveled to Philadelphia often, and although he didn't have much in common with Pat, the desire to be with Isabel reunited him with his old friend. He filled Elie in on all the latest news and his face lit up when speaking about the child.

While she listened, Elie felt relaxed, happy. The thirty-year relationship with Michael provided a cherished anchor in her life.

They finished their meal, skipped dessert and when offered tea, Michael asked if it was decaffeinated. Then he explained how his constitution was delicate and he absolutely could not fall sleep if there was even a drop of caffeine in his body. Elie resisted the urge to mention the caffeine in his beloved Diet Coke, or to scold him about hassling the waiter once again. She just laughed with him about how senior they had both become.

Back home, Elie felt content. With her two closest friends forming a cocoon around her, she had a sense that the future would be okay. She was fortunate; Philip had consented to the divorce without a major fuss, and the girls, although upset, had accepted it. So what if the job situation was a fiasco? Maybe Syd was right: that being in one's fifties wasn't so bad at all. Perhaps the changing of the guard at the magazine was just the push she needed, maybe it really was time to pursue something else.

In the morning, Elie awoke refreshed. She knew that she was finally ready to face her future, as uncertain as it may be. She walked into the kitchen to make coffee and remembered that there had been a message on the answering machine last night from Devi. She wondered if her friend knew all her news, but assumed not – Joshua would doubtless be discreet. It was mid-afternoon in Israel, probably a good time to call.

Ellen, the American Embassy Residence manager, picked up. "Oh, hello Ms. Stein, I'll put you right through to Mrs. Young. Hold on, please."

It took about two minutes for Devi to come on. When she did, Elie heard, "And please, just a steak and perhaps one of your divine salads for dinner, Colin. It's just the two of us tonight. Hey Elie, are you there?"

"I sure am. So, are you sure you want just a steak and a divine salad for dinner? You can order something a lot more interesting, you have your own private chef!"

"Sure, go ahead and tease me. We have events every night and an excessive amount of rich food. When we're alone, it has to be simple. How are you doing, my long lost friend?"

"I'm fine Devi, just fine. What a nice surprise to get your message. What's the occasion?"

"What do you mean? I can't call an old friend and ask how she's doing? First, I wanted to tell you that I saw Lexi. She came to the King David Hotel with little Gavri and they joined me for lunch. What a delicious baby he is. She really looks happy, El."

"That was so nice of you to invite her. And the baby is very cute, isn't he? I see them on Skype, but it's not like in person."

"Isn't that a wonderful thing? That in spite of the distance, we can communicate by computer? I love all this new technology. Anyway, I also phoned because I wanted to know what's up with you. My brother is way too discrete. He doesn't tell me a thing!"

"Ah, right. You and I haven't spoken for some time. I emailed you, Dev, about the divorce being final. Didn't you get my big announcement? Come to think of it, I wondered why I never got a response from you."

"El, you would not believe how often the guys from the tech department mess with my email accounts. They always suspect that my computer has been hacked or that the house is bugged. Umm, maybe not all this new technology is so wonderful. Apparently, I miss a lot of mail. So, the divorce is signed, sealed and delivered? You're ready to move on to a new life?"

"Hard to believe, but yes. A bit scary, but so far so good."

"So, *mazel tov*! And to think, you all predicted that my marriage would fail. Funny, huh? But you really are okay, Elie?"

The comment, and the irony, was not lost on her. When Devi married Lawrence, no one believed it would last. "You're right – look who couldn't make her marriage work."

"No, I didn't mean it like that. Really, are you all right? It can't be easy, what you've just been through."

"There are some unpleasant things happening, but I'll be okay."

"What do you mean, El? What's going on?" Devi's voice had a concerned tone to it.

"Why? I need more news? Getting divorced after twenty-eight years is not enough?" Elie laughed, nervously.

"Yes, it's plenty. But I know you, Elie, talk to me."

She sighed. "Actually, the divorce was almost the small news. I have new *tsouris* to worry about."

"I'm listening."

"My boss sold the magazine and the new owners want a different look. They didn't ask me to go, but the word out there is that my assistant will be promoted to the top spot. As a result, I've decided to resign." The moment Elie uttered those words, she was surprised. She realized that she had made a decision.

"That's not good at all! I'm so sorry, Elie. But you've been there forever. What will you do?"

"I have absolutely no idea."

Devi's voice was suddenly cheerful. "I do! Come to Israel!"

Elie laughed. "I couldn't possibly get away now."

"You could and you should. I mean it, Eleanora Stein. This is the perfect time to come visit. Do I need to remind you that you have a daughter with a new baby? You were here when he was born, and that seems like ages ago. You can visit with Lexi, and then with me. Yes, why don't you come? It will be great."

As Devi spoke, Elie started to entertain the idea. "Oh, Devi, it sounds wonderful, but I really shouldn't. I'll be out of work, no money coming in. This isn't a good time to take a trip."

"Nonsense! You are not going to give me a speech about being poor, are you? I am absolutely positive that you have enough money to manage a trip here. So what are you waiting for? I know you – you'll start something else soon and then you'll never get over here."

Elie was tempted. If she was going to leave the magazine, why not take a break to consider all options? She'd love to spend time with Lexi, and she could stay with Devi or even at Syd's apartment in Tel Aviv. Yes, the idea might not be bad at all.

"You know what, Dev? I'll think about it. Maybe it is a good time to come, and forget about everything here. My friend, I may just take you up on your offer."

"Great, do that! Now, you take care, and call me soon with good news."

Elie hung up and realized that the prospect of being spontaneous, and not planning her life down to the hour, sounded excellent.

Thirty-One

Once she verbalized her decision to resign, Elie realized that it had been simmering below the surface ever since the talk with Walter. Although her job had been wonderful, there was no way she could continue under the new management. She thought about Syd's advice – to concentrate on dreams.

Hoping for inspiration, she scanned business blogs, read self-help books and made pro and con lists. She analyzed what she liked about her work, and what she didn't. She considered turning her cooking hobby into something more serious, but realized that she was not cut out to be a caterer, nor did she have the inclination to study to be a chef. She thought about high-end retail, perhaps selling imported decorative objects. That idea was scratched when she figured out who her clients would be – dealing with the whims of the wealthy was not for her. She hoped that something submerged in her subconscious would bubble up to the surface. For one of the first times in her life, she allowed herself to take it easy, believing that the solution would appear. There were clues, her brain was formulating a concept, so she waited patiently.

And then, it happened! Elie had her eureka moment. She knew exactly what she wanted to do.

She felt a resolve, a determination not felt for a very long time. She decided to go with her gut, to listen to the voices inside her head and for once, not block them out or denigrate them. True, a venture like this had never successfully been tackled before. Furthermore, her experience, while wide, was not sufficient to handle all aspects of the work. She would need a great deal of help. But, if she had learned anything in the last few months, it was to go with your instincts. Listen to your heart, even when the outside world is thrusting obstacles in your path.

She would create a magazine for women over the age of fifty – a glossy, gorgeous, intelligent journal that catered to the needs and interests of the "older" woman. Elie was absolutely convinced that the market was ripe for the concept.

She thought about all the talented, wonderful women she knew. Most of them were above the target age for publications like *Cosmopolitan*, *Elle* and *Vogue*. They were way past the *Good Housekeeping* and *Ladies Home Journal* stage, and older than the average *O* or *More* readership. This magazine would be geared for the woman who had been there, seen it and done it, for the woman with worldly experience, who would appreciate a direct and realistic approach to beauty, fashion, health, culture and business.

The idea boiled like a pressure cooker inside her brain, she could not let it go. She decided to release some of the steam by talking to Walter; he would know instinctively if she were on the right track.

He was in his office, speaking on the telephone. He saw her, and motioned for her to come in and sit down. As she waited, fiddling with the brass tacks on the chair's leather upholstery, she thought about the many times she had done just that, sat in this chair. Only this time, the conversation would be very different from all previous ones.

He hung up and looked at Elie. "Hey kid, how are you doing?"

Elie nodded her head. "Good Walter. What about you? What's the latest?"

"Too much hassle over this sale. I'm in meetings all the time. Unbelievable. I started this magazine with Denise as my secretary and Leigh as my researcher and that was it. Now I need teams of attorneys to sell it. I detest this legal wrangling. All the MBAs walking around here, documents to sign, accountants to call in. You'd think I was selling Microsoft. What about you? I guess you've also had a lot on your mind."

"Yes, I'd say that's a pretty fair understatement."

"And? Have you reached a decision?"

"Yes, Walter, I have. I think I know what I have to do. Actually, I feel as if I have no choice. The decision was sort of made for me."

"Look, Elie, before you say anything else. No one expects or wants you to leave. I realize that it could be awkward for you here and that things may change a great deal, but you're a very vital part of this magazine. Honestly, I'm not sure they can pull it off without you."

"Thank you for that vote of confidence, but I believe they'll be fine. Or they won't. But it won't be my problem. I've decided to leave the company."

"I see. And that decision is absolutely final? You are really sure about this, Elie?"

"Walter, to tell you that I'm positively sure, would be lying. No, of course I'm not sure. I'm scared to death." She leaned forward. "Do you realize that this is the only serious job I've ever had? I've thought of little else since you dumped the news on me. Coming at a time right after my decision to divorce and all that, well, the timing was about the worst it could be. But I'll be fine. I think I've made the right decision."

He had been playing with a fountain pen on his desk, but stopped. "Elie, I'm concerned about you. You have a very generous retirement package here. You'll get a nice chunk of money that you can live off and do nothing for a while. But you cannot sit at home. It's not your style, kid."

She smiled. "I've given it tons of thought and I do have an idea. I would like to discuss it with you, that's why I came in, but you've got so much more important stuff to deal with now, I'm hesitant."

"Oh for God's sake, get over yourself." He looked annoyed. "I don't know how many more days I'll be in the office and anyway, I need a diversion. We're speaking off the record and in complete confidence. I have no bugging devices here, so just spill it. Tell me what your plans are."

"I don't have any specific plans yet, Walter, but if you want to know what I'm thinking, it's to start a magazine geared for the quote unquote older woman." She waited for a reaction.

"Yes and ...?"

"And what?" She couldn't understand why he didn't react in a stronger manner. She was afraid he thought it was a stupid idea.

"What kind of women's magazine, what's the target audience,

where's the money going to come from? I want details."

"You don't seem surprised. I would have expected you to be a bit taken aback."

"Then you don't know me well, Missy. I think you would be perfect running your own magazine. And if I hadn't been so selfish and insistent on keeping you here all these years, I probably would have encouraged you to do it ages ago."

"Now you tell me!" She couldn't conceal her delight.

"Elie, you have everything it takes. You're talented, you're professional, you have great instincts and you have style. You are a very classy lady, and if anyone can pull this off, it's you. But then again, you haven't told me what you're planning. *Nu?*"

"I'm thinking of an upscale lifestyle magazine for the over-fifty woman. It would be filled with features that women are interested in: health, beauty, culture, design, fashion, finance. It would highlight the work of great female writers, maybe short stories. There are a million ideas dancing disco in my head. I'm just beginning to put it all together. The message is 'gray is gorgeous', something like that."

"I like it and I think it fits a market niche. Take Leigh Fairchild and run with it."

"Now, that's an idea!" Elie was getting more and more excited, but she tried to maintain her cool. "Walter, it means the world to me that you support the concept. However, there is so much to consider. One not so insignificant issue is that non-compete clause I signed with you. If the new owners hold me to it, this magazine of mine won't be able to get off the ground for a few years."

"Non-compete clause? What are you talking about?"

"You know damn well what I'm talking about. When the unions approached us several years ago, you gave everyone contracts and mine contained a non-compete clause. It said that if I left the magazine, whether I was fired or quit, I could not go to or start another magazine for a period of three years. Remember?"

He looked her straight in the eyes. "I remember no such thing. And *if* such a contract did happen to exist, I am quite sure it no longer exists. Isn't that funny, how things have a way of disappearing just when you need them? Very funny, indeed."

"Walter?"

"Don't bother me with this nonsense, Elie. I would advise you to go home and if you happen to find a copy of such a ridiculous contract, rip it up. Okay? Do I have your promise on that? As far as I'm concerned, I never heard of such a thing. End of subject."

"You are amazing. If you weren't married to such a lovely woman, I'd make a great big pass at you. You know I'm a divorced woman now, right?"

"Yes, I know, and I thank you. You just made an old man a very happy old man. Elie, I support this wholeheartedly. Go with your instincts. You have the talent to do this and I will help you in any way I can. How do they say it? *You go, girl!*"

Elie couldn't resist. She walked around to his side of the desk and gave him a kiss on the cheek. Walter Lavigne was probably one of the finest people she knew, and she would miss him a great deal.

He was embarrassed and motioned her away. "Okay, enough of this sentimentality. Get out of here, so I can get some work done. We still have a magazine to put out. Get back to your office and work. Until the day I'm officially signed out of here, I want this magazine to shine. Shine, do you hear me, shine!"

Encouraging words from Walter Lavigne meant a great deal, but Elie knew she had to take her brainchild one step further. She hired a market research firm and presented them with the concept. She decided to sit tight until they completed their study.

When the results of the market research survey were delivered to her at the office, she could barely breathe. She held off opening the package, preferring to wait until she got home. More than once, she was tempted to rip open the envelope, but her newly found determination won out.

She entered her apartment, kicked off her shoes, poured a glass of wine and headed into the den with the envelope. She had to trust this firm, they were top notch and known to generate an analysis that was thorough and accurate.

She took a sip of wine. Then she put the glass on the coffee table and ceremoniously slid the letter opener under the envelope flap. She pulled out the document knowing that there, in black and white, was the key to her future.

The document was thick, but Elie did not have to get past the letter clipped to the first page. It said there was an unusually positive response to the idea of a magazine for women over the age of fifty. Every audience they tested was unwavering in its enthusiasm for the project. With the right kind of promotion, they believed that the magazine would meet a definite market need. It was signed by the CEO, with wishes for success.

Elie let out a huge sigh of relief and dropped the pages into her lap. Her face moistened with tears. She felt like she had been given the keys to the Emerald City. She may have been wearing the ruby slippers all along, but the Wizard had just blessed her journey home.

Fortified by the results of the survey, Elie was now ready to move forward. She met with Syd and shared her news, that she would be quitting her job and starting her own magazine. Her friend thought it was brilliant. Elie joked that it took her nearly thirty years to make one major decision, and now, in a matter of months, she was making them non-stop.

She also decided that she would go to Israel. She wanted to see Lexi and the children and she felt the need to breathe different air for a change. The time away would provide her with a blank slate to formulate ideas, work on a business plan and socialize with her old friend.

She debated whether or not to stay with Devi at the residence. In the end, she decided not to impose, knowing how hectic the life of an ambassador's wife could be. Syd was happy to hand over the keys to her apartment in Tel Aviv, and the arrangements were made.

She met with Chloe and told her about starting the magazine. Her daughter loved the idea and promised to help her mother in any way she could. She brought over gifts for her sister's family and sent her mother off with kisses, hugs and a promise to look in on things at home. Elie realized that Chloe had turned into a responsible and lovely young woman, and she felt very proud.

Elie handed in her resignation and informed Walter and the staff that she would be taking a two-week vacation and would return to wrap up loose ends. She refused the offer of a farewell party. She preferred to exit that part of her life as quietly as possible.

Thirty-Two

From the moment the plane touched down at Ben Gurion airport, Elie felt renewed. It was a cloudy March day, and in spite of the ominous look of rain, she was thrilled to be back in Israel. Dovey surprised her by showing up at the airport, and he was friendly and talkative during the ride to Jerusalem.

As the car drove up to the house, Lexi rushed out to greet them. She pulled her mother into the baby's room to show off her sleeping son and asked a million questions while kissing and hugging her. Elie was happily overwhelmed.

When the two older children came home from school, they shyly said hello to their step-grandmother and clung to their father. However, when Elie emptied her bag of presents for them, they started jumping all over her and pulled her into their room to show her the toys she had brought them the last time.

It was a lively household and Elie got into the swing of things, thoroughly enjoying being with her daughter's family. By the end of the week though, she was exhausted and craved privacy. She looked forward to the next, quieter phase of her vacation.

Syd's apartment was in a high-rise building in north Tel Aviv. As Elie entered the lobby and introduced herself to the doorman, he handed her a small shopping bag. Inside, were a bottle of pomegranate port and a beautifully wrapped package of dried fruits and nuts. The note accompanying it read: *Dearest Eleanora, We welcome you with just a few of the seven species of the land of Israel. For the other culinary delights, come to dinner! Can't wait to see you. Devi and Lawrence.*

Elie entered the apartment, looked at the magnificent view of the Mediterranean Sea, and smiled. For the first time in months, there was nothing specific on her calendar, no documents to sign, no articles to edit and no pressing decisions waiting to be made. It was time to recharge batteries and plan the future.

The apartment phone rang and startled her. Very few people knew she was here.

"So my dear, is your party dress ready?"

It took her a second to realize who the voice belonged to. "Devi, hi! That was so kind of you to send over those goodies. What a wonderful welcome to Tel Aviv!"

"Pleasure, dearie. Now tell me, you did bring something festive to wear, didn't you?"

"How festive?"

"We're having a big do at the residence on Saturday night. Last minute, but important. Interesting people and lots of men. Actually, I don't know if they're single, but we have more men than women so I need you to fill up a chair. I promise you'll have a good time. Ellen will call you with the details. Have to run, talk to you later."

As usual, Devi was brief. Elie was glad she was staying at Syd's apartment and didn't have to rely on her old and always busy friend.

After the phone call, she wondered what was the right outfit to wear when visiting the home of the American ambassador for a Saturday night dinner party. Who would be there? Formal or semi-formal? As this was Israel, she had some slack. No one dressed up as they did in New York, but it was still an important occasion.

Luckily, she didn't have to obsess for very long. Ellen called the next day and provided all the details: appropriate outfit, when to show up and what type of ID to bring. The security was strict and it was important to be prepared.

She changed her mind about outfits all week and fussed endlessly while getting ready. She finally chose a straight cut, raspberry colored jacket with an open Nehru collar over black tapered pants. She accessorized it with a choker and earrings of pink crystals and wore simple black pumps. Her hair, still wavy and chin length, was no longer colored. She had chosen to let the gray come in naturally, and she loved the salt-and-pepper look. When she made a final check in the mirror, she felt quite sexy, a feeling that had been sorely missing from her repertoire of late.

The driver from the car service was waiting outside the building. He opened the back door for her.

"Shalom, missus. To Herzliya Pituach, right?"

"Yes, to Galei Tchelet Street. We're going to …"

"Ah, I bet we go to the American ambassador's house. Right? I knew it. You see, I got a feeling about these things. You know him in person?"

Elie didn't answer him. She did not want to be rude, but she was certainly not going to discuss her friendship with the Youngs.

As he pulled out of the parking spot, the driver turned around and faced her. "Listen missus, maybe you could do me a favor? My boy Avi is in the U.S. now. He went to make some money, but he needs a green card. Maybe you can ask the ambassador for us, to help him? I'm sure with the snap of his finger he can make Avi a green card. Or maybe the missus ambassador can help?"

Elie didn't hesitate with her response. "I'm so sorry, but ever since September eleventh, no one has privileges anymore. Connections don't help as they did in the old days. Even the ambassador himself can't do anything. I'm sorry."

"Yah, you know this nine-eleven thing really did a screw up on everyone. Such a shame. Nice boys like my Avi can't get no rights in America. Ah well, that's what we get for being Jews. They are all against us, the rest of the world. What can we do, right Missus? We just have to be grateful for our health and hope that the good lord will take care of everything else." He touched the *hamsah* hanging from his rear view mirror and drove the remainder of the trip singing along with the radio.

As they approached the area, Elie could see that it was going to be a big event. The street was closed off to traffic and only those with invitations, or residents, were allowed in. Chauffeur-driven embassy cars were lined up all along the street waiting to discharge their passengers. She told the driver to pull over, wished him a good night and got out to walk the remaining distance.

After passing through the security booth, she walked up the

steps of the imposing house and felt the majesty of America: the bronze eagle perched on the roof, the American flag flying proudly on the portico, an Andy Warhol painting on one side of the entrance hall and a Norman Rockwell on the other. She enjoyed the irony of that, the works of two such diametrically opposed artists displayed together in this gracious home.

The ambassador and his wife stood in the entryway and greeted each guest with several words and a handshake or kiss. Devi looked exquisite in a turquoise, raw silk jacket and long skirt with a side slit, no doubt Bill Blass or Donna Karan. She made a point of wearing American designers when she appeared at official functions.

The guests were ushered into a large living room that overlooked magnificent gardens and the sea. It was furnished with sofas upholstered in tones of lemon and cream, coffee and side tables of the American Federal period, a Steinway baby grand piano and huge abstract paintings on the walls. The atmosphere was regal. As the sun set, the sky turned from shades of persimmon to scarlet to plum, and the guests were captivated by the spectacular view.

The reason for the celebration was the signing of a special trade agreement between the U.S. and Israel. The guest list included dignitaries from the business and academic worlds, celebrities and artists from both countries. The guest of honor was the American Secretary of Trade. Elie was flattered that she had been invited, and excited.

Once the greetings in the main foyer were completed, Lawrence and Devi joined their guests for drinks. Devi winked at Elie, but did not have a chance to chat with her. After fifteen minutes, a set of French double doors was opened to reveal a formal dining room.

The room was filled with round tables, draped to the floor with white damask tablecloths that were edged in gold. Centered on each table was a six-branched crystal candelabra, which had swags of English ivy hanging from it. Tapered white candles were lit and glowing and crisp white napkins held together with gold mesh ribbons were set on gold and white monogrammed plates. The room glimmered and sparkled and Elie heard more than one gasp of admiration as they entered. Leave it to Devi, the consummate hostess, to create such a breathtaking setting, she thought.

As each person found his or her place according to the seating chart, hearty hellos and slaps on the back were heard. Despite the formal surroundings, this was Israel – many men did not wear jackets, some women were less than elegantly dressed and the atmosphere was friendly and warm.

Ambassador Young, sitting next to the wife of the guest of honor, made the first toast. He raised his glass, thanked the guests for coming, and spoke a few words about the trade agreement. The Secretary of Trade stood up, thanked his hosts, spoke about the importance of mutual trade interests and acknowledged the guests.

A trio of musicians played a lively combination of classical, Israeli and American music. The first course of seared moulard slices over wild mushroom risotto was served, accompanied by a California Cabernet, and the conversations began to flow.

After the dishes were cleared away, Devi stood up and invited the guests to move around and mingle. Several people from Elie's table took the opportunity to search out their partners, who were seated at other tables.

As she was contemplating a trip to the powder room for a hair and makeup check, Elie felt a touch on her shoulder. She heard a man's hesitant voice behind her.

"Elie? Elie Stein, is that you?"

She was surprised to hear her name mentioned. Up until this point, she knew no one at the party. She turned around to face the person who spoke, but did not recognize him. Then it dawned on her, and she froze.

He pulled out the chair next to her and sat down. "It is you! I knew it! I saw you from across the room and I could not believe my eyes. I thought it must have been someone who resembles you, but it's really you, isn't it? Oh Elie, it's so good to see you." He was smiling, as he took her hand in his.

She was stunned, and her heart started to pound. How handsome he still was, how smooth and commanding his voice was. "Hello, David," she said. It was all she could manage.

His green eyes were even softer then she remembered, with

many lines around them. His dark hair was still thick, but generously flecked with gray. He had aged, but quite attractively.

Not letting go of her hand, he started to bombard her with questions. "What are you doing here? How long are you here for? How do you still look so beautiful?"

Direct questions are good, she heard herself thinking. I am capable of answering those.

"I'm visiting my daughter, who lives here in Israel and Devi, I mean Mrs. Young, the ambassador's wife. She's the one who invited me." She was having trouble formulating her words, and she felt a lump in her throat.

"Devi? Wasn't that the name of your roommate when you were here?"

She was amazed, and almost paralyzed. "Yes, I can't believe you remembered that. It's the very same Devi."

"This is remarkable. I cannot believe I am talking to you. How long has it been? Over thirty years, no?"

"Yes, just about." Feeling like a moron, she could not bring the conversation to a higher level. This was David Abarbanel, *her* David Abarbanel, sitting next to her, asking questions.

"How long are you here for? We must get together. I want to hear all about your life." He smiled and waited for her response.

Many years ago, Elie fantasized about this, meeting David spontaneously. And she often wondered whether he would harbor any resentment towards her for the way she had ended things.

"I'm due back in New York next week." She finally gathered up the courage to ask him a question. "What about you? What are you doing here tonight?"

"I know Ambassador Young. We've met several times here and in Washington."

"Are you involved in politics?"

He laughed. "No, not at all. Elie, you're still so beautiful."

She was overwhelmed. She felt that if he stayed next to her much longer, she might faint. She grabbed her glass of water.

"I want to talk to you, to find out everything about you. But this is ridiculous, we can't catch up here. Where are you tomorrow? Let's meet for lunch and review our lives from where we left off.

Can you meet me tomorrow?"

"I don't know. I have so much I have to do. I promised that I would ..."

"Elie Stein, you are not getting away from me. I refuse to take no for an answer, absolutely no excuses. Clear your schedule tomorrow and meet with me. Otherwise, I will kidnap you tonight." He had a glimmer in his eye. "It's your choice. Tonight or tomorrow?"

Elie relaxed a bit and laughed. "Okay then, tomorrow it is. Where and when?"

"Where are you staying?"

She told him the location of Syd's apartment.

"Okay, great. There's a nice place not far from there called The Bookworm. It's a book shop and café."

"I know it, near Rabin Square, right?"

"Yes, exactly. I have a meeting nearby in the morning, so how about if we meet there at twelve, for lunch? Would that be convenient?"

"Yes. No problem." She was speaking without thinking, she could barely hear his voice over the beating of her heart.

Just then the music stopped and the guests were asked to return to their seats. David stood up and whispered in Elie's ear. "Don't you dare leave this room tonight without giving me your contact information. I want your phone number, address, and anything else I need in order to get in touch with you."

The sensation of his breath brushing her ear sent shivers up and down her spine.

"By the way, what's your last name? I assume it's changed?"

"Yes, no. I mean, it was different, but I'm back to Stein again."

"Okay, tomorrow it is. Don't disappoint me, Elie Stein." David touched her arm, and walked back to his seat.

As her dining companions returned to the table, Elie stood up and excused herself. She headed to the bathroom, locked herself in a stall and took a deep breath. And then another. Her heart was only just beginning to slow down. She could not get his face and voice out of her head. She scribbled her phone number and address on a piece of paper and quickly slipped it into David's hand on her way back to her place.

She barely got through the rest of the evening. She was too excited to speak intelligently to anyone at her table, she just smiled and managed some small talk. She tried desperately not to steal glances at David. She left the event as soon as it was politely possible, with a quick thank you to Devi and Lawrence.

Elie arrived back at the apartment, got undressed and into bed, but sleep was not possible. She lay awake for hours, as her head filled with memories. David Abarbanel!

Thirty-Three

It was a Sunday evening, beginning of the second semester, and Elie had finally convinced her roommate to go to folk dancing with her. She walked with Devi across the campus and heard the music from a distance. When they approached the social hall, they came upon two young men engrossed in conversation, unintentionally blocking the entrance. Devi flexed her flirting muscles and went into action. Elie was horrified.

As the men turned to face them, Elie was struck by how good looking the taller one was – well built, with wavy, dark hair and olive-toned skin. When she saw his intense green eyes, she nearly swooned.

Introductions were made. The tall one was David, pronounced *Daveed*, a name Elie knew she would never forget. Eyal was the other young man, and he took an immediate interest in Devi. The ping-pong of quips started, while they were still blocking the door.

David must have sensed Elie's discomfort, because he yanked his friend's arm. "Eyal, get out of the way and let them pass." He looked at Elie. "I apologize for the rude behavior of my friend. Ever since we discovered him buried at an archaeological site, we haven't been able to train him properly."

The girls laughed and walked into the room. Elie tried to forget the incident by joining the people dancing in a circle, but the moment left a strong impression.

A man in the center was calling out instructions over the loud music. He was deeply tanned and muscular, wearing a T-shirt, tight jeans and sneakers. He had a thick handlebar mustache, a booming voice and was so virile that Elie understood why the Sunday night folk dancing was incredibly popular among the female students.

After several minutes, she decided to take a break. She joined the hands of her partners to each other, and headed over towards the refreshments table. Out of the blue, David appeared next to her. He started to speak to her in perfect English. She calculated that he must have lived in America or had American parents.

She suddenly wished that she had some of Devi's ease with guys. Her friend was much more experienced in matters of romance – she had already experimented with sex – while Elie planned to stay a virgin until marriage. She found it difficult to answer David's questions with more than one word answers, but he persisted.

After a few minutes of chatting, her shyness took over and she excused herself to return to the dancing. David also joined in and they found themselves being paired off several times.

At the end of the evening, he asked Elie if he could walk her back to the dorm. She agreed and they took the slow route through the star-lit campus. The fronds of the palm trees were swaying slightly and the air was delightfully warm for February. When they reached her building, they sat outside on the grass, talking until it got very late. Finally, David made movements to leave. He asked Elie for the telephone number of her building and promised he would call. He said good night, gave her a light peck on the cheek and walked off.

She floated up to her room and wondered whether she would ever see him again. She was smitten.

By the end of the week, spent mostly obsessing about David, Elie gave up. She was annoyed at herself for being so naive. Why *would* he call? It had been just a walk on the campus.

Devi was no help. She advised Elie to forget about him and move on. She said there were lots more hunky Israeli fish in the sea and there was no point wasting time thinking about one that got away.

Elie decided to cheer herself up by going to downtown Tel Aviv. She took the bus to the Carmel Market, the outdoor marketplace that was packed and bustling on Fridays. Vendors in the fruit and vegetable stalls were singing songs promoting their produce, butchers were holding up dead chickens and calling out to the shoppers. Bootlegged cassettes of the latest rock music were sold next to children's toys, cleaning products, flowers and freshly baked pastries. Old women were pushing their carts, housewives were doing their pre-*Shabbat* shopping and students and tourists were everywhere taking pictures. Elie got lost in the cacophony of sights, smells and sounds.

She started shopping and loaded up her net bag with fruits, vegetables and chocolate *rugelach* from her favorite bakery. She stopped off at the meat shop, where chickens were roasting on spits, and ordered one. She asked the butcher if he could cut it up for her, and he responded, "Sure, *motek*, anything for such a nice girl." The routine always made her happy.

By early afternoon, Elie headed back to the dorms. Devi had left to visit relatives and their two Israeli suite-mates went home to spend *Shabbat* with their families. She was facing a weekend alone.

As she arrived at the building, arms loaded with packages, she kicked open the door, and stopped dead in her tracks. Sitting on the stairs in front of her was David, looking devastatingly handsome in his army uniform. She almost dropped everything.

"Oh my god! What are you doing here?" Everything hit her at once: excitement, anger and nervousness.

"Well, what do you think? I just happened to be walking by the dorms and figured I'd hang around for over an hour. I'm waiting for you, of course!"

"But, how did you know where I li …?" She realized that he had walked her home that night, and immediately wanted to take back her words. "I mean, how did you know when I'd return?" That sounded even more stupid.

"I didn't, I just took a chance. I'm just back from the army reserves, which started the day after we met, and I came straight here. And you sure kept me waiting. So hello, Elie Stein!"

He remembered her name! She could not have been happier, more excited or more nervous. All previous thoughts of anger towards David for not calling evaporated. She suddenly realized though, that she had a problem.

Up until now, Elie had been rather prudish – no boys allowed in her room. It was a rule that her mother had established and she respected it. She had to make a decision, and fast. She decided – and whatever her mother would say, was irrelevant.

They entered the suite and she invited David to sit down. She made them both Turkish coffee, which she had recently started to drink, and they chatted. At one point he looked at his watch and jumped up. The public transportation would be stopping soon because of *Shabbat* and he needed to get home. He asked if he could see her the next day and they made a plan.

When he left, Elie was way too excited to eat. She put away all the groceries, lay down on her bed and took out her diary. This was a day to remember!

She awoke early the next morning. After showering, dressing and eating a small breakfast, she remembered the chicken from the day before and decided to pack it. At exactly nine, she was downstairs with a picnic bag, a sweatshirt and her shoulder bag. David pulled up in an old blue Dodge.

"Well, good morning to you. What's all this?" He leaned over to open the door for her.

"Our lunch. I didn't know if you planned anything, so I brought along something to eat." She was taken by how good he looked – he was wearing jeans, a denim shirt and sandals.

"Great! I thought we'd find a fish restaurant in Tiberius, but yours is a much better idea."

As they drove north along the coastline, David pointed out the sights. They stopped in the town of Caesarea and visited the amphitheater and the ruins of the ancient port. Then they drove east to Zichron Yakov, a charming little town that was one of the first in the country known for its vineyards. The radio was playing the music of Arik Einstein, and they listened quietly.

Elie finally broke the silence. "So, now we're heading towards the Sea of Galilee?"

"Yes, I thought that would be nice. We call it the *Kinneret* by the way, supposedly because it resembles the shape of a lyre."

"Oops. I knew that. We had a boat trip there with the university;

I've always wanted to go back."

"Well young lady, today is your day!"

Although David's English was nearly flawless, he used some funny expressions. No one under the age of sixty had ever called her young lady, but she chalked it up to him having to speak to her in a foreign tongue. She knew she would not manage very well if she had to talk to him in Hebrew, and felt grateful for his English.

The windows were rolled down and the fresh air was blowing a crisp wind into the car. Her long hair was flying and David asked if she wanted the windows closed. She said no, and pulled it back into a ponytail. She laughed to herself, thinking about how much time she had spent blow-drying it that morning.

The conversation got around to the differences between Israeli and American kids. David commented on the experiences he had going to school in Washington, D.C., while his father was stationed there. Elie mentioned the apparent closeness between Israeli teens and their parents, and an openness that was foreign to her. Her roommates often spent weekends with their boyfriends, with their parents' knowledge and approval.

She mentioned how strict her parents were. "I have to tell them where I am at all hours of the day and night. It's a miracle that they let me come to Israel. I think they're overprotective because I'm an only child."

Elie liked the way David spoke about his family. He held his parents in great respect and there was an obvious affection for his sister, Sara, and his younger brother, Guy. His mother was a teacher and his father worked for the government, in military acquisitions. The four years they had spent in the U.S. left a strong impression on all of them, and they often spoke English at home in order to maintain it.

As they drove into the Galilee region, David pulled off the road and told Elie to look down. The view of the lake, shimmering blue in the sunshine, was stunning. Sure enough, it was shaped like a lyre, and seemed to go on forever.

"Let's drive around to the eastern shore and stop somewhere for our picnic."

"I'm in your hands, captain, whatever you say."

"Watch it miss, don't offer me everything just yet – I may take you up on that."

She blushed and remained silent.

He drove down a winding road until they reached a junction, then turned right. They passed undeveloped sections, which afforded open views of the lake, and areas which were dotted with restaurants and campsites. After several minutes, David turned the car onto a dirt path that meandered through a grove of banana plants. The path stopped almost at the water's edge.

"This is it, our secret hideaway." He parked on the side and turned off the motor. "Come on, let's go down to the beach with the food." As she left the car, she pushed down the door button to lock it, which made David laugh. "Elie, this is Israel, no one steals cars. You don't have to lock the door."

They took their things and headed towards the water. The ground beneath was sand and rocks and brush. Elie had never seen a beach environment like this before. It was both wild and tame. David spread out a blanket, knelt down and motioned for her to join him. "Okay, let's see what kind of feast you prepared for us."

She was emptying the bags, when all of a sudden, she slapped the side of her head. "Oh no! I knew I'd forget something – no plates and forks! Some feast I've prepared."

David smiled. "We have fingers, don't we? Food always tastes better this way." He picked up a chicken leg, waved it in the air and bit into it.

They ate their meal and afterwards David got up and put his hand out for Elie. "Come on, we have to try the water."

"Are you kidding?" She looked at him incredulously. "It must be freezing in there. We may be having a warm spell, but it's winter, David!"

"Never mind, just stick your feet in and then you can say you've been in the Kinneret." He pulled her up by both hands and dragged her over to the water's edge. "Come on, take off those sneakers and wet your toes!"

Elie did as she was told.

The bottom of the lake was covered with pebbles. The water was perfectly clear, she could see their feet beneath the surface.

And it was cold!

"Yikes, it's freezing! Can I please go back now?" She pleaded with David, as if she needed his permission, and ran back to the blanket complaining about the rocks she had to hop on to get there.

She dove down into the blanket, put on her sweatshirt and made chattering noises with her teeth. David grabbed the blanket ends and covered her feet. Then he laid the blanket down, took her feet in his hands and rubbed them.

Elie felt a flash go up and down her body. It was like an electrical jolt that started in her groin and went up to her neck. Her whole body reacted by shivering.

David noticed and offered her his jacket. Fearing that she would absolutely faint if he touched her again, she declined. She couldn't get over the previous moment.

They both lay down on the blanket. David turned towards her and raised himself on one arm. "Elie Stein, I like you a lot. What are we going to do about that?" He brushed some sand out of her hair.

"Why do we have to do anything about that?" She laughed and sprinkled sand on his arm.

David moved his finger towards her mouth and outlined her lips. He touched her cheek with the back of his palm and caressed it. Once again, Elie felt her whole body tingle.

He moved his body closer to hers, put his finger under her chin and pulled her face towards his. Ever so gently, he kissed her. She closed her eyes as she felt the touch of his lips on hers. She kissed him back.

When she opened her eyes, she saw that David was looking at her. He pulled his face away and smiled. She did the same. She was grateful for the break from his kiss. She needed to catch her breath, to regain the composure she had almost lost.

David turned from her to lie back on the blanket. He moved his arm over towards her and took her hand in his. They lay like that, silently, for a long time.

Elie finally spoke. "This is heaven. Thank you for bringing me here."

"My pleasure. I love it here, too, but there are a few other places in the area I want to take you to. Are you ready to leave our little hideaway?"

"I guess, if I have to."

They gathered up their belongings and headed back to the car. As they drove around the lake, the radio station was playing Israeli oldies and Elie recognized many of them. She sang along.

"How do you know all these songs? I was born here and I don't even remember them."

"From summers at camp, and Hebrew school, and Jewish youth groups." She was glad that her background gave him cause to be impressed.

He pulled into several sites along the lake and explained their importance. There was Kibbutz Ein Gev, which was a popular place for volunteers who wanted to work the fields; there was the site where Jesus was said to have walked on water; and Capernaum where he healed people. David pointed out the ruins of the ancient synagogue there. Elie was impressed by his knowledge and obvious pride in his country.

As the afternoon wore on and the sun started to set, they headed back to the university. When they approached the dorms, David pulled the car over, but did not turn off the engine. Elie hoped that he would say something about getting together again.

She spoke first. "I've had a great time, David. Thank you for a wonderful day."

He put his hand on her shoulder. "Me, too, Elie. I'd like to see you again. I have two classes on Monday, can we meet then?"

They arranged a time and place, and he leaned over and kissed her goodbye. When she got to her room, she found Devi there. Elie breathlessly recounted the events of the day, telling her almost everything. She told about the kiss, but kept the electrical jolt to herself, wanting to secretly treasure that. She was sure she would remember it for a lifetime.

Elie and David became a couple, and the relationship exclusive. David was aware that this was Elie's first serious romance and he did not push her to have sex. Although they went further than the kissing stage, there was always a point at which he backed off.

Elie finally decided she was ready for the next step and asked for Devi's advice.

"Well, it's about time! I knew you wouldn't wait until marriage, that's so old-fashioned. So, what do you need to know?"

Elie was surprised by how far Devi had come from the religious girl she knew back home, but she was grateful for her knowledge.

Devi accompanied her to the gynecologist at the university clinic. Elie answered his questions, got through the examination, and left with a prescription for birth control pills. The whole experience of taking her first step towards womanhood was over in no time. She began taking the pills and planned her next step.

It was a Friday night and David was coming over for dinner. She had a premonition of how the evening would end.

He arrived with a bunch of sunflowers and a bottle of wine. "*Shabbat shalom*," he said as he kissed her. He looked handsome in an ironed white shirt, khaki pants and brown leather loafers. His hair smelled of shampoo and his face was smooth. Elie wondered how she would be able to survive dinner.

After they finished eating and washed up the few dishes, David suggested they go out for a walk to enjoy the star-filled night. Elie agreed, taking the edge off her nervousness.

They walked around the neighborhood, passing the home of Golda Meir, where he spoke about her years in power, and the Land of Israel Museum, where he referred to the collections it held. As the hour grew late, they headed back.

When they entered Elie's suite, David pulled her towards him and kissed her passionately. She responded in kind and led him into the bedroom.

They had spent a few nights there, when the other girls were away, even pushing the beds together, but they never went all the way. David pulled her down and started tickling her, breaking the tension that she had been feeling. After she faked a few screams and showed how indignant she was, he enveloped her in his arms. He started to kiss her and undid the buttons of her blouse. She did the same to his shirt.

After a few minutes, they were both in their underwear. Elie put her hands behind her back and undid the hooks of her bra. Then she leaned down and pulled off her panties. The wine she drank for dinner was still having an impact, alleviating her shyness.

David's reaction was delayed. He was kissing Elie's face and his hands were stroking her hair. Suddenly he saw that she was naked and he stopped. "Elie, what are you doing?" He moved away slightly.

"I'm on the pill and I want you to make love to me, David." She managed to get it out.

"But you never ... I thought ... Are you sure? I can wait. We really don't have to ..."

She moved towards him and kissed him, drowning out his objections. He understood and said no more. He moved his body partially on top of hers, while slipping off his underpants. Elie had never seen a man's totally naked body before, and certainly not in her own bed. She thought he was beautiful.

He continued to touch and kiss her, caressing her body with his hands and lips. He moved his hand between her legs and touched her gently. She felt as if she would die of his touch and could not control herself from letting out sounds of pleasure. He slowly eased himself inside of her, watching her face for any signs of pain.

Elie felt a momentary sting and she understood that she had just lost her virginity. David raised himself on his elbows and looked down at her. "Are you okay? Does it hurt?" She shook her head and kissed his face.

He began to move in and out, slowly. The sensation of having a part of his body inside of her was remarkable. Suddenly, his whole body quivered and he let out a sound. Elie felt a rush of something warm inside. Neither said a word.

He moved off her and propped himself up on his arm. "You surprised me. I had no idea that you were on the pill. Tell me something, Miss Stein, have you just seduced me? Did you plan this?"

"Well actually, I sort of did plan this. Is that a bad thing?"

He smiled broadly. "Not at all. Plan it anytime you want."

The rest of the semester breezed by. Elie kept up with her studies and spent her free time either with David, or thinking about him. He attended classes and did his military reserve service and they saw each other on some weekdays and most weekends. When her roommates were away, they slept in her room. On the rare occasion they were there, David usually found an apartment of a friend to borrow or they just didn't spend the night together.

Elie dreaded June, which meant the end of her year in Israel, and she began to think seriously about staying in the country and transferring to the regular university program. It meant a massive overhaul of her life: giving up her design studies, living away from family and friends, embarking on an intensive Hebrew course to improve her language skills. Although she loved being in Israel, it was not something she would have considered if David had not been in the picture. She wondered what he would say about her idea.

By early May, she decided to broach the subject. "David, we never talk about it, but I think we should. My ticket home is for June. What's going to happen to us?" They were at their favorite place on the beach.

David looked at her and said with a serious tone, "I haven't wanted to think about it."

Elie was surprised. Usually he was positive and talkative.

He continued. "I was hoping that I could convince you to stay for the summer."

"But how? I have to vacate the dorm." She was relieved that he seemed to be thinking like she was.

"You could stay with us; my parents would be fine with it. They like you a lot."

She had met his family several times and felt comfortable with them, but not with his idea.

"Maybe, but my folks wouldn't be fine with it." Just thinking of how her parents would react made her squirm.

"But why? They know we've been together, don't they?" He looked puzzled.

"David, it's one thing knowing there's a guy in the picture when their daughter is away at school. They don't really have any of the details. But, letting me stay with you, unsupervised, not part of the school program? That's another story. My parents are old-world, they're not like Israeli parents. They're much less permissive."

"I see. Well, what about you? Have you been thinking about us and what's going to happen?"

"Are you kidding? Constantly. I've even thought of transferring here, applying to the regular university program."

"Would you do that? Could you?" He stopped playing with the sand and looked surprised and eager.

"I'm not sure. It's a major decision. I just don't know. Truthfully, if it weren't for you, I would never think of it. I don't know if my parents would allow me."

"It would be a very big deal for you, wouldn't it? You'd have to give up your career plans, since there's no interior design program here that I know of." He stopped for a moment and then continued speaking.

"To tell you the truth, I was thinking of coming to New York, maybe to do an MBA program there. I would have to finish my studies here first. I don't want us to part, but I'm afraid I don't have a solution, Elie Stein. And usually, I'm very good at solutions."

Elie was touched that David had been thinking of coming to live in the U.S. It gave her an encouraging sign. She decided to write her parents a long letter, and explain to them what she was thinking of doing. She would tell them that she had fallen very much in love with David, and would like to stay in Israel and complete her studies there.

The response to the letter was a phone call with an absolute directive – under no circumstances was she to stay in Israel. Her mother was insistent that she come home according to the original plan. She was sensitive enough not to minimize the relationship with David, she said she was sorry, but the decision was final.

Elie was surprised by her mother's harsh reaction. She had rarely been so uncompromising. It was not like her. Elie resented it, but she realized that she did not stand a chance. Her only hope was to go home and convince her parents to let her return.

As the day of departure neared, Elie obtained permission to travel with David to the airport, rather than on the bus with the other students. She spent her last night in the dorm with Devi and their roommates in an emotional farewell pajama party. David promised to pick her up early in the morning.

When he arrived, she was taking snapshots of the suite. Devi had plans to spend the summer with relatives in Israel, so the two girls hugged for several minutes and promised to be in touch by frequent letters. Elie took one more look around, put the key on the table and walked out. She was sad to be closing such a significant chapter of her life, but was hopeful that she would return soon.

They had a few hours before she had to be at the airport and she allowed David to plan her time. Elie was quiet, her feelings were confused, her stomach jittery and she was filled with sadness. She did not want to part from David.

They drove the short distance to the beach, parked the car and David led her to their usual spot on the sand. As they approached, Elie saw that someone was standing at the edge of a blanket waving to them. The beach was crowded but there was no doubt that the person was signaling them. Elie looked at David and he smiled, but said nothing.

They reached the blanket and Elie saw that a picnic had been set up. There were also sunflowers in a jar weighed down with sand, two glasses and a bottle of champagne in a plastic bucket. A bunch of balloons was secured to the edge of the blanket with a pile of rocks. Standing guard over all this was Eyal. Elie could not believe her eyes.

"Madame, your feast awaits." David smiled at her and slapped Eyal on the back. "Good job, my man, you're the greatest."

"I don't believe this. How did you arrange all this? Eyal, you're amazing!" Elie was beaming.

"Not me, Elie, your boyfriend arranged it all, I just kept watch. Now, I shall leave you two to have your romantic breakfast on the beach. *Bon voyage* Elie. It's been a pleasure knowing you and I hope we meet again." He kissed her, high-fived David and went off.

Elie stood there with tears falling from her eyes. She felt that she could collapse with all the emotions that were gurgling inside of her.

They sat on the blanket and drank the champagne. She didn't care about arriving at the airport tipsy, she hoped it would help ease her sadness. She tried to eat some of the food but was too nervous. After a while, it was time to get moving. David scooped up everything from the blanket, except the flowers.

"Why don't we leave these? Maybe another couple will enjoy them." He smiled, but looked sad, as he put his arm around Elie.

They drove to the airport in silence. Elie tried to memorize every stretch of the road, the palm trees in the distance, the scattered neighborhoods, the exit signs along the highway. She wanted to burn the landscape into her brain.

They arrived at the airport and saw the busload of students ahead of them. She knew this was it. She would have to part with David in order to be with the group when they went through security.

He turned off the engine and got out of the car. He took Elie into his arms and held her for several minutes. Then he lifted up her face and kissed her. He reached into his pocket, pulled out a little blue box and handed it to her.

"Please don't open this until you're settled on the plane. I wanted you to have something from me. I hope you like it."

"David, I don't know what to say. Not just for this gift, but for everything. These months with you have been the best in my life. I ... I ..." She started to cry.

He wiped the tears from her face. "Elie Stein you are an amazing girl and I am crazy about you. Actually, I love you, Eleanora Stein."

It was the first time he had said those words. Elie felt like she would lose her composure. "I love you, too, David Abarbanel. I love you very, very much."

They stood at the curb holding and kissing one another. The other students started teasing them. Elie resented that her final moments with David were disturbed by the lewd comments of her friends, but it eased the tension. They both laughed and pulled away from each other.

David spoke. "Okay, I can't stay here any longer because then *I'll* start to cry. Have a great flight, get some rest and call me when you get home. I'll be at my parents' house so try me there, okay?"

Elie said yes and kissed him once more. She watched him get into the car and drive off. She looked at the box in her hand and put it in her purse. She would keep her promise not to open it until she was on the plane.

Thirty-Four

The book shop entrance was clearly visible but Elie nearly missed it. She entered, feeling nervous and self-conscious. She walked towards the café in the back and spotted him immediately. David stood up and pulled out a chair.

"Elie Stein, I hardly slept a wink all night and it's entirely your fault. I have so much to ask you, so let's get the ordering over with. What would you like to eat?"

He was wearing a black polo shirt and jeans, and looked even sexier than he did in a suit. She was having trouble accepting the fact that this was "her" David. He was still so handsome, and manly. Every one of her nerves seemed to be on high alert.

"Elie?"

She focused. "Oh, sorry. I don't know, David. I drank too much wine last night so I'd like to keep it light now. What do you suggest?" She was way too excited to think about making selections from a menu, especially one in Hebrew. "Why don't you just order what you know is good. I'll be fine with whatever."

"Good idea." He called the waitress over and ordered a plate of mini-sandwiches and two cappuccinos.

The drinks were brought over immediately and when the waitress walked away, David started to speak. "Elie, I want to hear about everything. I want to know what you've been doing with your life since you walked out of mine. I cancelled my afternoon meeting and I don't intend to let you go until I know absolutely everything. And then, only to let you rest, change, and go out to dinner with me." He looked directly into her eyes and smiled.

Elie put down the cup. "Where do I begin? What would you like to know?"

"Let's start with the social security details – marriage, children, work."

She provided a brief rundown of her life, keeping it to the basics. David showed interest and asked questions.

When the plates of food arrived, Elie felt grateful for the break. The rehashing was making her uncomfortable. Although eating was not really in the forefront of her mind, she realized that she was quite hungry when she saw the food. She had not been able to swallow a thing since last night.

She commented that the platter of mini sandwiches and dips reminded her of tapas dining in New York.

"I know what you mean. This place in general makes me think of New York. The whole area around here and over by Basel Street has been gentrified. It reminds me a lot of the Upper West Side, and what it went through in the eighties."

Elie put down her fork and looked at David with a quizzical expression. "How do you know about the Upper West Side in the eighties?"

"I do travel, my dear. And as it happens, quite often to New York. You don't need to be a native to appreciate the neighborhoods of Manhattan. Why the surprise?"

"I'm sorry. I guess that sounded condescending. It's just that I live on the Upper West Side, it's been my home since I married, and it jarred me to hear you speak about it so familiarly."

"You mean, during all the times I was there, we might have run into each other? We could have passed each other on Columbus Avenue?"

"Yes, very likely." She stopped to think about the possibility, but it seemed too bizarre. She needed to change the subject. "Okay, David, now it's your turn. What about your life? Are you married? Children? Work?"

"I'm divorced and I have one son."

"Oh, come on. You have to do better than that." She crossed her arms in a mock defiant gesture.

He laughed. "How did I know that you wouldn't accept my answer? I suppose I have to dredge up all the nitty gritty details?"

"You sure do."

"Okay. I was married in my early thirties. I finally gave up pining over you and married the first woman to ask."

"Oh sure. I bet it was just like that."

"You'd be surprised how much it was like that. The truth is that I was getting to that age where it was weird in Israel not to be married. It seemed easier to do the socially acceptable thing than to resist. Unfortunately, it was wrong from the beginning."

"Why?"

"Nothing dramatic. We both knew it wasn't right. Vered was recovering from a broken relationship, I was in the right frame of mind, so we got married. We had our son, Ben, but not long after that, we realized that our marriage was not working. It was an amicable split and we are on very good terms. It was years ago and since then I've managed to survive on my own quite well. She's remarried to a good man and the story ends happily."

"And your son? Ben is his name?"

"Yes, and he's amazing. Truly extraordinary and, no, I am not saying that because I am a prejudiced father. He's out of the army and just finished his first year at Hebrew University."

"Not Tel Aviv U.? Like father, like son?"

"No. Ben follows his own path. He wanted to be away from home, Jerusalem was just far enough."

"And your work? What do you do?" Elie could not eat anymore, she just wanted to look at and listen to the man opposite her.

"I'm a business consultant. I worked in computers for a while, made enough money, took a break and now I'm involved with several companies. I'm on a few boards of Israeli corporations and that's how I came to the ambassador's house last evening."

Elie had a feeling that he was minimizing his accomplishments, but she did not pursue the matter. She was dying to ask him the other questions on her mind. His family – were they all well? Did his little brother become the pilot he wanted to be? Did he really miss her after she left Israel, or was he exaggerating? She could not get the questions out, unwilling to open the compartment where all that was stored. Managing the present was doable, acknowledging and referring to the past was too painful.

After they finished eating, Elie began to feel claustrophobic in the café. She was about to suggest they leave, when David spoke.

"Elie, what are your plans for the rest of your time here?"

"I was thinking of doing a bit of Tel Aviv touring this week. But mostly, I want to give myself an opportunity to rest, to think things through and to make some decisions about my future."

"Good. Then I volunteer, no I insist, on being your tour guide. Let me show you around to some of the places you may not have been to before. And as you might have guessed, I won't take no for an answer."

"I'm your captive?"

"I like the sound of that. Why don't we start with the Tel Aviv Museum of Art? They have an exhibit of the Vienna Secession Movement on now and I heard it's wonderful. Can I convince you?"

Elie smiled, telling him that the museum was on her list. David paid the bill and they left.

"Elie, did you hear me? I asked what you thought of Gustav Klimt."

They were standing in a gallery, surrounded by the works of some of her favorite artists. She was totally lost in the Klimt in front of her – the extraordinary use of colors, the intricate patterns. There was something so deliciously seductive about his work.

"I love him. I've always been attracted to his paintings."

"Me, too. Some people think his work is a bit kitschy, but I don't. He was a fascinating man."

David shared what he knew about the Austrian artist; about Klimt's proclivity to draw the female body and the controversy surrounding him because his work was considered boldly erotic. He used symbolism in an overtly sexual way and many found it disturbing. But his colors! The vibrancy and the propensity to use gold leaf was new and thrilling. He was one of the founders of the Secession Movement in the late nineteenth century and came to be considered one of Vienna's greatest artists.

Their meanderings led them to the work of Joseph Hoffmann, an Austrian architect and designer. David mentioned that his work looked like a prelude to the buildings of Frank Lloyd Wright, who was known on the other side of the Atlantic. Elie was surprised by the wealth of his interest and comprehension of the subject.

As they walked around the museum, Elie found herself more and more drawn to David. It seemed that the handsome prince of her youth had turned into a man of great substance. She was fascinated by him, and enjoyed listening to his analysis of art, architecture, even the layout of the museum itself.

She could not help but make the inevitable comparison to Philip. It had been impossible to walk through a museum with her husband – he always behaved as if he was suffering. His appreciation of art went only as far as its investment potential or how it complemented a room's décor. Elie had long ago figured out that this was not something they could share, and she stopped requesting that he accompany her to museums. The difference in attitudes between the two men was glaring.

When they completed their tour, it was late afternoon, and Elie felt tired. She told David she'd like to get back to the apartment. They caught a taxi and as they rode there, she told him about Syd, and how fortunate it was that she could use her friend's apartment.

Suddenly David changed the tone of the conversation. "Elie, I'm a businessman, not a spiritualist. However, I can't help but feel that some force of nature brought us together again. I would like very much to see more of you. How about tonight, after you've had a rest, we go out for dinner? There's a great place on HaYarkon Street called Boccaccio – delicious Italian food. Do you know it?

"No, but I love Italian food. That sounds great."

"Good. Then, afterwards, maybe we'll head over to Neve Tzedek. It's sort of an artist colony, or Soho, if you will. Are you familiar with that area at all?"

"Now it's my turn to get huffy. I have been here before, you know. I am very much aware of Neve Tzedek and all its charms."

"*Touché*. So we'll have a wonderful dinner, followed by a walk around that neighborhood. If I pick you up at seven, does that give you enough time to have a nap and look even more beautiful tonight?"

She laughed. As she got out of the cab, she brushed his cheek lightly with her lips.

Upon entering the apartment, Elie didn't know what to do first: fall into bed, call Devi, try to find Syd in New York, or just sit and contemplate the extraordinary events of the last twenty-four hours. She picked up the phone and called Devi.

She was connected immediately.

"Hi, Dev. How are you?"

"Great El. Good to hear from you. Sorry we didn't get much of a chance to talk last night."

"No problem. I didn't think we would be able to. Devi, I want to thank you for inviting me. It was really a lovely evening, and I enjoyed it thoroughly."

"Good. I'm glad. Now tell me, who was that man I saw you sitting with? You two looked pretty intense in your conversation."

"You're not going to believe it. I have been dying to tell you."

"*Nu?*"

"Do you remember David, my boyfriend when we were students here?"

"Yes, of course."

"That was him."

"*No!*"

"*Yes! Yes! Yes!* He recognized me and came over. It was amazing. I just got back from spending the day with him."

"Oh Elie, that's fabulous! Imagine, you met him here! I wish I could talk more but we're going to a minister's house in Jerusalem, and I have to leave soon. We'll have to speak some more. I'll call you. Wow! Unbelievable!"

Elie hung up and felt frustrated. She wanted to talk, but as always, Devi was pressed for time. She got undressed, got into bed, and tried to relax. Just as her eyes were closing, the telephone startled her. She picked up the receiver next to the bed and could not believe whose voice she heard.

"Hey, Elie girl! How're ya doing? I just took a chance that you would be in the apartment now. How's it going?"

Elie smiled and thanked the gods of providence. "Syd, you have no idea how perfect it is that you called now. How could you have known?"

"Because we're on the same wave length, of course. We're too old to be getting our periods together, but I guess living in the same building has built up our energy radar, or whatever you call it. What's going on?"

Elie sat up in bed and leaned against the headboard, knowing that this was a conversation that warranted her full attention. She relayed the story, from the previous night through the events of the day.

"Oh my god! I absolutely do not believe this. This is just too marvelous for words. Actually, you know what? I do believe it. You so deserve this in your life. This man has been returned to you. A gift! And you better damn well accept it."

"Oh, Syd. I don't know. It's so confusing to me."

"Confusing, *my ass*. This is not confusing. This is a fucking miracle and you, my dear girl, are going to thank your stars or better yet – go to the Western Wall and put a note in one of the crevices. I'm not kidding, Elie. This is just what you need."

"Syd, seriously. I'll tell you what's bugging me."

"I'm listening."

"I could easily fall for this man. He's even better looking than he was then, he's sexy and mature and smart like you can't believe. Oh my God, Syd, we walked around the museum and he was an absolute fount of information. Can you imagine Philip in that situation?"

"Give me a break. Philip should not even be spoken about in the same context. So, the guy is not only a hunk, but cultured as well. I don't get it. What's the problem?"

"Syd, you know I'm at a crossroads. I really wanted to spend this time thinking about the next stage of my life. I'm serious about starting the magazine and I have to start planning it. I was hoping to do that here, as well as see Lexi, have a rest and be rejuvenated. You think I want to complicate things now with a romance? If that's what he's offering, I'm not sure. For all I know, he has someone."

"Listen. I understand you. Really I do. I know that it could be easy to fall into something with him and forget everything else. But why can't you have both? Tell me, why can't you have a wonderful romance with him now, then come home and start the magazine? Elie, we're living in a new age. You can have everything."

"I don't know. It sounds too good to be true. Syd, this guy was the love of my life. I know I was only a girl when we had our romance, but I'm telling you, it was something out of this world. I don't want my heart broken again. But then again, I'm really nuts. We had one afternoon together. Why am I carrying on like this?"

"Because, you're you. You're sweet and a tad naive. Elie, listen to me, and listen well. If you do manage to capture this guy and have a romance and your heart gets broken, so be it. At least you'll have one hell of a fling, and something to remember forever." She stopped for a moment, but then continued.

"But you know what? It won't happen. Because you're in charge now, you can control what's happening. You can travel, he can travel, there's email, video phones, Skype, all that ridiculous cyber stuff that makes communication between two people across an ocean feel like they're across the street from each other. You can do this, Elie. You have to trust me. This is meant to be. It's *bashert!*"

"Now who's getting carried away?" Elie laughed out loud. "Have I mentioned lately how much I love you?"

"No, you haven't, but I'll take that as confirmation that you do. How's the apartment? Did you find everything okay there?"

"Perfect. I couldn't ask for anything better. Your housekeeper was here, she filled the fridge, left fresh flowers. I love it here."

"Good. Enjoy it, but don't get too comfy. You have to come home and start a new life. Everything is fine here. I went into your apartment to check on things. Gloria was there and the place is sparkling. I spoke to Chloe and she's fine. So, do you need any other advice or can I hang up knowing that you're going to go for it with this David of yours?"

"What about you Syd? How are the doggies? Business? The situation at the office?"

"Dogs are fine. Work is more or less back to normal. Things have calmed down, but truthfully? I'm getting tired of this life. I'm really considering a change. Maybe it's time to retire."

"No way! You'd be lost without something interesting to keep you busy."

"Yes, I know. That is exactly the problem. I know I need to do something else, but just thinking about it gives me a headache, so I'm avoiding the subject. Anyway, I'd rather just arrange your life, if that's okay with you."

"It sure is. I can't think of anyone I'd rather have arranging my life."

"Okay, it's a deal. I have to get off now, but I am so glad I called. I was itching to talk to you and it looks like I found you at just the right time. I want you to go for it, Elie girl. Be with this luscious David and have a great time. Will you do that? Just enjoy yourself?"

"I promise you, I'll think about it very seriously. I'll keep you posted."

"You do that. Bye for now. Be cool."

Elie hung up. She reached over to the alarm clock, set it for six, and fell asleep, exhausted and happy.

She awoke groggy, unsure if it was day or night. Not used to naps during the day, it took a few seconds to realize where she was. She showered and dressed – deciding on pencil thin black pants, an off-the-shoulder, cream-colored sweater and silver hoop earrings. When the doorman announced David at seven, she was ready.

He walked into the apartment carrying a bouquet of sunflowers and presented them to her as he kissed her on both cheeks.

"Wow, you look gorgeous. All this just for me?" He moved back to admire her.

"Don't embarrass me. And thank you. You remembered that I love sunflowers."

"Yes, of course I did." As he walked in, he looked around. "Wow! This is some apartment. What a view!"

The huge windows had a commanding southwest view of Tel Aviv and the water. The lights of ancient Jaffa sparkled in the distance.

"I know. I love it here. Syd hardly uses it anymore since her husband passed away, but I guess she hangs on to it for sentimental reasons. I'm sure not complaining. Would you like a drink, David?"

"A glass of wine would be great."

"Coming right up." As she walked to the kitchen with the flowers, the situation reminded her of the date with Joshua. She returned with two glasses and a bottle of wine, and as David took them from her, thoughts of Joshua evaporated.

David poured the wine and raised his glass to hers. "Here's to a lovely evening. And, here's to finding you again. If you haven't already figured it out, I'm very excited about this."

When they left the apartment, Elie wondered if she should have called for a car. It was difficult to find a taxi on the street in the evening. But David guided her down the block, towards a red Alfa Romeo. She smiled, thinking back to the old car he used to drive around in.

"Quite a difference from the last time you rode with me, with that old blue Dodge of my parents. I promised myself that one day I'd be driving a sports car – it's not the Porsche of my dreams, but it makes me happy. My mid-life crisis, solved with a car." He held the door open for her.

They drove south along Tel Aviv's shoreline, passing hotels and restaurants on the left, and the promenade and beach on the right. He turned left onto a side street and parked the car in a lot.

He took Elie's arm as they walked up the two steps to the restaurant. The owner, Nizza, kissed David on the cheek, warmly greeted Elie and led them to one of the candle-lit tables near the window. The lights were low, the background music was a mix of jazz and classical, and only a few other couples were dining.

The waiter came by with the menus and offered them a drink. He recommended a passionfruit cocktail and both David and Elie nodded.

"I shouldn't have agreed so quickly; sweet alcoholic drinks go right to my head." She laughed nervously.

"Not to worry. I'll make sure you get home unharmed. And anyway, we're in no rush. Let's take our time and savor the evening. I want to make every moment with you count. Have I mentioned how beautiful you look tonight?"

"David Abarbanel, you sure know how to make a woman feel

special. Where did you learn to be so charming?"

"Why? Wasn't I charming when you knew me?"

"Yes, actually you were."

When the drinks arrived, David proposed a toast. Just then, the music changed and Elie became very excited.

"Oh, I adore this piece of music. It's one of my favorites. It's Pachelbel's ..."

"Canon in D Major. I love it, too."

She couldn't believe it. "David, we share a passion for so many of the same things – art, now music. I'm amazed." She was wondering if this man could be any more perfect.

"Well, if the truth be known, I told Nizza to play that piece. It's the only one I recognize. You needn't be so impressed."

"You didn't!"

He laughed. "No Elie, I didn't. I see you have not lost your naiveté. You're still so gullible."

"Don't you dare tease me while this is playing. I love it and don't want to be disturbed. Hush!"

He made a zipping motion across his lips and remained silent until the music changed.

They reviewed the menus and David made a few suggestions. Elie deliberated between the grilled sea bass in a Pernod cream sauce and the filet steak in a port and wild berry reduction. She asked David for his advice. His response was that they should decide what type of wine they felt like, and then choose the entrée.

"Well, I must say, that's an original way of choosing one's dinner. Why didn't I ever think of that before?"

"It's simple. White wine, we opt for the fish. Red wine, we go for the steak. On the other hand, we could mix it up a bit and do something daring, like a Bordeaux and seafood. What do you say to that?"

She laughed, appreciating David's easygoing manner. Philip was finicky about wines and his behavior in restaurants had often made her feel uncomfortable, and ignorant. She felt relaxed enough to divulge her honest preference.

"You know what? I like white better than red, especially Chardonnay or Viognier. Plus, I always find it easier to get up in the morning if I've had white wine the night before."

"Then Chardonnay it is and let's go with the sea bass and the seafood risotto. Sound good?"

"Sounds perfect."

Nizza walked over to the table, bringing a tray of her antipasti specialties, along with the homemade focaccia.

David thanked her in Hebrew and then switched to English. "Nizza, you never forget. How I love this focaccia of yours! Elie, the caramelized garlic is something one can only dream about."

David mentioned to Nizza that this was a reunion for the two of them. That the last time they had dinner together was more than thirty years before.

Nizza's face lit up. "How wonderful! You know – this is not the first time I have heard this. Many times we have Americans meeting here with old Israeli friends or lovers. I'm honored that you chose to come here tonight. Now, I must get back into my kitchen and see to your food."

As she walked away, Elie commented to David. "She's lovely. She radiates warmth and kindness. I am sure her food will be marvelous. How do you know her?"

"Since the restaurant is close to the American Embassy, whenever I have meetings with Americans I suggest it. I've been coming here for almost twenty years and I've never been disappointed. And you're definitely right about Nizza, she is a *balabusteh* of the first order. She makes everyone feel at home. She's that perfect combination of earth mother, Italian mama and sensuous woman. And her Boccancini salad and halvah parfait are to die for."

"David Abarbanel, you are quite the *foodie!*"

"*Foodie?* Okay, now you've got me."

Elie laughed. "Sorry about that. Guess I'm too influenced by American slang. A foodie is someone who loves to eat, to cook, to read about food, to talk about food. A gourmand, you could say, in the most positive sense."

"Umm. I wouldn't say I fit into all those categories, but I do know what I like. And I definitely like to eat!"

When their meal arrived, they exchanged tastes, and spoke about their favorite foods, the best dinners they ever had and their favorite restaurants in New York, Paris and Italy. It was an easy, flowing conversation, touching on many topics. After the waiter cleared the plates away, David's expression became serious. He wiped his mouth with his napkin. "Elie, you know there's an elephant here."

"Excuse me?"

"Maybe I said that wrong. My English is not always as perfect as I want it to be. I think there's an expression about an elephant being in the room? What I mean is, there's a topic we are dancing around and I think we need to get it out on the table."

She knew at once what he was referring to, but couldn't bring herself to admit it.

"I'm listening."

"You and I shared something very special. At least for me it was, and I thought it was for you too. I was sure the tracks of our lives would merge. That somehow, it would all work out, in spite of the geography. However, it didn't, and I've never been sure what caused the drifting apart. Well, maybe I do know, but I want to hear it from your lips."

Elie was taken aback. She had not expected him to be so direct. From her experience with Philip, men didn't open up like that. She was touched, and moved enough to let go of her inhibitions and speak the truth.

She put her hands on the table and played nervously with the ring on her right hand. "I will try to explain. First of all, David, I was out of my mind in love with you. I thought I would die when we said goodbye."

He looked at her intently, without interrupting.

"But when I returned home from my year in Israel, my entire world shattered. My father was very sick, he was dying actually, and it nearly destroyed me. My mother tried to remain strong, but I could tell it was eating away at her. I felt so guilty, that I had been enjoying my time in Israel, while they were suffering through his illness.

I lived in a constant state of dread. I knew my father was going to die, and I didn't know how my mother and I would survive. The three of us were so close as a family. When it came to thinking of you, I didn't want to consider my own happiness. I felt that I had no right to it. On a rational level I knew that my joy was not related to their suffering, but I couldn't resolve it in my heart."

Elie took a deep breath and fingered her glass, purposely avoiding his eyes. "I wanted more than anything to return to Israel, straight into your arms, but it was impossible. My father died soon after I got home. There was no way I could come back here and abandon my mother.

I decided to return to school and finish my design degree. My mother insisted that I live in the city, so that my final year at school would be a rewarding experience, but I was only a subway ride away from her."

Elie's eyes welled up with tears. David reached over and touched her hands. She continued to talk, but still averted his stare. His beautiful green eyes were piercing her soul, and she found it unnerving.

"I forced myself to let go of you. I would cry myself to sleep every night, but then wake up in the morning determined to get on with my life. I received your letters and debated whether to read them or not. Each time one arrived in the mail, I was ecstatic and miserable at the same time. I finally decided to force you out of my mind. Eventually I met Philip, he swept me off my feet and the rest is history. My history, anyway."

"Did you think about us after that?" He had a pained expression on his face.

Elie was beginning to understand how deeply she had hurt him. She felt sad and confused. "I would not allow myself to. Each time a thought of you came into my head, I made a huge effort to push it out. I was reading creative visualization books at the time, and that helped me place you somewhere in the far, far distance. I closed off that chapter of my life and moved on."

"I see."

This time she looked at him directly. "David, please don't misunderstand me. What you and I had was extraordinary. I will admit to you, that the feelings I had for Philip never compared to what I felt for you. I just convinced myself that I wasn't entitled to you. After a while, I thought that perhaps I had imagined how good it was with you. That maybe it was a big thing in *my* head, but for you just a fling. I started to think that maybe you had already forgotten me."

He smiled and shook his head. "And with Philip? Were you happy?"

She hesitated. "I can't say that I did not have a good life with him. I did love him at the beginning, and we raised two wonderful daughters. I don't regret marrying him. It would be a mistake to claim that. It was right for then." She stopped speaking.

David took up where she had left off. "I thought about you all the time. I even considered working in the States for a while just to be with you. I applied for a security position at the Israeli Embassy in New York and I got it, but at the same time, I was accepted into the Masters program here, which was a big honor. Very few made it. I chickened out about coming to New York because you did not give me the feeling that you were one hundred percent into us. I was not sure where it would lead, and since my reason for being there was you, I decided not to take the chance. I guess we all make decisions that will affect our lives, without really knowing what's absolutely right."

She looked up at him. "Am I forgiven, all these years later?" She wasn't sure she had to ask for it, but she very much wanted to hear that she was.

"Yes. Under the circumstances, I don't think you need to apologize. What happened, happened. I guess it was our fate not to be together then."

He took both of Elie's hands in his. "So, now that we're adults, with no encumbrances upon us, why don't we just let this go wherever it's supposed to go? I say we enjoy you being back in Israel and make up for lost time."

The feelings of sadness, guilt over hurting him, and all the years in-between, melted away. A weight was lifted. "I think that's an excellent idea. But David, I must ask you, don't you have someone?" Her mind raced towards a feeling of insecurity. How could such an extraordinary man not be involved? There had to be a woman in his life.

He laughed. "Let's just say that the timing is perfect." He took her hand and squeezed it.

She understood that there may have been someone, but he was not going into the details.

"I have a suggestion. Let's leave touring around Neve Tzedek for another time. Right now, I suggest we sample some of Nizza's divine desserts, perhaps the tiramisu and the famous parfait that I mentioned. Then we go back to your apartment for a nightcap."

Elie agreed with the dessert suggestion, but kept silent about the other. She conducted a debate in her head. If she invited him up, it would be impossible to let him go, and she was not sure she was ready for the next step. On the other hand, she sensed that before long she would go to bed with him, so why not tonight? She felt an urgency to do it, in order to stop the obsession she had been feeling. She heard Syd's voice in her head egging her on, and she made her decision.

On the way back to the apartment, Elie mentioned to David that he could park the car in the garage, in Syd's spot. She knew exactly how he could interpret the underlying message. Once inside the apartment, she invited him to get settled on the sofa while she brought out brandy snifters and Cognac. For several minutes, they sat together sipping their drinks and looking at the lights of the city. Then, suddenly, David put his glass on the coffee table and took Elie's glass from her.

He put his finger under her chin, pulled her face towards him and kissed her passionately. He pushed back the waves of her hair and told her she looked even more beautiful with the streaks of gray in her curls. He kissed her face and her neck. She became dizzy, lost in the thrill of the moment. The sensation of his soft lips on hers transported her back thirty years. It was as if it was happening for the first time, and it was happening with the same man.

David did not play coy. He stood up, put his hand out to take her's and told her to lead him to the bedroom. She did. She felt a momentary panic about her body being that of a woman of fifty-one, and not of the girl he had known. But once again the alcohol was doing its magic, and her nervousness faded.

Everything began to unfold like in a dream, and they fell into each other's arms as if they had always been together. David was gentle, and took pleasure in exploring Elie's body as he kissed and caressed her. He moved slowly and brought her to such a state of ecstasy that she lost almost all control. She had never experienced such a heightened sense of sensuality with Philip. This was something extraordinary.

The years, the hesitations, the shyness, all vanished as they made love. Elie began to understand what it meant to be at one with someone, to lose consciousness of where one person's body ends and the other's begins. She felt at home in this man's arms, and fell asleep with her body intertwined with his.

In the morning, she awoke first and looked at David. Here, in her bed, was the older version of the young man she had loved. His body had softened, the dark chest hairs were now mostly gray, and the extra weight that age bestows was obvious, but well distributed.

She slipped out of bed quietly and washed up. She peeked in on him again and then went to the kitchen to prepare breakfast. She was feeling more alive than she had for years.

"Good Morning!" He surprised her as she was setting the table.

"Hi! You're up. I tried not to wake you. Did you sleep well?"

He was wearing just pants. He hugged her and answered with a smile. "Perfectly! And you?"

"The same. I've prepared some breakfast. I don't know if your taste runs to a full Israeli breakfast or coffee and a pastry so I made a combination."

"And she cooks, too!"

"Well, I wouldn't exactly call this cooking, but you know what? I can cook! Remind me to invite you for dinner one day." She motioned for him to sit down.

"I will. This looks great. I'll just put my shirt on and be right back."

Elie felt exhilarated. She had no idea what would happen next, and she did not care. She was with David, she felt wonderful, and she decided her life was now in the hands of fate.

They ate breakfast as if they had done so for years, not at all like two people reuniting after three decades. They were relaxed, and totally at ease with each other.

"Elie, you said you have to get back home next week." He looked at her and smiled. "Any chance you can delay? Now that I found you again, I really don't want to give you up so soon."

She loved that he was asking. "Oh David, I don't know. I have so much to do when I return. If I'm going to start the magazine I've been dreaming about, I really shouldn't put it off. I don't want to lose the momentum and there's an enormous amount of work involved. I had hoped to take this time in Tel Aviv to start a business plan. So far, I haven't written a word."

"Hmm, I see. Okay. I have the perfect solution. I can help you with the business plan and that will enable us to spend more time together. I'll take a break from my work this week, and maybe next week I'll just go in half days. That way, we'll be able to see each other often. What do you say? I do know how to write business plans, by the way."

"My heart says yes, my head says no."

"Well, to tell you the truth, I always knew that your heart was on my side. Think about it, okay? I won't pressure you any more. Take your time – you can give me an answer as late as oh, let's see, ten minutes from now? When I get out of the shower?"

"Very funny. I will think about it. I promise."

Elie delayed her trip back an additional two weeks. When David was able to get away from work, they traveled to different parts of the country or just walked around Tel Aviv. When he could not, he came over in the evening and spent the night. During the days, she sketched out her business ideas and strategized about life after *Interior Design & Style*. In the evenings, David explained the fine points of a business plan and helped formulate her concepts into one.

She learned a new vocabulary, and was once again impressed by David's knowledge. He spoke to her about market potential and competitive edge, he asked about finance resources and key people and explained risk analysis. She got a mini-course in business and her head filled up with new information.

Being with David was so different than being with Philip. With her ex-husband, she had often felt like a sidekick, an accessory in his life. David made her feel vital. He discussed business ideas with her, and issues that were on his mind.

They had dinner with Devi and Lawrence at the American residence and it was a great success. The men talked about American and Israeli politics, and the women chatted endlessly about all aspects of life. Elie expressed her undying gratitude to Devi for being the reason David was back in her life.

The pair separated only when Elie went to visit Lexi. Elie was not yet ready to introduce her daughter to her new old lover. Lexi was still shaken from the divorce and Elie did not want to trouble her any further.

It came time to return home. Elie had delayed the trip once, and the ticket could not be changed again. She knew that as much as she was falling in love with David, her life was back in New York. She was tempted to forget it all and stay with him, but she resisted.

The events of the last months had helped Elie achieve a closer understanding of herself. She knew that this was the time to go for it, to establish something totally of her own, to squash her fears and make her own way in the world. As much as she wanted to stay with David, she believed, for the first time in her life, that she could have it all. At least, that's how she felt most of the time.

David understood her decision and supported it, although he made it very clear that he would not accept her disappearing from his life again. He brought her to the airport and they both talked about the last time he had done so.

"But this time, Elie, you're not leaving my life. Either you will have to come back here soon or I will come to New York. When do you think you'll have some free time for us to be together?"

"I have no idea. I assume I'm going to be crazy busy in the coming months. Maybe the summer?"

"No way, I am not going to wait that long. We'll have to meet somewhere. On the other hand, I can come to New York and just sit and watch you work hard, while I put my feet up on your coffee table. How does that sound?"

"Good, as long as you wipe off the prints."

They both laughed, realizing they were nervous, and he took her hand.

David walked with her to the security lines, where he was asked to stand aside. Once she had checked in and her baggage was sent off, she went with him for a cup of coffee.

They spent the hour talking about the last few weeks, the miracle of finding each other and the practicalities of what Elie needed to do to get the business off the ground. She knew David would continue to be a source of comfort and advice when she was back in New York.

Finally, it was time to board. David walked Elie to the security point, held her and gave her a long, passionate kiss. He pulled away, looked at her and said, "You are the greatest, Elie Stein. Now go home and start that magazine of yours. I want weekly, if not daily updates. You got that?"

"Sir! Yes Sir!"

"And while you're at it, make some room in your closet for me. When you give the green light, I'm coming to visit."

He hugged her once more and sent her off.

She barely thought back to the last time he said goodbye to her at the airport. This time she was a grown woman who knew just what she wanted from life and had her list of priorities straight. And David Abarbanel was very high on the list.

Thirty-Five

Elie was so energized on the plane ride home that she worked non-stop, until the battery of her laptop gave out. Then she started scribbling in the notebook she always carried around, and by the time she got home in the early morning, it was more than half filled. She felt glorious, not at all like someone who had just gotten off an eleven-hour flight.

It was a cold, cloudy day in New York but she didn't seem to notice. The sun could have been shining brightly for the way she felt. She took a taxi to her apartment and as soon as the clock hands struck eight, she called her dear friend.

"Syd, Syd, Syd, I'm home! I have so much to tell you! Let's meet!"

"Ah, the wandering Jewess returns. And happily too, it sounds. May I take a shower first? Aren't you exhausted?"

"I am but I don't care. I'm dying to see you and tell you everything. Can I invite you for breakfast? Meet you in twenty minutes in the lobby?

"Make it thirty."

Elie was waiting downstairs when Syd walked out of the elevator. She laughed when she saw how fabulous her friend looked. "How is it that you're so gorgeous in sweats, even at this hour of the morning?"

"Because they're sweats by Donna Karan and cost me a bloody fortune. I had better look good in them! Come here and give me a kiss, you old broad." Syd reached out to her friend.

As they hugged, Elie felt a tremendous feeling of warmth towards her friend. She put her arm through Syd's and they walked over to the Popover Café on Amsterdam Avenue.

Soon after they settled into a cozy booth, the basket of warm popovers and strawberry butter arrived.

"I know I shouldn't be eating these, but I'm dying for one. *Oy*, I'm in such trouble – you would not believe the amount of humus and tehina I've gorged on these past few weeks. And here I am, eating a popover!" Elie split open the pastry and a gush of steam spewed out.

"Oh, just forget it. Let's splurge and think about our bodies later. Maybe you'll finally join me at the gym, now that you're a lady of leisure. Okay, I want to know everything. Start talking."

"Syd, I have so much to tell you, I'm bursting. As far as gyms, I don't think so! I won't have time. But first, your news. I started to worry. I tried you by email and phone and couldn't find you. I know you can be in a do-not-disturb mood, but this was weird because it was more than a week."

"I went to my retreat. It was the anniversary of Julian's death and I felt like being off on my own somewhere, sort of as a commemoration. Nothing but fruit, vegetables, yoga and meditation. I thought I told you I was going. Probably you forgot. I guess you had more important things on your mind." She looked at her friend and winked.

Syd continued, "It was heaven and helped clear out my head. I feel much better now. And, *tada!* I lost four pounds! The disaster at work is over and I'm clean. But it took a chunk out of me. Dogs are fine but getting old. Like me. I met Chloe and we had a lovely dinner, that's it. Now, your turn."

They ordered omelets and Elie told her friend everything about David. How it was to see him again, to be with him, to make love with him. She talked about him being with her every night and supporting her plans for the new magazine. She detailed how he helped her develop a business plan.

"*Whoa!* I thought we were going to talk about your new romance, but now I understand we're advancing into you becoming a magazine mogul. You got laid *and* got business advice?"

"*Did I ever!*" Elie talked on and on about her experiences with David, visiting with Lexi's family, the new scene in Tel Aviv. She couldn't stop.

Syd listened with a big smile on her face.

"And that's not all. Besides the whole David thing, I have something else to discuss. It involves you. Ready?" Elie took a sip of coffee and geared up to pounce again.

"Well, aren't you full of surprises today? Go ahead, I'll brace myself."

"Syd Sorenstein, you're a wizard when it comes to all things financial. I've always thought you were a bit wasted working for those big shots. You should be advising people, women especially, on what to do with their money."

Syd interrupted. "Elie, why do I have a feeling that you have some plans for me?"

"I do. I'm getting there, let me finish. I want you to head up a financial column in the magazine. I truly believe you would be brilliant at this. Imagine, women getting professional advice about how to choose stocks and bonds, deal with overdrafts, repay loans, make the best investments, analyze retirement plans, buy insurance. What convinced me is that when we spoke from Israel you admitted that you're somewhat tired of what you've been doing. What do you think?"

"Christ, Elie, you're not kidding! You're going way too fast, even for me. You're really serious about this?"

"I am indeed and I think you should be too. I'm not talking about a community newsletter, Syd. I'm talking about a major magazine with national, hopefully international distribution. With all the women's magazines out there, there's nothing good that focuses on women our age. It's needed in the market, I'm certain of it."

"Elie, you don't have to convince me of the importance of the magazine, I'm already with you on that. I'm just not sure this is a direction I want for my life. I should be slowing down, not getting involved in a new project."

"Nonsense! If you don't have an interesting project to keep you busy, you'll go crazy. I can just see you staying up all night baking scones and tarts. Maybe you'll add popovers to the repertoire. Then you'll have to open a bakery, but you don't like people and won't like serving them and then the bakery would shut down, because all the customers would run away from you, and then you'd be miserable again."

"Wow, when did you become such a bitch?" Syd laughed. "Here, *schmear* some strawberry butter on your popover and shut up for a minute."

She handed Elie the ramekin of butter and continued. "What about others? Do you know the people you want for this venture? You need a very talented staff, a strong Internet presence, a solid public relations firm, the works."

Elie explained her plans and mentioned the names of the people she wanted. Among them were Leigh Fairchild from the magazine and Michael, who would be brilliant for a design section. She wondered how Syd would respond to that idea.

"Are you okay about that? About Michael being part of the group?"

"Oh Elie, really. Who cares anymore? I don't hold anything against him. He's a persnickety prig with a stick up his ass, but so what? We all can't be perfect like you and me. Besides, getting together with him when we had that intervention with you really helped clear the air."

"Okay, great. I wouldn't want there to be any duels. Are you saying that you'll do it? You'll join the project?" Elie was excited, but afraid to hold out too much hope.

"Let's say, I'll take it under very serious consideration. Moreover, I'll be happy to attend a meeting to meet the others. What about Chloe?"

"What about Chloe?" Elie wasn't sure what Syd meant.

"She would be perfect for your magazine. She's smart as a whip, she's got her MBA and from what I understand, she's doing great things at Philip's company. Honey, that daughter of yours is a dynamo."

"Thank you, I feel the same way. Funny you should mention her. I did think of her. I have no doubt that she would be amazing, but what about the mother-daughter thing? Couldn't it present problems? I mean, her rebellious period is over and we've gotten closer in the last few years. I wouldn't want to jeopardize that. Also, Philip would kill me if I plucked her away from Sands Furniture."

"Elie, she's a gem and she'd be great for the magazine. And Philip, for once in his life, will have to think of someone else besides himself. In my humble opinion, as if any of my opinions are humble, she'd do a sterling job. See if she's interested."

"You know what? You're right! I will talk to her."

"El, what about the money? This will take an enormous amount of capital. What do you intend to do about that?"

"It's a problem. I'll probably have to take out a loan and dip heavily into my savings. I said I wouldn't, and it's the only money I got from the divorce, but if not for this, then for what?" Elie brushed the hair away from her forehead and continued.

"I can live off my package from the magazine for a while, as well as the interest from what's in the bank. The girls are taken care of, so I don't have to worry about them. It's a big risk, but I'm ready to take it. So what if I'll have no money left? You'll take care of me in my old age, won't you?"

"Honey, by the time you're elderly, I'm going to be fighting with everyone in the old age home where they'll stick me. So you better not count on me. At least not for that."

The two women kept talking, as they finished their breakfast. After a few refills of coffee, Elie began to feel jittery.

Syd saw the jet lag hitting her friend. "El, you look like you're fading. Let's go home, and we'll talk again after you're refreshed."

"Good idea. I'm starting to feel the effects of the journey. Let's ask for the bill and get out of here."

After allowing herself two days for jet lag recovery, Elie began to get busy. She went to the office and saw that everything was fine. They were managing without her and although it hurt a bit, she understood that her presence was really no longer needed. She spent two hours tying up loose ends and left for home, taking a few personal items with her.

She concentrated on returning phone calls, answering emails and stocking the house with food. Finally, she was ready to embark on her journey. To enhance her mood, she loaded the latest Sarit Hadad CD into the player. David had teased her when he saw what kind of music she was buying, but she ignored him and threatened to buy several more discs of the popular Middle Eastern, Oriental style music so popular with Israeli youth. She picked up the telephone and began to execute her plan of action.

"Hey Syd, how are you doing?"

"Other than the quarter of a million dollars I just lost in a commodities trade, I'm fine. What's up with you? How are the plans coming along?"

"Good. As a matter of fact, more than good. I am assembling a get-together. Thursday evening, dinner at my apartment at seven. Can you make it?"

"Sure. I haven't made a decision yet, but I'd be happy to come and offer my pearls of wisdom. Who else are you inviting?"

"As we spoke about, Chloe, Michael and Leigh from the magazine. And you!"

"Okay, I'm in. See you Thursday."

She dialed the next number.

"Hey Michael, how's my favorite interior *dreckorator?*"

"Oh sure, you just go ahead and make fun of those of us in the profession that you couldn't compete with. *Dreckorator* my ass! And how are you my sweet? How was your trip to Israel? Darling Lexi and company doing well?"

"Trip was great. Lexi is great. Lots to tell you, including a very exciting l-o-v-e story. I am absolutely, over the top excellent, especially considering I divorced my husband and lost my job. Must be all that medication I'm on."

"Yeah, as if you would actually take any. I'm telling you, a little Valium or Prozac and you'll be a very happy girl. You should trust me on this dearie. Wait, did you say l-o-v-e? Do tell!"

"No. First tell me about you. Daniel, darling Isabel, your mother? Are they all good? Fill me in."

"Good, good and good. Happy to report that all is fine. Love my man, love my granddaughter – ooh that sounds so funny – Mother is fine. Blah, blah, blah. *Nu?*"

"My love story comes later. First, I have another matter to discuss with you. I need you for a very important project I have up my sleeve."

"And what would that be, precious?"

"Remember I mentioned to you, that I have an idea about starting my own magazine? That I'm thinking about making this dream of mine come to fruition?"

"Yes ...?"

"So, I want to do it. At least I'm at the stage of planning a meeting with people I trust and consider crucial to that dream. And I want you there."

"Me? Little *ole* me? Are you offering me executive publisher? Chief Stud? What's my position?"

"Be serious! I have a few ideas and I really, really want you to be a part of this. Or at least hear me out. Maybe they're wild and unachievable, but I will lay my cards out on the table and see what happens. Are you in?"

"Sure. Name the time and place."

"My apartment, this coming Thursday evening, dinner at seven. I think there will be about five of us."

"And who else among the invited guests?"

"There's Chloe, Leigh Fairchild from the magazine, you I hope, Syd and me."

"What was that name you mentioned after mine? I don't believe I ever heard it before."

"Cut it out, Michael. You two are over that thing already. Remember?"

"You expect me to sit in a room with that Tzarina of the Tongue? Really?"

"Yes, I do, and more than that, you're going to be civil and give her a kiss and make nicey-nice. You and Syd are my closest friends. I need you both now and you have to be there for me. And anyway, you called a cease fire."

"Okay. Okay. I'm just joking. We've already done the kissy-kissy thing. Of course, I'll be there, dolly girl. What shall I bring?"

"Nothing at all, just you." She laughed to herself, knowing that he could not cook. "You are a true friend. Thank you, Michael, see you Thursday. And please try not to be late."

"Late, *schmate*. He who shows up early obviously has nothing better to do."

"Whatever. See you then." Good, Elie thought. She had already spoken to Chloe, so four down, one to go. She phoned Leigh, who was delighted to accept her invitation. Next, she considered what to serve for dinner.

The ringing of the telephone interrupted her thoughts.

"How did I forget? You didn't tell me the love story. *Nu,* speak up girl. I'm waiting and I don't have all day. Spill it!"

She laughed as she realized that Michael would never let her get away with keeping a secret from him, especially one so juicy. She began to retell the David story and despite his interruptions and exclamations, she managed to get it all out.

"*Holy mother! I am in heaven for you!* My girl Eleanora has a boyfriend! And a hot one, it seems. Is he as handsome as me? What does he look like undressed? Describe his body."

"Okay, enough. That's all the info you're getting now. Come over early on Thursday night and maybe I'll fill you in on some of the tastier tidbits." She hung up without giving him a chance to harangue her any more.

She scribbled down menu ideas. She actually strategized about how to exploit her culinary talents to her advantage. Nothing too heavy, so they would not feel stuffed. Something a bit on the gourmet side, to entice, but not overwhelm. She sang along with the music and wrote down the ingredients she needed to buy.

On Thursday, everyone arrived more or less on time and the greetings got off to a good start. Leigh had never met Syd, knew Chloe slightly and was well acquainted with Michael since his work was often featured in the magazine. Michael was an absolute gentleman, and Syd was relaxed and friendly, not displaying any of the haughtiness she could command at will.

Both Syd and Michael made a big fuss over Chloe. Michael had always been crazy about Elie's girls and remembered to send them birthday and Hanukkah presents every year. Syd's closeness to Chloe was well known, so it was no surprise to see them acting chummy.

Aiming for a relaxed, casual atmosphere, Elie had set up dinner in the kitchen, rather than the dining room. She used the brightly patterned placemats and napkins from Provence and her Fiesta dinnerware – a different colored plate at each setting. In the center of the table was a squat orange pitcher filled with zinnias.

After a few minutes of chatting in the living room, she invited her guests into the kitchen. She was anxious to get to the main topic.

"How marvelously festive!" Leigh was the first to comment on the table.

"Hey doll, you missed your calling. Martha Stewart, watch out! This looks fab!" Michael clapped.

Elie beamed. "Thank you one and all. Now, please be seated wherever you like and let's get started."

She placed a soup tureen on the table and ladled gazpacho into each bowl. She passed around a plate of bruschetta and asked Chloe to pour the wine. When everyone was served, she tapped her wine glass with her knife and asked for silence.

"I would like to make a toast. I have asked you here today because you are all very precious to me. Precious in my personal life and vital in what I hope will be the continuation of my professional life. I want you to remember this day as a milestone in your lives, as I hope it will be in mine. To you, my newly appointed Kitchen Cabinet – at least I hope so – *L'chayim!*"

The guests raised their glasses, mumbled about the kitchen cabinet line, repeated the toast for good life and drank. Elie was smiling from ear to ear and she had a premonition that her dream was about to come true.

The guests started to eat and Michael commented on the soup. "Oh my lord in heaven, this gazpacho is *absolutely* divine. I know there's something special in here, speak up."

Elie smiled. "My secret."

Before she had a chance to explain, Syd interrupted. "Will someone please tell me why I shelled out buckets of money for private cooking lessons, which I ever so generously shared with my friend Elie here, and she becomes an artist in the kitchen and I can't cook for shit!"

Everyone laughed and Elie responded, "Enough of your

complaints, Syd. I've been hearing you bitch about those cooking lessons for years. At least *I* learned something and put your money to good use. And you can so cook."

"Come on Elie, spill. What's in the *delicioso* soup?" Michael asked again.

She smiled. "Cilantro and ouzo. Those are the secret ingredients."

Michael raised his glass. "Well then, three cheers for cilantro, ouzo and Eleanora's creative inspirations. Hear! Hear!" The glasses were raised once again and the meal was off to a cheerful start.

As she served the main course, Elie began to outline her ideas. "You all know that I've been in the magazine trade forever. I can't imagine doing anything else. But I could not continue with *Interior Design & Style* under the new regime, so I took a long hard look at myself and came up with what I think is a great idea – a magazine geared for the over-fifty woman. I believe that there is a huge market niche, one that has been sorely neglected. But this part you all know."

She continued. "The concept is a slick upscale journal that covers every topic a woman of a certain age, and I use a certain age in quotations, would like to be informed about. That means: beauty, fashion, interiors, health, literature, finance, culture, shopping – you name it. I don't think we'll get into politics, but I would be open to discuss it. Every month we cover another theme, or maybe we cover the same themes month after month. I haven't yet decided. I just know in my gut that this can work. I am certain of it, and I have not been certain of much for a very long time."

Syd was the first to pipe up. "Bravo girl. I think it's a genius inspiration. Put me down for the first subscription!"

Leigh joined in. "And me for the second. I think it's a brilliant idea, Elie, and if anyone can make it happen, you can."

"Hold on there. I cannot make it happen without a team and I would like each and every one of you to be a part of my team."

"Mom, what are you talking about? Explain please." Chloe had a puzzled look on her face.

"That's just what I intend to do. I did not invite you all over here tonight to impress you with my culinary skills. I had an ulterior motive. Each of you has a very particular talent and I would like to exploit that talent."

The guests looked at each other.

"Syd is a financial genius. She can make money in her sleep, other than the quarter of a million dollars she lost before breakfast the other day."

"Not to worry, I made more than that back by lunchtime" Syd said dryly.

Elie smiled and shook her head knowingly. "I want Syd to write a monthly column devoted to money issues. We all know that many women rely too heavily on their husbands or their husband's accountants for financial matters. Then, when they find themselves alone, whether by divorce or widowhood, they're lost. I want Syd to address that need."

Elie put her hand up, to prevent anyone from interrupting her. "Michael, there isn't a more talented designer on this planet. But let's face it, you're not the best when it comes to customer relations if you know what I mean."

"I'll say!"

"Quiet, Syd. You, my dear Michael, would be perfect heading up the interior design section. I want a serious look at design today, a critical eye reviewing what's happening. Maybe we take big designer projects and hack them or rave about them. I'm not sure, it's your baby. You need a break from the wacky world you've been living in and this could be it. Don't say a word. I'm not done yet."

"Now, Chloe. Sweetheart, you've done wonders with your job at Sands and it's not for nothing they selected you for it. Although you're nowhere near the age category, I think you'd be a natural in this business and I'd like you to consider running our marketing and public relations division. I promise you it will be more exciting than furniture and it will give you an opportunity to start something from scratch."

"But Mom…" Chloe looked astonished. "I think I need another drink. Michael, would you pass me the wine please?"

He poured her a glass.

"Let me finish, before you voice your objections." Elie pushed her chair away from the table and continued.

"Next, Leigh. Ladies and gentleman, there is no one, I repeat, no one, who knows more about the world of fashion and interiors than Leigh Fairchild. I thought she was a genius when it came to furnishings, and then I found out she's got a fully stocked library of fashion in her head. She can spot trends and react to them from the perspective of the older woman. Leigh, I would like you to be our style editor."

Leigh looked stunned.

Finally, Elie took a breath. "Now I permit you to talk. What do you all have to say?" She drank her wine and smiled smugly.

"Mom, you're not kidding about all this, are you?"

"Chloe, I have never been more serious in my life. I believe with all my heart that we can pull this off."

Leigh spoke. "Elie, I am really flattered that you would like me to join you. Truthfully, I do not see myself staying on at the magazine under the new management. But I'm close to retiring, I feel too old for this kind of assignment."

"Leigh, don't be ridiculous. You're indispensable and way too spirited to retire into obscurity. You are a national treasure. No doubt in my mind. You have to be part of this. Next?"

Michael piped up. "General, may I speak?" He didn't wait for an answer. "I think it's great what you're going to do. But I've never written. It seems so far from what I'm doing. Although I am intrigued by the thought of it. And I am certain I would be *excellente* at it."

Elie responded. "Good. Stay intrigued and stay with me. I know you've never written. That's where I come in. Obviously, my editorial talents, as they may or may not be, have to come into play here. I will organize the topics for the issues, edit the stories, and in your case, Michael, I will re-write them. In addition, I plan to do everything else that has to get done in a magazine, which means I may not be sleeping at all for the first year or two. That would leave us with Chloe and Syd. So?"

Syd was unequivocal. "You know what? Count me in. I love the idea. I've always wanted to put my ideas down on paper and force people to listen to what I have to say. What the hell? Where do I sign up?"

"I'm delighted! And Chloe?" Elie looked at her daughter.

"Mom, I'm flabbergasted. I knew you were cooking something up, and I love the idea, but I don't know if I could really help you with it. I feel too inexperienced."

"Chloe, with what you'll be getting paid, your inexperience will be no problem. Just joking, honey, you'll be great. I am so very certain that you will be perfect for this. Otherwise, I would never have dreamed of asking you to leave your father's company."

She hesitated for a moment and then went on. "You know what else, Chloe? It's more important that *you yourself* realize how perfect you are for this. I don't want you to make the same mistakes I made until now, not knowing what I was really worth. You have to believe in yourself, and go for the life you want, which of course I hope will be with this magazine.

I realize that you have a great job now, and I wouldn't have suggested switching if I didn't think this could be something important for you, a career you could really grow with. I know I'll have to deal with your father on this issue – he'll probably want to slaughter me – but what the heck."

Chloe glanced at Syd and then back to her mother. "Well, maybe it would be better for me to disengage from Sands Furniture. I love the idea of being involved in a start-up and I've never really been crazy about armoires and credenzas, to tell the truth."

Everyone laughed and Leigh spoke. "I hate to be a party pooper, and this may be none of my business, but, Elie, what about the finances? This is going to require a huge investment of capital."

"You're right and I'm working on that. Not to worry."

Elie turned to the others. "Now, let's talk about logistics. For the time being, the magazine will be created out of this apartment. We might need to requisition your old room Chloe, or maybe I'll take it and convert the master bedroom into an office. I know we'll have to move out of here soon, but for the immediate time being, I want to save money, so this is the office."

"But Mom, you live here! How can you manage to both live and work out of this place?"

Leigh responded. "Chloe dear, Walter Lavigne, his secretary, and I started *Interior Design & Style* out of an office the size of this kitchen. And look at what it grew into! Your mom can do it. We can do it. I was just wondering, does it include meals prepared by our new publisher and editor-in-chief?" She turned towards Elie.

Everybody laughed and Elie answered. "You bet! When I'm not busy doing about a million other things. We're still far from having everything we need. Photographers, layout people, a graphics person, another editor, an advertising person, a foodie who can review recipes and restaurants, I could go on and on. We have a long way to go. We'll work with freelancers, until we can afford to hire more professionals."

"Mom, what about the Internet? We all know that many magazines are not doing so well these days. I think you need to consider an interactive website."

"Yes, of course. Put it on the list."

"My friend's brother is a graphics and Internet genius. He just sold his company and he's hanging around waiting for something challenging to come along. Would you like me to see if he's interested?"

"Yes and no, Chloe. I do believe we need a strong Internet presence but I was hoping we could hire mostly women. You know, support our market."

"Well, *excuse me*. I'm not a woman and if you want me, I'd say you should consider some other testosterone on the team. Of course, if he has a nice ass and knows how to wiggle it, that would be even better."

Elie raised her hand to quiet Michael. "Hush up, you. Okay, Chloe. Please call him and arrange a meeting for us. Any other suggestions?"

"Yes, I have one." Syd took the floor. "You don't need a foodie person. We already have one. Elie, you'd be perfect. You know every recipe in the world, you've studied the history of cuisine as a hobby and you're a genius in the kitchen. Every restaurant you have recommended or warned me to stay away from has been right on. You dearest, should be the food editor."

Elie shook her head and laughed. "That too I have to add to my plate? Metaphorically speaking."

"Mom, Syd is right. You'd be great." Chloe said.

"Thank you, my fan club, but let's put that up for discussion at a later date. Do I have your word, all of you, that you're in? And that for now, this stays among us?"

They instinctively held hands around the table and echoed their agreement.

"Well then, that makes it unanimous. I believe this ends the official part of our evening. I say we break open another bottle of wine and keep drinking until we have a whole first year of issues cranked out." Elie was smiling from ear to ear and as she raised her glass, everyone joined her in another toast.

Later that evening, Elie phoned David and updated him. They were in touch frequently and she felt that he was very much a part of this new endeavor. He was delighted with the progress she was making and told her he was not only in love with her, but proud of her as well.

Thirty-Six

There were two messages on the answering machine that she had not returned. One was from Tillie, the other from Joshua, and she avoided them both.

A month earlier, Elie would have been excited to hear from Joshua. But now that she had reunited with David, she felt awkward. She knew she would have to see him and explain the situation.

Joshua was happy to hear Elie's voice on the phone and they arranged to meet for dinner. It was the same restaurant they went to before, only this time she insisted on meeting him there. She was too nervous to wait until after the meal to tell him her news, so she started as soon as the drinks arrived. She explained what she was doing with her life, the business plans and then finally, she blurted out the David story.

"Joshua, I felt I had to tell you, but it feels strange." She thought she saw a look of disappointment on his face.

"How do you mean strange, Elie?"

"I know that you and I had only that one date, but yet I was thinking that maybe ... this feels so silly to be speaking about."

"Nothing is silly. Go ahead."

"Quite frankly, I wanted to see where things would go with you. I was very much looking forward to seeing you again."

"As was I."

"I didn't go to Israel expecting anything other than a well-needed rest and a chance to clear my head. But seeing David at your sister's party shocked me to the very core. He was the most significant man in my life, other than Philip. I had unfinished business with him. I guess I ..."

"Elie, you don't owe me any explanations."

"But I feel that I do. You've been such a gentleman. You were wonderful during the divorce process and you were so kind in your approach to me afterwards."

"Perhaps that was a mistake. Now I'm thinking that I should not have been so chivalrous. Perhaps if I had let my feelings be known earlier, we would not be having this conversation." He looked at her intently.

Elie felt that she had to handle the situation with complete honesty. "Joshua, I used to have a little crush on you. In case you didn't know it, this is a confession. And my mind took me to all kinds of places after that kiss of ours on Columbus Avenue."

"Mine too."

"I am so sorry about this. But running into David ignited all my previous feelings for him. It's as if I was given a chance to get back what I lost thirty years ago. A gift, in a way." She looked down and played with the napkin on her lap. "This sounds arrogant, but if David hadn't shown up that evening, I would have loved to come home and let things develop with you. If, you would have had me."

"I definitely would have had you." He laughed. "Now *that* wasn't so gentlemanly. Let's say, I would have loved to see where a relationship with you could have gone. You're quite a woman, Elie Stein."

She smiled and reached out for his hand. "And you're quite a man, Joshua Strauss."

"So in the end, we can blame my dear sister Devi for ruining the potential of our budding romance. I think I shall have to kill her."

They laughed, ordered their food and enjoyed a nice dinner. Joshua wished her well with her business and offered to help in any way he could. They parted with a friendly kiss and promised to be in touch with each other.

Elie delayed returning the other call. A few days earlier, Chloe had sheepishly admitted that she had a confession to make. At a lunch with her grandmother, she had mentioned Elie's idea about starting her own magazine and Tillie had shown great interest. She hoped her mother did not mind.

Elie didn't. She knew that her daughter was close to her

grandmother and anyway the edict about keeping quiet did not apply to family. Elie reassured her that it was no problem.

Tillie telephoned again, and this time caught Elie at home. Without pretense of small talk, she asked for a meeting, stressing that it was important. She suggested lunch at Jean George. Ever since the closing of Café des Artistes, Tillie had switched allegiance to the famous chef's restaurant at Columbus Circle. They arranged a day and time and Tillie offered to take care of the reservation.

It was raining and Elie arrived at the restaurant wet and cold. She took off her raincoat, tried to shake off her umbrella without causing a flood on the floor, and handed them both to the woman who greeted her. She felt a bit discombobulated as she was escorted to Tillie's table.

There sat Tillie Sands, looking as elegant as always. She wore a St. John red knit jacket with leopard collar and cuffs, and black pants. Her makeup, hair and nails were perfect. The air around her was scented with Shalimar and she was sipping a martini.

"Hi. Sorry, I'm late. What a mess getting here. No cabs when it rains, but I guess you know that. I started to walk, got soaked and finally found one going uptown and got him to turn around for me. Whew." Elie was almost out of breath.

"Sit down and relax dear. Shall I order you a Chardonnay?" Tillie was composed, as usual.

"Yes, that would be great. I'll try to find the waiter." Elie took the chair facing Tillie and turned her head around.

"No need, here he is." She half raised her hand and a waiter appeared immediately.

"So, how are you, Tillie? How is Max?" She caught a glimpse of the watch on Tillie's hand, made up entirely of baguette-cut diamonds and rubies. "Wow, that's some watch! Gorgeous!"

"Thank you dear. It's Bulgari. Lovely, isn't it?

Elie unconsciously fingered the Swatch on her left hand.

"We're just fine. Max is doing great – watching his diet, exercising. He's been a perfect patient, or after-patient. But, I want to know how *you're* doing, Elie dear. That's why I asked you to meet me today."

Steering the conversation away from herself was unusual.

"I'm doing okay." Elie did not feel like sharing the news in her life.

"And what about my darling Alexis? I know you were just in Israel. How is she managing with her little family?"

"Everything is great with her. Gavri is a little angel and the other children are so sweet, they're really darlings. It's a lot to deal with, but you know Lexi. She can handle it and a lot more. She sends you her love of course."

"I'm glad to hear she's doing well. We must get back to Israel, there's so much to see now. That short visit for the *brit* was not enough."

"Lexi would love that." Elie was beginning to get impatient, wondering about the point of the lunch.

"Elie, Chloe told me what happened at the magazine. I think it's unspeakable what they did to you. I was very sorry to hear about it."

"Thank you. It was a big shock, but I'm coping."

"I'm sure you are. I think you have an enormous capacity to survive and even flourish in adversity. I have no doubt that you will be fine."

Elie was surprised, and flattered, by Tillie's comments.

"You know, ever since you and Philip divorced, I wanted to meet with you. Just to catch up. But when Max had his incident, I couldn't concentrate on anything else."

Elie grabbed the glass of wine that had arrived and took a big gulp.

The waiter came by and recited the specials. Tillie, never one to take suggestions very well, ordered one dish, instead of the combination of two offered on the lunch menu.

"I would like to have the salmon with the watercress gremolata. Do not bring me the apple-celeriac puree and please make sure the salmon is fully cooked."

"Yes, ma'am. And for you?" The waiter looked at Elie.

Elie, as intimated as ever when around this woman, also ordered only one dish, but decided to make it a substantial one. "I would like to try the grilled beef tenderloin, with crunchy potatoes." When the waiter walked away, Elie looked at Tillie, as if she had to explain. "It comes with a pear-horseradish puree which sounds too divine to pass up."

"Well dear, you could have ordered just the puree with another dish, since they have it anyway. I'm sure they don't make it up special when the steak is ordered."

Leave it to Tillie, Elie thought. The only person in the world who could make her feel like a hillbilly in a Manhattan restaurant. On second thought, there was something to be admired about the woman – no one intimidated her or made her feel uncomfortable. She always did exactly what she wanted and never seemed to worry about what others might think.

Tillie continued. "Now, before they come back with our food and bother us, let's get down to business. First, taste this roll, it's new – they're making it with whole wheat flour and a variety of seeds and grains. I think it's excellent." She offered the breadbasket to Elie.

"I'm sure you are wondering why I invited you to lunch, besides catching up of course. And dear, you needn't butter the roll, waste of calories. It's tastes lovely without."

Elie stopped buttering her roll and looked up.

"I have a proposition for you. I would like you to hear me out and give it some thought before you decide."

"Okay, I'm all ears."

Tillie leaned forward, pushed the breadbasket to the side and folded her hands together on the table. "Chloe explained your situation to me. From what she said, or didn't say, I made some assumptions of my own. What I understand is that the magazine has been sold, the new owners want a different look and your assistant would have become your boss. Is that more or less the scenario?"

"Yes. That's it in a nutshell." Elie was beginning to feel uncomfortable. She knew she was fidgeting in her seat, which she tended to do when she sensed trouble.

"And Chloe mentioned something else, that you were seriously thinking about starting your own magazine. Is that correct?"

Elie debated how much information to give Tillie. She did not like the idea of her knowing too much.

"Elie? Are you listening? Is it true?"

"Yes. But there are issues." She hesitated to go on.

"What issues? What does it depend on?"

"On a few things actually. Market needs for instance. I hired a company to do research and although they came back with a positive response, it's still risky." She was not yet ready to admit to Tillie that the project was a go. She didn't want to jinx it.

"And ...?"

"I guess the other problem is money. I need a tremendous amount of capital to get it going. Other than that minor detail, I'm golden."

"I see. From what I gather then, it's all about the money. I know you have the courage, guts, and capability. That's clear to everyone and it should be to you. Market survey, well, you got that answer and it was positive. You need seed money and lots of it. And you don't have it?"

"Tillie, this conversation feels strange. Why all the questions?"

"I will explain in due time, my dear. Now as I was saying, I assume you do not have, or do not want to use, your own capital?"

"I have savings in the bank, but it's earmarked for my retirement. I don't really want to touch it." Elie certainly did not want to get into the details of her settlement with Philip. It had not taken into account a situation such as unemployment and starting a new business, but there was nothing she could do about it now.

"And you shouldn't. One should never use one's own capital for such a business venture. You know what they say – OPM is best."

Elie could not believe her ears, hearing the term OPM coming out of the mouth of this eighty-something-year-old woman.

"Tillie, you amaze me. How do you know about OPM?"

"Elie, I might be getting on in years, but I've been around. What do you think I do when I'm getting my hair and nails done? You think I have patience to listen to those *yentas* in the salon? Of course not! I read the business pages of the newspaper. I have a subscription to *The Wall Street Journal*. And anyway, I ran the business with Max. I may have been in the background, but we discussed everything. I know a lot of business expressions and I certainly know that for a large cash infusion it's always best to use *other people's money*."

Tillie continued to speak about Sands Furniture and how it was run. She explained that they never took loans which were not repaid, that the company grew slowly and wisely by adding one showroom at a time, and in the end, what a fine business model Sands had become. As she spoke, Elie listened quietly, wondering where the talk was headed. Finally, Tillie broke the monologue.

"Look Elie. I'll get to the point ..."

At the worst possible timing, the waiter arrived with the food and Tillie looked annoyed. "Do we eat first, or get to the meat of the matter?"

"Well, I would like to know what you have to say, but the meat of the matter will get cold."

Without responding to Elie's pun, Tillie declared, "Then let's eat fast!"

During the meal, Tillie proffered her opinion on the state of modern restaurant dining. The egos of chefs were getting too big, portions too small and too artfully constructed, prices were exorbitant, lighting was insufficient and ingredients were esoteric. She complained that the average person needed a dictionary in order to feel comfortable choosing from a menu.

Elie laughed and thought to herself, she's right. She agreed with many of Tillie's sentiments, but refrained from verbalizing her opinions. There was still a part of her that had to remain silent, lest she be seen as partnering with her old adversary.

Since she was anxious to learn the purpose of the meeting, Elie rushed through her meal, although she enjoyed it immensely. She knew that Tillie would likely not finish her fish and they'd be able to get back to the main topic soon.

Tillie wiped the corners of her mouth with her napkin and pushed her dish away. "Okay, we're done here. Let's get back to the real business. But first, I want a clean table to discuss this over." She looked for the busboy.

Once again, the commander-in-chief was leading her troops. Just as she waved her bejeweled hand, a young man appeared and cleared off the table. She instructed him to hold off on the coffee. He took the little tunnel-shaped knife out of his breast pocket, swept the crumbs off the table and disappeared.

"Now I feel better. Elie, I'll come right out with it. I believe in what you're doing and I want to help you. I would like to fund this project. That's it. That's why I asked you to meet me today."

Elie opened her mouth but Tillie beat her to it.

"You look like you're in shock." She said it matter-of-factly.

"Yes. I'd say so. I cannot accept, of course, but I thank you for the gesture. It's very kind of you." Elie was totally unprepared.

"Oh, yes you can accept it, and you will. You have to let me put my money up for this. I insist on it."

Elie winced. The woman was pushing her way into a situation that was none of her business. How could Tillie dare think she was going to get her hands on her magazine? It was her baby and no one else's. For decades she had suffered with this woman's arrogance, but that period was over. Enough! Then she calmed herself, realizing that she was divorced from Philip, and his mother could no longer wield any power over her.

"Tillie, what's behind this? Where does this offer come from?"

Tillie was obviously prepared with her response. "There are several reasons why I want to do this, Elie. First, I want to because I think it's a great idea, and I believe in it. If I understood correctly from Chloe, you want to target the over-fifty woman. You plan to produce an upscale journal containing all kinds of information and stories relating to the older woman. It would be a beautifully designed magazine focusing on areas of women's interest. Am I correct?"

"Yes ..." Elie felt suspicious and a little hostile.

"So, let me just say that I like it, and I believe in it. I've always felt that the older woman is ignored by society. As she gets on in years and her children leave the house, she is ripe and ready for a new life, but there is hardly anything out there that can inspire and excite her. You can do that with this magazine. And I assume you are looking at an Internet site and international distribution as well?"

"Yes, it's all being taken into consideration, but I'm only at the development stage now."

"Okay. Good. Next reason. I think I owe it to you, to support you in this venture. Because if you want the absolute truth, I feel guilty when I think about you. I am sorry that I did not support you or appreciate you enough during your marriage to my son. But now that you are divorced from Philip and there is no longer that official in-law bond, I can say what's on my mind. I am speaking to you woman to woman, not woman to former daughter-in-law."

She continued. "I misjudged you. I didn't think you were good enough for my son and I probably made that far too obvious. You came from a nice middle-class family and you were raised with good values. But you did not come from a family like ours and I suspected that you were marrying Philip for his wealth. I could not have been more wrong."

Elie was stunned at what she was hearing, but remained silent.

"In retrospect, I think you were an exemplary wife and mother. When Philip and Sandy were young, we had enough money to hire help. So they were practically raised by our housekeeper. I was busy with the business, with my charity work and social commitments, with keeping up the apartment here in Manhattan and later the house in Palm Beach. I guess I came from a generation that didn't think we had to be overly absorbed in our children's lives. I had a lot of expectations from them, but I wouldn't say I was doting or terribly involved." She stopped to drink some water and continued.

"You, on the other hand, were very involved – even though you had enough money to hire help. You gave up a very nice job when you had Alexis and continued to stay home and be there for the girls as they both grew up. Then, when you went back to work, I know I more than once gave you a hard time for trying to balance motherhood and career. I think I could have been a lot more supportive. I regret that I was not."

Elie started to say something but Tillie interrupted.

"I'm not finished." She was sitting up straight in her chair with her hands folded on the table. "I am very well aware, that living with Philip was not easy. He is a self-involved man who was not around enough, not for you, nor for the girls. I know he traveled excessively and did not participate in as much of your family life as he should have. From what I could see, you put up with it and did not make a stink. You could have raised hell, demanded that he be home more, or you could have just escaped and done your own thing. You did neither. You stood by him and made a beautiful home and raised two lovely young women that I am proud to call my granddaughters. I think you did an excellent job under less than perfect circumstances."

Elie listened to Tillie's words and felt ashamed for her previous thoughts. To hear this larger than life woman be so remorseful touched her. "Tillie, I really don't know what to say. I'm very moved by your words, truly."

"Please, don't say anything yet. Quite frankly, we should have had this talk a long time ago, but what's done is done and there's no point regretting the past. I don't hold it against you, that you divorced Philip. I would have preferred that you stayed married, because I believe that once you've made that commitment, you should honor it. But that is my opinion, and today's generation obviously does not agree with me. Finally, I was impressed that you did not try to take the business from Philip during your divorce proceedings. I think you were a *mensch* about it, and you know I don't say that about many people. Elie, I only want to see you succeed and move on with your life. You deserve true happiness, my dear." She looked directly at her ex-daughter-in-law and smiled.

"I can't tell you how much that means to me, coming from you." Elie kept hearing Tillie's words in her head. Just when she thought the woman had finished, she spoke again.

"There are other reasons, too, why I want to do this. You know I was always with Max one hundred percent in the business. We started with something small and modest, and developed it into something huge. I may not have been in the office all the time, but every night, during dinner, Max and I would discuss what was happening. We made all the decisions together."

She folded her hands under her chin. "I know I come off as the big boss and I like to tell everyone what to do. However, Max is the genius and he has always had the right instincts. He is a natural with business and I like to think that I picked up some smarts from him along the way. Quite honestly, it was exciting. If the times were different, I would probably be running that company with him as a full partner, instead of being the silent partner at home. I took the business very seriously and seeing it ride the wave of success has given me great satisfaction. Now that Philip and Sandy are working well together and the grandchildren are also involved, I feel that we really did the right thing. We handed them something substantial and I have had the pleasure of watching a second and third generation take it to even greater success. They are the guarantees that it will continue to flourish. I would like to offer you that same opportunity."

"Are you saying you want a part of this magazine? That you want to be involved?" Elie's insecurity popped up again.

"No, no! Not at all. I have done enough in my life. I am quite happy now to cater to my husband, nag him about his health and continue with my charity work. You know I love criticizing all those women I work with. What would I do without that? Who would I look down upon?" She stopped to take another sip of water.

"No, Elie, this is your project, and yours alone. I want to see you succeed. You're doing a great thing and I want to read the first issue and say, '*Voila!* I helped put that magazine on the map!' I just want to give you the money with absolutely no strings attached."

"Tillie, I need a lot of money. We're talking six figures here and there's no telling when I could repay you."

"My dear, I am not ignorant of these things. I know you need a lot of money. Say the number and I will write the check. And I do not need to be repaid. It's an amount I can miss. My poppa, may God bless his soul, always used to say that if you invest wisely, you will see a return on your investment in ways beyond financial. I think he was talking about raising children, but the example fits."

"Tillie, I'm just curious. Does Max know what you've just proposed to me?"

"Yes, of course. I rarely do major things without discussing them with him. And he's absolutely fine with it."

Elie began to feel a bond with Tillie. She sensed that perhaps they could move beyond the relationship they once shared, and develop something new. She thought that she might even grow to like the woman.

"So, Elie, will you take me up on my offer?" She folded her hands on the table, looked her straight in the eyes, and waited for a response.

"Well, you certainly have given me something to think about. In my wildest dreams, I would never have imagined that we would be sitting here having this conversation. I must tell you that my immediate reaction is no, it's too generous an offer. However, you've presented some very good arguments. I am really touched by it. May I have some time to think it over? I promise you I will consider it very seriously."

"Yes dear, of course. You should think it over. I would not expect you just to jump up and down and say yes right away. As I said, there are no expectations and there's no time limit. The money is yours, as much as you want and whenever you need it. Enough said. How about a little chocolate cake for dessert? Don't we deserve it? To hell with my diet!"

Elie laughed and agreed.

Thirty-Seven

It was time to cash in her last chip, to speak to an old advisor and make absolutely sure she was on the right track. He picked up the phone after several rings.

"Hi, Walter, it's Elie. How are you?"

"Hey kiddo, what a nice surprise. How're ya doing? How was your trip?" As always, he brought the subject back to her.

"I'm fine, and about to do much better. I have a plan and I'd like to discuss it with you. Would it be possible to come up to the country and talk?"

"I'd be delighted. When's good for you?"

"As soon as possible. Name the day. As you know, I'm a free woman now." She was hoping it could be soon.

"Yes, don't remind me. If ever I had a guilty conscience over anything, it's you. How about this Wednesday? Do you remember how to get here or should I send you the directions?"

"No need. I remember. Anything special I can bring you from the city?"

"No, Elie, we're fine. Just bring yourself. Come for lunch. I've become quite the cook these days. You'll be impressed. Say around noon?"

"I'm there. Thanks, Walter. See you then." Elie hung up and felt a huge sense of relief. Why she always assumed the worst she didn't know, because things usually worked out for the best, as she had learned in the past few months.

On Wednesday, she headed upstate with a bag of home-baked goodies, a bottle of Courvoisier and her ever-expanding notebook. She was excited about talking to Walter, and hoped that his reaction to her plans would be positive. She trusted his opinions and steeled herself for what he might say.

When she arrived at the property, she saw a man puttering in the garden. He was wearing a red baseball cap, khaki trousers, a white polo shirt and moccasins. He looked so different from the impeccably dressed, eminent publisher, that she did a double take before realizing it was Walter.

She removed the packages from the car and called out to him. "Hey Farmer Greenjeans! Is that you? Am I in the presence of the great Walter Lavigne, publisher and editor-in-chief of *Interior Design & Style?*"

"No. Just Walter Lavigne, *schmendrick* gardener. I'm checking on my cabbage and onions. Come see."

Elie walked over, kissed him hello and looked down at the ground. He proudly explained how he had planted them, what type they were and what was required to grow them organically. She laughed at the change in the man.

"Come on, let's go into the house. Katherine's having a good day and is waiting for you. What's all this?" He looked at the bags in her hands.

"Oh, nothing much. Just a few of my specialties and the Cognac you like. I need to butter you up, so I've brought offerings."

"I see. Am I required to drink some before we get down to business?"

"Required, no. Advised, perhaps. You decide."

He took the bags, put his arm through hers and escorted her into the house.

Walter had prepared a simple, but delicious meal of roast beef, roasted rosemary potatoes and a tomato and mozzarella salad. Katherine joined them and was alert and friendly. After lunch, she excused herself and went to her room to rest. Walter gave Elie his undivided attention.

She described her progress with the magazine. He asked many questions and she had answers for all of them. When she finished, Walter declared that it had his full blessing.

Elie was elated. They chatted on and on, and then Walter asked the one question that she did not have a good answer for.

"Advertisers, Elie. What about advertisers?"

"That's a bridge I have yet to cross. I'm going to hire a firm and let them take care of it. I see no other way for the time being."

"I see another way and I'm surprised you didn't think of it."

"Really? What?"

"Elie, I've been in this business since I was in knickers. Didn't you realize that I have connections? I can make a few phone calls and you'll have the biggest companies at your doorstep begging to take out full page ads." He waved his arm, as if it was already taken care of.

Elie couldn't believe it. He was solving one of her biggest problems, handing her the solution on a silver platter.

"I, I'm … I don't know what to say."

"Really?" He smirked. "That's so unlike you."

"Walter, how would you be able to? You may be out of the business soon, but your magazine is still running. You can't take business away from it. I'm sure you have a non-compete clause that this time no one is going to rip up."

He winked. "No problem kiddo. Your magazine does not compete with ID&S. Anyway, it's the least I could do for you. This magazine is going to be a great success and if I can do one small thing to help get it off the ground, I would be delighted. Please leave it to me, Elie. I'm sure I can help you with this."

Elie hardly paid attention to the drive on the way home. Her head was filled with thoughts of magazine names, logos, and features for the first issue. Without a moment's hesitation, she did something extravagant. She called David from the car phone.

"Hey there! Just wanted to let you know everything is falling into place. I'm happy, I have a great team and I'm going to make a huge hit out of this magazine."

"Tell me something I don't know," he replied.

"I love you, David Abarbanel. And this time, I will not let you out of my life. Bye bye!"

She hung up without giving him a chance to respond. She turned up the radio and sang the rest of the way home, almost missing her exit.

Thirty-Eight

The months following were packed with activities. Elie barely slept five hours a night and yet she had never felt better. She spoke to David frequently and he continued to be a source of encouragement and advice.

She decided to accept Tillie's offer and the first installment of money was transferred to her account. Although she knew there was more where it came from, she tried to limit her expenditures. She met with Tillie to update her on the progress, and was often impressed by the woman's business acumen.

Chloe announced her decision to leave Sands over dinner with her father. His first reaction was anger and resentment, but after carefully listening to Chloe's reasons, he came around.

Elie hired a few necessary people, moved the magazine out of her apartment and into office space, and managed to get the first several issues on the boards. A name for the publication had still not been decided on, but she was certain that a good one would materialize.

Walter came through and brought in major advertisers. Syd slowly eased herself away from several of her clients, steering some who were willing towards a trusted colleague. Leigh sketched out ideas for six months of issues and brought in fashion students from FIT and Parsons the New School of Design to work as interns.

Michael scored several impressive projects owned by people willing to publicize their homes. He concentrated on residences of women above the age of fifty, and obtained the cooperation of a widowed millionaire in a Fifth Avenue penthouse; a divorced mother who had renovated an old mansion in Princeton, New Jersey; and a single CEO living in a condominium in South Beach, Florida. The magazine's design department was taking shape.

Philip called Elie and asked to meet with her. She was curious about what he wanted, and felt proud of herself for not panicking. If Philip didn't like what she was doing, or objected to his mother funding the project, it was just too bad.

They planned to meet at Il Divino. Elie actually looked forward to the evening. She hadn't seen or spoken to Philip for some time.

She ran into him as she entered the restaurant, he was surprisingly on time. He kissed her and as she took off her coat, he complimented her on how great she looked.

"You look different, Elie. What is it? New makeup? Did you lose weight? Did you have a facelift?"

Elie laughed. Leave it to Philip to think it had to be some sort of artificial means that contributed to her radiance.

"No Philip, no new makeup or weight loss or facelift. Actually, I let my hair go natural – I don't dye it anymore. I'm happy, content with my life and very busy. I feel good, I guess it shows."

"It sure does. I hate to think that divorcing me caused the change, huh El?"

She didn't know what to say. Agree with him and hurt his feelings or let it go? She chose the later.

"Well, here's to you, Elie Sands. Sorry, Elie Stein. I wish you all the best in this new venture of yours. I mean it, you deserve every happiness."

Elie was touched. "Thank you Philip, that's kind of you. I had no idea how you would react, but I must admit that I didn't think you'd be too keen on the idea."

"Why not?"

"Well, to be perfectly frank, you were never very supportive of my ideas. Anytime I came to you with a concept for something new, you usually negated it. You were not very encouraging when it came to my career, Philip."

"No, I wasn't, was I?"

"Not really." She decided not to belabor the point. "And I was sure you would be angry at me for asking Chloe to join the magazine. I know you wanted her for your business, but I think she has a great future here and that it will be perfect for her."

"Yeah, at first I was really pissed off. But Chloe spoke so highly of it, she loves the idea of working for the magazine, so how could I object? She's my daughter after all, and I want what's best for her."

"It's good you see it that way."

"You know Elie, to be honest, I'm aware that I made a lot of mistakes. Now that we've been apart all this time, I've had a chance to think things through. I'm going to therapy you know."

"You're *what?*" Elie nearly choked on her breadstick.

"Okay, I deserve that reaction. I figured you'd get a kick out of it. The truth is, our divorce hit me harder than I expected. I figured my life would go on as it was, with some minor changes. But it was tough for me, too tough. I figured I'd give therapy a shot."

"Philip, I had no idea. You were always so against therapy. You made fun of me when I suggested couples counseling."

"I know. What can I say? I was an ass. I think I screwed things up royally. I definitely forfeited a lot when I lost you, Elie. Want to try again?"

She heard his comment, but was not sure how to interpret it. He could not possibly have invited her tonight to try to get back together, or could he?

He noted her silence and continued speaking. "Relax. I know you probably won't consider it. Would you? I mean, I figured you have a new life by now and you've probably moved on. I have too. I have a girlfriend."

Ah, there it was, the old Philip hedging his bets. He could throw out an idea like getting back together, but he would also make sure to have someone around, so that he would not have to be alone.

She felt at ease. Now that enough time had elapsed to process the disintegration of her marriage, she was confident that she had made the right decision. She ignored Philip's question and pursued the girlfriend angle.

"I'm glad for you, Philip. You also deserve to be happy. Is it the woman with the earrings?" She knew she shouldn't ask, it had an air of bitterness to it, but she could not resist.

"No. That was over a long time ago. This is someone new I've met. She's really sweet."

"Divorced?" In spite of herself, she was curious.

"Yes, with a kid, a boy. Look El, I'm not telling you this just out of the blue. I wanted you to know because I'd like her to meet the girls. I want to set up a meeting with Chloe and I've been thinking of inviting Kirsten to Israel to meet Lexi."

Making a quick judgment based on the name, Elie assumed that Kirsten was both young and not Jewish. He has to be in someone's company, she thought, good for him.

"You certainly don't need my blessing. Our daughters are grown women, you should have them meet Kirsten, if it's important to you."

"Thanks. I'm glad you're good with it. And listen, I know that my mother has given you money for this project. She told me about it as an established fact. I was quite surprised. And boy, you should have heard her give it to me. That I was a rascal and a *no-goodnick* and that I didn't deserve you and that I really messed up. I couldn't believe she was defending you so much."

"Nice to hear. I hope she didn't disinherit you over it." Elie smiled.

"No, of course not. As soon as she finished letting me have it she invited me up to the apartment to feed me. She said I looked too thin."

"Once a Jewish prince, always a Jewish prince."

"You bet. You know, Elie, this is nice. Having dinner with you with no arguments, no hostility. I'm glad we can do this."

"Me, too."

They continued to talk – about their daughters and Philip's business. He didn't ask her for details about the magazine or if she was seeing anyone and that suited Elie just fine.

Thirty-Nine

Everything was falling into place, except a name for the magazine. Whenever someone asked, Elie sheepishly admitted that she had not yet decided on one. The truth was, she didn't even have an idea. Nothing sounded right or had the impact of what she wanted the magazine to represent.

It was mid-morning and she was scribbling notes for the Editor's Page of the first issue when the phone rang. It was Philip, but she barely understood him. It sounded like he was crying.

"Philip, I don't understand you. What is it? What happened?" She felt a rush of fear run through her body.

"She's gone, Elie. She's dead."

"Oh my God, who is dead, Philip? Who are you talking about?"

He was babbling. "Just like that, nothing could be done. She's gone. I'll never see her again."

"Who, Philip? Who?" She almost screamed at him.

"My mother, Elie. My mother is dead."

Her body went numb and she almost dropped the phone. She had just had lunch with Tillie the week before. She was vibrant and healthy. How could this be?

Elie had trouble forming a sentence. "What happened, Philip? Can you tell me what happened?" Her tone was soft, as if she were talking to a small child, but her voice cracked.

"It happened last night. They were getting ready for bed, she was sitting in the chair and she just fell over and started mumbling. Pop called an ambulance, but by the time the EMT crew got there, she was out of it. They brought her to the hospital, but the doctors could do nothing for her. It was a massive stroke. I'm at their apartment now with Sandy and my dad. I don't know what I'm going to do, El. I'm devastated."

"I'll be right there."

Elie put down the phone, told Leigh she had an emergency and rushed out.

When she arrived at Max and Tillie's building, the doorman waved her in.

Sandy answered the door looking exhausted, her eyes bloodshot.

"Sandy, I'm so, so sorry." She hugged her tightly.

"I'm glad you're here, Elie." She wiped her eyes with a wad of tissues she was holding in her hand. "My brother is a basket case. I thought he was going to lose it in the hospital."

"Where's your dad? How is he?" Elie worried that the shock might be too much for Max.

"We put him to bed. They gave us a sedative for him. He's not doing very well."

Elie walked over to Philip, who was sitting on the couch with his head in his hands. He looked awful – unshaven and disheveled. He was a man who kept up a perfect appearance and to see him with a creased shirt hanging out of his pants stunned her. She hugged him, which caused him to break down and start sobbing. She picked up a glass of water from the coffee table and instructed him to drink.

Philip did as he was told, then he put the glass down and looked at her. "I can't believe it, El, she wasn't supposed to go like this. We all expected my dad to go first. He was the sick one, she was the rock. I thought she'd live forever. What will we do without her?"

"Shh, Philip. Just try to take it easy."

"I can't believe I called you. You probably have a million things to do with your magazine and all."

"Nonsense, Philip. I have to be here. We should call the girls, if you haven't already."

"Oh. I didn't even think of that. My poor girls, they really loved their grandmother."

"Yes, Philip, they loved her very much. She was an extraordinary woman. Really. I've come to know her so much better lately. She was becoming my hero, you know."

Philip looked at her and smiled. "Thank you for saying that. She was a hell of a broad, wasn't she?"

"She sure was."

The next two days were a blur. Elie cancelled all her meetings, asked her staff to handle things at the magazine, and put herself at the disposal of the family.

Friends and associates were informed. The rabbi met with Philip and Sandy to gather information for the eulogy. There were endless phone calls and people stopping by. Tickets were arranged for Lexi, Dovey and the baby. Miriam kindly offered to stay with the older children.

The funeral chapel was filled to capacity for the service. People from all walks of life attended, from cleaners who had long ago retired from Sands Furniture, to the mayor of New York.

In addition to the rabbi, each of Tillie's grandchildren spoke. There was hardly a dry eye in the building and sniffling could be heard throughout the service.

When Elie finally got home at the end of the day, she collapsed on the sofa and started to cry. All kinds of feelings came pouring out of her: the hostility she had felt towards and from this formidable woman, the years of struggling to be a dutiful daughter-in-law. But mostly, the unforeseen friendship that had developed between them over the last few months.

The week of *shiva* helped ease the shock and pain. Many people visited and told stories about Tillie. They related how she would visit the synagogue nursery school and read stories to the children; how she ran the charity bazaar and forced all her friends to give up at least one designer handbag; about her efforts with the city to elevate the reading level of children from disadvantaged homes. There were many such anecdotes, along with some spicier Tillie tales. The family was heartened by them all. Lexi's baby was a source of joy and a big fuss was made over Gavri and Lexi with each new visitor who arrived.

For Elie, the sense of loss was intense. She knew that grieving for Tillie would consume her for a long time.

When the seven days of mourning were over, Elie immersed herself back in the magazine, hoping that the enormous amount of work would keep her distracted. She suggested that Chloe might want to take a break, but her daughter refused, also feeling that being busy would ease the pain.

She called together a meeting of the Kitchen Cabinet. As promised, it had become a monthly habit and was eagerly awaited. It gave each member of the team a chance to be updated on what was happening in every department.

Elie always prepared something interesting to eat, a recipe she had developed or picked up from one of her many cookbooks. She knew the likes and dislikes of her group: Chloe was a vegetarian, Michael was fussy, Leigh was allergic to shellfish and Syd ate everything. Either she cooked something the whole group could eat or made substitutes for those with issues.

Since the funeral, she had been craving home-style food and decided that the next dinner for the group would be loaded with comfort and calories. Her tomato basil soup came out perfect and with the addition of crème fraîche, it was an instant hit – everyone had seconds.

Next came out the *pièce de résistance* and Elie felt the need to apologize to Leigh, whom she assumed would never have chosen such a dish. She figured Leigh for an epicurean, who might turn her nose up at such a blue-collar meal.

"Okay gang. This may well be the most politically incorrect, outrageously fattening, and thoroughly gooey, main course you have ever had, but we are about to feast on my nouvelle cuisine version of ... a tuna casserole!"

Equipped with silicone oven mitts, she pulled the steaming hot casserole out of the oven and placed it on a trivet she had set in the middle of the table.

They all laughed and Leigh admitted that it was her second favorite meal, after chicken potpie. There ensued a discussion about fashionable foods, and what people secretly love to eat but are afraid to admit. Chloe came up with the idea of an article on the subject. Everyone started talking about his or her ideal meals, their secret snacks, and their all-time favorite comfort food. As often occurred, the relaxed conversation around the table added to the enjoyment they all felt towards their common goal of creating something wonderful together.

As Elie scooped out big portions of tuna and noodles oozing with Gruyère and Emmental cheeses, and topped with fried onion rings, the reactions of her guests confirmed that her instincts were right. Syd poured a Chenin Blanc and everyone dug in.

In between bites and second helpings, each person gave a status report on their department. Chloe related that preliminary accounts on pre-publication subscriptions looked good. Walter, she confirmed, had come through and the magazine already had enough advertisers for the first six months of issues. Syd described a litany of financial subjects and described the direction of her columns. Michael was using his influence all over town to amass a list of spectacular design projects. He was also developing a series for the magazine on illustrious female designers and architects.

Leigh suggested that Michael work with an interior design student and offered to bring someone in to assist him. She also reported that for the first few issues, she had researched and was considering the life accomplishments of Donna Karan, Caroline Herrera and Coco Chanel.

Chloe's friend came through with a concept for the website and a small team was assembled to get it started. Everyone kept nudging Elie about a name for the magazine, but she still hadn't settled on this important element. Word spread in the media and Elie was invited for interviews, which she declined, preferring to keep silent until right before the launch. Her silence added to the buzz, generating even more free publicity.

Conversations with David took place almost daily, unless schedules and the time differences could not be coordinated. Although they kept discussing a trip, they were both too busy to get away for an extended period. They finally decided to take a long weekend in Paris.

They stayed in a boutique hotel on the Left Bank and spent their days walking around the city, visiting museums and eating at charming cafés. Their nights were consumed with lovemaking and endless conversations. Elie returned radiant. She no longer worried about the future, because she had a sure sense that it would be fine.

David was ensconced in her life and her heart, and there was no way he would disappear this time.

On a few occasions, she drove up to Scarsdale to visit Max, who had moved in with Sandy and Richard. Although it felt strange to be there without Philip and Tillie, she enjoyed the visits and was pleased that her presence made Max happy. She spoke to him about how her business was going and although he didn't have the curiosity and spirit he once had, he was able to ask pertinent questions and offer advice.

One of the biggest surprises Elie had was a phone call from Keira, who requested a meeting. She couldn't imagine what her former assistant wanted – she had certainly made sure that all her files and records were left in perfect order. She also assumed the young woman had her hands full with her new position at *Interior Design & Style*. Why would she want to meet with her?

Keira was sweet on the phone, even a bit overdoing it, offering to come up to Elie's apartment. Elie suggested a café near Lincoln Center. Although up to her ears in work, she was curious.

They met in the late afternoon a few days after the call. "You look really good, Elie. I love the new hairstyle. It suits you." Keira was obviously easing her way into what was on her mind. She was stirring sweetener into her coffee.

"Thanks Keira – I guess it's all part of the new me." Elie waited patiently.

"Look, I know you're probably really busy, and I am too, so I guess I should just get to the point. I've had something on my mind for a while and I need to get it out."

"I'm all ears." Elie thought the girl sounded nervous.

"I'd like you to know that I didn't campaign for the job. Actually, I was sure it was yours, and when they asked me, I was shocked. You and I never had a chance to discuss this. I just wanted you to know that it didn't sit right with me." She swallowed hard.

"I'm sure you'll do a good job, Keira. I know you're a very serious and committed worker."

"I am. But perhaps not because of the best reasons." She took a deep breath. "For the entire last year, I was in a horrific relationship situation. My boyfriend dumped me, and I kind of lost it. Then he wanted to get back together, and I agreed, but it wasn't good. I know it seems juvenile, but the situation got so out of hand that I just dove into my work and took on way too much. It was my method of coping with my shitty personal life.

Perhaps the new owners noticed, and thought I was an incredibly dedicated worker. But Elie, the truth is, the job is huge and I'm not so sure I can handle it. In some ways, I'm really excited about it. But in others, I sort of wish you got it, and just took me up the ladder with you."

Elie thought that Keira looked like a child, who was about to go on stage for her first school performance. Maybe the meeting was more about reassurance, than apologies.

"You will be absolutely fine." Elie touched Keira's hand, which was fingering the coffee cup. "You have all the right instincts, and for whatever reason you worked so hard, your efforts paid off. You did, and will do, a great job, and you should not doubt yourself. You have a terrific staff – don't hesitate to ask them for help when you need it."

"I was afraid to come to you. But I so much wanted to clear the air. I feel guilty about what happened. How did *I* end up being the editor-in-chief of *Interior Design & Style,* instead of you?" She laughed nervously.

"To tell you the truth, Keira, I was also taken aback by the decision. I was not at all happy. But, it enabled me to do something else with my life, and for that I am very grateful.

You should look at this as a marvelous opportunity. Don't think about how you won't be able to cope. Be positive and think about what a great job you will do. The owners obviously want a new direction for the magazine, and they believe that you are the one to create it. Just go for it and make me proud." She caught the waiter's eye and motioned for the check.

Elie felt good. There had been lingering doubt about Keira – she always wondered if the young woman had planned a coup and she had missed the signs. She said goodbye to Keira with a kiss and sincere wishes for success.

Elie gained an important insight. The problem had been her own self-doubts and insecurities, not Keira's aggressiveness. Her assistant had not been out to get her or her job; she was just lost in her own personal state of turmoil and handled the situation as she knew best. There was a lesson to be learned here – people are usually too busy with their own lives to strategize on how to mess up the lives of others. It's always best to stick with positive thoughts, and trust in the universe. Things will usually work out for the best.

Another tiny little chapter had just closed. Elie left the café with a very calm feeling.

Forty

Early one morning, when she was still at home, Elie received a phone call that troubled her. It was from Nathaniel Brandt, the Sand's family lawyer, asking to meet with her. She became alarmed, fearing that it had to do with Tillie's investment in her magazine. Then she felt ashamed for thinking that.

She had no idea what Mr. Brandt wanted, and she was uptight about the meeting. When she arrived at his office, she felt even more uncomfortable. She had seen plenty of beautiful offices throughout her years at the magazine, but this place was extraordinary: wood paneling on the walls, English antiques, leather Chesterfield sofas and Persian carpets. It radiated decorum, and affluence.

She was acknowledged by a receptionist and led into a private waiting area. When the door to the inner office opened, she was greeted by a tall, silver-haired man who seemed to be in his seventies. He looked vaguely familiar; she thought she recognized him from the funeral. He guided her into his office and motioned for her to sit down. He took his seat at his desk.

"Mrs. Sands, or is it Ms. Sands now?" He looked at her over the upper rim of his glasses.

"Actually, it's Ms. Stein."

"I see. On second thought, would you mind if I called you Elie? I feel like I know you from my conversations with Tillie."

"That's fine." Elie's reaction must have shown on her face.

"I see you're surprised by my familiarity. Allow me to explain. I've been representing the Sands family in certain matters for several decades. They don't use my services for the usual run of business matters, more for very special needs."

"I see." She was getting that fidgety feeling again.

"And in the course of the last several months, I had a few

conversations with Tillie about you. She came to see me not long before she died."

"Why?" Elie made a conscious effort to stop the nervous tapping of her foot.

"She wanted to make arrangements for you, to discuss the funding of your magazine."

Elie interrupted. "Mr. Brandt, Tillie was extremely generous. She expressed a desire to help me get my magazine off the ground and I'm sure she would have honored that commitment if she were alive. Now that she's gone, I have no expectations. She has a living spouse, children and grandchildren and I am sure they would like the money to remain in the family."

"That is where you are very wrong, my dear. That is not at all the scenario."

"I don't understand."

"Elie, this may come as a shock, but Tillie knew she was ill. She had several tests done and, among other problems, she had high blood pressure and a weak heart. Actually, she had a minor incident not long ago, but she kept it a secret."

"She did? What kind of incident? I don't think anyone in her family knew."

"And that is exactly how she wanted it. She did not want to take medication, and she refused to change her lifestyle. She made it very clear when she came here, that no one was to know. She said she would rather live her last day gossiping with her girlfriends or dining with her husband, than start fussing over her health and be treated like an invalid. I tried to talk her out of it, but she was insistent. She came to me when she knew her time was running out. I am sorry to be the bearer of this news, but it might help you to understand what her thoughts were. She was quite a remarkable woman."

"Indeed, she was." Elie didn't know what else to say.

"Why don't I just get to the point? First of all, you should know that Tillie made arrangements for each of her grandchildren. Your daughters are taken care of handsomely in her will. But, *that* is not why you are here. There are also special arrangements for you."

Elie listened.

"Tillie left you two things. One is a monetary gift and one is a piece of jewelry."

He opened a drawer, took out a black leather box and an envelope and handed them to her. "She wanted you to have this and asked that you wear it to the opening party of your magazine. She hoped you would plan a big event and she said she would be honored if you would remember her by putting it on then."

Elie wondered if she should open the box. She looked at Mr. Brandt and he nodded.

She lifted the lid of the box and gasped. Inside was a ring, a large cabochon ruby surrounded by diamonds. It was stunning and Elie had never seen anything like it before. She gently took it out of the box and held it between her fingers.

"There is a letter for you in the envelope. I suggest you read it when you get home. You might also want to consider putting the ring in a safe. It is an extremely valuable piece."

"I would imagine so." She cleared her throat.

"Now, as to the matter of the money. You are right, Tillie did want to have money for your magazine. And whether she had the foresight to plan in advance because of her illness, or just because she was a smart businesswoman and didn't want to leave any unfinished business, I cannot say. But she has left you a significant amount of money."

"But I couldn't. This ring is enough. I shall treasure it always."

"She thought you would. Especially when you understand the circumstances under which she purchased it. But the matter of the money is indisputable. You see, Elie, she left you a sizable sum. Two million dollars, to be exact."

Elie's body stiffened. She grabbed onto the arms of the chair and just stared at him.

"Would you like a glass of water?" He leaned forward and looked concerned.

Elie just shook her head back and forth.

"I can see that this is a shock for you. Take a moment for yourself." He folded his hands on his desk and then he continued to speak.

"Tillie left you this money to do with as you see fit. She hoped you would use it to build up the magazine. She was very proud of you, and wanted to help you achieve your dream. It comes from her private account, which she had been investing wisely for many years."

Elie finally spoke. "Did you say two million dollars?"

"Yes, I did." He smiled, for the first time. "She also told me to tell you that the first thing you should do is go out and buy yourself a decent coat, preferably one from Bergdorf Goodman. She said you were wearing some old *schmateh* the last time she saw you."

Elie laughed, and it broke the tension. Then, the tears started to flow. She fumbled in her purse for a tissue.

He waited for her to compose herself. "That's it, Elie. I assume the letter will explain Tillie's thoughts. I have carried out her wishes. There is a bank account set up with your name on it, and only you have access. Here are the documents." He handed her another envelope. "Do you have any questions?"

Elie had trouble mouthing the words, but when she finally came to her senses, she said she could not think of anything. She put the envelopes and the box in her purse and held it close to her chest. She got up, shook the lawyer's hand and walked out of his office in a daze.

My dear Elie,

If you are reading this letter, it means that I am no longer on this earth. I hope that my demise was in good taste. I am putting all my affairs in order and I wanted to share a few thoughts with you.

We are both aware that over the years I disapproved of many of your decisions and, unfortunately, I made that way too obvious. I deeply regret my behavior and if I could retract those errors, I would. I hope you have forgiven me.

As I recently made clear to you, I wholeheartedly support this new endeavor of yours. Of course, you do not need my blessing, nor would you have sought it. But it is important to me that you know how very proud I am of you, of what you have already done with your life and what you are about to accomplish.

I believe your new magazine is going to be a big success. I told all my friends about it and you can be sure that at least the sisterhood of the temple and all the women in the charities I belong to will sign up for subscriptions. I ordered them to do so!

There is nothing to write about the money I am leaving you. That is my wish and I am sure you will put it to good use.

As for the ruby ring ... many years ago, when the future of Sands Furniture was on solid footing and we had just opened our seventh store, I decided to buy myself a present. I neither asked Max for permission nor informed him about it. I chose not to go to our family jeweler – I wanted to buy it retail and anonymously. I made an appointment at Harry Winston – intimidating even for me – and met with a lovely saleswoman there. I told her I wanted to purchase a piece of jewelry for myself, and that price was not an issue.

I chose the ruby ring that you now own, not just because of its beauty, but also because of its uniqueness. The stone is from an exotic place (they told me, but I don't remember) and the setting was a replica of one designed for a queen in the last century. The story was probably nonsense, but I didn't care. I think the ring is one of the loveliest pieces I own, and I wanted you to have it.

The ring represents what it means to be an independent woman, a woman who can buy an expensive (very!) piece of jewelry without the approval, money or accompaniment of her husband. The example of my ring applies to life in general.

You should always remember, my darling Elie, that you can fulfill your dreams. You own them and you can achieve them. All you have to do is believe in yourself. I hope the ring will remind you of that. Do not doubt yourself, just follow your heart, and you will be surprised how far it will take you. Do not let anything or anyone stand in your way.

I am certain that you will build a wonderful new life for yourself. I am sorry that I won't be there to witness it. But know, my dear girl, that I am somewhere up above smiling down on you. You have all my blessings.

Now go out a buy a gorgeous evening dress – call my personal shopper, Miss Regine, at Bergdorf. Make a party to end all parties and go get them with that new magazine of yours!

With my deepest love and admiration,

Tillie

P.S. If either Lexi or Chloe should have a daughter in the future, I would insist that they NOT *consider naming her Tillie. That is not a name for the next generation of Sands women. However, Tea might be nice.*

Forty-One

It was time. All the articles were all edited and polished. The advertisers were on board. The photography was checked and re-checked, and it was as perfect as it could be. The staff was working nearly round the clock and they were proud and excited about the way the magazine was turning out. The first issue featured Donna Karan as a role model for the over-fifty woman.

Elie knew it was time to launch. On less secure days, she felt intimidated by the enormity of her decision and wondered what she was doing. She feared that not a single soul would buy the magazine or even agree to glance at the first issue. But she tried hard to squelch those thoughts. Deep down, she maintained the belief that she was creating something important. When clouds of doubt hung in the air, she re-read Tillie's letter.

During one of their many "after a long day at the office" dinners, Elie and Syd recapped the latest goings-on in their new, shared world. Syd was a full-fledged member of the staff, but she stuck to her financial world and didn't interfere in other matters. Elie wanted to discuss a launch party.

"Yes! A launch party – let's have a great big soiree!"

They were sitting in Elie's kitchen feasting on ceviche and Cava.

"This magazine is going to be something, Elie, and you need to introduce it to the world with a New York *über*-bash. What are you considering? Where? How many people? What kind of food?"

"Who's had time to deal with all that? I really haven't given it any thought. I'm stumped."

Syd scooped up a bit of the ceviche with a pita crisp. "Man, this is to die for!"

"Thanks. I added some preserved ginger to it. *Nu*, what are we going to do?"

"Okay, let's deal with this party. First – how many people do we want to invite?"

"A few hundred, I guess. Everyone involved in the start up of the magazine, their partners and the advertisers. Then there's the press. Chloe has the PR list. Gee, now that I think of it, there has to be a lot of people invited. Some hired hall wouldn't be the right image and the museum spaces are too big. I think it should be artsy and not black tie, something more casual. On the other hand, maybe black tie and casual – so women know that however they are dressed, they will be welcome. I've been to and planned dozens of parties, no hundreds maybe, but mine? *Oy*. Help!"

"*Eureka!* I have it!"

"I'm listening." Elie smiled, knowing that Syd always had a solution to every problem.

"Gallery 30! It's perfect!"

"And that is …?"

"Don't you remember? It belongs to Rafael, Julian's son. It's an art gallery in Soho. It's a lovely, open space, minimalist in design. It's large, can accommodate many people and has a well-equipped kitchen. It was a restaurant before he took it over. I don't know what show is on now, but I'm sure we can get him to agree to host the party. It would be good publicity for the place. What do you think?"

"That could be perfect. But wouldn't he feel under obligation because it's you asking?"

"Yes, and your point is? I'll just remind him how much his father adored me. Seriously, I'm sure it'll be fine. And if not, we'll find another place. Leave it to me."

"Okay, great. Thank you for taking that off my list, one less thing I have to worry about. You know Syd, since Tillie's death I've lost some momentum. I so regret not really knowing who she was sooner. I feel sad for all the years we wasted."

"Ironic, isn't it? Obviously, you needed the divorce from Philip and the distance from her, for both of you to re-evaluate. It certainly gave her a chance to know you as a person, and not as the woman who snared her son. She was quite the hero in the end, wasn't she? I still can't get over the ring and the money. You are going to wear it to the party, aren't you?"

"Of course I am! With hopefully a gorgeous dress to go with it. I was even thinking of calling her personal shopper at Bergdorf for something special. She asked that I do so."

"Then I'm going with you. Okay, we've solved two problems. The party is at the gallery and the perfect dress shall be purchased with the wise counsel of Tillie Sands, from above. Take out your diary – we're making a date."

Miss Regine was called and a meeting was arranged for Saturday, in two weeks time. Then Elie had another idea. Why not invite Michael to join? He was the ultimate fashion connoisseur, and the three of them could have so much fun. Syd agreed and so did Michael.

When it came time for the appointment, Elie was nervous, as if she were applying to a sorority. The irony of the situation did not escape her. Here was the publisher of a magazine for older women, telling them that they should be confident and strong, and she felt intimated in a classy store.

She brought the ring with her, and she hoped that with Tillie's wardrobe mistress in tow, she would be able to make her proud.

Elie and Syd were in the waiting area of the personal shopper department when Michael walked in with Isabel. "Eleanora Stein and Syd Sorenstein, I would like to present the most important young lady in my life, the famous Isabel. Isabel, you already know Ms. Stein, this is Ms. Sorenstein."

Isabel's blonde hair had grown back and it was swept back by two red barrettes. Her big blue eyes were shining brightly and she had the most captivating smile. She wore black and white polka dot pants, a white Ralph Lauren polo shirt, and red ballet slipper shoes. A red patent leather purse was slung over her shoulder, a perfect match to the barrettes and shoes. Both she and Michael wore matching red silk scarves. The change from tomboy to girly-girl was dazzling.

"I know this is your gig Elie, and you need my full attention – after all we can't leave this important decision to Syd here – but I just had to have Isabel with us, because she has incredibly good taste and, she's never been to Bergdorfs. Together we shall help you select the most perfect outfit!"

Syd made a face at Michael, reached out for Isabel's hand and invited her to sit on the sofa next to her.

When Miss Regine walked out of her office to greet them, Elie was surprised. She had expected someone young, French and haughty, someone who could elicit the fear of the fashion gods. That was not at all the case.

Miss Regine was well into her sixties, her straight gray hair pulled back in a chignon and her black dress simple, but beautifully tailored. She wore low heels, Paloma X earrings and a wide silver bangle bracelet. A pair of tortoiseshell bifocals swung from her neck on a silver chain. She exuded elegance.

"How do you do. I'm Miss Regine and it's a pleasure to meet you all." She shook hands with every member of Elie's party.

"I understand that we will all be participating in Ms. Stein's experience today. Wonderful! I am certain we will find something together that will be just right. Let me take you into our fitting room, where we can sit and chat."

The fitting room looked like a luxurious boudoir. It had the air of 1940's Hollywood written all over it and just needed Joan Crawford walking around in a peignoir to complete the picture.

"Wow, what a room! I'd be willing to buy anything if I got to shop for it from here." Syd was the first to speak.

"We do try to make our clients comfortable. You know, Ms. Stein, your mother-in-law was a very special client of ours. She will be sorely missed by many in this store."

"I'm sure of it. Please, won't you call me Elie?"

"Yeah, *ole* Till must have dropped quite a wad in this place." Syd couldn't resist and Elie shot her a look.

Miss Regine took the reins. "I've taken the liberty of sending for some refreshments. They should be here shortly. Why don't we discuss your special event and what sort of ensemble you would like to wear?" She motioned for everyone to sit.

Elie and Michael settled into Bergère-style armchairs, while Syd stretched herself out on a hot pink chaise lounge, and motioned to Isabel to join her.

They were all chatting, when a woman walked in wheeling a cart.

"Ah, here are our sweets. A little champagne, chocolate and strawberries never hurt anyone before a shopping expedition, did it? And for you Miss Isabel, I've ordered a strawberry ice cream soda."

"Oh, it's my very, very favorite!" Isabel folded her hands together and glanced at Michael, to request his permission. He nodded with a smile.

The friends looked at each other and laughed. Any woman who would offer Belgian chocolates, strawberries and champagne before trying to turn them into fashionistas, was their kind of woman. They all relaxed.

A discussion was held regarding the event, the location, the time of day and the people who would be attending. Miss Regine understood that Elie needed to look magnificent, without being over the top. She guessed Elie's size and made some notes. She took off her glasses and looked directly at her new customer.

"Very well, I have more than enough information. I will have my assistants bring in several pieces, which I think are appropriate. It will take a few minutes, may I offer you any additional food or drink?"

Elie responded. "No thanks, we're fine. Take your time, we'll sit here and enjoy the wait."

"That's the idea, my dear." Miss Regine walked out and left the group alone in the room.

While Isabel played with the fringes on the upholstered chaise, Syd spoke. "So, Ms. Stein, while your personal shopper is foraging among the racks of retail heaven, what do you say about us being here? Isn't this just the coolest?"

"Excuse me, Ms. Sorenstein, but *I'm* the one who brought you here."

"Yeah, yeah. Okay, so you did. Must say I could get used to this personal shopper business. I don't know why I never considered it before. It just figures, I discover it *after* I've given up meeting important clients. Who needs designer clothes for writing financial columns?"

"Don't give up, Syd. When the magazine goes international, we'll have to fly overseas to meet with our contacts there. And of course, we'll have to look gorgeous so there will be plenty of opportunities to meet with Miss Regine then."

"Ah, but Ms. Wise One ..." Syd looked at Elie, "when we are in Europe, as in Paris, Europe, I shall take you to my favorite designer shops. We can do much better than Bergdorf. I know that city like the back of my hand. And then, when we get to Rome ..."

"Oh hush up, you yapping *yentas*. I've already forgotten what you two think you know about fashion. Goodness, you'd think you were having an audience with Queen Liz herself. My word, you are both so *pedestrianic*." Michael made a clicking sound with his tongue.

"*Pedestrianic?*" Syd was about to give Michael a lecture about his vocabulary.

"Can I come to Europe, too? Please? Please? Please?" Isabel looked at Syd. "I've never been there, but *grand-père* said he would take me."

"*Grand what?*" Both Elie and Syd looked at her, with their mouths open.

"*Grand-père*. That's what I call Michael. He's sort of like my grandfather, but he's not."

Syd looked directly at Michael. "Are you *effing* kidding me? You're making this child call you *grand-père*? What white horse did you ride in on?" She threw a velvet pillow at him.

"Don't you dare start with me, you dried up old prune. I think *grand-père* is a lovely name. And Isabel likes it, too. Don't you, my *petite chèrie?*" Michael blew Isabel a kiss.

Syd stuck her finger in her mouth as if to gag and Michael threw the pillow back at her. Elie was shaking her head and Isabel was laughing and sipping her soda.

Michael was determined to get the last word. "I promised Isabel that I would take her to Paris to teach her all about style and good taste. We must get her started in the ways of the world early. It may be too late for you ladies, but not for my darling Isabel. We'll go to Versailles, and the Petit Trianon, and the Louvre, and we'll drink café au lait with croissants and ..."

"Sweetheart, does everyone call you Isabel?" Syd said, purposely interrupting Michael. "Don't you have a nickname?"

"Well, to tell you the absolute truth, I do have a nickname. It's Izzy. But *grand-père* said it's vulgar and I shouldn't use it."

"Well *grand-père* here sometimes needs a good kick in his *derrière*. I think Izzy is a fabulous name and I would like to call you that."

Elie shot both Michael and Syd a warning look and then turned to Isabel. "Isabel, I have two daughters and neither one was crazy about their name when they were little, but now they love them. I think your name is very beautiful."

"Thank you, Ms. Stein. I like the name Elie a lot, too!"

"Then please call me that. Ms. Stein is so formal."

"Ooh, here she comes. I'm so excited I could just spit!" Syd clasped her hands together.

"Don't you dare! I will not have you embarrassing me, here in the holy of holies!" Michael looked aghast.

Elie glanced at Isabel and they both giggled.

Miss Regine entered the room smiling. "Okay, Ms. Stein, we're all set. I've asked the girls to bring in several outfits. I am sure that you will find something to your liking."

Within a few minutes, two young women wheeled in a rack with clothes hanging all along the length of it. As they left the room, Miss Regine closed the door behind them and suggested that Elie start trying on the clothes. She escorted her behind a screened-off area and handed her the first outfit.

Elie emerged wearing a black pants suit and Michael did not waste a moment. "Oh no, that will definitely not do. You look like the Bride of Frankenstein. You're just missing the long horrible hair. Off with it!"

A navy blue silk suit garnered a thumbs-down from both Syd and Michael. Elie went back to the dressing room and back out. She swirled around in a long pleated skirt and V-neck sweater.

Syd's response was: "I don't think so. It reeks of evening at home with the *Ladies Home Journal*. Forget that one."

Elie went through outfit after outfit, each time emerging from behind the screen thinking, this might be it. She looked at Miss Regine, hoping for guidance, and got more and more frustrated while her two friends enjoyed every moment of her discomfort. Each had a monologue about why the latest outfit was not suitable and Elie began wondering aloud why she had invited them. She was just about to settle for one of the acceptable choices when Isabel cried out.

"This one! I found it! I found it! You have to wear this one, Elie." Isabel was tugging on a dress hanging at the end of the rack.

It was a black camisole dress with a boldly patterned, silver floral appliqué, under a sheer black tulle overlay with a bateau neckline and slit kimono sleeves. Miss Regine smiled knowingly, mentioning that the dress was Marchesa, and an exclusive of Bergdorf's.

"I think this is the most beautiful fairy princess dress I have ever seen. And it has silver parts! And flowers! And it's black! Isn't black what you're supposed to wear to grown-up parties?" Isabel crossed her hands across her chest and just waited for everyone to agree with her pronouncement.

They all cracked up. Isabel was right – the dress was a knockout. Miss Regine slipped it off the hanger and handed it to Elie.

Elie went behind the curtain and when she came out, she got exactly the response she had been hoping for. Syd let out a wolf whistle and Miss Regine nodded and smiled.

"*Magnifique*! Eleanora Stein you have never looked more stunning." Michael was bowing to Elie as he walked around her to view the dress from all sides.

"Well, my friend. What do you have to say?" Elie looked at Isabel.

"You look like the most beautiful queen I have ever seen. I want to come to the party, too. Can I? Can I please, *grand-père*?" She put her hands together in a begging pose.

Michael smiled and bent down to kiss Isabel. "I shall escort you as if you were the finest princess in the land! That is as long as your grandmother says it's okay."

For the first time in her life, Elie exclaimed that she would take it, without asking the cost or looking at the price tag.

"Not just yet. I think I may have a surprise for you." Miss Regine reached for the cell phone that was discreetly hidden in the pocket of her dress and pressed one number. "Kate, please bring me the black Louboutin sandals, you know the ones. Just a minute." She looked over at Elie. "Ms. Stein, your shoes are a size eight?"

Elie nodded.

"I thought so, yes, size eight."

"I think I know how Cinderella felt." Elie glanced at Syd and Michael.

"Me too! I even think Cinderella would like to come here to *Birdoffs*!" Isabel was swirling around the room.

Kate walked in with a box and Miss Regine ceremoniously opened it. As she removed the shoe from the tissue paper, Elie and Syd gasped. It was black high heel sandal with diagonal straps over the open toe and three crystal-studded rings going up the vamp. As with all of Christian Louboutin's shoes, it had a completely red sole. It looked more like art than footwear, and Elie glanced at Miss Regine before daring to try it on.

"My dear, they are only shoes. They may be priced like jewels, but they are to be worn, I assure you. Please, why don't you slip your feet into them? They are lovely, are they not?" Miss Regine looked very pleased with herself.

Elie did as she was told and the shoes were perfect. They were much higher than she usually wore, and she was not sure she would be able to stand in them all night, but she did not care. She was a goner for the complete outfit.

"Done! I'm in love." She curtsied to all in the room.

"Well then, that completes the outfit. I won't even suggest a purse because as hostess for the evening, you should not carry one. I would suggest you make arrangements to have your personal necessities handy somewhere if you want to spruce up your makeup."

"Miss Regine, you have made my day. And week. And month. I believe I shall look exquisite for my launch and I have you to thank. I am most grateful."

"That is very kind of you to say. But please let us not forget Mrs. Sands. It is to her credit that you are here."

"You are so right." Elie took the glass of champagne and held it up. "Here's to Tillie Sands. May her memory be a blessing forever and ever."

Forty-Two

The magazine had a working title, but a definitive name had yet to be announced. In her deliberations, Elie wanted it to be symbolic, representing the qualities of a woman who had reached the age of fifty. She wanted it to project an image of clarity and wisdom, of experience and inner beauty. It had to be savvy, but not cute. It had to exude an aura of confidence, and perhaps even a bit of indulgence.

Elie did not like relating to a number, as in Fifty-Plus. She could not associate it with goddesses, because most had an evil side. She searched for a name that was sexy, a bit mysterious and intriguing. And one that would project beauty.

She thought about Tillie during the process. She had been a woman who took good care of herself and kept abreast of what was happening in the world. A woman with a full life, who had learned from experience and was very self-aware. She was a woman filled with confidence and determination. She had been proud of who she was, and it showed.

Elie touched her ruby ring. It functioned as her amulet, her icon of independence and strength. She thought about how Tillie looked, with her perfectly coiffed silver hair and her exquisite fashion sense, and how she behaved with elegance and poise. Elie wanted there to be a connection, even if it was only she who understood it. She finally came up with a name she loved, but kept it under wraps until the very last moment.

You are cordially invited to attend the launch of

Silver & Sage

A magazine for savvy & spicy women
of a "certain age"

Please be among our honored guests
Saturday, October 15 at 8:00 pm

Gallery 30
30 Wooster Street
New York, New York

RSVP: www.silverandsage.com
Eleanora Stein
Publisher and Editor-in-Chief

Forty-three

The date of the big event was approaching. The first issue had been printed and the subscription department was buzzing. Elie instructed the printer to run off several hundred extra copies for distribution at the launch party.

Elie had hoped that David would fly in for the celebration, but he was not certain he would be able to. He explained that there was a critical business meeting with overseas investors that had been arranged months before, and it would involve a major undertaking to reschedule.

The night before the launch, Elie called her small staff together. She thanked them for their tireless work on behalf of the magazine, and handed each person a small gift.

As the tightly knit crew began to open the boxes, their reactions delighted her. Each received a silver pin that was a replica of a sage leaf, with a tiny diamond set into one of the flowers.

Elie addressed the group. "You all are the heart of *Silver & Sage*, and it could never have gotten off the ground without you. Please consider this gift a token of my gratitude, and a symbol of what we have accomplished together. Now go home and get some rest, because tomorrow we party all night!"

Huge spotlights focused on the building, illuminating the entire facade of Gallery 30. A tuxedoed guard stood at the door and discreetly asked for invitations. Chloe had done her job superbly and there was a media frenzy outside. Paparazzi were everywhere and curious on-lookers were lined up to see what was going on. A trio of jazz musicians played just inside the entrance and people were made to feel welcome from the moment they walked in.

Symbols of the magazine had been embedded throughout the interior. Imposing ficus trees were set in silver jardinières and ornamented with twinkling silver lights. Hors d'oeuvres were passed around on Baroque silver trays that had been decorated with sage leaves. Sage plants set into silver pots were placed on surfaces throughout the space and the walls were covered with blown-up pages from the first issue.

There was a pulsating atmosphere. As she stood near the entrance to greet her guests, Elie was delighted to see Miss Regine among the first to arrive. One wink from her and Elie was confident that she looked beautiful.

Chloe was stunning in a DKNY shawl-collared tuxedo, and she worked the crowd like a professional. Lexi couldn't fly in, but sent a framed photograph of the whole family posing with a sign that read: *'Mazal tov! We love you Savta Elie.'* A limousine brought Sophia who, looking beautiful in a midnight blue suit, beamed proudly as the publisher's mother. Sandy and Richard escorted Max, who was walking with a cane. When she went to hug them, Max kissed Elie's hand and declared, "Tillie would have been so proud of you. Only someone with your kind of moxie could have pulled this off. Bravo to you, my darling Eleanora." Elie had trouble keeping her eyes dry.

Syd wore a shimmering, pewter-colored, asymmetrically cut jacket over a straight skirt – the latest from Vivienne Westwood. True to her trademark, her ears were almost completely covered with abstract-shaped silver earrings. Rafael, the host, wore a silver embroidered shirt and flowing sage green pants. His outfit was perfect for the part of eccentric art gallery owner.

Michael looked handsome in a beautifully fitted Italian suit, a pale gray shirt and a silver, sage and cream tie. He was accompanied by Daniel and Isabel. The little girl's hair was piled on top of her head, her black and white dress sported a silver belt and she wore silver Mary Jane shoes. She ran up to Elie, gave her a hug and whispered in her ear. "See, I told you the dress would make you look like a queen. I'm your matching princess! And no baseball cap tonight!" Elie hugged her and brought her over to meet her mother.

Philip showed up with Kirsten, and Elie noted to herself that she seemed very sweet – and young. Leigh, arriving with another woman, was elegantly dressed in a vintage Saint Laurent suit. Several employees from *Interior Design & Style* came, including Keira, and Elie was delighted to see them.

Walter was there, without Katherine, and he made the rounds, greeting everyone and acknowledging the advertisers. Elie was delighted to see that Joshua had accepted the invitation, and that he was with a lovely looking woman. He gave Elie a big hug and whispered in her ear that she looked stunning. He carried a package from Devi that he instructed her to open immediately, as per his sister's orders. It was a botanical print of a purple sage plant, printed in Jerusalem in 1892. Elie was touched that Devi had paid tribute to her in such a special way.

The only disappointment was that there was no sign of David. She had not received any last minute calls to pick him up at the airport, so she understood that the meetings in Europe could not be cancelled. She rationalized that this was her night, there would be many other nights in the future with him.

Partway through the evening, Rafael pulled Elie aside and brought her into his office. Sitting on his desk was a gigantic bunch of sunflowers in a glass vase. "I don't know where these came from. It's hard to find sunflowers now, but someone must have really wanted you to have them. Here's the note that came with it. I wasn't sure you'd want me to put them out in the gallery since they don't fit the design scheme." He winked as he handed her the note.

I am so proud of you. I'm with you in spirit tonight and love you always. David.

She kissed the card, put it back in the envelope and returned to the crowd. He had not forgotten. He was indeed with her.

The outpouring of love and enthusiasm in the gallery was overwhelming. Elie soared on a high that could only come about when all the people in the world that one cares about show up to lend their support. She could barely speak when the time came for her speech.

The musicians were instructed to stop playing. Chloe got up on a platform, took the microphone and asked for silence. She looked around the room and then spoke with complete ease.

"Tonight is about an extraordinary woman, who happens to

be my mother. Eleanora Stein, you did it! You created something remarkable and we are all so proud to be a part of it.

Before I bring you up here, I have a special announcement to make. We've been holding out on you, those of us in the marketing division. But as of late this afternoon, *Silver & Sage* has passed its subscription target! Sales have taken off and we've had an incredible response. I am very proud to tell you that *Silver & Sage*, the magazine for women of a certain age, is a hit!"

The crowd roared and Elie started to shake. It took her a few seconds, before she could regain control and take the microphone from Chloe's outstretched hand.

She started slowly, clearing her throat a few times. "I do not know how to properly express what I feel. So please bear with me while I try to find the right words." She took a few deep breaths. "This evening represents a moment in my life that is straight out of a fantasy. It is the fruition of a dream that for a long time I did not even know I had. A dream that has come true tonight with the help and support of all of you here in this room.

I have been so fortunate in my life. I was raised by extraordinary parents, enjoyed a solid marriage for many years that produced two incredible daughters, and I had a career that I loved. My family and friends have always been there for me. What I lacked though, was a strong belief in myself – but I can tell you that at the ripe old age of almost fifty-two, I found it!

And that, ladies and gentlemen, is the essence of *Silver & Sage*. We would like to be there for women finding their own place in this world. They are remarkable human beings as caretakers and nurturers, but sometimes they forget that they also have many other talents. It is time for them to open their eyes to the wonders that await them, to say yes to all the possibilities this universe has to offer and to say no to the little voice inside them that says: you cannot, you should not, you must not. This is a magazine for women who, you should pardon the expression, have been there and done that. They are ready to take on the second half of their lives with enthusiasm and wisdom. They are both gorgeously silver and extraordinarily sage.

Please accept my most humble gratitude for helping me make

this dream come true. I would like to dedicate the first issue, and this evening, to my remarkable mother-in-law, Tillie Abramoff Sands, of blessed memory. Although she is no longer with us, I am absolutely certain that she is here tonight in spirit. Tillie, this one's for you!" Elie raised her hand with the ruby ring and threw a kiss upward. She waited for the crowd to stop clapping before continuing with her speech.

"I thank you all for being here, I am ever so grateful for your support and your belief in me and *Silver & Sage*, and I look forward to continuing this wonderful journey with all of you. Now let's party!" She stepped off the platform to a roar of applause.

As the crowd cheered, a DJ hired for the evening took control. The music started pounding out of the sound system, ranging from Disco to Motown, rock and roll to reggae. Food and wine flowed and an exhilarating atmosphere permeated the gallery. Elie tangoed and boogied until two in the morning, when the last of the guests finally left.

In the cab ride home, she could not contain her excitement. The launch of *Sliver & Sage* had been flawless – a success way beyond her dreams, and a fairy tale ending to an arduous journey. If the evening was any indication of what was to come, it would be pure sailing from now on.

As Elie entered her building lobby and greeted the doorman, he pointed in the direction of the seating area. She didn't understand what he wanted, until she saw the back of a head she recognized. She gasped, not really believing it could be, but it was. She walked over to the sofa, and into the waiting arms of David Abarbanel.

"I'm a little late. Did I miss anything?" He smiled. "I knew I wouldn't make it in time for the beginning of the party, and I wouldn't dream of crashing, so I figured it would be okay to meet the publisher at home. Any problem with that?"

Elie grabbed him around the neck, drew his face towards hers and kissed with all the passion that was stored up inside of her.

Boy, had she ever just launched a life of her own!

The End

Acknowledgments

First and foremost, thanks go to Karine Wagemakers Kahn. She suggested that I write a novel and pushed me until I did. I invented the characters, she enhanced them. She nurtured every page and scrutinized every chapter, endlessly. She is the best editor a writer could ever hope for and I thank her from the bottom of my heart, for sticking with *Menopause in Manhattan,* and with me.

The literati: I was fortunate to have found such talented people to proofread the book. Carol Novis was the first, and she kindly gave it a thumbs up. Sharon Wolf read it and suggested a movie. Deborah Delin dug in, while developing an on-line English learning program (www.strivney.com), and she found copious commas and colons that needed correcting. Anne Usher agreed to on-site and on-call editing, Miriam Shaviv had a peek and offered encouraging words and Guy Frawley tweaked the traits. My forever bosom buddy, Saralee Boshnack, discovered errors when we all thought it was perfect.

The experts: Exercise ace Veronique Shenkar determined the extent of Syd's workout, Hillary Avitan clarified Lexi's preterm contractions, Avi Amsili contemplated the likelihood of Syd's massage and Anton Delin provided a quick lesson in finance. Debbie Walker kindly shared her story, Rachel Alkalay years ago advised me to start a website and Karen Moloney tried to get the book into the right hands. The erudite Hans Kahn noticed inaccuracies that, fortunately, could be rectified in time.

The technorati: Graphic designer Ofra Lerner put together the covers, Gai Haephrati rescued me from InDesign disasters and Iris Fahrer and Catherine Reich took a swipe as well. Yael and Josh Schlenger taught me cool keyboard tricks and Apple Discussions pro Peter Breis supported me during formatting freak-outs. Web wizard Kelli Brown (www.pixelpointpress.com) shared her endless knowledge about on-line marketing and website design.

The support team: the beautiful (inside and out) Pazit Dan makes me feel as if I can do anything, her husband Meir is my on-call Internet advisor and her mother Wilma was the inspiration for Sophia. Dahlia Peyser keeps me laughing and lovingly reminds me about what I tend to forget. Orna Landau de Shalit maintains an eye out for me and my soul sister Claudia Camurati Langworthy makes sure I'm updated on New York happenings. Sefi Kerem is my go-to person for design opinions and her mother Linda keeps me stocked in homemade pomegranate syrup. Aml Bisharat Hana keeps me smiling, Natalie Amor Ohana keeps me organized, and the women of the International Women's Club keep me on my toes.

Robin Levine Cassity, Laurie Gafni, Dina Kussoff and Matthew Kussoff were never properly credited for the help they provided on my cookbooks, and they so deserve it. Yonatan and Anna, Michael and Dana supply encouragement – and the cutest kids! Nizza Ben Shalom, of Boccaccio Restaurant, is just as sweet in person as she appears in the book. And to Dr. Ziva Levite and Dr. Refael Levi – expressions of gratitude are just not enough.

The marketing mavens: Kudos to Jane Krivine for her ideas, Ruth Geva for her filmmaking talents, Renaissance man Ardyn Halter for thinking up the best names, and witty and wise Greer Fay Cashman for *the* name. And to Harte Feldman who promises to keep those Menopause Martinis and Hot Flash Toddies coming.

The icing on the cake: I am indebted to Julie Maner, Director of Museum Editions, Ltd. I asked if I could use part of my Fazzino "Greetings from New York 3D" for the cover – she offered me an original! I still can't believe it. Thank you to Patrick Fagan for putting it together, and a giant kiss to the coolest pop artist in the world – Charles Fazzino (www.fazzino.com).

Last, but certainly not least, to my husband. His love, support, and belief in me is limitless, and it doesn't get much better than that. Thank you, Oded, for giving me the time and space to write this book.

Anne Kleinberg

To purchase copies of *Menopause in Manhattan*
or to learn about the:

Characters
Fashions
Jewelry
Food
Restaurants
Missing Scenes
& more

please visit:

www.menopauseinmanhattan.com

To contact the author, please visit:

www.annekleinberg.com

Other Books by Ann(e) Kleinberg

Gifts from the Kitchen
Parragon Books Ltd., 2007

Flavored Oils & Vinegars
Parragon Books Ltd., 2007

Pomegranates - A Celebration of Recipes
Penn Publishing Ltd. & Mishkal, 2004

Pomegranates
Ten Speed Press, 2004

Edited & Translated by Ann(e) Kleinberg

Easy as Cake
by Ruth Jolles
Sterling Publishing Co., Inc., 2005

Sandwich
by Yisrael Aharoni
Ten Speed Press, 2004